The Rose Stone

TERESA CRANE was born in Hornchurch, Essex. She had always wanted to write, and has been doing so professionally for ten years. She began with short stories, which were published in *Woman*, *Look Now* and other magazines, and then wrote her first novel, *Spider's Web*. *Molly*, which is partly based on Teresa Crane's own family history, was her second novel, and *A Fragile Peace* was published in Fontana in 1984.

D1342461

Available in Fontana by the same author

Molly

A Fragile Peace

TERESA CRANE

The Rose Stone

FONTANA/Collins

First published in Great Britain by
Victor Gollancz Ltd 1985
First issued in Fontana Paperbacks 1986

Copyright © Teresa Crane 1985

Made and printed in Great Britain by
William Collins Sons & Co. Ltd, Glasgow

CONDITIONS OF SALE
This book is sold subject to the condition
that it shall not, by way of trade or otherwise,
be lent, re-sold, hired out or otherwise circulated
without the publisher's prior consent in any form of
binding or cover other than that in which it is
published and without a similar condition
including this condition being imposed
on the subsequent purchaser

For Rita

PART ONE

Russia, Poland, Amsterdam, 1874–1875

CHAPTER ONE

The rutted and waterlogged road that had started in death and terror and that led — so far as the exhausted child could tell — to the promise of little better, stretched bleakly to a cloud-smudged horizon that seemed never to change, never to come any closer no matter how the travellers laboured. The girl bowed her head, and fixed her eyes despairingly upon the rough ground just a yard in front of her, trying not to see the endless, awful miles ahead. For how many days now — how many weeks — had they been following this hateful ribbon of potholed mud and stone westward? She could not recall. She only knew that sometimes now it seemed that she could barely remember a time when this had not been her life: the freezing rain and foul, squelching mire, painful feet and cruelly aching legs, and always the necessity, the compulsion, to tramp on. To what? Day after day in raw cold that chilled her to the bone despite the overlarge and moth-eaten fur jacket that Uncle Josef had managed somehow to acquire for her she trudged blindly on, the origins of this fearful journey often blessedly forgotten, the possibility of an end unimaginable. They slept at night in any haven they could find — a noisy tavern, a hayloft or byre, or at best, when some peasant woman took pity upon a child's pinched and weary face, upon the beaten mud floor of a crowded hovel before the fire. The girl drew a long, trembling breath, watched muddy water slurp around her ruined boots as she plodded through an ice-filmed puddle that she was simply too tired to avoid, and wondered how much further they must struggle today before the relief of roof and rest. Despite the cold, despite the movement, her eyelids drooped as she walked. She would not even mind if, as so often before, there were nothing to eat — she was simply tired to death, the ankle she had twisted yesterday paining her badly. Her eyes closed again, the comforting dark at least some refuge from the misery around her, and against her own volition she found herself drifting into that waking dream world that was both her sanctuary and, if she were unwary, her terror.

A small white bed. Fragrant sheets. The last rosy blush of an evening sun lighting the familiar ceiling of the night nursery. The comforting sound of a lullaby as one of the Georgian maids crooned to baby Olga in the room next door. The calling of her brothers as they tumbled on the lawns below —

Don't think of it.

She was conscious of a faint lift of sound in her head, a sound that had its source somewhere in the base of her own skull; a keening, an echo of misery that if she allowed it — and in the worst of circumstances she had discovered that it could be almost a relief to allow it — would overwhelm her, drown her, beating from her brain all thought, all terrible memory. Once — it now seemed long ago, for the sun had been shining and the roads had been dry, and dusty — when they had been travelling with the gypsies, the terrifying boy with the rat's face whose greatest pleasure had been to torment the frail, pale little stranger who had fallen in with them on the road, had discovered her horror of fire and had chased her with a burning brand. That had been the worst time. The sound had risen to a crescendo to burst her head. Stumbling from him, the brutal smell of burning flesh in her nostrils, she had begun to scream, had screamed herself to blessed, mindless oblivion until the feel of Uncle Josef's hands upon her shoulders, the urgent sound of his voice had brought her from terror to silence. She opened her eyes now, blinking against the windblown sleet's razor edge, and glanced up at him. He walked as always, grim-faced, eyes fixed upon the muddy track ahead, her hand tight in his, his heavy sack bouncing rhythmically upon his shoulder. She knew that the burden chafed with every step through leather and cotton to the skin beneath, had seen once the raw redness of his back beneath the torn and dirty shirt where the tender skin had been flayed to blood. Yet she knew that, next to her own hand, his grip upon that dirty sack would be the last thing he would relinquish. And she knew why. The dop, the tang, the heavy wheel known as the scaithe, the small precious leather bag — if they had a future, here it lay. Night after night she would doze off to the sound of his voice talking of a far-off and unimaginable place called Amsterdam, of a new life, of a home and warmth and rest and comfort. She flinched from the thought. A home? Without the gentleness of her mother? Her glorious, graceful, bright-faced father? Her brothers and sisters and baby Olga? Grandfather, with his stern voice and twinkling eyes? Sometimes she told herself — yes, they will be waiting, and we will be together again, and happy. But sometimes the truth would not be denied, and she knew they would not. The eldritch ringing began again in her head, distant, insistent.

Don't think of it.

Bright-eyed faces, laughing. The flower-filled fields of spring. Picnics, and games across the fields. The musical running of the silvered river as the winter snows melted. Her brother Josef — named in friendship after this same man who now strode silently beside her — his brown, serious face gentle as he lifted her to see a perfectly woven nest securely enclosing the dear, funny little fledglings with their blinking eyes and gaping beaks —

Don't think of it!

Too late. Blood now and screams. A soft baby head crushed like rotten fruit. A brutal hand in her sister's long, flying hair, that stopped her flight and dragged her back to death. The unspeakable things that the devils had done to her mother — her father's pleading, anguished and desperate as, laughing, they had held him to watch. And then, after that nightmare of blood, the fire. The smell, that had crept to her nostrils as she had crouched, half dead with terror, in the water barrel behind the workshop, her secret hiding place in their children's games.

Don't think of it.

Too late now. Much, much too late.

She stopped walking. From some far distance she heard someone screaming; a thin, shrill sound like the cry of an injured animal.

"Tanya!" Josef was on his knees in front of her, his grip on her shoulders painful, the precious sack fallen disregarded in the mud beside him. "*Tanya!*"

The sound subsided. She stood quite still, trembling, tears

pouring soundlessly down her face. He gathered her fiercely to him, crushing her, hurting her. The leather of his jacket was hard and cold. Something sharp dug into her cheek. Passively she stood, still shaking, unresisting in his arms, an unhappy, docile little doll.

Josef Rosenberg drew back, looked into the huge, haunted eyes of the child and cursed savagely the land of his birth.

Later he watched her in sleep, the thin little face a pale, beautiful mask within its haloed cloud of hair, the enormous eyes closed, violet-shadowed within an arch of bone. Occasionally she moved or muttered, restless even in her exhaustion. Josef sat by her, setting himself between the child and the crowded room, fervent guardian to her safety. No further harm would come to this, the only surviving child of his murdered friend, if the body and strength of Josef Rosenberg could prevent it; he owed that at least to a lifetime of comradeship and near brotherhood. And more, much more. To the Anatovs he owed his life, his loved ones, his very existence — the least he could do in exchange for so great a debt was to try to preserve this small, damaged flower, the last of their line. Thirty-five years before, Tanya's grandfather, Count Boris Anatov, had rescued a dying baby from its dead mother's side on the bitter winter road to Kiev and had brought it to the house of Solomon Rosenberg, his best friend. The elderly childless couple had believed the child a gift from God and the nameless, abandoned scrap had become Josef Rosenberg, a much-loved son, secure within the framework of the two families, a companion to the Anatovs' own son Alexei, an unlooked-for treasure to bring light and happiness to the Rosenbergs' old age.

Tiredly Josef rubbed the heels of his hands into his reddened eyes. The atmosphere was thick with smoke, the stench of unwashed bodies and with the unappetizing reek of the cabbage soup which was the only sustenance, with black bread, that the tavern had to offer. The noise was deafening. In one corner a small knot of men gambled, faces avid in the lamplight, the group dominated by a giant of a man in the homespun blouse and dirty, baggy trousers of the Polish peasant, with hands that dwarfed the dice to pea size and a voice like a bull. Josef detested having to bring Tanya into places like this and made a point of avoiding them whenever possible; but tonight the child had been on the brink of pure exhaustion. He had had to carry her for the last difficult mile, together with his other burden. At the thought his hand moved instinctively to the sack, unaware that from across the room a pair of bright, hot eyes had lifted from the dice and were watching him in crafty speculation. Through the rough cloth he felt the reassuringly familiar outline of the wheel. Here was yet another gift from the Anatovs — for in taking him to the Rosenbergs old Boris had not only presented him with loving and devoted parents but with a skill and a livelihood that had, as the years progressed, become a true passion. Diamonds. He allowed himself, fleetingly, to remember a small boy standing by his foster father's knee watching in wonder the spinning wheel, hearing the sweet note of the singing stone, seeing and envying even then the skill and deftness, the sureness of touch that turned what looked like a small shapeless lump of clouded glass into a piece of living, sparking fire. With delicate accuracy the planes were cut, measured by eye to a fraction of a degree, then polished on the spinning wheel until within the gem the light would glance and gleam, rainbow spears of colour to delight the eye. Often Boris Anatov would be there, watching his old friend at work, for this love of the diamond was one of the things that drew the two men, so disparate in most things, together in unlikely friendship. One of the things. Josef sighed. If it had been only that, if they had not also shared a passionate hatred for injustice and oppression, had not become enmeshed in that dangerous movement that advocated reform and revolution in a country where, Josef was convinced, neither would ever come about, then Tanya Georgievna Anatov would at this moment be safely asleep in her nursery in the lovely old house that had been her home on the estate just outside Kiev and he, Josef, would be sitting downstairs in the house in Charnov Street, quietly with his wife Anna, the children, those little innocent ones martyred for their name and their religion, asleep upstairs —

All gone.

Bitter words, bitter thought, almost impossible to accept even now as the truth. God of my father, where are you now? If you exist, and I pray that you do not, how could you possibly encompass such viciousness, such barbaric cruelty, such mindless horror — not once, but a thousand times? For the carnage of Charnov Street was, Josef knew even in the agony of his own loss, just a small drop in the ocean of the suffering of his parents' people, the Russian Jews.

His parents' people.

Why, after all these years, did he still think that? Why, after a lifetime in a Jewish family, after marrying the good, Jewish wife that his foster mother had so desired for him, did he still feel, in the depths of his being, an outsider? Why could he not believe? Why, for all these years, had it been necessary, in gratitude and love, to pretend? Of one thing he was certain — the feeling of alienation had not been simply due to the circumstances of his birth and adoption, nor yet to the fact that he in no way physically resembled the people amongst whom he had lived; it had been rooted deeper than that, somewhere in the darkness of an unbelieving soul that still now denied him the comfort of faith, never revealed to those who loved and cared for him for fear of hurt. Alexei had known — but then, in the intimacy of near brotherhood, Alexei had known everything about Josef Rosenberg. They had shared everything from their thoughts and dreams as boys to their first whore as students in Moscow. Alexei had been Josef's other, more flamboyant self. He could see him now in the pure lines of the face of the child who was his daughter, in the living halo of her hair, saw his shadow each time he looked into the dark-fringed violet eyes. Alexei, laughing, careless, daredevil who had inherited his father's passion for revolutionary politics without the old man's good sense and restraint, and who had been the undoing of them all. Josef knew beyond doubt that the attack on the house in Charnov Street had been instigated and stage-managed by agents of the police and the Imperial government. The Anatovs had had too much influence, were too well regarded and protected upon their own ground — how much more vulnerable were they there in the Jewish quarter of the city, unarmed, unprepared, at a family party celebrating a child's birthday? How regrettable, people would say, that a family such as the Anatovs should have been caught up in one of those sporadic spasms of Jewish blood-letting that were, if unpleasant, so necessary to the health and well-being of the city of Kiev. But then — a man was known by his friends, was he not? And if he chose to befriend dogs above his own kind, should he be surprised to find himself hunted with them?

Josef thanked the God in whom he could not believe that Solomon and Sarah Rosenberg had been safely at rest for more than a year before the Cossacks had come, laughing, to that neat and prosperous house in Charnov Street, to ravage, to kill and to burn —

A shadow loomed, blocking the light. Josef looked up, eyes still clouded with recollections of that terrible day. The giant who had been dicing with the others in the corner grinned down at him, exposing wolfish teeth. He held out a massive hand in which nestled two ancient bone dice, yellowed with age and worn almost spherical by use.

"You like this?" His Russian was horribly accented, almost unintelligible.

Josef shook his head.

The other man frowned, jerked the hand that held the dice. "You like," he said again, and moved his head towards the corner in which his friends were sitting, grinning, watching the entertaining sideplay. "You play." He mimed the rolling of the dice, grinning his canine grin in crafty encouragement.

"No," Josef said again, firmly, his eyes steady though his hands were slick with the sweat of anxiety. He had no doubt at all that this Goliath could break him in half with one hand, even less that the other occupants of the room would watch him do it with no concern and little more than a passing interest. "No." He looked away, deliberately dismissive. The big man did not move. His huge hand hung level with Josef's eyes. Josef tried not to look at it, at the callouses, the ingrained dirt, the filthy, bitten nails. His own hand seemed coldly welded to the rough sack beside him. Still the man made no move; his shadow, enormous and somehow threatening, lay across the sleeping child. Josef stiffened, the sickness of fear stirring the pit of his stomach as the huge hand reached towards Tanya, touched the fair, tangled, sleep-damp curls.

"Nice," said the Pole in his heavily accented Russian.

"Pretty."

Josef, very still, lifted his head and watched the other man as he stood contemplating the small, angelic face. The stirrings of terror lifted the hairs of his body. He knew himself not to be a brave man — in their years together at university in Moscow he had never managed to acquire Alexei's gay appreciation of a good fight, his disregard for physical hurt — but nevertheless he bunched his legs beneath him, ready to launch himself at the giant at the first threat to his sleeping charge. Tanya murmured and turned her head, her fingers curled loosely close to her smooth cheek. She was small for her eight years; asleep she looked younger. Another fearsome grin spread across the man's face, exaggeratedly sentimental. He said something in his native tongue which Josef did not understand. The man smelled like a pigsty and his breath was foul. At a table not far away an argument had started and a knife flashed. The big hand closed upon the dice, rattled them gently, close to Josef's ear.

"You play." The words were soft, confident. "Yes? You have a good time. A man is not a — what? — a nursemaid, no? You play."

"I've no money."

"You win some." The words were coaxing, the bright eyes disturbingly derisive, disbelieving. The Colossus dug his hand into the pocket of his trousers and produced a handful of small coins, rattling them enticingly in his fist as he had the dice. The altercation at the next table rose again. A man stumbled across the floor and cannoned into Josef's tormentor. He had blood on his face. Without taking his eyes from Josef the big man planted a hand in the man's chest and shoved him back with the force of a steam hammer the way he had come.

Josef waited, sweating.

The giant watched him with bland eyes and an unfeeling smile.

"I've no money to gamble," Josef said at last, in desperation.

The man sniffed noisily, cuffed his running nose. One of his friends in the far corner of the room, bored with the lack of action, called impatiently. The hot, speculative eyes watched Josef for a silent moment longer before, with no other word, the man turned and pushed his unceremonious way back across the crowded room to his table. Before he sat down he looked back, once. Josef turned hastily away. When next he hazarded a glance the man was once more intent upon his game. Almost paralysed with relief Josef moved closer to Tanya. Protectively he leaned to the child, tucking the fur jacket closer about her, trying to still the painful racing of his heart. No Alexei to take his part now — nor ever again. Had he been here, Josef found himself wondering, what would he have done? Taken the dice, more than likely, and happily beaten the brute at his own game. Or, depending upon his mood, cheerfully accepted the implicit challenge to violence and proceeded to destroy the tavern stick by stick. Many a man had been misled by that deceptively pretty face and slight build. Roused, Alexei Anatov had not been noted for his restraint. Indirectly it had, in fact, been Alexei's volcanic disposition that had earned Josef a place at university with him, sponsored and paid for by a Boris Anatov who had hoped — vainly — that the steadier Josef might temper the extremes of his son's volatile temperament. As if anything or anyone could have done that, Josef thought now, ruefully. Even after Alexei's marriage to a girl he truly loved, even after the birth of children, the passing of years and the responsibilities of taking over his ailing father's estate, the blithe recklessness of his youth had never truly left him, neither in action nor speech. And so the intellectual polemic of the father had in the son given way to rash action — and the inevitable end that came upon the blades of the Cossacks in Charnov Street. Blind chance had decreed that Josef should not share the bloody fate of his friends and family, and even now he could not for his life decide if fortune had favoured or duped him. Might it not after all have been better to have died with the others? With Anna and the children, with Alexei and his family. Even old Boris Anatov's years and standing had not been spared. When, hurrying late from an appointment in the city, Josef had come to the house in Charnov Street after the brutal storm had passed, the old man's savaged body had been the first he had found. Of the others, those that remained after the flames, he still could not think without sickness. By then the violence, unleashed and uncontainable, had spread through the Jewish quarter and slaughter was everywhere. Ancient fires of hatred had blazed again, endless retribution exacted from a despised race.

"But Jesus was a Jew," Josef had pointed out, just once, in argument at the university in Moscow. "And He, surely, hated no one. If you believe, as you say you do, how can you think that He would countenance such cruelty perpetrated in His Name?"

"Watch what you say, bastard Jew," had come the reply. "If you want your tongue slit, just take His Name into your filthy mouth once more —"

Josef's decision to flee after the attack on Charnov Street and after he had found the terrified, speechless child in the water butt had been instinctive — but still, now, he believed it to have been right. He had known, had been warned, that Alexei's — and through Alexei his own — involvement in subversive activities had come to the notice of the authorities. He had no doubt at all as to the motive of the attack. But the violence had not stopped there: others, innocent, had died and Josef Rosenberg, always despite his efforts the outsider, would rightly be held responsible when the community recovered from this latest outbreak. He could expect little help or support from anyone. And Tanya — what of her? She had lost every living relative in the massacre, apart from a distant cousin in Amsterdam. Her father's estate would undoubtedly be forfeit now that Alexei's strong arm was no longer there to defend it. The child had been shocked almost beyond reason. Harsh treatment now, Josef was certain, might have deranged her mind for ever. And so, with the small leather bag of rough stones that he had been carrying with him that day and the old tools of his trade that, discarded in favour of new, had been stored almost forgotten in the garden shed, he had taken the child and fled, following that arduous refugee road to the west that had been trodden by so many before them. Had he guessed the enormity of the task of shepherding a young, delicately nurtured mind-sick child across a continent, would he still have attempted it? He looked now at the pale little face and knew beyond doubt that he would, despite the danger and hardship that had brought him more than once to the brink of despair. With little or no money they had had no choice but to face more than a thousand miles of rough country on foot, travelling sometimes alone, or sometimes — as with the gypsies — falling in with a group of travellers for safety's sake. Josef earned their bread where and when he could along the way. The stones he carried were worth nothing in terms of food, shelter or transport. A Russian or Polish peasant offered these baubles in place of hard cash would scorn the fool who tried it; and, unsure of pursuit and terrified of rousing suspicion, or getting himself arrested and so being forced to abandon Tanya to a lone existence which she would certainly not survive, Josef had avoided the towns where he might have sold one of the small gems. Apart from anything else, as the weeks had passed, the stones had become to him a kind of talisman, a charm of promise for the future. Here lay their fortune — he would not endanger it by forfeiting a single gem. Let them just survive the gruelling present and, in Amsterdam or maybe London, their future was assured. A small business, prosperity, safety — perhaps even complete recovery for poor Tanya. For the moment, with winter advancing fast and the weather worsening by the day, they must endure, keep moving and avoid the dangers of the road.

The thought brought his mind back unpleasantly to the present. He turned his head. The big man who had accosted him earlier was staring across the room through the smoke, eyes narrowed, probing into the dark corner where Josef huddled over Tanya. As Josef watched, one of the man's companions, a boy pretty enough to be taken for a girl, spoke and laughed uproariously, slapping the table, rattling the bottles and glasses. The giant nodded, smiled briefly. But his eyes across the hazy room were calculating and absolutely mirthless.

They were waiting for him the next day just a few miles along the road. They made not the slightest attempt to hide themselves or their intent. The giant sat upon a stone, elbows on knees, rain-damp towhead lifted, watching the man and child as they approached, his cronies disposed around him on the muddy grass verge of the track. There was no one else in sight. Josef's heart took up the steady, heavy beat of fear at the first sight of them, but he walked on unfaltering, Tanya's hand firmly in his, the sack bouncing on his shoulder. As he drew closer he saw that in one huge hand the man held a rough cudgel which he slapped rhythmically into the vast palm of the other as he sat and waited.

Tanya, frightened, hung back when she saw the men. Josef squeezed her hand reassuringly. "Come along, my pigeon. It's all right."

She shook her head, her feet dragging.

He dropped to one knee beside her, still holding her hand. "Don't be afraid, little one. They won't hurt us."

Brave words.

She bit her lip and nodded uncertainly. He straightened, braced his shoulders and started forward.

With no words the giant stood and barred the path, the cudgel swinging gently beside him.

Josef stopped. "Good day to you." The words were calm, civil, spoken in Russian.

The man smiled his predator's smile and held out his hand, palm up. "Give."

Josef, swallowing, stood his ground, gripping his sack and the child's hand, knowing himself lost. "I have nothing."

The smile faded. The three other men were on their feet now, two behind Josef and the third, the slim, slovenly beautiful young man that Josef had noticed the night before, at his leader's elbow. "*Give*," said the man again and took a threatening step forward.

Tanya cringed, whimpering and clinging to Josef's coat, her huge eyes terror-filled.

"Please — don't frighten the child. There's no need to frighten the child —" Despite his efforts fear threaded Josef's voice. He heard it himself, and hated himself for it. He gritted his teeth and met the giant's hot eyes with his own as steadily as he could manage.

The Pole snapped something in his own language. The boy stepped swiftly forward and caught Tanya's shoulders, trying to drag her away from Josef. She screamed shrilly and fought like a small animal, kicking, spitting, biting, holding like grim death to Josef's hand.

Josef let drop the sack to reach for her.

Deftly the giant caught it before it hit the ground, upended it, spilled its contents into the mud and pushed them around with an enormous, booted foot. The young man who had grabbed

Tanya swore luridly as her sharp teeth sank into his skin. He lifted a hand to strike the child. She screamed again, her breath sobbing in her throat. Before the blow could fall the bandit leader's huge hand shot out and, with enormous strength simply plucked the sobbing, struggling child from Josef's grip and tucked her beneath his arm like an oversized doll. His fears for himself forgotten, Josef froze.

"Please. Don't hurt her."

A great, dirty palm was extended, open, waiting. The calculating eyes were unblinking.

"We don't have anything," Josef gestured, his empty hands graphic. "I swear we don't have anything."

Josef's tools lay at the giant's feet in the mud. There was no sign of the leather bag. The man pushed the scaithe again, uninterestedly, with a booted toe. Grunted. Thrust forward his hand once more.

"I tell you we don't *have* anything!" Frantically Josef began to turn out his pockets, showing them empty of valuables, his eyes on Tanya's hanging head. The child's body had gone ominously limp; even the sobs had stopped.

The giant watched Josef's pantomime of emptying his pockets with unimpressed eyes, snapped an order at the girlish-looking young man. The lad grinned salaciously, stretched filthy, slender hands with long, effeminate fingers and advanced towards Josef. One of his companions laughed, harshly. Josef stood like stone as he was searched slowly, meticulously, painfully obscenely. The long fingers probed, caressed, investigated every likely and unlikely place where valuables might have been concealed, whilst the boy's companions looked on, laughing and calling encouragement. Like the whore he obviously was, the lad explored Josef's body, his bright, pretty eyes fixed upon his victim's face. Josef stood like rock. At last, regretfully, the boy stood back, shaking his head. Tanya moaned a little, tried to move. The big man who held her looked down at her almost in surprise as if the small comedy he had just witnessed had driven the thought of her from his mind. Josef, his face burning with humiliation, raked his numb brain for the Polish words.

Unexpectedly gently the giant set the child on her feet. She staggered from him, then finding herself free she flew to Josef, flinging her arms about him, burying her face in his patched coat. Josef's arms closed about her, his eyes on the robber leader. The man was gazing thoughtfully at the implements that had fallen from the sack. Curiously he bent to pick up the dop with its rounded heap of solder, the tiny indentation at the top. He regarded it for a moment with puzzled eyes, then tossed it back into the mud. He shifted the big metal wheel once more with his foot, and pounced upon something that was revealed by the movement. Josef's heart sank. The big man straightened. In his hand he held not the leather bag but Josef's loupe, his jeweller's eyeglass, a tiny magnifying glass set in a brass surround and frame. The man held it cradled in the palm of his hand, crafty eyes thoughtful. Then he said something in Polish and reached again for the sack, shaking it, turning it inside out.

The little soft leather bag landed at his feet.

The small sound that Josef made was hardly audible, a simple, swiftly indrawn breath. But the man heard it. He bared his yellowed teeth, danced the bag in the air in front of Josef's eyes, tutting softly, his eyes dangerous.

"Tch, tch. Bad boy," he said in his mangled Russian.

Josef said nothing.

Huge fingers fumbled with the fine leather thong, tore it at last in impatience. The small, dull stones tumbled into a dirt-ingrained palm. The man frowned. This was not what he had expected. Pieces of dirty glass? Of what possible use were they?

And yet —

He glanced at his victim. In the man's eyes as he looked at the glass-like pebbles was a despair he could not disguise. That was enough. Jan Kopelski was no man's fool. He tucked the leather pouch into his pocket and then eyed the man and the child, his mind moving with slow deliberation to the next problem.

What to do with them?

The man was whey-faced, the child clinging to him in terror. In truth they made a sorry pair. Behind them Lech the whore, who had just so much enjoyed searching the man, was waiting with bright expectancy on his face, long fingers flexing. For some reason Kopelski felt a spasm of irritation at the naked bloodlust in the boy's face. Stupid child.

The little girl was weeping softly, helplessly, the great, oddly empty violet eyes drowned in tears.

Never let it be said that Jan Kopelski was not a generous-hearted man; let them live. Why not? The child looked like an unhappy angel — perhaps if he left her unharmed one small candle might be lit somewhere, sometime, for his besmirched soul. Kopelski, nothing if not superstitious, took the thought as an omen. A good deed warmed the heart. Leave them be. They were harmless enough. In all probability they'd die on the road anyway. Let some other son-of-a-whore take the responsibility for that. With a sweep of his arm he gathered his comrades to him. They came, eager for sport.

"Leave them," he said, and took malicious pleasure in the disappointment in young Lech's girlish eyes.

"But —"

"Leave them, I say. They can do us no harm. Come." He turned and strode down the road, knowing his command of them. Reluctantly they followed. At the brow of the hill he turned back. The man had sunk to his knees in the mire, the child clasped in his arms. Even from this distance there was defeat in the bowed shoulders.

"Pah!" he hawked, spat, considered for a moment going back and finishing the job after all, then shrugged. Why bother? Let the wolves have them.

CHAPTER TWO

AMSTERDAM 1875

The city, on this February evening, was a place of glimmering reflections: the dark, wind-rippled waters of the canals shimmered beneath bridge and wall, never still, mirroring the gleam of lamplight from the tall, gabled houses, glittering in the bitterly cold darkness and creating a deceptive beauty from the narrow, squalid streets behind the city's waterfront.

Josef Rosenberg, head down against a biting wind that cut through his threadbare coat like a butcher's new-honed knife, noticed neither the beauty nor, for once, the squalor. He walked fast, blindly, his fury carrying him forward. Turning a corner too fast he slipped on rain-slick cobblestones and cursed in a manner of which he would have been incapable twelve months before. At least, he reflected bitterly, past experience was teaching him something.

Ahead lay the familiar little bridge which crossed a narrow canal to a street where stood a row of dirty tenement houses much frequented by the sea-vagrants of the port. In one of these, to his shame, in an unhealthily damp semi-basement he and Tanya had lived since arriving in Amsterdam a few months before. He slowed his steps a little, fighting for control of a temper which, if slow to kindle, had always been equally slow to die.

Thrown out by a servant! After all he had been through — to be literally thrown from the door of the house of the man upon whom he had pinned his hopes, with no chance to explain himself. He almost choked with mortification to think of it. He could still feel the rough hands on him, still see the sneer on the servant's face. "Out, beggar!"

Josef stopped on the bridge, leaned over the crumbling parapet and, sightless and sullen, contemplated the night-dark waters of the canal. Was nothing ever going to go right again? Was this nightmare never to stop? They had survived a massacre, a gruelling journey, attack, theft and — he was certain — near murder. Left bereft and helpless by the vagabond thieves of Poland, they had stubbornly struggled on, step by step, yard by yard, always westward, always somehow keeping hope alive, until at last, against all odds, he had dragged himself and the helpless child to Amsterdam — the goal that in those last terrible weeks on the road had shone before them like a golden beacon in darkness. He uttered aloud a sharp bark of self-mocking laughter, and turned to contemplate with a disenchanted eye the dingy tenements and narrow, unpromising streets that surrounded him. Not for them the wide waterways and pretty, tree-lined avenues of fashionable, prosperous Amsterdam. From the day they arrived their ill-luck had continued to dog them. Even without their precious small store of diamonds Josef had felt reasonably certain that he would be able to find employment in the diamond cutting and polishing centre of Europe. But those last grim weeks on the road had taken a much worse toll than he had realized. To feed Tanya he had himself eaten nothing, to clothe her he had gone all but naked, and his body, unused to privation, had finally rebelled. By the time they had reached the city, in company with a band of players from whom Josef had earned a few coppers helping to set up and dismantle the stage, he had been a very sick man indeed. Their first night had been spent in the open, their second here in the comfortless room in which they still lived, the only accommodation that Josef could afford. By that second night Josef had had a fever, and those first few days in the city were still a confusion in his mind, a nightmare of pain and restless half-sleep punctuated by terrible hallucinations. Amazingly, it had been Tanya who had cared for him then. His few lucid moments had been lit by her sweet smile, tended by her small, careful hands. She had in her gentle way made friends for them amongst the other tenants of the crowded building — the woman on the first floor had donated worn and none-too-clean blankets, the man who worked on the fish quay supplied fishheads for soup, another a few lumps of coal. And Pieter van Heuten — Josef's brow furrowed a little as the name came to him — had shared his bread and sometimes his ale. For a time the world had seemed a more friendly place. As soon as he was enough recovered, Josef had set out hopefully to look for two things — the house of Tanya's distant cousins, whom he felt sure would be ready to give the child a decent home again, and work. In the first task he had expected some difficulty, whereas in fact the discovering of the Anatovs' whereabouts had proved relatively simple; in the second he had expected none and been savagely disappointed.

Amsterdam was not a big city, and it had not taken long to discover the more prosperous centre. It was on the evening of the second day of combing the streets, scanning brass nameplates and letterboxes, that he had, to his delight, found the Anatov offices on the Rokin. The building in which they were situated was magnificent, the nameplate discreet and well-polished. Only too aware of his beggarly appearance Josef had hesitated, ineffectually smoothed his hair and then, somewhat apprehensively, had rung the bell.

It was a very long time before the door opened to reveal an obviously astonished young man in high collar and frock coat, his black hair oiled to the sheen of metal, whose supercilious gaze summed Josef up and dismissed him out of hand before he had even opened his mouth. Disparaging eyebrows lifted.

"Wat blieft u?"

"I'm — I'm looking for — for Mr Anatov. Mr Sergei Anatov," Josef stammered in his native tongue. At university he had been considered an outstanding student of languages — his English and French were, though rusty, near perfect. However, under present conditions — not too surprisingly — he had discovered that of the Dutch language he could not yet make head or tail.

The superior young man shook his head dismissively, spoke again, briefly, in Dutch and made to close the door.

In an almost involuntary action Josef jammed a desperate foot in the closing gap. "Please. Please! I must see Mr Anatov! I have — a little girl —" In his anxiety to have himself understood he found himself, ridiculously, raising his voice as if sheer volume might bring comprehension.

The man spoke again, quietly and icily, and with an

undisguised threat in his voice that needed no translation. Neither did the expression on the face of the uniformed flunky who answered the young man's call. Josef stepped back. "Mr Anatov," he repeated urgently. "Sergei Anatov. *Please.*" He spoke slowly, willing them to understand.

The door closed sharply in his face. In angry frustration he stared at it.

"You're looking for Anatov?"

The voice was young and hard, the words spoken in Russian. The speaker, who had apparently appeared from nowhere, was as unkempt as Josef himself, younger, the face sharp-eyed and bitter.

"Yes."

The young man considered. "What's it worth?"

Josef shook his head. "I have nothing. Wait —" This as the youth lifted a nonchalant shoulder and turned away. Josef hunted in his pockets. The day before Tanya had given him a few coins that Pieter van Heuten, the sailor who spent so much time with the child, had given her. "Here. I have this. That's all."

"Pah!" A dirty finger flicked in disgust.

"It's all I have."

The youth watched him for a moment, speculatively. He put his head on one side, eyes cunning. "You got trouble for Anatov?" A voracious eagerness threaded the tone and gave Josef, gutter wise now, his cue. Here was a grudge.

"Could be," he shrugged.

"Then I tell you. That bastard deserves trouble. You going to try to get something out of him?"

Josef almost found himself shrugging again, that involuntary, very Jewish gesture that he had intended to shed with his shaved off beard and ingrained way of speech. He had had a lot of time to think of such things. "Perhaps."

A short sharp sound that could have been laughter. "I wish you luck. It's the tall red brick house on the east side of the Herrengracht. The one with the black door and the eagle gablestones. Anyone will tell you. Everyone knows the Anatov house. Hey —" This as Josef turned away with muttered thanks. A dirty hand extended, the fingers clicking. Josef deposited the coins in the grubby palm. "There's no one there just now," the boy said, in grinning afterthought as he pocketed his profit. "They've all gone off on some stinking trip. Paid for with other people's money, of course." The words were vicious.

"When will they be back?"

"God knows. Or the Devil. Ask him."

Josef sighed now, shivered as the wind gusted across the water, sending ripples of yellow light dancing beneath the bridge. Perhaps he should have taken note of the young man's bitterness. He had found the Anatov house, but as the youth had said it had been locked up and deserted, the shutters firmly closed, not even a servant left to answer the empty ringing of the doorbell. The only thing to do was to wait, watch the house until the family returned and, meanwhile, to find work.

He had reckoned without the trembling hands of deprivation, the disability of his wrecked appearance and his lack of the Dutch language. Time and time again he was turned away, sometimes sympathetically, mostly less so. Not even the influx of gemstones from the new and exciting discoveries in South Africa had made jobs easily come by. No one was going to employ a worker, however skilled he claimed to be, whose hands shook like a drunk's. No one could be bothered to listen to his pleas and promises in mangled Dutch — they had no need. Skilled men flocked to Amsterdam, men with steady hands and eyes, and with proof of their prowess in handling the precious adamantine stone. The last months had made of Josef a physical wreck, his tall frame weakened and stooping, his brown hair peppered with grey, his eyes red-rimmed and often painful. There was no work for such as he. At last he had to accept the bleak truth and had taken to haunting the docks, begging, accepting any work he could find, eking a living of sorts for himself and the child and praying that when the Anatovs returned to Amsterdam help would be forthcoming, at least for her.

Then at last, yesterday, on one of his regular visits to the Herrengracht, the miracle had happened; there were lights in every window of the house with the eagle gablestones, a bustle of servants, a stream of tradesmen and visitors to the handsome doors. The family were back. Happily he had hurried home to tell Tanya, who for the past few days had been poorly — now, at last, everything would be all right. When the Anatovs saw Tanya, living image of her dead father, surely they could not deny their aid?

Arriving home, he had known the minute he put foot on the doorstep that the child's cough was worse. He heard it, a racking, painful sound as he hurried down the dank passage to their door. His heart sank — Tanya had had a niggling cough for days, but this was more than a mere childish illness. He opened the door. The slatternly woman known as Bea who lived in the room above with a tribe of children — no two of whom looked alike — was there with Tanya, one of her snivelling, fatherless offspring as always clinging to her dirty skirts. She beckoned to Josef impatiently, speaking rapidly in ill-accented Dutch of which he could understand only one or two words. Tanya huddled on her mattress in the corner, bright flags of fever flying in her cheeks, the racking cough shaking her slight frame every few minutes. The woman fussed around her. Josef sat, helpless, and watched, cursing again the goddess of fortune who baulked him at every turn. His plan had been to take Tanya to the Anatov house, where the sight of her, regardless of relationship, must be certain to melt the hardest heart. Now, looking into the bright, fever-lit eyes, he knew that to be impossible.

And so, this afternoon, he had gone alone.

It had begun better than he had dared to expect; the imposing black door at the top of the steep flight of steps had been opened by a slight, pretty girl in neat dark dress and apron. To his relief, for he had not ventured to hope that the Anatovs would employ Russian staff, she spoke Russian with a strong Ukranian accent, and after only a moment's hesitation shyly invited him into the house while she went off to find a servant of some higher degree and experience to deal with this confusing visitor. He realized later, and to his cost, that only the still-disorganized state of the newly-arrived household had allowed him so far. He stood in awe, despite himself, at the flamboyant splendour around him; not for the Anatovs the steep, narrow stairs that characterized most of the houses of Amsterdam, but a sweeping, graceful staircase in gilt and white, its banisters and rails wreathed with swathes of golden leaves and flowers, intricately wrought. There were echoes of St Petersburg in the glittering chandeliers, the tall mirrors, the soft, jewel-coloured rugs and carpets: the house had all the hallmarks of taste and of immense fortune. Across a wide landing at the top of the sweep of stairs a pair of tall white and gilt doors stood half-open, through which from his view-point below he could see enough to guess at the size and magnificence of the room beyond. As he stood, a drably incongruous figure in the midst of splendour, servants hurried by, most eyeing him in open curiosity, some with a glint of not quite smothered amusement. As he watched a woman in elegant afternoon dress — a gracefully bustled affair of brown velvet and cream silk which set off to perfection a stately figure and haughty carriage — swept across the landing and disappeared into the magnificent drawing room. The small, scurrying maid in neat black and white who followed her shut the door behind her mistress with a click.

"You!"

Josef turned to find himself confronting a uniformed manservant whose demeanour suggested anything but welcome.

"What are you doing here?"

Like the little serving girl, this was a Russian. Josef allowed himself a lift of relief — at least he could make himself understood. "My name is Josef Rosenberg," he began politely, and with as much dignity as he could muster. "I've come to see —"

"Out."

Josef stared.

The man stepped forward. "Out," he said again, simply and with great emphasis.

"But — wait — you don't understand —" The serving man had grasped Josef's arm, painfully firmly. On an unexpected spurt of temper Josef wrenched himself free. "I insist that you listen to me."

Something in the sharp, well-educated voice gave the servant pause. He hesitated and Josef took advantage of his uncertainty.

"I must see Sergei Anatov. It is of the utmost importance. My name is Josef Rosenberg —" He saw again a flare of dislike in the man's eyes. How many times had he suffered that reaction at the mention of his name in this anti-Semitic world? Grimly he ploughed on, "I have in my care Mr Anatov's young cousin, Tanya Georgievna, daughter of Alexei Anatov of Kiev —"

He got no further. From the stairs above him came a voice, sharp and irritated. "What's going on here?"

A few steps from the top of the lovely staircase a man stood, immaculate and well-groomed in black morning coat, dark trousers and snow-white linen shirt.

Josef's heart stopped.

"Well?" The voice was not the same — Alexei's had been light and pleasant, this was harsh, a voice with nothing in it of laughter at all. "Well?" the man asked again, and his fingers drummed upon the patterned handrail.

The face and figure was Alexei, from the fair hair and darkly violet eyes to the slim build and long, impatiently tapping fingers.

"Sir, please —" Regaining his voice Josef moved eagerly forward, ignoring the threatening movement of the man beside him. "I am Josef Rosenberg, come from Kiev. I have in my charge a young relative of yours. Tatiana Georgievna Anatov, daughter to Alexei, my friend, your cousin —" He faltered a little as the harsh expression on the familiar face above him neither softened nor changed, then rushed on, "You must have had news of the tragedy that overtook the family? Tanya and I escaped and fled. We've been on the road ever since — I brought her to Amsterdam in the hope that —" Thunderstruck he stopped as, with a dismissive flick of his fingers, Sergei Anatov turned away.

"Throw him out."

"No — please — you must listen."

"This way, Jew." The manservant's hands were like steel. He was quite evidently enjoying himself. "Like I said the first time. Out." He forcibly propelled Josef towards the door.

Josef dragged himself away. "No. Mr Anatov — listen! The child is ill —"

The double doors of the drawing room shut decisively. The front door opened. "Out, beggar."

From top to bottom of the steep steps Josef tumbled, painfully, and lay sprawled in the road. A pair of urchin children, huddled for warmth by the house wall where the vent from the kitchen was situated, giggled and pointed.

The shining black door had slammed shut.

Josef hardly remembered the rest of the day: dazed with fury and with a disappointment that had been like a sickness, he had wandered the streets of the city unwilling — unable — to face the eager questions of the child whose implicit faith in him had led her to believe what he had believed himself — that Sergei Anatov would be their salvation if they could once reach him. With the blind stubbornness that he knew to be one of his biggest faults he had, over the past months, resolutely ignored the mental voice that had reminded him time and again that the two branches of the family had never seen eye to eye — on the contrary that Alexei had openly detested the man he had described as his 'money-grubbing cousin'. That on one occasion, brought nearly to ruin by two bad harvests in succession, old Boris had, against his better judgement, applied to these, his only living relatives, for help — only to be told that he must, like any other borrower, put up his property as security for the loan and pay exorbitant interest. In fact, it had been the Jews of Kiev who had saved him on that occasion, and Boris had cursed his kin as soulless usurers. But somehow none of this had seemed of any great significance when weighed against the tragedy that had overtaken the Kiev Anatovs, and the perils of the past months. The Amsterdam Anatovs had seemed to Josef to be the only hope. He had been unable to believe — still, in truth could not really believe — that any man, no matter what the circumstances, would deny a child of his own blood, condemn her to poverty and to likely death, leave unchampioned the man who had spent himself to save her.

Thought of Tanya jogged his memory. He felt in his pocket to check that he still carried the small bottle of medicine that he had at the last minute remembered to purchase at the Sign of the Yawning Man — the sign of all apothecaries in the city — for the sick child. He took it out and surveyed it moodily. He was not fit to care for the child. Even this, the medicine she needed so badly, he had not been able to supply. It had been purchased, as so many of their necessities were purchased, through Pieter van Heuten's doubtful charity. A man in whose debt Josef would rather not be. The brutish seaman's attentions to Tanya were, despite the welcome generosity that attended them, a source of worry to Josef. There was something disturbingly unnatural in the way the man's eyes followed the child, in the way that his hands reached greedily for her when ever she came close to him. He sighed defeatedly. In this, as in everything else, there was nothing he could do until he could free them from the rathole that had been their home for the past awful months. And how, now, was he going to do that? With shoulders hunched to his ears he walked from the bridge into the narrow, wind-scoured street.

The first thing he noticed as he came to the tenement door was that the child's cough, unexpectedly, sounded a little better. The terrible rattle had eased and it no longer sounded so rackingly painful. A small mercy, but one for which to be more than grateful; he pushed open the door of their room with a forced smile.

Two pairs of eyes met his — Tanya's, enormous, trusting, disturbing as always and Pieter van Heuten's, pale and avaricious. Josef tried to suppress the surge of dislike that the sight of the man brought. Van Heuten had helped him when he was ill, had spent hours entertaining the sick child, had paid for her medicines and most of the food she ate. Yet dislike and distaste persisted. Pieter van Heuten was a man of medium height and enormous bulk, as strong as an ox and strangely ugly — strangely because the ugliness lay not so much in his features, which were unremarkable, as in an indefinable brutality of expression, a twist of the heavy lips, a rapacious light in the pale eyes. He was of middle age and boasted of having been to sea since he was ten years old. His other boast was that he had travelled to every country in the world and could curse recognizably in every language in existence — a patently exaggerated claim that Josef was in no position to challenge. Certainly the man's Russian — swearwords and all — was understandable, and he had also managed to teach Josef some small smattering of Dutch so that their conversations, if polyglot, were at least comprehensible to each other. Van Heuten had sailed in on a ship home from Cape Town at just about the same time that Tanya and Josef had arrived in

Amsterdam and had taken up residence in what was apparently his permanent home on the top floor of the tenement, where he lived, if in equal squalor, certainly in a great deal more comfort than most of the other occupants of the building. Josef assumed him to be living off the proceeds of his last voyage — presumably when they were squandered he would be off to sea again. Despite the man's apparent generosity, the day could not come too soon for Josef. Pieter van Heuten was not the friend or companion he would freely have chosen for himself, let alone for Tanya. From the moment the seaman had seen the strange, lovely child, the unnaturally light eyes had devoured her, following her every movement, watching her for hours. Even whilst holding a conversation with Josef, van Heuten's eyes would invariably be on Tanya. He took every opportunity to touch her, pulling her roughly on to his lap, fondling her as he might a small animal, while Tanya, sweetly docile as ever, suffered silently the man's advances for the sake of friendship. Young and hurt as she was, a kindly voice, presents of food, sweetmeats and even occasionally playthings were too precious to sacrifice simply because she disliked being handled so. Always sweet-tempered and anxious to please, it was not in her nature to protest at an action that she believed in her innocence to be kindly meant. But Josef saw sometimes the effect that the child's soft body had on the man and despised himself for allowing it, for accepting still the man's company and help. Yet he, too, found it hard to turn away support and friendship, however suspect its source. Pieter van Heuten's generosity to them was no part of a naturally giving nature — van Heuten had confided, spitting, that to the other tenants of the building he would not give the clippings of a dog's hair. Nor was it, Josef was certain, altruistic — sooner or later the man was going to expect some reward for his help. But for now and for the immediate future Josef could see no way that they could survive without him, so in this, as in so many other things, he lived necessarily for the day and left tomorrow's troubles for tomorrow. But the man disturbed him unpleasantly. Like or trust him he could not, and his heart sank at the sight of him.

"No luck?" the seaman asked, at sight of Josef's face.

Josef, shaking his head, perched upon the end of Tanya's

mattress — van Heuten was sitting in the only chair in the room and had made no move to vacate it.

Tanya lifted great, uncomprehending eyes. "Are we going to the house on the Herrengracht?"

Josef hesitated. "Not yet my little one. There's — a little difficulty."

The child frowned. "Are my cousins not at home after all?"

"I — yes, but — they're very busy. I — couldn't get to see them today."

"Ah." van Heuten's eyebrows were raised sardonically.

Josef ignored him. "I thought — we'll wait till you're better, little pigeon. Then you shall come with me." Last hope. Sergei Anatov, surely, could not refuse the evidence of his own eyes.

The shadow on Tanya's fever-bright face lifted. "I should like that."

Josef pulled the medicine bottle from his pocket ransacked the drawer for their one spoon and gently poured the foul liquid into the obediently opened mouth. Pieter van Heuten looked on, eyes expressionless. When Josef had done playing nursemaid the seaman searched behind the chair upon which he sat and produced, with his habitual unpleasant grin, a bottle three-quarters full. "Here. You look as if you need it."

The spirit burned fiercely and hit Josef's empty stomach in a flood of fire. He swallowed again.

The Dutchman, still grinning, stood up and patted the chair in invitation for Josef to sit, then disposed himself comfortably at the foot of the mattress, one hand apparently accidentally resting upon the foot of the almost-sleeping child. "Tell Uncle Piet all about it."

The telling did nothing to ease Josef's humiliation-fed anger — neither did the entire remaining contents of the bottle. Pieter van Heuten fetched another. Half-way down that one, "Shits," he said unsteadily, breaking unexpectedly into a gloomy silence. "Shits the lot of them. Dutch, Russian, English — bloody Chinese for all I know."

Josef lifted an aching head. "Who are?"

"Them in the shitting diamond business. Shits the lot of 'em. Rob an honest man an' leave him dead any day of the shittin' week."

Josef did his best to focus his glazed eyes, then shook his head with drunken deliberation. "No."

Van Heuten leaned forward belligerently, "What do you know about it, eh? Eh? Tell me that. What — do — you — know?" He rubbed his eyes with the heels of enormous, calloused hands.

"As a — matter of fact —" Infuriatingly Josef found himself not quite master of his tongue; he knew exactly what he wanted to say, but, confusingly, the effort of putting it into words was almost beyond him. "As a — matter of fact —" he began again, obstinately, "I know a very great deal. A very — great — deal." He thought deeply for a moment, then leaned forward gravely and confidentially. "What do you think I used to do in Kiev, eh? Answer me that. What do you think?"

The Dutchman yawned prodigiously. "How the hell would I know?"

Josef extended his right hand. His thumb showed the leathery burn mark that was the brand of his craft, scarred by the many times he had smoothed the hot solder into the dap and set firmly into its hot mass the stone to be ground and polished. "Have you never seen that before?"

The Dutchman yawned again. "Never."

Josef's eyelids drooped.

Van Heuten, none too gently, nudged him and he almost fell off the chair. "Well?"

Josef jumped awake. "Well what?"

"What is it? The mark? What's so special?"

Josef told him, at great and rambling length. Half-way through the narrative the seaman went back to the bottle. But those strange eyes regarded Josef with every sign of sudden, rapt interest.

Josef planned very carefully his fresh assault on the Anatovs. This time he must make as certain as he could that nothing could go wrong. To this end he prepared the way by writing a letter — and cursed himself for a fool not to have thought of something so simple before. Surely the only possible explanation of Sergei Anatov's behaviour was that he did not know the true situation. Who could blame him, if that were the case, for distrusting a stranger, a vagabond, who turned up from nowhere with no child and no proof of her existence? So Josef reasoned and reassured himself, resolutely ignoring misgivings. Tanya was getting better each day. Soon she would be able to go out. In his carefully worded, beautifully scripted letter he requested, politely, an audience with Sergei Anatov the following Friday afternoon.

To his enormous, if hidden, relief the uniformed footman who opened the door to them at the appointed time made no demur, but stepped back, his expression frigid, in invitation to them to enter. That hurdle crossed, Josef breathed a little easier — right to the last moment he had more than half-expected to be turned away. Tanya, pale now with the aftermath of illness and transparently beautiful as a small angel, clung to his hand as if to her hope of salvation as they entered the great house. With a lack of deference that amounted to outright insolence and deflated a little of Josef's fledgling optimism, the servant led them up the sweeping staircase, past the magnificent drawing room to another set of double doors further along the ornately decorated landing. The footman knocked, and a peremptory voice bade them enter.

"The man and the child, sir." The footman's face was wooden.

"Thank you, Brazanov. You may go."

The man bowed himself out, leaving behind him a silence that bred foreboding and started a faint, sickly tremor of nerves deep in the pit of Josef's stomach. Tanya might have been a small alabaster statue; she stood still, scarcely breathing, her pain-filled eyes fixed upon the man who sat behind the vast mahogany desk. The room was furnished as a study, a comfortable, expensive masculine retreat. A fire burned brightly in the big fireplace. The heavy draped curtains shut out the darkening afternoon, and in the shadowed winter room Sergei Anatov's bright hair caught the glint of flame and reflected it red-gold. As did Tanya's.

Josef opened his mouth to speak.

"No." Anatov held up an imperative hand. "You are not here to speak. You are here to listen."

At the sound of the harsh voice the child flinched, physically. Josef tightened his already vice-like grip upon her hand.

Sergei Anatov stood up and walked around the desk, then leaned upon it surveying his visitors. In his hand he held a piece of paper which Josef recognized as his letter. He lifted it, his eyes cold.

"Perhaps we should begin by getting something absolutely clear. I have no intention whatsoever of being blackmailed by a cock and bull story into accepting this — child — into my household or my family. Is that understood?"

For a moment, Josef could not speak.

"I cannot imagine that you could truly believe that I would allow myself to be taken in by this pack of lies —"

"No!"

"— this pack of lies, I say," the man continued evenly. "My distant cousin and his family —" the chill eyes flickered very briefly to Tanya's stricken face "— his *whole* family — were killed, tragically, when their house caught fire and burned down."

Josef gaped.

"Now you come to me with this fabrication, besmirching the family name — *my* family name — with sedition and filthy Jewish lies, and expect — what? That I should welcome you with open arms? Recognize the child as —"

Josef found his tongue. "Recognize her? That, surely, is the word, yes. Just look at her." Josef thrust the silent Tanya forward. The man's eyes flicked to her and away.

"Do you take me for a fool? Of couse I see the resemblance. Who would not? A bye-blow, no doubt. A bastard, taken from the streets of Moscow to further your schemes." He gave a small, caustic laugh. "Didn't you know my cousin Alexei? He was notorious —"

"He was the best friend I ever had."

There was a moment's silence. The uncharitable, assured eyes raked Josef from toeless boots to uncut, shaggy hair. "Oh, really? You expect me to believe that? Come, now." The tone was deliberately, quietly offensive. "I've already told you that I'm no one's fool. It will be easier for us both if you simply realize that there is absolutely no point in your persisting in these outrageous lies." He paused. "Perhaps I should explain something. If your purpose is, through this little impostor, to lay some claim to her libertine father's estate, then your efforts have been for nothing. You'll both be sorely disappointed. The estate has been confiscated —" the chill eyes looked for a moment directly into Josef's own "— in payment of debt. There's not a rouble, not a blade of grass left. Now let me make something else plain. Unless you retract this — this lunacy —" he struck the open palm of his hand with the letter in a sharp movement that belied his apparent calm "— in writing, you'll get not a guilder from me. I must tell you that when first I read this my reaction was to have you arrested." He paused, allowing the words to sink in. Josef watched him, expressionless. "However, having now seen the child and knowing too well my cousin's — regrettable — reputation, I might be willing, in charity, to offer you a small sum. I would not have it said that I allowed my cousin's bastard child to starve. However, on one thing I insist. Not a penny will you receive from me until you admit in writing that you have fabricated here a pack of lies."

The slow fire of Josef's anger was building. "Never!"

The man stood up. "Then there is nothing else to be said. You'll get no second chance from me. Go back to whatever hole you crawled from and ponder the rewards of good sense —"

"The rewards of treachery, you mean."

For one still moment violet eyes met brown with the faintest spark of acknowledgement flickering beneath steel-cold determination. In that moment Josef knew this was no case of an honest mistake. "A melodramatic word, I always think. And, unlike most Russians, Mr Rosenberg, I am not much given to melodrama. It will get you nowhere." Anatov turned away. "Enough. Will you leave of your own accord, or do I have you thrown out again?"

Josef clung to the shreds of his self-control, his concern now to get Tanya away with no more hurt. "We'll go," he said tightly, adding more in defiance than hope, "But you'll hear from us again."

Fair, assured eyebrows raised. "I think not. At least — not until you've swallowed your pride, written your retraction and come begging for the charity that is the only thing you'll get from me."

With enormous restraint in deference to the presence of the

child, Josef refrained from telling him, bitterly and inventively, what to do with his charity. With no word he turned and strode to the door, towing Tanya with him. In the doorway he almost cannoned into the elegant woman he had seen on his first visit.

"Sergei," she asked sharply, "what on earth is going on?"

"Nothing to worry about, my dear. A little unpleasantness —"

For the first time the woman caught sight of Tanya. "Good God!" she said faintly.

Josef saw his chance to plead Tanya's case again, this time perhaps to a more tender heart. "Madam — please — I beg you. The little girl is daughter to your husband's cousin who died in Kiev last year. She is quite alone in the world —" New hope died still-born. There was not the faintest flicker of warmth or sympathy on the woman's face, just, somewhere almost hidden, a shadow of pure relief quickly masked, before she turned from Josef to look to her husband.

"A pack of lies of course, my dear," he said quietly. "Though, as you can see, the child is undoubtedly Alexei's — a bye-blow sired God knows where. It is an ill-conceived attempt to extort money."

Madame Anatov looked again at poor Tanya, distaste and dislike written clearly upon her attractive face. "What are you going to do with them?" She spoke as if neither Josef nor Tanya were in the room.

Her husband shook his head. "Nothing. They're leaving. They know better than to come back."

Josef saw a flicker of doubt in the woman's face. She looked at Tanya again and this time he saw, as clearly as if she had put it into words, the reason for her concern; no woman could be happy to see in her own house a child who was the living image of her own extremely attractive husband. A small, unpleasant thought was born.

Anatov joined them at the door. "I asked you to leave."

For the moment there was nothing left to say. With what dignity he could muster, Josef took Tanya's hand and turned from the pair, marching down the splendid staircase stiff-backed, aware of their eyes upon him. In the hallway below a manservant waited, beneath his veneer of impassivity a hint that there would be nothing to please him more than for Josef to make trouble.

In a moment they were out in the street, enveloped in a soft, blowing rain that could not disguise the tears that glistened on the child's face.

That night, morosely, Josef sat in the dirty, ugly little room that had become home and stared into space, silent, comfortless. Three times he had refused the bottle that Pieter van Heuten had proffered. Now he did so again, with an impatiently shaken head.

Van Heuten shrugged, tipped the bottle to his own mouth, not for the first time. "Face it, Josef. You handled it all wrong."

He spoke in Dutch. Josef understood enough to grunt angrily in reply, but so far gone in depression was he that he could not be bothered to speak.

Van Heuten continued expansively, in the mongrel tongue he and Josef shared. "These diamond people — I told you — they're farts. Won't give nothing. You have to take, Josef, my friend. Take. The man's frightened, you say, to be associated with the girl's father? Use it. Frighten him more. Take him —" van Heuten reached into thin air with his hand and grasped an imaginary object "— and squee-eeze him." The huge hand closed, graphically slowly into a fist.

Josef shook his head. "He doesn't strike me as being the type to be — squeezed — as you put it. He's a man of wealth and influence. God knows what he might do if I tried to make trouble for him. Always supposing that I could." He went back to his gloomy contemplation of the wall.

"But he did offer you something?"

"Charity." Josef spat the word.

The seaman shook his head in exaggerated wonder. "Charity, you say? Well, God's teeth, what's wrong with that? You can afford to be that choosy? Get *something* from the pig —"

"No!" Josef's fist smacked the table, almost waking Tanya, who was asleep in her corner, her face still swollen and tear-streaked. She stirred and murmured. Josef, with an effort, lowered his voice. "No. To accept his terms — to fall in with his lies simply to save his face means branding Alexei's daughter bastard for the rest of her life. I won't do it. I swore she should suffer no more — swore that she would live again, safely, securely. She needs love and happiness —"

"We all need that my friend." The words were sardonic, but Josef ignored them.

"She needs healing! What chance would she have living on the charity of a man like that? God only knows what might become of her."

"What chance has she anywhere else?" The Dutchman walked from the dark window where he had been standing, to where the child slept and hunkered down beside her. Josef watched him. "Pretty, pretty little thing," the seaman said, and reached a hand.

Something in his eyes stirred the hairs on the nape of Josef's neck. "Don't touch her," he snapped.

The broad, hairy hand stilled for a fraction of a second and unfriendly eyes flicked to Josef's face. Then the man continued his arrested motion, tucked the thin blanket beneath Tanya's chin and straightened, shrugging. "My friend, you're on edge. What you need —" he lifted the bottle high "— is a drink."

This time Josef drank, long and deep. The Dutchman, grinning, waved an inviting hand and Josef took another swig, felt the rough liquor course down his throat. Van Heuten lifted his head and drank with relish, smacking his lips. "Josef," he said, his voice oddly confidential, "tell me something." He watched Josef for a long moment. "You say you know diamonds."

Josef nodded grimly. "For all the good it does me."

There was a short and somehow significant silence. Josef glanced up. The light eyes were upon him, speculative and crafty. "I was thinking more, perhaps —" the Dutchman said in careful Russian, "— of the good it might do me." He stood up, swayed a little. It came to Josef that the man was perhaps more inebriated than was immediately apparent; though when he spoke his voice was steady and his words unslurred. "Come. I show you something. Something beautiful, to cheer you. And then, well, we'll see. Perhaps you help Piet, eh? Perhaps you know a way —" He jerked an imperative head, "I show you. Come." He picked up the guttering candle from the table and led the way to the door.

Curiosity impelled Josef to follow the man, his shadow flickering giant-like upon the running walls, out into the passage and up the narrow dark stairs, past doors behind which voices were raised and children cried. Josef started as a stray cat, disturbed at their passing, suddenly shot from the darkness through his legs and away down the stairs. A few steps on he averted his eyes from the half-dismembered rat that had been the animal's meal. Jovial with drink, Pieter laughed loud and unpleasant, and slapped his shoulder.

"You're too finicky, my friend. Like a girl, eh? Me — I *like* this place. Wouldn't live anywhere else. I could be a rich man — oh, yes, as God is my witness I could — you'll see — I could live anywhere. In a palace. Yes. A palace. But I *like* it here." Laughing uproariously now he fiddled with his key in the lock of his door. The key never failed to astonish Josef — no one else in the building had such a refinement, nor even thought of it. He followed the other man into a foul-smelling room that was lair-like in its filth and chaos.

Van Heuten held the candle high, and cleared a chair with a wide sweep of his hand. "Sit down, eh? Sit down. First — another bottle. Here. Ah — that's good." He rolled the drink upon his tongue. "Now, I show you. I show you my fortune." He set the light upon the table, began to turn away, then stopped, his expression suddenly drunkenly wary. He pushed his face close to Josef's. Josef recoiled from the evil breath. "You listen to me. You say nothing about this. You hear? To no one. Or I kill you, eh?"

Looking into the brutal face, Josef did not for a moment doubt the threat. He said nothing.

"You hear me?"

"I hear you."

The Dutchman watched him for a moment, still belligerent. "You better hear me. You cross me — I break you in half —" he raised a hand, snapped dirty fingers beneath Josef's nose "— like that. Believe me."

"I believe you."

The silence stretched a few heartbeats longer. The man gave a sudden shout of laughter. "Of course you do. You're my friend. My good, Russian friend. My good Russian friend in the diamond business." Still chuckling, he went to a small cupboard in the corner of the cluttered room. "Now. Now, you see — wait —" he came back to Josef, something cradled in his cupped hand. In the act of holding it out for the other man to take he hesitated for a moment, as though he might after all change his mind and snatch the thing back. Then, "There." He deposited something the size of a small egg in Josef's hand, where it lay, heavy, gleaming, lucent in the unstable light, opaque yet lustrous as lit ice.

In the silence a barge hooted outside, a lonely sound.

"It's beautiful, eh?" The voice was still soft, somehow lustful.

"I — yes, it's beautiful."

"A man would kill for such a stone, eh?" the Dutchman snickered boastfully, watching Josef for his reaction.

Josef hardly heard the words. He was staring in wonder at the thing that nestled in the palm of his hand as if it belonged there. It was beyond doubt the biggest and most beautiful rough diamond he had ever seen.

CHAPTER THREE

From the first moment he saw it, in the darkness of that stinking, dirty room, the light of the candle glimmering deep in its heart, Josef coveted the stone as he had never coveted anything in his life before, nor ever was to again. Here, cradled within the grasp of his open hand, was the means to change his life and Tanya's at a stroke, the glittering key to a future of which he had all but despaired. He had no doubt at all as to its value, needed no minute examination to convince him of the diamond's flawless quality; he knew it, would have staked his life upon it, felt it in his blood the moment he held it. Yet — it was not simply the fantastic value of the thing that drew him, the knowledge of the fortune that must surely await the man who could release the living fire that smouldered within it. From the start it was as if the gem bewitched him, called to him, revealed to him, and to him alone, planes and angles and the rainbowed refraction of light that an unpractised eye could never have recognized. From the moment he held the stone, his fingers ached for the feel of the tools that would discover the beauty that lay dormant within it. So rapt was he in those first moments that he hardly heard the rambling, drunken tale that accompanied it — a story of treachery and murder and betrayed friendship that later he was to sicken of hearing; for, once the Dutchman's tongue had loosened, it was as if a vicious compulsion urged the telling and retelling of the tale, often with added, lividly embroidered details — but always with the same core that Josef came to recognize as the barbaric truth.

Eighteen months before, on shore leave in Cape Town, van Heuten had embarked upon a drunken orgy that had ended in the cutting of the throat of a ship's officer. Judiciously, he had decided the time had come to leave the sea for a while, and he had jumped ship in the hope of trying what he saw as the easy pickings of the newly-opened diamond fields upcountry. Lacking in experience, equipment and luck he had at first been disappointed. But not for long. In such a place and at such a time there would always be alternatives for a man like Pieter van Heuten. Leaving the hard work to others he gambled, swindled and cheated his way from the Orange to the Vaal and back again, finally going into dubious partnership with a German called Weitner — a man from all accounts as villainous as himself — with whom he had entered into the lucrative business of stealing sheep and cattle from the vast farms that surrounded the diggings, slaughtering them and selling the meat at hugely inflated prices to the hungry men of the mining camps that had sprung — mushrooms of timber and corrugated iron — along the banks of the diamond-rich rivers of Southern Africa. But they had badly underestimated the tough farmers of the veldt; the day came when van Heuten and his partner had stolen one sheep too many — on their next foray an unfriendly reception committee awaited them. Weitner was taken and hanged on the spot with no ceremony. Van Heuten was luckier — though slightly wounded he managed to escape and make his way towards the newly christened town of Kimberley, centre of the new diamond rush and a good place for a wanted man to lose himself. A few miles from the town, however, he collapsed, weakened by his wound, and was found by the roadside by a young American, Johnny Burton, who, unlike most in his position, neither left the stranger to die nor robbed and finished him off himself. Believing, to the Dutchman's private amusement, van Heuten's fabrication about being attacked and robbed, the young man befriended him, took him in and nursed him back to health. More fool him, said van Heuten with a grin; and predictably had repaid the young man's misplaced generosity with a conscienceless betrayal that had cost the American his fortune and his life. It had been almost a month after van Heuten had moved into Johnny's corrugated iron shack — an oven in the heat of the African sun, but a haven nevertheless for a hunted man — that the American had at last found the stone that all along he had been convinced was waiting for him. Flawless, weighing nearly seventy carats, it was every diamond man's dream of swift fortune. Sitting that night with the

Dutchman around their small cooking-fire he had, with naïve elation, shown the man he considered his friend his find, had sat till the early hours dreaming aloud of his future — a cattle ranch somewhere in the Western States, marriage to the girl he had left behind, a family — twenty-four hours later Johnny Burton was dead, battered almost beyond recognition with his own shovel and Pieter van Heuten was on his way to Cape Town, the diamond in his pouch. He had, however, made one bad miscalculation; Johnny Burton was not, as were so many of the men that haunted the diamond diggings, a friendless down-and-out to be left for the vultures and no one to care. Even among the hard-bitten men of the mining camps his good nature and friendly open-handedness had won him many good friends, among them a dour, tough Canadian known simply as Bull, who had detested and mistrusted van Heuten on sight. As luck would have it, Bull it was who found Johnny's battered body within an hour of the Dutchman's departure and, drawing the only possible and absolutely correct conclusion, immediately set out to hunt the man who had killed his friend. So it was that van Heuten, to his astonishment, had found himself the subject of a grimly single-minded manhunt that had, as well as disturbing his peace of mind, effectively prevented him from disposing of the diamond. Finally reaching Cape Town with the stone still in his posession and with Bull right on his heels, he had signed on to the *Marie Anne*, a freighter bound for Amsterdam, and had fled to safety.

"Why haven't you sold it here?" Josef asked that first time, weighing the diamond in his hand, turning it gently upon his palm with the tip of his finger.

"Pah!" The sound was a compound of disgust and anger. "Do you think I didn't try? Cheats! Cheats and thieves!" He snatched back the stone, brooded over it. "Can I go to the ponces that live on the Herrengracht with something like this? Clearly not. Questions would be asked, eh? Questions I should not be happy to answer. So I went —" he paused, shrugged "— elsewhere. To the smaller dealers — to the ones who don't ask so many questions. Pigs. They thought they could cheat me. Told me the stone was worthless. You know what they offered me?" He spat, too close for comfort to Josef's boot. "A stinking six thousand guilders. Six thousand! Do they think I floated in to Amsterdam on the last tide?"

"I suppose they guessed that you wouldn't dare try to sell it on the open market."

"I suppose they did." The light eyes gleamed in the guttering light, glinting malevolence, fixed upon Josef. "But perhaps — now — they're wrong, eh? Now I have a friend — a friend who knows diamonds — a friend who can tell these cheating jackals that Piet van Heuten knows the value of this stone and won't be made a fool of by misbegotten sons of bitches who think they can pull the wool over a man's eyes."

Exactly when the overwhelming desire to own the stone became a resolve — an astonishing resolve — to steal it, Josef was never sure. The thought must have been there, he realized later, from the very first moment he held the thing, must have lain quietly in the recesses of his mind waiting for the moment when desperation and necessity finally exerted themselves to transform the unthinkable into the acceptable and the decision could be taken. Certainly within a very short time he found himself to be completely obsessed with the stone. In his dreams, waking and sleeping, he handled it, worked it, watched its transformation from clouded crystal to living, lustrous gem. The thought of it lying neglected in that pigsty of a room above his head was more than he could bear; the knowledge that all of his own hopes, and Tanya's, could well lie in that festering filth was far worse, and not even an innately honest nature could long remain proof against such enormous temptation.

But if he could not recall the precise instant of decision regarding the theft itself, he never forgot the moment he saw, in Tanya, the means to that end.

It occurred on an evening when van Heuten, as so often, turned up at their door with a bottle of schnapps and a present for Tanya. Carelessly at home as always, he flung his coat on to the hook on the back of the door, handed the bottle to Josef, his eyes already searching for the child.

"Hey, my little Russian princess. Come see. Come see what Uncle Piet has for you." He drew from his jacket pocket a prettily-dressed, slightly tattered rag doll with round blue eyes and smudged red cheeks. Grinning, he dangled the doll in the air, just beyond Tanya's reach. She looked at it, pleadingly.

"Say 'Please', now." He taunted her as he might a puppy, keeping the doll just beyond her reach.

She lifted her arms. "Please," she whispered.

"Please, dear Uncle Piet."

She turned her great eyes for a fleeting moment to Josef. Her colour was high. Then, "Please, dear Uncle Piet," she repeated obediently.

"Give it to the child if you're going to," Josef said shortly. "Why make her beg?"

Van Heuten ignored him. He dropped to one knee and handed the doll to Tanya, catching her round the waist before she could grasp the doll and flee, as had been her obvious intention. "Doesn't your Uncle Piet deserve a kiss then?"

The child's hesitation was barely noticeable. Then she allowed herself to be pulled on to his knee and petted.

"That's my good little girl. A kiss for Uncle Piet — just a little kiss."

It was then that it struck Josef that these times — when he fondled and played with Tanya — were the only times when he ever saw the man so relaxed, so unguarded. Vulnerable. He tried to push the thought away. To contemplate stealing — even from such a rogue as van Heuten — was bad enough. To consider involving the child, surely, was unthinkable. Yet the thought, once lodged, would not be dismissed. Through the long nights when he lay unsleeping, discarding first one impractical plan, then another, he came constantly upon the same stumbling block — van Heuten's constant vigilance. The man trusted nobody, and though he treated Josef's room as his own the compliment — if compliment it were — was in no way returned. Never did Josef find himself in the other man's room alone, never on those occasions when the man was out of the house was his door ever left unlocked. The only way to get at the diamond was to get hold of the key. That, Josef thought, might be easy enough. But then he had to arrange for something — someone? — to distract the man's attention, keep him safely downstairs, out of the way.

He tried time and again over the next few days not to think of using Tanya as a decoy, yet no matter how he tried the thought would not be dismissed; on the contrary, as the days passed, he found himself reasoning with himself, justifying the unjustifiable. The child could not possibly come to harm. If he — Josef — stole the key from van Heuten's pocket, made some excuse to slip out, went straight upstairs, took the diamond — why the whole operation would not take more than five or six minutes. What hurt could befall the child in such a short time? And she, after all, would partake no less than he of the new life that could follow. If the choice were between a life that had a meaning and a life that had none — what true choice was there? His plan to dispose of the diamond using the Amsterdam Anatovs meant using the child, and he had no scruples about that — where, in heaven's name, was the difference?

So he reasoned, knowing the devil's voice, helpless to withstand it, a man driven against his nature to dishonour. His resolve faltered only once, when the woman Bea, with seemingly uncanny timing, chose to warn him against letting Tanya associate with van Heuten. Josef had noticed that there was intense bad blood between these two; the reason for it became clear on the day that the woman stopped him on the stairs with a crook of her finger and a conspiratorial jerk of her head. "A word with you."

Josef by now understood enough Dutch to follow most of what she said. He stood politely, waiting.

"Him up there —" She jerked a fat thumb graphically towards the top landing. "Don't let him near your girl. He's filth."

Josef was more than a little taken aback at the directness of the words. "He's been very kind to Tanya," he began.

The woman snorted. "Kind? Hah! I dare say he has. As he was to my little Hendrikje, eh? Giving her presents. Telling her his filthy stories. And me not knowing what was going on under my very nose! Till the day I caught him with his hand up her skirt —"

Josef felt hot colour rise to his face. Ridiculously he felt as guilty and humiliated as if it were he himself the woman discussed with such contempt. "I don't —"

She ignored his attempt to speak. "I tell you the truth. His hand up her skirt. His fingers —" She stopped, eyeing the expression on Josef's face, "Well, no need to say, eh? I tell you — he was lucky I didn't chop them off, and his other parts with them. Filth!" she said again, with quarrelsome force. Then she softened. "Your little one, she's an angel, a little angel, But," sorrowfully she pointed a finger, screwed it illustratively into her own forehead, "she's not quite right in the head, huh? And her so gentle. How would she know how to behave with such a man? What would he do to her, filth like that?"

Josef fled. But though the woman's words haunted him, still the compulsion, the necessity to acquire the stone, the key to their escape from savage poverty and indignity, drove him; and he could see no other way. He'd be a fool and worse than a fool not to take this chance. A heartless fate had kicked them in the teeth more than once this past year — now was the time to take fate by the throat and redress the balance. The man to whom the stone truly belonged was dead, foully murdered by van Heuten. It now belonged to anyone who could possess it. And who had a better right than the man who knew instinctively the secrets of the stone, and who could release its captive beauty to the world? The child would not be harmed.

So he told himself, and so he more than half-believed.

Josef Rosenberg turned thief one gale-swept March night while the loose, ill-fitting shutters of the building crashed against the rotting brickwork in the wind, and small, chill drafts, sprites of cold mischief, scurried along passages, up stairs and beneath doors. He had laid his plans as far as he was able, and then simply and fatalistically waited; who knew, perhaps the opportunity would never arise. But when, on this windy evening, van Heuten put his head round the door and Josef from the other side of the room smelt the raw spirits on his breath, he knew with a disturbing mixture of dread and anticipation that the gods had indeed decided to tempt him.

The Dutchman, grinning foolishly, stumbled into the room, divested himself of his coat, tried unsuccessfully to hang it as usual on the hook on the back of the door and watched in drunken surprise as the garment slipped to the floor in an untidy heap.

"It's all right. I'll do it. Here — sit down before you fall down," Josef to his astonishment heard his own voice, even and self-contained as ever, betraying nothing of the sudden thumping of his heart, the dryness of his throat. He pushed the rickety chair forward, catching the Dutchman behind the knees. Giggling and wheezing, van Heuten collapsed into it. Casually, Josef stooped to pick up the coat. "What in God's name have you been doing to yourself?"

Van Heuten tossed back his head and roared with laughter. "Drinking, my friend! What else? Drinking a scoundrel under the table! Did I ever tell you of Hennie van der Post? The bugger who damn near got me cut into collops in Athens three years ago?" He launched into a garbled story, the slurred words almost unintelligible. Josef watched him, not listening. The man was drunk as a pig — surely he must soon slip into insensibility? Slowly he walked round behind the chair, and hung the coat he was still holding on the back of it. The room was far from warm, but a sheen of sweat stood on his face.

"And then — you'd never credit it —" the Dutchman stopped, peered around. "Dammit, Josef, where the hell are you?"

"I'm here. Here," Josef said, soothingly.

"Ah. Well, then I said —"

"Uncle Josef! Uncle Josef — Hendrikje's found a kitten. A poor little lost kitten. May we —" Tanya's precipitate entrance into the room took her almost into the arms of Pieter van Heuten before she could stop herself. As he reached for her, she froze. Van Heuten stopped talking, his bleary and reddened eyes upon the child's suddenly still face. He licked his lips.

Tanya, abashed, stepped back, pulling away from him.

"Come now, little one. Little flower. Come to Uncle Piet." The tone was maudlin, the hot eyes obscene.

The child looked to Josef in desperation. His heart took up the slow hammer beat of tension. "Where have you been?" he asked severely.

"Upstairs. Playing with Hendrikje. She's —"

He interrupted her. "You're late."

The child looked surprised. "But —"

"You're late" he repeated sternly. "I've been waiting for you. I told you — I have to go out. To see a man about a job."

She looked puzzled. "You didn't —"

"Tanya — will you stop arguing?" Guilt made his voice sharper than he intended. "I tell you I have to go out. So come along now — get undressed and into bed."

The child glanced at the watching van Heuten, then, pleadingly, back at Josef. A poppy flush of embarrassment had risen in her cheeks. "Must I? Couldn't I wait till — till you get back?"

Josef hardened his heart. Five minutes. Nothing could possibly happen in five minutes. He saw the way van Heuten was watching the child, knew beyond doubt that the man would offer to stay with her. "Come," he said again, severely, "into bed."

Reluctantly Tanya walked to the corner where her small mattress lay, turned her back on the room as she wriggled out of her threadbare blouse and skirt. van Heuten watched. Outside, the wind moaned, whistling through the cracks, bringing the child's pale, pearl-smooth skin to goosebumps. In her petticoat and without turning round she slid swiftly into the cold bed, pulling the dirty blankets close up around her chin.

"Don't be so hard on her, Josef my friend," van Heuten slurred. "She's not ready for sleep yet. Are you my pet?" He lifted a drink-flushed, brutal face. "I'll tell you what — you go about your business. I'll stay with the child. I'll tell her a story. Eh? You'd like that, wouldn't you, little one?" He staggered to the mattress. She watched him come with wide, stricken eyes.

Almost, then, Josef abandoned his plan. His conscience and his heart impelled him so — his brain told him that no such chance was likely to come again. The key in his hand might have been made of red hot metal. "Please yourself," he heard himself say. "I shan't be long. Five — ten minutes at the most. Make yourself comfortable. But Piet —"

The Dutchman looked up, surprise in his eyes at the sharpness of Josef's tone.

"— if you're going to tell stories, make sure they're suitable for young ears."

"Hah!" The man made a gesture of injured irritation. "You

been listening to that cow upstairs? I know decent stories. Go — off you go." He waved an unsteady hand at Josef. "Don't worry. I'll look after her. Uncle Piet will look after her." He turned back to Tanya, who lay, mute, her face in shadow.

Josef cleared his throat. "Yes. I'll go. I won't be long. Five minutes at the most —" He hesitated at the door.

Van Heuten grunted and did not turn. Josef let himself out into the dark, draughty passage. The key he had taken from the Dutchman's pocket had left a painful imprint upon his palm, so fast had he clutched it. He stumbled up the unlit stairs. A feral glint of eyes was followed by a skittering flight — cat or rat, it could have been either. The top landing where stood the Dutchman's locked door was faintly lit by the lamps of the city that shone, diffused, through a narrow, dirty window. With trembling fingers he jammed the key into the lock. It rattled loosely and would not turn. Cursing, he forced his shaking hands to steadiness, guided the key more carefully into the keyhole. This time it caught, clicked, and the door yielded. Up here at the top of the house the wind noise was demented. The gale buffeted the windows, clattered the shutters, whistled down the chimney, found every crack. Like the landing, the room was lit dimly from the outside. Josef went straight to the cupboard where he knew van Heuten kept the stone.

The wind screamed across the roofs, hit the window as if intent upon breaking into the room.

The diamond was not there.

Frantically he hunted, blinded and deafened by the imperative need to find it. He could not — *could not* — come this far, take this risk, only to fail once again. The stone was here, somewhere. It had to be.

The minutes ticked by. To the floor at his feet, abandoning caution, he threw dirty clothes, an untidily coiled length of tarred rope, an unwashed tin mug, a tangled ball of string —

It had to be here.

He glared around the room to where another cupboard stood against the wall. Careless of noise, he ran to it, colliding in his haste with a chair and knocking it flying. The cupboard was empty of all but a mouldy loaf and a few hard unappetizing-looking sausages. His eyes picked out in the gloom a chest of drawers. He dragged the drawers open, flung their contents aside.

Nothing.

The wind shrieked, derisively.

And then he saw it in the shifting light — a familiar small box standing in full view on the cluttered mantelshelf. He reached for it with a shaking hand. A moment later the object of his search was in his hand, heavy, cold, wonderfully familiar. He closed his fingers over it, stood for a long moment, eyes closed, perfectly still, the stone clenched in his fist.

It was then he heard, high above the banshee howl of the wind, Tanya's piercing scream.

The staircase was a pit of darkness. The diamond still in his fisted hand he half fell, half leapt down the first steep flight. The child screamed again; no door opened, no voice was raised in question — in this area of the city, indoors or out, a cry for help was best ignored. Josef slammed hard and painfully against a wall, knocking the breath from his body. He regained his balance, gasping for air, continued his breakneck descent. As he slipped and stumbled down the stairs he rammed the diamond into his pocket.

The foot of the stairs was marked by the lighter square of the open street door. Wind buffeted along the passage, deadly cold.

He reached the door of the room that he shared with Tanya, hurled himself through it. One glance took in the child's white body, her terrified eyes, the smears of blood on thighs and belly. Van Heuten's brutish face as he lifted it to the shrieking Josef was a picture of drunken astonishment. His trousers were around his ankles, hampering his movements. With no thought, Josef let his momentum carry him on across the room. He heard his own voice roaring outrage. Blinded by fury and a terrible guilt, he launched himself upon the much heavier man like an attacking animal, bearing him over by the sheer unexpectedness and ferocity of his assault. Van Heuten's head cracked hard against the floor. The man squirmed, massively strong, beneath Josef's lighter weight. Tanya screamed again, shrill and piercingly as the fighting men rolled on to her legs.

"Swine! Vile animal!" Josef screamed the words in Russian. He beat at the perspiring face beneath him, heard the agonizing crack of bone. With a roar van Heuten gathered himself to throw his assailant off. Tanya scrambled silently into a corner, weeping silently now, collecting the shreds of her torn petticoat around her. Josef fell against the table leg, giving his shoulder a blow that normally might have half paralysed him. Bellowing, and still hampered by his tangled trousers, the seaman came after him, murder in his eyes. Josef rolled away, came up awkwardly on to his feet. The other man tried to stand, tripped and tumbled. For a moment he lay, prone and dazed, at Josef's feet. In a move that was pure instinct Josef reached for the chair that stood by the table, swung it high in the air and brought it down with savage force upon van Heuten's head. The man collapsed without a sound, sprawled obscenely, half-naked and bloody.

Josef retched.

The child sobbed, desolate.

The door opened.

"God in heaven." Bea stood, hands on hips. "What's this? What in Christ's sweet name is this?"

Josef straightened, wiping his mouth with the back of his hand. He did not look at the woman; his eyes were upon the shuddering, whimpering child.

Van Heuten did not move.

For a long moment the room hung, suspended, in shocked silence. Then Josef moved stiffly to the child. He gathered her to him, rocking her back and forth, muttering her name over and over.

Bea advanced into the room and with a dispassion that amounted to callousness grasped van Heuten's hair and turned his face to the light of the lamp. "You've made a mess of this one." Her tone was quite unruffled. "If I was you I'd be away before he wakes up. If he ever does."

The words brought Josef back to his senses. He stood up, fighting the weakness of reaction that invaded his muscles and turned them to water. He bent to wrap Tanya in the dirty blanket that lay crumpled upon the mattress. The child stood as if mindstruck, no longer crying, the violent trembling her only movement.

"Poor little mite." The woman moved towards her. Tanya

drew back, shrinking against Josef. "Can't say I didn't warn you, though. Filth!" This last, viciously spoken word she spat at van Heuten's prone body.

An almost paralysing calm had settled over Josef. Ignoring the woman he settled the blanket around the child, lifted her frail weight in his arms.

"You got somewhere you can go?"

He looked at her then, dark eyes burning in a face bone-white in the lamplight. He did not reply.

The woman nodded, stood aside. "You're right. Best I shouldn't know. Just make sure it's a good long way away."

Holding the still child as he might a baby, Josef walked past her and past the sprawled body at her feet without a glance, out into the windy darkness.

The house on the Herrengracht was ablaze with light. Despite the still gusting wind, the front door stood open and there was every evidence that a well-attended social gathering was in progress. Josef allowed himself a faint, grim lift of relief. All the better. Walking through the night-dark, gale-swept streets he had tried not to think of the consequences if this, the second half of his plan, went as badly as had the first. The sight of the lit windows and queueing carriages cheered him a little; an audience could surely only make his chances of success stronger.

He entered the house by the simple expedient of marching up the steps and through the open doors with a crowd of elegantly attired arriving guests. He was almost half-way up the staircase before the astonished servants had grasped what was happening.

"Hey!"

He neither stopped nor looked round. His body ached, his face smarted where van Heuten's clawing nails had caught him, the child's light weight after the walk from the waterfront was leaden. Doggedly he climbed the wide, shallow stairs, the focus for a dozen pairs of astonished eyes.

"What's this?" On the landing above, flanked by several openly intrigued guests, stood Sergei Anatov, his harsh voice tense with the same rage that whitened his handsome face to the tone of ivory in the light of the glittering chandeliers.

Josef neither spoke nor stopped until he reached the landing and stood eye to eye with the man he had come to confront. A liveried servant stepped forward. Sergei Anatov, his eyes flicking from the perilously challenging face of the man before him to the blanket-wrapped child that he carried, held up a restraining hand. For a moment they stood so, the two men, the one resplendent in perfectly cut evening clothes, diamonds sparking in the studs of his shirt and at his snowy cuffs, the other thin, shabby, his face scratched, his eyes exhausted.

"My dear Sergei —" A slim, blonde young woman in shimmering pink, frill-bedecked, draped and exaggeratedly bustled, her bare shoulders gleaming in the light, leaned to Anatov and tapped his arm playfully with her fan. "How very entertaining! A charade. It is a charade, isn't it?" Her voice was piercing, her pink mouth smiled, her eyes were sharp and avidly curious as she quite unashamedly craned her neck, trying to see the cowering child's face. "What are we supposed to do? Is this," she laughed spitefully, "some kind of Russian game?"

"It's no game, Madame." Josef's eyes remained fixed steadily upon Anatov. "I'm going to talk to you," he said, simply and quietly to the other man, "either here in public or elsewhere in private. The choice is yours."

For a moment it looked as if Anatov might unleash the anger that simmered beneath his surface calm. Then, with an obvious effort, he spoke softly in Russian. "In the study."

"Sergei — Sergei, for Heaven's sake, what's —" Madame Anatov's gay voice died and she stopped, staring dumbfounded at the tableau. Music drifted through the open doors of the drawing room. Very slowly, deep colour rose, mottling her shoulders and throat and staining her cheeks.

"Look to our guests, my dear." Anatov's voice, to his credit, was now totally under control, "I'll see to this." More people had gathered around them, the women gowned and gleaming with jewels, the men elegant in evening clothes, their faces without exception lit with the same voracious interest that the girl in pink had shown. Here was something that promised to lighten the boredom in the salons of Amsterdam — something to make a change from the latest love affair, the latest scurrilous gossip. Eyes moved from one face to the other, trying to probe beneath the filthy blanket that hid the child from view.

"The study," Anatov said again, tightly, and moved from the crowd, past Josef, to the study door. Looking at no one, Josef followed. As if a spell had been broken, everyone moved then, the guests being ushered into the drawing room by Madame Anatov — though there were some still to send speculatively curious glances towards the study door as it closed sharply behind the two men.

The study was in darkness, lit only by the glow of firelight. Anatov, his movements brisk with the anger he would not show, lit a lamp that stood upon the wide desk, adjusted it so that its light sent shadows dancing on the walls and drawn curtains. Josef gently laid his silent burden upon a leather couch, tucked a cushion beneath Tanya's head and folded the tattered blanket tenderly about her. The child's eyes were open, unblinking. She made no sound. The sight of the small white face hardened his resolution. He must not fail.

Anatov watched in silence, frowning. "What's happened to the child?"

"She's been — hurt." Josef's voice held a faint tremor. "Please — she needs some decent clothes — perhaps also a bowl of milk?"

"Certainly," Anatov said coldly, paused, and then added very quietly, "but I doubt that that is all you have come here to demand."

The door opened, and the sound of music and laughter swelled as Madame Anatov entered the room, closing the door quietly behind her and leaning upon it, her eyes on the two men.

Josef straightened. "I have come for two things," he said. "A loan. And — a favour."

"I see. And if I refuse to grant either and have you thrown out on to the street as you deserve?"

In answer Josef leaned to the child and drew back the blanket from the bright head. What might have been Anatov's own eyes looked at him, emptily and apparently without understanding. "Your guests seemed very interested in the child," Josef said quietly. "I very much doubt if you could have us thrown out of the house in such a manner as to arouse no curiosity. And —

even if you did — it would be an easy matter for me, I think, to discover their names — contact them later —" He let the words fall gently into the silence of the room. Anatov watched him contemplatively. His wife stood tense as a strung wire at the door.

"To what purpose?" The man's voice was even.

"To — shall we say — satisfy their curiosity. To beg a little help for the child — to explain the sad circumstances of her birth — the shame of her parenthood —"

"Ah," Anatov said.

The woman by the door drew a sharp breath, her eyes on her husband, doubt and question open upon her face. The man ignored her, watched Josef with an unfathomable gleam in his eyes. "I thought we might come to something like this," he said softly. "Come, explain to us the — shame — of the child's birth."

"It's a sad story. My poor sister, seduced, ruined, abandoned, died giving birth to the love child of the man who betrayed her. All these years it has taken me to track the scoundrel down, and now — despite the evidence of anyone's eyes — he repudiates the child, abandons her as he abandoned her poor mother to poverty and death."

"All lies."

Josef lifted suddenly peaceful eyes. The woman by the door visibly held her breath, watching him. "Of course," he said, and the woman's eyelids fluttered, veiling her relief. "But since the truth served for nothing but to get me thrown from your door — what else is there for me but to resort to deceit? It isn't of my choosing."

"Is it not?" Sergei Anatov walked to where another lamp stood upon a small table in a corner by the window. His movements studied, as if unaware of the eyes focused upon him, he lit it, carefully adjusted the wick to his satisfaction. The silence stretched on, punctuated by the muffled sounds of music and laughter, the crackle of a burning log. The man turned. "Money you said. And a favour. What favour?"

Josef hesitated. Here was the final throw, the gamble upon which all might be won. Or lost. He held out his hand, palm up, to Anatov. The man stood for a moment, absolutely still, his eyes upon the stone that lay in Josef's open hand. Then very slowly he reached for it, held it between two tapering fingers towards the light. "Where in God's name did you get this?"

Josef shook his head. "You don't need to know that."

Anatov was regarding the stone in rapt admiration. "What do you want of me?" he asked at last, softly, after what seemed to Josef a very long time.

"Your word that, after I've cut and polished it, you'll help me sell the stone, above board and no questions asked. I'll want you to substantiate the story that I obtained the stone legally and brought it from Russia with me. I plan to go to London. There I'll work on the stone. But I need someone of good standing to dispose of it for me."

Sergei Anatov nodded thoughtfully, turned the stone this way and that, his attention and his connoisseur's eye totally taken by it. He looked up at last. "Now tell me this. What is to stop me from simply appropriating this and turning you over to the authorities?"

Josef's voice did not falter; here was the true test of nerve. "The child. The scandal. And your own self-esteem. You may be hard, Sergei Anatov, but I don't believe you to be cruel. Nor dishonest." Fair eyebrows quirked at that. "I would of course be perfectly willing to negotiate a commission upon the sale of the diamond."

"How much?"

"Ten per cent."

The man barked laughter. "Thirty."

Josef shook his head, trying not to let the relief that washed over him distract him.

"Twenty-five."

"No."

"Well cut and polished it will be worth a fortune."

"I know."

"Twenty per cent."

Josef hesitated. "Twelve-and-a-half."

"Sergei —" said the woman from the door.

"Fifteen," her husband said, his eyes intent upon Josef. "Or you find yourself another seller. Fifteen."

Josef let out his pent breath. "Done."

"And the money to take you to London —"

"— would be a loan. Oh yes —" Josef added, as he saw the open disbelief on the handsome face. "A loan. I too, believe it or not, am an honest man." He pushed from his mind the thought of those sickening moments when he searched for the diamond, and of the events that had followed. "I'll not be beholden to you. And neither will Tanya. Don't worry — after this transaction is finished you'll hear from neither of us again."

Anatov watched him for a long, unnerving moment. "You're assuming that I've agreed to the transaction, that you've blackmailed me into helping you."

"Yes."

"You really believe that people would take your word against mine in the matter of the child?"

"Yes. In fact," Josef hazarded a shot in the dark, "I suspect that some would be glad to —"

The woman, who still had not moved from the door said now again, sharply, "Sergei! For heaven's sake!"

He made a quick, irritated movement. "Supposing I did agree." He held up the diamond. "How do I know you can handle this? How do I know you won't ruin it? I'd rather have it prepared in our own workshops —"

"No!" Josef's voice was sharp. He held out his hand, thumb turned to show the leathery burn mark that was the brand of his craft. "You'll have to trust me in that. No one is to work the stone but me. I can handle it, I promise you."

"The cutting?"

"That too. My father taught me well."

There was a short, nerve-racking silence. "Very well," Anatov said softly. "Then I agree." He lifted a hand as Josef began to speak, and continued, his voice brisk. "We'll feed and clothe you and the child. Tomorrow we will agree a sum to take you to London. It will not, I warn you, be princely. Enough to get you there and to live on for — shall we say three months?"

Josef nodded.

"That should give you long enough to prepare the stone for sale. It will also give us time to manufacture some story as to its source — I imagine you have no desire to tell me or anyone else the truth of it."

Josef remained silent.

"As I thought. It's South African?"

"Yes."

"Then it shouldn't be too hard." Anatov handed the diamond back to Josef. "If stones like this aren't exactly two a penny, at least there are enough of them turning up not to create too much fuss. It seems to me that the best thing would be to say that you brought the stone with you from Kiev. The less we lie the better. And if you produce the stone that you promise, it would be impossible, I think, to keep from its buyer the name of the man that worked it." He turned to the mirror that hung above the splendid fireplace, straightened his white tie meticulously, turned as he caught Josef's eye in the mirror. "Understand this," he said, softly, "I want you, the child and the stone out of this house by tomorrow evening, and I want your solemn word that you'll not bother us again after this business is finished." He stood for a moment over Tanya, looking down, his face sombre. The child lay, as she had since Josef had put her there, a silent doll. He lifted his head, searched Josef's eyes. "What in God's name happened?" he asked quietly.

Josef maintained a bitter silence. Something that would not have happened had you helped us in the first place — he did not say it. What purpose in recriminations now? Relief was giving way to exhaustion. He needed to be alone. To think. To rest — yes, above all to rest.

Anatov stared down at the child for a moment longer, then shrugged and turned away. "Well, Mr Rosenberg — I trust you have no further objection to our rejoining our guests?"

"Rose," Josef said, his voice tired.

The man turned. "What?"

"Rose. The name will be Rose. In England. An English flower. An English name. I'm not just going to England, you see. I'm going to be English. I'm going to forget everything that has happened, everything that I've known. A fresh start. A new name. Rose. Josef Rose."

"The man's rambling." Madame Anatov laid her gloved hand upon her husband's extended arm. They left the room in silence.

"Josef Rose," Josef said again softly into the flickering shadows, then walked unsteadily to the sofa, sat beside the silent child, buried his face in his hands and wept as he had not since Charnov Street.

INTERLUDE

LONDON 1876

London, Tanya and Josef were to discover, was as heartlessly indifferent as any large city; friendless they arrived and friendless they remained — at least until the empty rooms above theirs were taken some weeks after they moved in. Not that their solitary state bothered either of them — on the contrary, each for their own reason welcomed it. For Josef there was the diamond — it filled his mind and his dreams. He held it, studied it, all but talked to it. He would sit for unmoving hours in silence as the days lengthened and pale spring crept almost unnoticed through the strange city streets, the stone held before him, gazing at it as if by sheer concentration he would dissolve the adamantine surface with his eyes and enter the crystalline structure of the gem. Many times he took out his tools — cradled the stone in malleable solder, picked up the stick ready-set with the cutting diamond — called a sharp — that he had brought from Anatov's workshops in Amsterdam, ready to begin the operation. And each time, slowly, he would lay the tools down again. The time was not right. He had not yet discovered the soul of the stone. So the meditation would begin again.

Tanya, for her part, did not seem to notice their isolation from the world. For the first few days after her hideous experience she had been as if struck deaf and dumb. She had neither spoken nor, apparently, heard a word said to her. She had not eaten, neither had she slept and Josef had been distraught, believing her mind and body finally to have broken. But from the day that they had taken the ship from Amsterdam the child had appeared to improve quite miraculously, her usual sweetly docile nature had reasserted itself, submissively she had allowed herself to be fed, she had begun to acknowledge Josef's presence, to respond when spoken to. During the whole of the crossing she had refused to go below but had stood at the rail, her wide eyes fixed upon the swelling sea with the first signs of understanding or pleasure that Josef had seen. By the time they were settled in their small but quite comfortable room in the Gray's Inn Road her improvement was remarkable — she seemed almost to have forgotten her brutalization at the hands of van Heuten. Josef, thankfully, accepted the outward appearance of her healing and indulged his preoccupation with the stone upon which their future depended. His plans were made — the execution lay now within his own hands. At last, one late April afternoon, with watery sunshine breaking through the shower-clouds that had dulled the day, he knew, simply and with no doubt, that the time had come. With steady hands he lit the charcoal fire in the hearth to soften the solder, and dragged the solid table to the light of the window. Whilst waiting for the fire to draw he set up the worn scaithe and the small flywheel, bolting them through holes he had made earlier, ready for the operation of grinding and polishing after the stone had been cut to shape. Then, with the solder softened, he took the diamond and cemented it into his cleaver's stick. He pulled on his leather gloves and flexed his fingers, knowing how brutishly painful the coming task would be, especially for hands so long unused to it. He pushed a small wooden box to the table's edge to catch the precious chippings. Tanya, her attention caught by the unusual activity, moved from her corner and stood by his shoulder, watching as he picked up the two sticks, the one set with the sharp for cutting, the other with the stone she had seen Uncle Josef handling so often. The sight was enough to arouse even her passive curiosity.

"What are you doing?" She spoke in Russian.

Josef, his building concentration broken, frowned a little. Then, with an effort, he turned to the child, his voice gentle. "In English," he said.

Her brow furrowed worriedly, white teeth buried themselves in her soft, childish lip. "What — do —" she stopped.

"What — are — you — doing?" he prompted.

"What — are — you doing?"

Speaking the words simply and clearly in English he showed her, pantomiming the actions. "With this —" he held the sharp stick next to the diamond and mimed a vigorous rubbing action "— I will cut this —" he held up the large stone "— to the right shape. Then —" he pointed to the wheel. "You remember? You've seen it before, in Kiev." He stopped. She watched him, impassively beautiful, apparently unmoved. He could not tell for his life what she understood, what she remembered. He pushed the flywheel gently with his finger. It swung easily, turning the scaithe. "Later — you'll turn the wheel for me?"

She recognized the questioning tone of voice if not the words, looked at him intently, trying to make sense of what he said. Josef pointed, first at Tanya, then at the wheel. "Tanya — will turn the wheel — for Josef?"

This time she understood. Gravely she nodded. "Turn wheel," she said.

He turned from her, picked up the two sticks again in his gloved hands. Now was the moment. From the split second that he set one stone against the other he was committed — to success or to failure. Beyond the window pale sunshine washed the old brick walls to gold. A hansom clattered by. A flower-seller called.

Josef willed his weakened, unpractised hands to strength and set the stones together.

The nerve-racking operation took the whole of that day and part of the next, during which time Josef ate little, slept less and spoke hardly at all. The child, tending at the best of times to silence, sensed his need and did not interrupt him except to bring him the simple meals she prepared. She watched from her corner as he cut painfully away the uneven corners of the stone, bruising his fingers to the bone even through the gloves. Then silently she stood and turned the wheel when, at last, the harshly laborious job was done and, with the scaithe primed with diamond dust moistened with olive oil, Josef set himself to the skilled task of grinding and polishing the gem to perfect fire.

By the evening of the second day he knew he had done it. The rain had started again, silently drifting along the busy street beneath the window. Drops chased themselves down the small panes of glass. Josef, tired to exhaustion, held the scintillating gem between his fingers. It was a stone of fine make, no one could deny that, and, as Anatov had said, worth a small fortune.

Now he could plan — really plan — for the future.

Firelight glimmered in the brilliant-cut stone, speared dazzling spectrum colours to the eye. Tanya let out a small, almost inaudible breath of wonder.

"Here." Josef lay the stone on a piece of paper, gestured her closer. She looked at it in awe. Rainbow light danced upon her face. Josef tried not to think of another face, brutal, bloody, lifeless. "What do you see?" he asked in English.

Gamely she tried. "Pretty," she said. "Pretty light."

"More than that, child," Josef said, very softly. "Oh, I see more than that. I see a business. A jewellery shop of great repute and great respectability. I see a home. Comfort. I see security." The child's shadowed eyes were uncomprehending. He gathered her to him suddenly, rocked her wearily, finding himself unexpectedly and absurdly close to tears. Faces rose in his tired mind: the faces of the dead. Anna. The children. Alexei. He screwed his eyes up painfully. The past was dead. It had, for sanity's sake, to remain so. His only hope was to look to the future.

As if to encourage him to do just that, Grace Sutcliff and her mother moved into the rooms upstairs three days later.

They met on the stairs on occasion, passed the time of day politely. Josef liked the plain, rather shy young woman on sight, was attracted to her slow, peaceful smile, her quiet voice. Within a couple of weeks of meeting her and her strong-minded mother he had begun to form the resolution that an alliance would be no bad thing for all concerned. Grace was of impeccably respectable family, good education, sweet temperament and no means at all, her recently dead father having been gulled into investing the family's money in a fly-by-night money-making venture which had collapsed, leaving him ruined and in debt. However, Mrs Sutcliff, Grace's mother, was not a woman to allow such misfortune to overwhelm her. She was a person of singularly staunch character, as was her daughter. Josef admired enormously their lack of self-pity, their obstinate determination to keep up appearances no matter how far down in the world they appeared to have slipped. That Grace's mother saw very quickly in Josef a means to ease the difficulties of their situation he readily accepted — indeed, having already seen those same possibilities himself, he encouraged her to see him so. That Grace was nearly twenty years his junior was no drawback — indeed in both the ladies' eyes it was a positive advantage. As for Josef — he had a future now and he intended to secure it. He needed a home, and within that home he needed — and very soon would be able to afford — a wife to take care of himself and of Tanya. He courted Grace hardly at all; the delicate negotiations were carried on almost entirely through her mother. This was not, after all, an affair of passion, but a civilized agreement of mutual benefit to all concerned. Nevertheless it pleased him that shy Grace appeared not to be at all averse to the idea. He liked her and he liked her mother. Both of them got on well with Tanya — indeed one of the best aspects of the whole affair was the quiet and unexpected devotion that the child offered to the tranquil Grace almost from the first moment they met. The kiss that Josef bestowed upon his affianced wife's cool cheek upon the day that Mrs Sutcliff acceded graciously to his request for her daughter's hand was the first they had ever exchanged. A month later they were married, quietly and with no fuss. On the day before the wedding Josef received the news from Amsterdam that the diamond had been sold for a little under twenty thousand pounds, to the elderly Count Nic Shuvenski as a bride-present for his new and very lovely young Countess.

Grace Rose neither had such a present nor missed it; on the day following the wedding she and Josef were inspecting the premises of a small shop in Hatton Garden, and Grace, with gentle guile, was allowing Josef to believe that in this, as in the recent matter of their wedding, the decision was entirely his.

PART TWO

London, 1885–1898

CHAPTER FOUR

Anna Amelia Rose — small, tow-haired, twig-thin and nearly eight years old — surveyed with a regrettable lack of remorse the dirty tidemark inflicted by the mud of the pond bank upon her shiny black buttoned boots and then, with equal disregard for the voluminous velvet tiers of her flounced skirt, dropped to her knees in the damp grass the better to observe the lovely insect she had been pursuing. The dragonfly, settled for a transient moment upon a narrow leaf, quivered wings that were like gossamer in the September sun. Its body glimmered an iridescent green-blue that reminded the child of the gems she had seen last week during her much-anticipated birthday visit to Papa's workshop in Hatton Garden. Emeralds and aquamarines, and turquoise and topaz — the child loved the very sound and colour of the words.

The dragonfly's head, too, gleamed like a precious stone. Its narrow, elegant wings, veined with gold in the sunlight, looked too fragile to carry that metallic, shining body.

"Anna! An-na!"

She ignored the call, not even turning her head. One of the very best things about the new house, after the overcrowded rooms above the workshop in which they had lived for as long as Anna could remember, was the garden which, miraculously, although it was not really very big, had corners to hide in. Corners like this one, that encompassed the small, overgrown pool that she and her brothers had christened rather grandly 'the pond' — much to her Papa's amusement. He, in his funny accent, called it 'the puddle'. Anna put out a thin, tentative finger to the dragonfly. It quivered, but did not fly. For a moment it seemed that the insect would allow her to touch it. Utterly absorbed, she moved her grubby finger a little closer —

"Anna!"

Her brother's voice was a bellow in her ear; she almost fell over in shock. The dragonfly lifted and swooped across the water into the darkness of undergrowth on the other side.

"Alex! You beast! You frightened it away!"

"Why didn't you answer? You must have heard me calling." Her older brother, at nine as strong and stocky as a young tree, towered above her.

She turned her head, looking away from him. "I was doing something else."

"You still have to answer when a person calls you." The words were truculent. She felt the familiar frisson of irritation that any contact with Alex was likely to produce in her.

"That's only for grown-ups," she said subversively, knowing very well the provocation she offered. "I don't have to answer you if I don't want to."

He glowered. "We're waiting for you to come and play."

She shook her head, drew her knees up to her chin. "I don't want to."

"We're going to play French and English." His tone was wheedling, the necessity to have an extra participant to even up the teams overcoming his ruffled temper. "You like French and English, you know you do."

"Not with the silly Smithsons," she said with a dismissive sniff. "That Christopher's such a ninny. He'll get knocked over, and he'll cry and he'll run and tell his Mama and we'll all get into trouble. Especially me."

Since this was indeed exactly the chain of events triggered off by the last occasion that they had played the boisterous and all-but-forbidden game with the visiting trio of Smithson boys Alex, never usually at a loss for words was, for the moment, nonplussed.

"You shouldn't have pushed him so hard," he said lamely.

With one of those swift changes of mood that so characterized her, Anna giggled. Christopher Smithson was a year her senior and at least twice her weight, a pampered, plump mother's boy with an adenoidal voice whose corn-coloured, carefully arranged curls and band-box clothes always put her in mind of an overlarge and rather silly-looking doll. The remembered sight of his wrecked appearance at the end of that riotous game more than made up for the painful slapping she had received from Nanny Brown for being the cause of it. Nanny Brown thought little girls should present a civilized example to the young gentlemen around them, not take them on and occasionally even beat them at their own games. Anna heartily detested Nanny Brown, who had joined the household after the recent move; and she had more than good reason to believe that the feeling was mutual.

The dragonfly swooped again, darting through the dappled shadows. Both children watched it.

"Come on, Anna. Be a sport."

"Nanny Brown won't let us play French and English anyway."

"She isn't there. She's gone for tea and a gossip with Nanny Smithson. There's only Trudy. She won't stop us."

Tempted, Anna scrambled to her feet. Her white stockings were grass-stained, her pinafore smeared with mud. Her brother looked at her with something approaching admiration and whistled — an accomplishment he had only just managed to acquire. "You're *filthy!*"

Anna shrugged.

"Anna? Alexis?" Tanya's clear voice, unmistakably accented, calling from the terrace at the back of the house.

The children exchanged glances. "That's torn it," Alex said in disgust. "If they're all back then we won't be able to play after all. Honestly, Anna, you are a pain — if you'd just come when I called you —"

Anna, hardly listening, had stooped to pick a feathery spray of grass. She stood quite still, studying it, moving it so that the laden head bowed and danced.

"Come on," her brother nudged her roughly, "they're waiting."

Irritated again she pulled away from him.

Alex snatched at the stem of grass. "Come *on*, I say —"

Suddenly scarlet with fury, she turned on him. He took an entirely involuntary and slightly humiliating step backwards; Anna's temper was something for even him to reckon with. She hung on to it by a thread.

"Temper cat!" he taunted her with childish malice, seeing the efforts she made to control herself, but nevertheless judiciously poised for flight. "I'll tell Nanny. You know what she says about young ladies and their tempers — you'll get another good hiding."

Still she managed to restrain herself. "Tell tale tit, tongue shall be slit," she chanted, pulling a ferocious face.

"Baby!" he riposted. "You'll be crying in a minute. You're always crying —"

"I am not!"

"You are!"

"I'm not!"

"You are, —"

"Alex! Anna! What are you doing?" A tall slim figure hurried towards them, fine white muslin blowing as she moved. At eighteen, Tanya Anatov had fulfilled all the promise of her childhood and was a truly lovely young woman. Her face, the wide brow furrowed now with concern, was pale and pointed as an elf's, the great, oddly expressionless eyes fringed with long fair lashes. Her rare smile was like sunshine. "Your Mama and Papa are back. They wait on the lawn for you. Oh — Anna!" She lifted narrow, frail-boned hands in genuine shock, "You are so *dirty!*"

Anna shrugged exaggeratedly, feigning an indifference that in fact, at the thought of her mother, had suddenly deserted her. Nanny Brown was not the only one who disapproved of unladylike behaviour. More than anything in the world she wanted to please Mama. But, so often, she found herself doing exactly the opposite.

Tanya, disregarding her own dress, dropped to one knee and began anxiously to brush Anna down with her hands. Anna suffered the attentions with good grace. After Mama and Papa she loved Tanya best in the world.

"There. I think that's a little better. Take your pinafore off — at least your dress is clean underneath. I'll come back for it later." Tanya used the discarded pinafore to rub the worst of the mud from the small buttoned boots. Then she folded the apron, laid it upon the grass for later recovery and stood up, smiling a little. "You are almost presentable. Smooth your hair — so —

that's right. Now, come see what Mr and Mrs Smithson have brought for you."

"Oh! Is it a birthday present? Is it? May I have it now, do you think?" Anna fairly danced beside the taller girl, holding her hand. Alex, still put out, glumly brought up the rear. Alex found anyone's birthday apart from his own a bore.

Tanya smiled. "I don't know. Let's see."

On the small lawn that led from the terrace at the back of the tall, narrow town house Grace and Josef Rose waited. Their other children were already grouped around them — six-year-old James, four-year-old Ralph and baby Michael asleep in his pram in the September sunshine. The visiting Smithson boys and their parents made up the party. Josef, as he so often did, found himself surveying the scene around him with a tinge of superstitious disbelief. Could this all indeed be his? Could his dreams have come true so absolutely? Or was it all some kind of monstrous joke played by a malignant fate that lurked somewhere, waiting to take it all from him? Behind him was the lovely house for which he and Grace had worked so hard and waited so long. In this, as in so many things, Grace had been right. She it was who had found the house: in one of the rather less fashionable squares of Bayswater it stood on the corner, had a fair-sized garden and was a little removed from the noisiest thoroughfares. Yet it was within easy and pleasant walking distance, through the park, of the new shop in Piccadilly. Each morning with clockwork regularity he followed that route — along the Serpentine to Hyde Park Corner and thence to Piccadilly; and hardly ever did he fail upon his arrival to stop for a moment, survey the small, expensively tasteful shop-front and wonder at the strange twists of fortune that had transformed Josef Rosenberg, penniless and desperate refugee, thief, possible murderer — he had never attempted to discover if van Heuten were alive or dead, nor did he ever intend to — into Josef Rose, naturalized Englishman, family man, respected, wealthy, a jeweller patronized by the rich and the titled, dealer in precious stones.

He glanced at Grace, who was gently scolding James for some slip in etiquette regarding their young guests. Here, astonishingly, was the rock upon which his success and his content rested. Who might have guessed, all those years ago, at the strength, the foresight, the good sense that resided beneath that gentle and self-effacing exterior? He had married for convenience and discovered boundless energy, sagacity and — most amazing of all — devoted love. He had no doubts as to the debt he owed her. Grace it had been who had supported him in those early, difficult days, who had shown him how to harness his energies, his resources and his talents to such good effect that ten years had seen the firm establishment of a family business of repute and solid worth. This house was but another step upon a ladder he had once despaired of climbing. Not that it had been easy. He had worked hard — very hard — and Grace with him. She it was who had sat night after night, a baby often asleep beside her, an older child in bed in the room next door, helping him with accounts and time-consuming paperwork that his labours during the day and her duties to the growing children precluded their doing in the daylight hours. Stubbornly she had refused to squander any of their growing savings upon help. The time would come, she would say, and very pleased she would be when it did — but money made money and spending it made nothing, so work she would until such time as they were secure and established. The bitter lesson she had learned in watching her father's ruin and disgrace now stood her in good stead. She had never despaired, never faltered, and her faith in him had spurred Josef to greater ambition than he had known he owned. Step by step their objectives had been achieved — culminating in the opening of the Piccadilly shop and the buying of this house. Now at last, and with enormous pleasure, he saw her in the situation that was hers by right; settled in a home that she ruled with a firm but gentle hand, with an adequate staff to aid her, her children growing around her. This was the ideal of the age — and neither of them saw any reason to question it. As for their rather more newly acquired aspirations — evidence of an advance in them stood here upon the lawn with them: Grace's small coup in engaging the interest and affection of Hermione Smithson, wife of an M.P. and stalwart, as was Grace, in the Society for the Relief of the Deserving Poor, might well have been envied by a more practised social climber than she.

Grace, sensing Josef's eyes upon her, lifted her head to him and smiled slightly before turning back to their son. She looked a little tired. For a moment Josef's thought strayed to the new life that stirred now within her. Unlike the others, Michael's birth had not been easy. He could not but wonder if he had been wise to allow her determination to conceive another child so early —

"Where's the birthday girl?" Jovial Obadiah Smithson, M.P., beamed around the garden. Tucked under one arm he held a large, prettily-ribboned box. "Have to be goin' soon, you know — business to attend to — like to see the little 'un before we leave." Obadiah had fathered three boys, a fact of which he was inordinately proud, but nevertheless he had a man's weakness for the frills and furbelows of little girlhood, and spoiled Anna as if she were his own.

"Here they are."

Josef looked up at his wife's words. Coming through the small shrubbery in the centre of the garden were his eldest two children, flanking Tanya's tall, slim figure. As always, at the sight of her, his peace of mind — so apparently assured, so fragile in fact — shattered. No matter how much he loved and cared for her he could not escape the fact that she was a constant reminder of the ugly past, the keeper of his unquiet conscience. That no one else in the world was a party to their never-mentioned secret helped not at all — like a flaw in an otherwise perfect jewel she — lovely, sweet-natured, vulnerable — was the blemish upon his life. He could not look upon her without guilt. He had told no one the true story of his acquisition of the stone that was now known as the Shuvenski Diamond. Even Grace believed that, in trouble with the secret police, he had fled Russia and smuggled the diamond with him. The Amsterdam Anatovs, in what they saw as their own interests, had been more than ready to back that story. As for Tanya herself — over the years her stable surroundings and the companionship and affection offered to her by Grace Rose, who though in fact only ten years her senior had happily accepted and successfully filled the role of foster mother, had apparently healed the worst wounds in the delicately unbalanced mind. She appeared to have forgotten the terrible events of her eighth year, together with the happy childhood that had preceded it. Yet still there was a strangeness about her, an aura of pitiful melancholy that disquieted others and distanced her from those about her. Most people — even, indeed, Grace herself — assumed her to be a little lacking in wits. Josef knew well that this was not so. She still suffered nightmares, both waking and sleeping, of that he was certain; she had simply learned to curb her screams. The knowledge racked him. Never by word or deed did she indicate to him that she remembered what had happened, or if she did that she in any way blamed him. On the contrary, it seemed to him that her occasional deep bouts of depression appeared to be turned entirely against herself. Yet she was, and always had been, wonderful with the children and they, accepting her unquestioningly, as children will, adored her. Companions of her own age she neither had nor apparently missed. She walked now, grave and graceful, holding Anna's hand, towards the waiting group, and not for the first time Josef felt a surge of shame at his own faint and unjust antipathy.

Anna, excited, broke away from Tanya and dashed forward, then — seeing the expression upon her mother's face — stopped short and dropped a hasty but creditable curtsey.

Her mother smiled.

Obadiah Smithson bent to her, beaming. "Happy birthday, my dear."

She pecked at his proffered cheek. "It isn't until tomorrow, actually." She hated people to get things wrong.

"I know, I know — but seeing that I'm busy tomorrow, and can't get to your shindig," with a flourish he presented the brightly-beribboned box to her, "I brought my small offering along today."

"Oh — may I open it now? May I?" She looked pleadingly at her parents. "May I, Papa?"

Josef glanced at his wife. "My dear?"

Grace hesitated, her face solemn, a twinkle in her eye. "It is a rule of the house, is it not, Mr Rose, that presents shall not be opened before the proper occasion."

"Oh — Mama — *please!*"

Her mother's plain-featured face lit with a smile. In her blue satin afternoon gown, stylishly trimmed with dark green satin ribbons and insets, a small dark green bonnet embellished with a cluster of violets perched upon her tightly-curled hair, she looked to her daughter the very image of elegance. Beside her, large Mrs Smithson in a fuss of red velvet and gaudily flowered satin looked positively vulgar. Anna was suddenly aware of her own slightly wild appearance, but for once her mother seemed willing to overlook impropriety for the sake of occasion. Grace inclined a neat head to Obadiah Smithson. "What do you think, Mr Smithson?"

"My dear Mrs Rose, of course the child must open it. Indeed, it would spoil my pleasure if she did not."

Anna needed no further prompting. In her haste she fumbled with the ribbon that tied the box, tangled it into a knot.

"Tch, tch, Anna, why must you always be so impatient? Here — give it to me." Gently her mother took it from her, untangled the ribbon and took the lid off the box. "There."

Revealed lying in a nest of tissue paper was a plump-faced doll, the size of a human baby, dressed daintily and expensively in christening gown and bonnet. Anna regarded it as much in awe as in pleasure. Tentatively she put out a small, dirty hand.

"I should think not, Miss!" Her mother's voice was sharp, "What a dirty paw it is! Whatever next? Don't dare to touch the pretty thing until you've washed your hands!"

Anna withdrew the offending hand, stared at the doll, who stared back with flat, blue, unimpressed eyes.

"Have you left your manners at the bottom of the garden with your apron?" Sharp eyes — sharp tongue — Mama, whatever the appearances, missed absolutely nothing.

Anna flushed. "N-no Mama. Thank you very much, Mr Smithson. Mrs Smithson." She reached dutifully to kiss them, hoping fervently that Mama would not insist that she extend the thanks to the rest of the Smithson family. She wouldn't kiss awful Christopher, birthday present or no.

Grace, however, was satisfied. She turned briskly, offered her arm to Hermione Smithson. "Before you go, Mrs Smithson, do please come in and inspect our new pianoforte – I believe you play very well. We plan a musical evening quite soon — I'd rather hoped that you might join us. Anna!" This over her shoulder to Anna who, gingerly, had reached into the box to lift the doll's lacy white skirt.

Anna froze. For goodness' sake — did Mama really have eyes in the back of her head, as Trudy said Nanny Brown had?

"Don't touch that until you've washed your hands. Go with Trudy now. Give the doll to Tanya for a moment." She resumed then, without taking a breath, her conversation with Mrs Smithson. "I was saying just the other day to Mr Rose how pleasant it would be —"

"Run along, poppet." Josef tousled Anna's already untidy hair. This, for no reason that he could clearly define, was his favourite child, named for the wife he had lost in another life, another world. He followed the children and the nursemaid across the lawn to the small terrace. Once there something impelled him to look back. Tanya, alone, had seated herself upon the grass, her skirts spread about her like the petals of a flower. As he watched she took the doll carefully from its box. Something in her attitude unexpectedly twisted Josef's heart. She held the doll for a moment, sitting herself as still as a carved image then, very slowly, she enfolded it in her arms, holding it as she might a real child, in the crook of her arm, her head bowed. Pain moved within Josef, blurred his eyes.

"Mr Rose? Our visitors are leaving."

He turned. "I'm coming."

Anna's birthday party had for weeks been the subject of much anticipation and in no way did it disappoint. With the fine weather holding, the youngsters were banished to the garden for the more boisterous games, whilst the adults partook of tea and sandwiches indoors. A gaggle of nursemaids and nannies sat beneath the chestnut tree and watched, fondly or otherwise, their various charges as they stampeded about the garden playing Hunt the Slipper, What's the Time, Mr Wolf? and other energy-consuming games; then they too repaired for tea in the kitchen, whereupon Armageddon was let loose as the young male guests, left almost unsupervised, took the opportunity afforded by breaks between games to even up old scores or, here and there, to create new ones, and rolled around on the grass kicking, biting and punching whilst the girls, by and large, gathered their pretty skirts and fled. By the time tea arrived many a white sailor suit was grubby and grass-stained, many a pair of stockings torn. On the whole, Anna reflected, presiding over a gargantuan feast of sandwiches, cakes and lemonade, the occasion was going remarkably satisfactorily.

After tea the games were restarted on the lawn.

"Now then," said Trudy who, for her sins and to her disgust, had been left in charge of the proceedings while still more tea was served in the kitchen. "What d'yer want ter play? Somethin' nice an' quiet I should think, after what you lot 'ave just eaten."

"I Sent a Letter."

"Grandmother's Footsteps."

"Sardines!"

The suggestions, deafening, came from all quarters, but it was the last one that was taken up with enthusiasm.

"Yes, Sardines. Let's play Sardines!"

"I'm 'It'," Anna bellowed across the pandemonium, "because it's my party."

Such logic was irrefutable. Alex opened his mouth. Trudy put a quick hand over it. "Fair enough, Miss Anna. Off you go then. Come on, you lot. Hide yer eyes. An' no peekin' now. We'll count together. *One — two — three —*"

Anna flew off down the garden. "*Nineteen — twenty.*" Where to hide? She dashed to the potting shed, hovered by the door. It was so obvious. Where else?

"*Thirty — thirty-one —*" Behind her the chant rose, simple and rhythmic. Excitement churned. Where?

She ran along the garden wall, past the small gate, always bolted, that led out into the Square. Overhanging it was an old apple tree.

"*Seventy-nine — eighty —*"

Disregarding her party dress she scrambled up the tree and perched upon the wall.

"*Ninety-five — ninety-six —*"

Almost giggling with excitement, she hunched into a small ball, arms wrapped around her knees. They'd never find her here.

"*Ninety-nine — a hundred — coming!*"

It was a long time before anyone found her. They wandered beneath the tree, calling; Anna stuffed her hand into her mouth to stop herself from laughing aloud. Beyond the wall the life of the city rode by — a costermonger with his fish-barrow, calling his wares and swearing inventively at his undauntable escort of cats; hansom cabs and carriages. "*Got you!*"

She nearly fell from the wall. It had to be Alex, of course. "Get up!" she hissed. "They'll all see you."

Too late. "There she is!" several children gathered beneath the tree.

"You're sposed to hide with me," she said, glumly.

"We can't, Anna." It was Christopher Smithson, his brow furrowed, "We'd all get awfully dirty climbing up there."

"Oh, fiddle!" In their disgust, for once Alex and Anna were in accord.

"Mother's calling anyway." Anna jumped from the wall. "Come on, we'd best go."

They streamed back on to the small lawn where stood Josef, Grace and several other parents. Josef was organizing chairs for the adults. "We've come to watch the fun —"

The fun, after that, necessarily, was considerably tamer, the most excitement occurring when young Ralph, rushing enthusiastically back and forth in the game Nuts in May, was very sick indeed. That diversion over, it was decided that things should perhaps take a quieter turn.

"One more game," Grace held up a single finger, "and then it's time to finish. What shall it be?"

The pandemonium started again. Grace, theatrically, put her fingers in her ears. The riot subsided. Grace looked at her daughter. "Let the birthday girl choose — Anna, what shall it be?"

Anna, not averse to having all eyes upon her, pondered. Truth to tell she was tired and would not now be sorry to see the back of her guests. She could not for her life think of a game that she really wanted to play. But she could certainly think of one that Alex had always detested, and that would do just as well. "In and Out the Dusty Bluebells," she said, and smiled innocently into her brother's black face.

"What a good choice. Come along, children — Dusty Bluebells. Get in line —"

The children linked hands, boys and girls alternately, Anna on the end. Grace began to clap and to sing in a high, tuneful voice, and the other adults as well as the children joined in.

"In and out the dusty bluebells, In and out the dusty bluebells, In and out the dusty bluebells, Who will be my master?"

Anna led the winding dance, in and out of the raised arms of the line of children, ducking and clapping. Then, as the others stood still, she skipped around the circle —

"Tippety tip-tap on your shoulder, Tippety tip-tap on your shoulder, Tippety tip-tap on your shoulder, You shall be my master."

The boy whose shoulder Anna had tapped slipped out of line and, blushing, pecked her upon the cheek before taking his place at the head of the line.

"In and out the dusty bluebells, In and out the dusty bluebells —" As the singing began again, Anna ran to the end of the line but stopped as a movement caught her eye. Sally, the little housemaid, was bustling across the lawn. Behind her came two young men in shabby, foreign-looking clothes. One of the lads was tall, handsome and with a mop of fair hair that seemed to Anna somehow familiar, though certainly she had never seen its owner before. The other was smaller, slighter and dark. Unlike the fair boy, he was unsmiling. He had the darkest eyes Anna had ever seen in a thin, intense face . No one else had yet noticed the newcomers. Anna watched them. The fair boy caught her eyes upon him and winked gaily. The dark one looked through her, his straight mouth tense.

"— Who will be my master?"

Josef had turned now and was staring at the approaching boys. The dark one stepped to him. Anna heard him speak — the language was strange, rapid, difficult to the ear.

"Tippety tip-tap on your shoulder, Tippety tip-tap on your shoulder —"

The dark young man was still talking, still unsmiling, using his hands to punctuate the words. Tanya had glanced up and, seeing them, had stilled, her face white. Then Josef let out a great shout and flung his arms wide. The two young men stepped into them and were enfolded in a bear-hug of delight. Anna saw the gleam of tears on the face of the dark lad.

"— You will be my master."

Tanya's brothers. Against all hope, here, ten years after the massacre, were two of Tanya's brothers, Josef and Boris, the one a year older than Tanya, the other a year younger. Much later, when the over-excited young guests had at last departed and the first ecstatic excitement had died down, the bare bones of their story emerged, told in Russian to Josef and translated for the rest of the family. Over the weeks and months that followed, the tale was enlarged upon, but on that first night enough was told clearly to show what the two boys had suffered over the past years.

A short while before the Cossack attack on the house in Charnov Street seven-year-old Boris — always in mischief even then — had disappeared. His mother, as so often before, had sent the more responsible Josef to find him. After much fruitless searching Josef had discovered his brother at last, a skull cap upon his fair head, singing songs he had no right to know and even less to understand, to an enthralled audience of Jewish children. Before Josef could persuade him away the Cossacks had swooped and murder was being done. Terrified, they had watched the slaughter of their kin from an upstairs window. The Jewish family with whom they had thus accidentally taken shelter knew only too well that the bloodlust of the killers, once aroused, would not be satisfied with the victims they had cornered in the Rosenberg house: a well-rehearsed plan had been put into action and they had escaped across the roofs of Charnov Street to the river.

"The Abrahams," Josef said, his voice quiet. Then, "They took you with them?"

Young Josef shook his head. Boris snorted. "They wouldn't. They drove us off. Said we were trouble-makers; that we'd brought the Cossacks on them —"

"They were not to be blamed for that." His brother said softly.

"What did you do?"

Josef Anatov's thin face showed remembered pain. "At first? We watched. What could we do? We were two children, unarmed —" His voice died. His brother reached a hand to him and rested it for a moment upon his arm before taking up the story himself.

"Josef it was who saved us. We knew the others had gone over the roofs — we followed them. He found the way. Behind us we saw fire." He glanced at Tanya, quiet and pale in her corner, "We didn't believe that anyone else could have survived."

Josef gestured. "Of course not. And then?"

"We made our way home. We couldn't think of anywhere else to go. It was terrible — no one came near us — no friend — no servant —" A short silence, an expressive shrug, long fingers, uncannily like Tanya's, spread. "The next day the soldiers came. They beat us, called us names, turned us from the house. They said the house and land belonged now to the Tsar — that the Anatov family were attainted traitors and that we were lucky to be allowed to live —"

As Boris spoke Josef glanced at the older brother's face. The dark eyes were suddenly bleak with hatred, the line of the straight mouth harsh. Involuntarily, the thought passed through Josef's mind — God help the man who crosses this one.

"What did you do?" He asked the question directly of Josef, the son his best friend had named after him.

With an obvious effort the young man broke his brooding silence. "We went to the city. Joined the other beggars." His voice was deeply bitter.

"That's how you lived?" Josef's probing was gentle.

Young Josef shrugged. "That and other ways. There are always ways."

"Yes."

"We learned most of them." In his own self-absorption the boy completely missed the significant note in the older man's tone.

Boris, unable to remain silent for long, took up the tale again. "It was Josef's idea that we should leave Kiev. He said there was no place for us there — that one day the Tsar's soldiers would come looking for us, too."

"We went south first of all — to Bucharest. Then," Josef shrugged, "Budapest. Vienna. Prague —"

"We got into trouble in Prague," put in the irrepressible Boris with a grin, shaking his hand as if he had burned it.

His brother grimly half-smiled. "We got into trouble everywhere. What else would you expect? Prague was just — a little more difficult. So, then we were on the move again. Westward this time. For I had remembered something —"

"There was a Dutchman in the jail in Prague —" interpolated Boris "— who spoke of Amsterdam. And Josef remembered — our father's cousin —"

Light dawned. "Ah," Josef said.

"It took us almost two years to reach Amsterdam." The dangerously hostile light had again appeared in the dark eyes. Josef remembered his own reception in that city and did not wonder at it.

"And when you got there?"

"We were not made welcome." The words were flat.

Josef nodded. "No more were we. But, at least, they did tell you that Tanya and I were alive and living in London?"

"Yes." Boris again, blue eyes bright and dancing. "And what a day that was, eh, brother? To discover after all this time that we had a sister —" His bright gaze flickered to Tanya, who had been watching him and Josef, her grave face absorbed as she tried to follow what they said in a language she had long forgotten. Meeting his eyes she smiled a little, racked dim memory. "Brother," she said, softly, in her mother tongue.

"That's right! Brother!" Laughing, Boris caught her hands and swung her to her feet. "Brother! Sister! Uncle! Friend!" His exuberance was irresistible. Even the sombre-faced Josef smiled.

"Sergei Anatov told you where to find us?"

"Yes, and offered us money to get rid of us." The hawk face lifted. "We did not take it." The bitterness was back in the young eyes. Josef looked with compassion into the savage dark face. Nineteen years old, and the lad bore a burden of hatred that could destroy many a grown man.

Anna, in her corner, quiet as a mouse in case someone noticed her and sent her out, watched the dark one named Josef after her father with wide, fascinated eyes. He looked so fierce.

Josef stood up, moved to where the lad sat, laid an arm across his shoulders. Still in each others' arms, Boris and Tanya stilled, watching. When Josef spoke, he spoke to his namesake alone, willing him to believe.

"It's over. You're home. You're wanted here. I promise you."

Anna thought she had never seen anyone's face so transformed as was young Josef's when he smiled.

Her father turned to her. "Here's a thing, my Anna. What a birthday present, eh? Josef and Boris — come to live with us."

CHAPTER FIVE

Josef Anatov stood by the barred nursery window. The street below was bleak with winter. Black ice made pavement and roadway treacherous; horses clattered and slithered awkwardly upon the uneven cobblestones, their breath condensing in clouds of steam in the cold air. The tree outside the window where Josef stood, stripped by inclement wintry winds, reached bare, soot-darkened branches towards a leaden February sky.

In Kiev the snow would be deep. Troikas would skim the packed surface, bells jingling in the frost-clear air.

The young man smiled caustically at the pretty thought. And someone, somewhere, he added grimly to himself, is probably being butchered —

Before the house stood a small gig, the blanketed horse between the long slender shafts held by a boy of about eight who was dressed in ragged trousers and a man's jacket that reached to his knees. A cap that had certainly done past service for his father, or perhaps an older brother, kept slipping over his eyes. Every now and again the child stamped his ill-shod feet, blew on his fingers and looked longingly towards the closed front door, torn between his desire to escape the biting cold and his need for the penny the doctor had promised him for holding the horse.

"Joss?"

The doctor had been here too long. Much too long. Even Josef knew that babies should not take this long to be born; nor should the constant attendance of a man of medicine be necessary.

"Joss!"

Behind him Alex and James squabbled. Always, he thought with a touch of irritation, they squabbled. Did they not realize how lucky they were? How fortunate in their security, in the comfort of their lives?

"Joss!"

A small, bony hand caught his and tugged. He looked down into Anna's thin, anxious face. Joss, she had called him — the pet name she had given him within a week of his arrival and which had been taken up by the rest of the household in order to distinguish him from the other Josef. In six months he still had not quite got used to it. "What is it, little one?"

The small face was grave. The blue eyes within their nondescript fringe of light lashes showed a desperate shadow of worry. If the boys had not sensed the atmosphere of the house, Josef reflected, the same could not be said of their sister.

He crouched down beside her, still holding her hands. On Nanny's instructions Trudy had tried — not very successfully — to curl her fine, straight hair in the fashionable way and had tied it with wide ribbons on either side of her head, an inappropriate style for a child as thin-faced and peaky-looking as Anna. Unthinking now, she wriggled a finger into the tightly-pulled roots of her hair and loosened the bunches. Several strands of stubbornly straight tow-coloured hair escaped restriction and straggled down her bony neck.

"What is it?' Josef asked again.

Anna, chewing her lip, turned to the windows and pushed her face between the bars, her breath misting the cold glass. She looked down at the gig. "If," she said at last, "the doctor is bringing our new baby in his black bag, why is he taking so long to give it to us? And why can't I go to see Mama? Is she ill? Iller than she was yesterday? I was allowed to see her yesterday. But Grandmama won't let me in her room today. I heard — I think I heard — Mama —" she stopped, and blinked rapidly. "I tried to ask Nanny but —"

"But what?"

The child looked hopelessly puzzled. "She slapped me and told me to stop asking wicked questions. Joss — why is it wicked to ask about Mama and the baby? And why, oh why, is it taking so long?"

"I don't know, little one." Unexpectedly touched by her miserable face he pulled her to him, tousled her untidy hair. The child looked pathetic, the unattractive blotchiness of unshed tears had reddened her face and her mouth drooped miserably. "I think — sometimes — the doctor has to look after the baby for a little while after he takes it from his bag."

"But *why?* Is the baby ill too? Is that why Papa has stayed home from work? He never stays home from work."

Behind them, Alex and James had for the moment stopped quarrelling and were laying out their fort and tin soldiers on the nursery floor. Ralph, as always, was curled quietly in a chair, his nose in a book.

On impulse, Joss perched on the windowsill, lifted her bird-weight on to his knee. "It won't be long now. I'm sure it won't." His English after six months, if passable, was nevertheless still heavily accented. Anna, however, understood him with the ease of a practised ear. He cast about for something to distract her. "What would you rather have — another brother or a sister?"

She pulled a face. "Oh, a sister! I don't want any more brothers!"

"Bags I'm General Gordon," Alex said loudly, right on cue. He was lying flat on his stomach on the floor, a small cavalry officer on a rearing charger galloping across the desert of the carpet between his fingers.

"No! That's not fair. You're always Gordon! I want to be him. You be the Mahdi for a change."

Ralph, without lifting his eyes from the page, put his fingers in his ears.

"Don't be daft! Gordon gets killed, doesn't he?"

"Well, then, why do you want to be him all the time?" asked the younger James smartly and with a belligerence that presaged another storm.

Anna slipped from Josef's lap, took his hand. "They're going to start fighting again. Come in the other room. Tell me a story —"

"Anna, my dear, your father's expecting me —"

"Please." Her face was woebegone, her lower lip wobbled, though she tried to hide it. He sighed. Ever since he had arrived this little one had followed him like a small puppy — why, he could not imagine. Somehow he had fallen into the unexpected habit of telling her the folk tales of his own childhood, that he had thought long forgotten.

"Please," she said again, and in conscience he could do nothing but comply. They went into the night nursery. She towed him to the chair by the fire and climbed on to his lap.

"Which story would you like?"

"Ivan the Ninny," she said at once.

He put a hand to his head in mock despair. "Anna, Anna! I've told you that a thousand times at least!"

"Oh, please. It's my very favourite." She cuddled into his shoulder. Josef held her awkwardy. He cleared his throat. She lifted her head.

"Joss?" Her voice was very small.

"Mmm?"

"It is all right? Mama, I mean — and the baby?"

What else to say? "Of course. Quite all right. You'll see. Now — I can't remember — how does this wretched story start?"

She settled herself back against his shoulder, closed her eyes. "Once," she said, her voice softly sing-song, "long ago in the Northern Steppes, where the wind blows a thousand miles before it greets a tree —"

Joss, as he himself had more than suspected, was wrong. It was not all right. For twenty-four hours the household waited in tense and worried silence as Grace struggled to give birth to a tiny scrap of humanity over whose chances of survival when she did finally fight her way into the world the doctor shook a solemn head. On his advice a priest was called and on that bitterly cold late February day Margaret Jane Rose, named for Grace's mother, was baptized by the bedside of her desperately weakened mother. Deep anxiety for mother and child made the next few weeks a nightmare. The whole house went on tiptoe, its thoughts and activities centred around the stuffy, darkened room on the first floor where Grace lay victim of childbed fever, and the small room on the next floor where the daughter she had brought so painfully into the world struggled for life. A wet nurse was brought in, a large, lugubrious woman who, like the doctor, shook her head knowingly over her small charge. Winter's grip loosened, the first pale haze of life appeared upon the trees in the park, strong spears of green pushed through the grass in Kensington Gardens as spring worked her yearly miracle and the first flowers reached for the light — and though Grace, at last, began to recover some of her strength, the baby still ailed.

One who, to her own guilty dismay, could not find it in her heart much to care about that was Anna. Her first reaction to the much longed-for baby sister had been anti-climactic disappointment. Here was not the playmate that she had imagined but a sickly, ugly, pale-faced scrap smaller than the doll that the Smithsons had given her, that did nothing but whimper, sleep and — worst of all — take up everyone's time and attention. For the first time in her life Anna felt totally left out. Her father, her grandmother, even Tanya — none of them seemed to have time for her any more. Anna knew, too, that in some mysterious way her mother's illness was connected with the arrival of Margaret Jane, which increased her resentment and antipathy towards the new arrival tenfold. The sight of her mother — a fragile, pallid face upon a vast white pillow, shadowed eyes, small, clawlike hands — horrified her. And it was the baby's fault. She knew it was. Each night, on her knees by her bed in the night nursery, she prayed to Jesus aloud under the stern eyes of Nanny Brown for the recovery of both invalids; privately she indicated her willingness to strike a bargain — if He had to take one of them, then He could take the baby and welcome. If He would just let Mama get well and let things go back the way they used to be she, Anna, would never do another naughty thing as long as she lived.

It seemed, however, that it was to her public rather than her private prayers that He listened. First Grace's health improved, then, gradually, the baby's. But to Anna's bewilderment and deep disappointment life still did not revert to its former happy pattern. For although her mother, once on the road to recovery, regained a good deal of her strength with a speed that was remarkable to anyone who was not familiar with the iron will that resided within Grace Rose's rather frail-looking frame, her absorption with the new baby was such that as spring turned to summer and the blossom drifted to the ground like snow, her other children saw little of her. Her own crisis over, Grace became obsessed by the need to ensure her child's survival. Everything else became subordinate to that as, over everyone's protests, she took personal charge of the nursery and exerted every ounce of her own hard-won strength to that end.

By that time Anna truly hated the baby. She tried not to, prayed that she would not, was haunted by the visions of hell that Nanny Brown was in the habit of painting with relish when she spoke of what awaited naughty children when they died. And Anna knew that the way she felt about Margaret Jane was more than naughty; it was truly wicked. But she could not help it. There seemed to be no one to turn to — the boys seemed not in the least affected by the changed circumstances — they went their private, noisy, cheerfully quarrelsome ways and seemed to notice nothing. Bereft and miserable with that self-centred misery of childhood that can see no end to unhappiness, rebellious at what she saw as an undeserved and unlooked-for rejection, made wretched by the savage pangs of jealousy and lonely by her own sullen touchiness, Anna became naughty, slipshod in her lessons, quarrelsome with her brothers, unbiddable in the nursery — where the fierce-tempered and autocratic Nanny Brown was inevitably more than a match for her. All of which simply served to make a miserable situation worse.

"Really, Anna, I don't know what's got into you! I wouldn't claim that you were ever the best-behaved child in the world, but lately — Go to your bed at once and wait till your father comes home!"

Supperless again, Anna would crawl into her narrow bed and sob herself to sleep, comfortless and — as she saw it — loveless. Practical and usually level-headed, Grace, strung to breaking point by the knowledge that the baby, though holding her own, was not improving as she should, punished the child in the way of the times, harshly. The strap and the cane were considered the only remedy for a badly behaved child and Anna received both in good measure. She did not know, then or ever, of the tears her mother shed after these painful sessions. She only knew that her world had turned upside down and she was wretchedly unhappy. And it was all the awful baby's fault.

It seemed to Anna that only Josef — now known universally by Anna's pet name of Joss — had not changed towards her. Joss, indeed, would certainly have been surprised had he known how largely he figured in his young foster sister's life. In truth he saw little of her, for he was now utterly absorbed in his new life, and the problems of a child were none of his concern. He, together with Boris, was working for Josef, and — unlike Boris — he was passionately enjoying it. Josef had planned a kind of apprenticeship for both of them, so that the two young men should learn every facet of the business, from the running of the workshops to the management and finances of the business. It was this last that fascinated Joss. Considering his lack of formal education, he had an astonishing head for figures, although his reading was and always would be hesitant at best — and though, to Josef's exasperated amusement he could not tell diamond from paste and was not particularly interested in learning to do so, the possibilities of the trade, the sums involved and the opportunities for investment and profit absorbed and excited him. So it was that his involvement with Anna's problems was slight — but, because he quite liked the child, odd little thing that she was, with her straight, wispy hair and plain, solemn little face, when he did see her he was casually kind, an attitude which, perhaps understandably in the circumstances, brought in return from Anna a devotion that would have astonished him had he suspected it. In fact only three people in the world really meant anything to Josef Anatov — his graceless little devil of a brother whom he had shepherded and fiercely protected through their dangerous youth, his newly discovered sister Tanya, whom he considered to be the most beautiful girl he had ever seen, and Josef, who had saved her and who now offered a new life to her brothers. Joss's life had not been one to encourage open-heartedness or easy, loving relationships. Lessons hard-learned in a bitter school were not easily forgotten. And so he had little or no understanding for Anna — though for her the day was lightened if he so much as smiled at her.

"I'm going to be like Ivan the Ninny," she told him one day, very seriously. "I'll go away, and I'll do something very clever — and everyone will be very sad because I've gone, but then I'll come back, rich, and —"

He grinned. "Ivan married a princess. Will you come back married to a handsome prince?"

She glanced at him sideways. She had her own very private ideas about handsome princes. "Perhaps."

Joss had picked up the piece of paper upon which Anna had been drawing — the only activity lately that she still seemed truly to enjoy. "Why Anna — how very pretty." A dragonfly swooped across the page, wings exaggeratedly long and body tapering to a graceful, curling curve. Beneath it was a spray of leaves, inaccurate in detail but delicately drawn.

Anna flushed and took the paper from him. "Miss Spencer says I draw very badly. She says I don't draw things the way they are." Miss Spencer came to teach the young Roses each morning in the school room above the nursery.

"Does that matter?"

"Miss Spencer says it does. So does Nanny."

Her tone reached even his insensitive ear. "Ah. Then I suppose it does, eh?"

She nodded.

"Well," he said abstractedly, gathering his papers, "I like it. You can tell your Miss Spencer that, eh." He laughed, totally oblivious to the devotion in her eyes.

It was less than a month to Anna's ninth birthday. No one this year talked of a party — her parents were too occupied with the still-ailing baby and, "Only good little girls have parties," Nanny Brown informed the child, sanctimoniously. "Naughty little girls don't deserve birthdays at all. What's this, Miss?" — with smugness in her tone as she turned smartly and caught Anna with her tongue out, "asking for another hiding, are we? I'll have something to tell your Mama when she comes up this afternoon. As usual." Nanny Brown was that product of an age that provided little employment for its women outside domestic service or slave-labour in a sweatshop or factory, a child-minder who did not particularly care for children.

In her strongly held opinion they should be seen and not heard, kept clean, quiet and out of the way, taught their manners and their A.B.C., their wilder natural instincts kept firmly under control by threat, intimidation or physical punishment. She had come highly recommended from a minister's family — the Reverend Mr Bassett having assured her future employer of her absolute competence in all matters appertaining to the care and discipline of children. She had been taken on as the family had arrived at the new house, and Grace — pregnant and then ill — had been only too pleased to leave the running of the nursery in her obviously capable hands. Needless to say, the opinion of the children of the house was never consulted. They, with one accord, all detested her, a fact that, had Grace known of it, might have given her pause for thought. Anna was a sore disappointment to Nanny Brown. She never expected much from little boys — ill-mannered little savages that they were bound by their sex to be, but girls, ah, girls were different. Or should be. Anna should have been the pride of the nursery — Nanny's pet, demure, well-mannered, pretty, a credit to Molly Brown's loveless dedication to her position. Instead the child was a constant source of irritation — untidy, plain, ill- mannered, disobedient. In Molly Brown's opinion her father and mother were far too lenient with her. Punishment made the child — the beatings that this one did receive were in no way severe enough. Why, the Bassett girls, good dear little lambs that they were, had meekly submitted to a beating regularly each Sunday morning before church, in case any unadmitted or forgotten weekday sin might be besmirching their pure little souls. That was the way to subdue a child's spirit properly. Anna, Nanny considered, got away with murder with her indulgent mother and father. But not in the nursery — oh, no, Molly Brown made sure of that.

The battle was a ferocious one, and one that poor Anna had no hope at all of winning.

Three days before her ninth birthday Anna awoke feeling even more miserable than usual. Her head felt like lead and her nose was running. She snapped at James over breakfast and was reprimanded for it, burst into tears when Trudy, in a hurry as usual, tugged too hard at her hair as she was attempting to tidy it, could not concentrate upon her seven times table and had her knuckles painfully rapped by an exasperated Miss Spencer. Lunch — eaten in the nursery with Nanny and Trudy — brought no respite. Half-way through the unappetizing meal — Nanny having very firm views upon the diet suitable for growing children — her nose began to run again. She felt in her pinafore pocket for her handkerchief.

It was not there.

She sniffed surreptitiously, frantically searching her sleeve, but of the missing handkerchief there was no sign.

She sniffed again, loudly in the silence. Alex looked up, nudged Ralph who was sitting next to him, and suppressed a forbidden giggle.

At the end of the table Nanny did not lift her head but applied herself to the mountain of food upon her plate.

In desperation Anna sniffed again and dashed the back of her hand across her face. Alex's shoulders heaved. He was scarlet with the effort not to laugh aloud, something absolutely forbidden at the nursery table. Trudy looked at Anna, frowned ferocious warning, jerked her head towards Nanny.

Anna had no choice. She sniffed again.

The table held its breath. Eyes flickered from one face to another. Very slowly Nanny lifted her head. She was a large woman with a florid complexion and fierce eyebrows. She fixed Anna with a withering eye.

"Anna. Your handkerchief."

"I — can't find it, Nanny."

This disturbing news was greeted by a moment's heavy silence. Anna was scarlet with mortification as, with all eyes upon her, her nose began to run again, and lifted a hand to her face.

"No! How dare you! Dirty child!" The hand was slapped sharply away. The tears that rose to the child's eyes made her predicament worse.

"Here. Come here." A stubby finger pointed to a spot beside Nanny's chair.

Anna obediently did as she was bid, leaving her chair and moving to stand, eyes downcast, beside her tormentor. "Please," she said softly, hating herself for begging so abjectly, "please, Nanny, may I go and look for my handkerchief?" As she spoke she could taste the mucus on her lips. She shuddered, her stomach churning.

"You had a handkerchief, then?"

"Yes."

"This morning?"

"Yes." The word was whispered.

"Then," Nanny spread blunt, elaborately surprised hands, "where is it?"

"I — don't know." Anna was desperate. She felt hot and her

head ached terribly. The tears ran unchecked. Even Alex, suddenly, looked away. "I think —"

The woman did not allow her to finish. "I see. And do you believe that your good Papa goes to work each day in order to buy things for you that you may simply go out and lose them?"

"Nanny, please —"

"Do you?"

"No! No, of course not. I had the hanky. I had it upstairs in the schoolroom. My nose was running. I must have left it up there."

"Your nose?" Nanny smirked, heavily, sarcastic, "Oh no, Miss. I'm afraid that your nasty nose is very much here with us."

"My handkerchief," Anna said wretchedly. "I must have left it there. Please — may I go and look?"

There was another moment's oppressive silence. Then, "No. You may not," Nanny said. "You know the nursery rules. No one leaves the table until all are finished."

"But —"

"No. Return to your place and finish your lunch."

Anna trailed back to her chair. Picked up her spoon. Her steamed fish had got cold, the lumpy mashed potatoes were unappetizing. She swallowed. Her stomach churned.

"What now?" asked the harsh voice from the other end of the table.

"I don't feel very well."

Nanny appeared to consider this. "Is that so?"

Anna nodded, not looking up.

"Perhaps a good dose of syrup of figs is called for?"

Anna flinched.

"Well?"

Anna, in great discomfort, ate her lunch.

Later that afternoon, alone and miserable, she wandered the garden. Finding herself in her favourite spot by the pond she sat down, rested her chin gloomily upon her knees. She felt wretched and lonely. No one cared. No one.

In the distance she heard the others playing. She huddled herself smaller. Who wanted to play with them anyway?

Close to her hand a small spider scurried across the blades of grass. Lucky spider. Lucky thing. You don't have a Nanny. Or a mother who doesn't love you any more —

Self-pitying tears burned her eyes. She'd run away. Then they'd be sorry. She'd run away, and they'd think she was dead. Perhaps she *would* die — how they'd all cry then. They'd like her better than the beastly baby then. They'd at least notice what she'd done.

September sunlight glimmered on the pond. She jumped to her feet, ran to the gate in the wall. It was securely bolted, the bolts rusted in place. She could not budge them. The apple tree stood sturdy beside her. She remembered last year's party — the game of Sardines when she had hidden for so long on top of the wall. She scrambled up the tree, swung herself on to the wall, sat with her feet dangling, watching the passing traffic. It was cool for the time of year despite the sun, and the wind gusted playfully. Dust flew, stinging her eyes. She wiped her nose with the back of her hand. No one to see her here.

In her pocket she had sixpence that her Grandmother had given her. She was supposed to have put it in her money box, but she'd forgotten. Nanny would slap her hard if she found out.

Not if she wasn't here.

A gust of wind blew, plastering her skirt against her legs.

With a quick twist of her small body she jumped from the wall and landed like a little cat on her feet on the pavement.

There was still enough of the afternoon left for Kensington Gardens to be thronged with children, their parents, nannies and nursemaids. It was a familiar sight to Anna — a familiar sight made strange and somehow more exciting because for the first time she saw it alone. Upon the Round Pond little boys sailed their boats, fighting ships and merchantmen skimmed in the rising wind from bank to bank, swooping like birds upon the water. Anna scrambled to the edge of the pond — no one to call her back today — and watched. Not far from her two boats collided, masts and rigging tangling. Their young owners, calling in the wind, disentangled them with long hooked poles. One splendid craft dipped and flew across the rippling surface of the water, its sailor-suited master racing along the bank beside it. Anna, hastily removing herself from harm's way, reflected not for the first time upon how much more fun it must be to be a boy than a girl: "Come back here, Anna — don't do this — don't do that." Well, she'd do this and that now, just see if she wouldn't. Except — she cleared her throat, which was feeling distinctly sore. When she had told Nanny Brown that she was not feeling well it had been the plain truth. Her cheeks burned in the wind. That was it, of course — the wind. That was what was making her nose run and her eyes feel so funny.

Nearby, a mother and her small children were feeding the ducks, to the intense excitement of a small Scottish terrier who strained at his lead in a frenzy of barking. A neat nursemaid, the wide white ribbon of her hat streaming jauntily in the wind, pushed a large, bouncing pram along the path, trailing a small procession of well-dressed children holding hands and walking in twos. Anna caught the eye of a girl of about her own age. The girl stuck her tongue out. Anna stuck her thumbs in her ears and waggled her fingers rudely, pulling a ferocious face. That made her feel considerably better.

A gust of wind buffeted her. Leaves skittered by her feet. Infected by the swirling movement, she picked up her skirts and ran, tangled hair streaming, into the wind. She ran until she was breathless and then leaned against a tree, panting. Not far away a boy flew a bright yellow kite with a long, snaking tail. She watched with rapt interest, admiring the skill with which he controlled the thing, tugging gently at the string, turning the kite like a bird in the windy sky. Anna considered for a moment asking him if she might try it, but something about him reminded her of Alex, and she thought better of it. She looked at the kite again. The sky was darkening behind it as the rain clouds built. The boy was reeling it in now, against the tug of a storm-wind. Anna shivered a little. Her nose was running again and the exertion of running had brought back her headache. Her sudden spurt of energy had deserted her. She wandered back towards the pond. People hurried by in the opposite direction, eyes cast up at the building clouds. An old woman was selling lollipops from a tray — "Two a penny — two a penny." Anna bought two, pocketed her fivepence change. She licked one of the lollipops and grimaced. Something in her mouth made it taste strange. Oddly enough, though earlier she had felt quite hungry, now her appetite seemed entirely to have deserted her. The Gardens were emptying. She climbed up on to a bench and sat, legs swinging, watching the departing procession of prams, children, dogs and nursemaids.

Suddenly she felt very lonely.

She'd have to go back, of course. She hadn't really meant to run away. Not — not for ever.

The wind had risen in earnest now, large spots of rain blowing in it. The pond, bereft of its proud flotilla, rippled emptily. The water, reflecting the sky, looked dark and cold.

They'd be having tea in the nursery now. They must have missed her. But — did anyone care? Were they just carrying on without her, as if she had never existed? She envisaged a familiar, florid face, "Good riddance to bad rubbish, I say. Eat up, young James, there's more for everyone now she's gone." Tears welled. She felt awful: hot and cold at the same time, her head splitting, her bones aching.

"Well, well. What's this, eh?"

She looked up. A figure loomed beside her, a man in tattered coat and muffler, his baggy trousers filthy, his boots laceless and unmatching. His dirty unshaven face looked to the sick child like a vision of the devil. Dumb with fright she stared at him. He seated himself beside her. His teeth were horribly discoloured and his breath smelled. "What's this, little Miss? All alone, are we? Lost our Mummy?" He leaned to her, "Come, my pretty, tell Uncle —"

She scrambled from the bench, eluded the dirty, grasping hand and fled. Sobbing she flew along the path to the gate, not daring to look back to see if he were following, utterly convinced that he was. Once in the comparative safety of the street she did not stop her headlong flight but in a panic ran blindly on, following the way more by instinct than thought, cannoning into people, gasping for breath, crying with fright. The city streets seemed suddenly vast and horribly hostile. Whatever punishment awaited her at home could not be worse than this. She wanted her mother. Sobbing harder, she cried it aloud, "I want my mother." Then she turned a corner into a blessedly familiar street and crashed full tilt into a slight figure whose hands caught her firmly to stop her from sprawling upon her face.

"No!" She struggled against the grip, "Leave me alone!"

"Anna — Anna, in God's name, what is it? Anna? It's Joss —"

She stopped struggling, stood like a small statue for a moment, her reddened, streaming eyes fixed on his face in sheer disbelief.

"Anna — whatever is it? What are you doing here, alone?"

The world tilted and she staggered, would have fallen, but for his hands. Tears ran unchecked down her face. "I ran away," she whispered between hiccoughing sobs. "I thought — I wanted —" the words became incoherent.

He remembered two small boys alone in an unfriendly world. Remembered the fear. He held her until the sobbing died a little. "Ssh." Her cheek flamed against his. He drew back, frowning, touched her forehead. "You feel unwell?" He thought he had never seen a small creature look so pitiable.

She nodded. "And Mama and everyone is going to be so angry. I shall get into such trouble —"

Joss Anatov, for very good reasons, did not consider himself a softhearted man. But the misery in the flushed, tear-drenched little face touched him unexpectedly. He remembered again that child with no one to turn to, no one, ever, to help —

"I ran away —" Anna was still sobbing, but the words were clearer "— because no one loves me since the baby came. They just think I'm a wicked nuisance. And now — and now —" she could not go on.

"Anna."

She sobbed still.

"Anna!" He shook her gently. She looked at him. "Listen to me. You are afraid that you will get into trouble for being out so long, and without permission?"

She nodded.

"No. For — we shall tell a small untruth."

Her sobs had quietened. She watched him with wide, half-hopeful eyes. The rain was falling in earnest now, blowing down the darkening street in gusts. She shivered. He stood up, took off his coat and wrapped her in it, scooped her lightly into his arms and started down the street, talking as he went. "We shall say this: that I, coming home early from the shop, found you playing in the garden and took you to the park, stupidly forgetting to tell Nanny where we were going. Then — we forgot the time — it started to rain — you felt unwell, and I had to carry you home."

"But then *you'll* get into trouble." Her voice was muffled. It felt so good to be in his arms, so warm and safe. She just wished that she did not feel so frighteningly unwell.

"No matter," he said, quietly. "Josef Anatov has talked his way out of worse trouble than this. So — remember — I took you to the park — you felt unwell, and it has taken me a long time to carry you home."

"Will it be all right?" She dared not hope it.

"It will be all right. I promise. And — Anna?"

"Yes?"

"I want to hear no more of this nonsense of no one loving you. If the day comes when you are truly unloved, cry then. But now? Foolish one — watch your mother's face when she sees you."

She laid her hot cheek against the wet roughness of his jacket. A small happy thought had lodged in her fevered mind, and she smiled at it. Whatever the disasters and alarms of this afternoon's adventure, like all good stories it had at least had a happy ending. Her handsome prince had rescued her and brought her home, to safety.

CHAPTER SIX

Measles. The disease swept through the house like fire; first Anna, then her brothers and finally — fatally — the baby. Grace watched helplessly as the small flame of life that she had fought so hard to preserve flickered and died. Her calm acceptance of the tragedy amazed those who watched and worried over her. Only she knew that in her heart she had suspected all along that her weakling child would be unlikely to survive the first onslaught of infant illness. After the difficult birth she had been told that she would never be able to bear Josef another child — knowledge that had made the small scrap doubly precious. But no matter how hard she had tried, not even her fierce motherly instincts had been able entirely to overcome the clear-sighted common sense that was so much a part of her make up, and she had been unable truly to deceive herself. So, when, despite her own constant care and attention, the disease took its inevitable toll of the frail constitution she, with painful stoicism, bowed her head and accepted at last that for His own good reasons God had not willed the child to live. Acceptance, however, did not preclude grief, and she never forgot the ordeal of her child's funeral. They followed the pitifully small white coffin through the October streets to the churchyard, the glory of autumnal red and gold a sharp contrast to the mourning black of the small cortège. The funeral plumes of the horses tossed in a chill wind that also stirred the white wreaths and flowers. Josef sat sombre beside her in the carriage, his hand clamped around hers in a hurtful grip. He had taken the loss of his little daughter very badly indeed — whilst beneath her black mourning veil Grace's eyes, if reddened, were dry, he wept openly, in a man's painfully silent way, for the new life extinguished before it had truly begun. She laid her free hand gently upon his arm. No love in her life, she knew, could ever equal that she felt for this man — old enough almost to be her father, uncommunicative in the extreme about his life before he met her, hardworking, emotional, indulgent — there was nothing about him that she would change. Grace Rose believed with utter and unquestioning faith in her God and in His designs — however obscure — and His benevolent omnipotence. She had no doubt at all that it had been His will that had sent Josef to her so strangely and so fortuitously, as it was His will that Margaret Jane had been taken from them. It worried her that she suspected that Josef had no such prop. As was right and proper he accompanied her, the household and the children, to church each Sunday morning and took his appointed place at the end of the pew; but she, who knew him so well, detected within him none of the joy and the certainty that her own communion with God brought her. On the contrary, though she would not dream of questioning him about it, she sometimes feared that she sensed a scepticism that concerned her always, but most of all now, when the sight of his contained but violent grief hurt her almost as much as her own loss.

Late that afternoon, back in the darkened house, he sat in the cluttered, shaded drawing room staring bleakly at the black mourning ring upon his hand within which was curled a small whisp of the baby's hair. Grace laid a hand upon his shoulder. "Our little one is with God, Mr Rose. We must remember that and try not to grieve too much." Her voice, despite the words, was not quite steady. "We are still blessed with the other children."

Her husband lifted reddened eyes and seeing the intent and worried look upon her still-thin face did his best to smile. "You're right, of course, my dear. It's just that it seems so hard —" The words fell into a silence made deeper by the whispers of a house in mourning.

She nodded. "Yes. It's hard." With her customary neat movements she stood up and walked to where the tasselled bell pull hung by the draped mantelpiece. The low late October sun slanted through the crack of the drawn curtains, glinting upon a small table with a long, fringed tablecloth upon which stood a collection of glass and china knickknacks that gleamed, spotless in the light. "Now — a cup of tea, I think? And then we'll visit

Anna."

The mention of their surviving daughter's name had exactly the effect that she had hoped. Grief for the dead child was, for the moment at least, overcome by concern for the living. "She's no better?"

"It would seem not. The last lot of medicine that Doctor Thompson gave her has done no more good that the first."

He stood up suddenly, strode to the fireplace. "I don't understand it. She was very ill, I know — but that was weeks ago. The boys have recovered long since. Yet there she lies — doing nothing, hardly speaking, eating nothing at all."

"Doctor Thompson says she is quite cured of the measles. It is, he says, the after-effects —"

"After-effects? What's that supposed to mean? After-effects?" The day's emotions exploded into the relief of anger. "The man's a charlatan. The child is ill. Fading to nothing. And he talks of — 'after-effects'?"

He stopped as the door opened and a small, uniformed maid tripped into the room. "Yes, Ma'am?"

"Tea, please, Sally."

"Yes, Ma'am."

Josef waited until the door closed behind her. "I want a second opinion," he said then, more quietly. "We've lost one child. We aren't going to lose another."

Grace nodded, seated herself, straight-backed upon a chair, her eyes upon her tightly-clasped hands, still sheathed in the black lace of mourning; and the tears that she had resisted all day, welled from her eyes and slid soundlessly down her cheeks.

The new doctor, however, did no better for Anna than the old. He examined her, tapped her chest, looked in her eyes, ears and down her throat and professed himself — in suitably professional language — mystified. As far as he could see there was no reason in the world why the child should decline so. Privately — for he had seen such apparently inexplicable cases before — he believed it likely that the girl would soon follow her small sister to the grave. Who knew why such things happened? God moved in a mysterious way. He took his fee, tipped his hat and left.

And Anna lay, bedevilled, slipping further into her nightmare world of guilt, contrition, terror and self-punishment.

In caring for her sick daughter Grace found at least some ease from grief. For while she believed absolutely in the will of God, she also believed — as she had demonstrated at and after Margaret Jane's birth — that He was occasionally found to be open to persuasion. Here was a daughter she would not easily let go. That her own loving ministrations actually added to the child's guilt-ridden distress never occurred to her, no more than did the fact that Anna, though ill, had been progressing perfectly satisfactorily until the baby had been taken ill and that her desperate decline had begun from the moment of her small sister's death.

Oddly, it was Joss who discovered the truth.

Trudy it was who begged Joss to visit the sick child. "Honest, Mr Joss — I wish you would. She thinks the world of you, you know. I'm sure it'd 'elp." Trudy was truly fond of Anna. She was also not averse to the thought of a daily visit to the sick room by this quiet, rather intriguing young man whom she found a lot more attractive than his more flamboyant brother.

Joss felt himself to be an unlikely comfort in the sick room. Also he was busy: Josef, recognizing his remarkable business acumen, had begun to allow him more scope in his activities within the company, encouraging him more and more to take into his own hands the financial side of the business, which had never been Josef's own forte. The thought of spending precious time with a sick child did not greatly appeal. "I think you exaggerate, Trudy."

"No. As God's my witness, Mr Joss, it's true. Your visit the other day did 'er a lot more good than that there doctor does, I can tell you that." Trudy crossed her fingers behind her back — it was, after all, in the best of causes — and added, "She's always askin' for you." In fact Anna never asked for anyone.

In conscience, there was little Joss could do but accede, and so it was that he took to dropping in on Anna each evening. As much to Trudy's surprise as her pleasure these visits did have a beneficial effect. The child came to look for the young man each evening. She even, at last, began to talk. It was a couple of weeks after the baby's funeral that Joss asked, very politely, to talk to Grace alone.

Grace agreed to this unusual request with some surprise and not a little reluctance. She and Joss were not close — indeed, if pressed, she might have admitted to an actual antipathy for the young man. She was ill at ease with him, and had been from the first moment he had stepped into the house. His brother Boris — handsome, lighthearted, feckless as a child and good for nothing but laughter — had found an immediate corner in her heart: but Joss disturbed her strangely. She never could fathom the thoughts behind those coal-dark eyes, nor find any warmth in the harsh line of his mouth. She supposed that to some he might appear as attractive in his slight, tense way as was Boris in his, but for herself his habitually sombre expression and long, disconcerting silences made him a difficult companion. Although the older by nine or ten years, she felt awkward and uncomfortable in his presence, an experience she was not used to in her own house and which, not unnaturally, she found herself resenting intensely. Always, to her, he gave the impression of an intolerable superiority, of sitting in judgement on those about them and mostly finding them wanting. Her husband's preference for him over his more extrovert brother puzzled her. She smiled now, a little coolly.

"Sit down, Joss. How may I help you?"

He sat in a large, overstuffed wing armchair, leaned forward, frowning a little. Irritation moved in Grace. Why did the boy always have to be so intense?

"I should like to talk to you about Anna," he said.

"Oh?" The last thing she had expected. She waited.

Unusually, he seemed for the moment uncertain of how to proceed. He touched long fingers to his mouth in a gesture that in another she might have thought of as nervousness.

"Well?" she prompted, her impatience barely concealed by her good manners. Rain trickled in dismal furrows down the windowpane.

"I think I may have discovered the reason for Anna's illness."

"She caught measles — really Joss, we all know —"

"No." Joss stood up. In God's name what was he doing here? The child's predicament was really nothing to do with him. Then the vision of a thin, flushed face and frightened eyes rose in his mind. Poor little devil. Someone had to do something —

"Anna believes that she is responsible for the death of the baby. She is desperate with guilt. She thinks you all hate her for it. She thinks she deserves to die."

Grace was on her feet. "What?"

"It's true. She told me. I thought it would help if you knew. I think you should talk to her. She needs to be reassured. To be convinced that it wasn't her fault that the baby died."

There was anger in her, and confusion. How should this — this stranger know such things about her daughter when she did not? He sensed her antagonism, half turned from her, then stopped. Joss Anatov was not one to shirk a self-appointed task. He had come so far, it made no sense to stop now. "Mrs Rose — I think there is something else you should know — something that might help you to understand."

"Oh?"

"On the day that Anna fell ill she had run away."

That was too much. "Nonsense," she said sharply. "Run away? We all know what happened on the day that Anna fell ill, Joss. You took her to the park. You forgot the time. You allowed her to become wet, and cold, and overtired —"

"No. I found Anna outside in the street. She was very distressed. She told me she had run away because she believed that no one loved her since the baby came."

Grace opened her mouth, shut it again.

"We lied, both of us. Now I've broken my word to her in telling you. But I thought you should know." He walked towards the door, turned with his hand on the knob. "I'm sorry if you think I'm interfering. I simply thought that someone should at least be aware of the child's state of mind. And since I have so obviously upset you, for which I apologize —"

Why, she thought, in furious exasperation, did he have to be so wretchedly polite?

"— then there seems little point in holding back the other thing I came to say."

"Which is?" Grace asked, faintly.

"If Anna were a child of mine, I'd not have her tended by a woman who obviously dislikes her. In my opinion, a lot of what ails the child comes directly from her treatment by that detestable Nanny you employ." He could hardly believe the words he spoke himself. He knew the influence Grace had with Josef, was absolutely unsure how she would take such undeniable impudence.

She regarded him for a long, cool moment. "Thank you, Joss," she said, "I'll look into it."

He knelt beside the child's narrow bed, the young man — slight, dark, graceful, his face serious, as always. "You must understand, Anna — I had to tell them. We must finish this nonsense once and for all. You're punishing yourself for nothing. It wasn't your fault."

She turned her head from him. "It was. It was!"

"No."

Very very slowly she turned back to him. "You don't know what I did."

"You caught measles. The baby caught measles —"

"No. Not that. Something else. Something — horrible."

He waited. Tears dribbled down the thin cheeks and dripped on to the pillow. Joss had a meeting to go to. Diamond prices were fluctuating crazily — if he could just persuade Josef to let him go to South Africa.

"What? What did you do that was so horrible?"

She lay quiet a long time. "I —" she began at last and stopped, swallowing painfully. "I — I prayed that —"

His straying attention was caught. "What?" he asked gently.

"I prayed to God that the baby should die. I wanted her to die! I told Him I did." The words were tumbling out now. "I wanted things to be the way they used to be. I wanted Mama to love me again — so you see it is my fault! It is! I asked God to let the baby die — I'm wicked. I'll go to hell like Nanny says — and, oh, supposing Mama finds out how wicked I am?"

"Oh, Anna. Anna." Very gently he drew the sobbing child to him, rocking her as he might have rocked a baby. "Listen to me. And think. Do you truly believe that God has time to listen to all the naughty little prayers of all the naughty children in the world? Don't you think He knows what's really in your heart? Was He not a child Himself? Did He not speak of and to the little children? Do you have such little faith that you believe He would do something wicked because you asked it of Him?" She had grown very still against him, listening. "You caught measles accidentally. The baby caught measles accidentally. And she wasn't strong enough. We all knew that. I believe that your mother knew it. It had nothing to do with your prayers."

"Perhaps the devil heard them." The words were whispered. Be sure the devil will take you, Miss, Nanny had said numberless times in the past for the slightest misdemeanour. Hell's flames haunted the imaginative child.

"Fiddlesticks to the devil. There's no such thing," he said.

She lifted her head, her eyes enormous. "Nanny says —"

"And fiddlesticks to Nanny too," he said shortly, and with finality.

Even in her distress a small spark of scandalized delight glinted in her eyes at that.

He laid her back upon the pillows. "Enough of this nonsense, little Anna. Your mother is coming to see you. Listen to what she tells you. Believe her and me. And as for the devil —" he leaned forward, spoke quietly "— spit in his eye and forget him! He'll have to wait a long time for you." Smiling one of his rare smiles, he tucked her in and made her comfortable. Already it seemed to him that her eyes were clearer and more peaceful, her cheeks a more healthy colour. The cleansing of confession, he thought a touch wryly, perhaps the men of science and of medicine should not too quickly dismiss the ministrations of Mother Church.

"Joss?"

"Yes?"

"You'll come and see me again? Soon?"

"Only — absolutely only — if you promise to get better."

"I will. I promise I will."

He left the room with a lift of relief that now, surely, his involvement in the child's problems was over. Before he had reached the bottom of the stairs he was rehearsing arguments in his mind to convince Uncle Josef that Rose and Company needed to invest some of its profits — he was so old-fashioned in this desire to have money lying in the bank, accumulating, doing nothing.

He had absolutely no idea that in the past moments childish devotion had in Anna given way to a depth of emotion far beyond her years: the first stirrings of a passionate and possessive love that would haunt them both, in one way or another, for the rest of their lives.

Grace's visit to the sick room following her talk with Joss was a better tonic than anything a doctor could have prescribed. To her credit, despite her initial outrage at what he had told her, she was ready after only a few minutes' talk with her daughter to admit her mistake. And to rectify it. Her efforts were rewarded with satisfying speed. With the wound that had festered so long in her mind lanced and cleansed, Anna's physical health began to improve steadily, though it was some weeks before the doctor believed the evidence of his own eyes and pronounced her out of danger. Nor was Grace small-minded enough to ignore Joss's other piece of advice. After she had spoken to each of the children, had a quiet interview with Trudy and an extremely stormy one with Nanny Brown, the latter, with bad grace and mutterings of spoiled brats and over-indulgent parents, packed her bags and left. The children were delighted — and Anna, when she was strong enough to rejoin her brothers in the nursery where Trudy now held much less repressive sway than had her predecessor, found herself something of a heroine, she having been given credit for the dismissal of the ogre. Life, at last, resumed its even tenor — for if grief for the lost baby still shadowed the hearts and minds of the adults of the family, younger memories were shorter and yesterday's trials and sorrows soon forgotten. Anna soon found herself slipping into the now pleasant nursery routine, happy to be well again, happy in her reinstatement in her parents' lives, happy above all to nurse secretly in her heart her devoted love for Joss, her handsome prince who once more had saved her. That she saw little of him as he became more and more involved with the business bothered her not at all. Her love had not as yet acquired the adult vice of possessiveness.

Christmas came and went and the new year of 1887 — Queen Victoria's fiftieth year on the throne — was ushered in with the usual celebrations and expectations. With Khartoum conveniently forgotten, the British people knew their Empire secure and their right to 'rule the waves' inviolable. Confidence, prosperity and expansion were the watchwords. To be sure, in the new year, there were some ugly disturbances in the streets of London and soldiers had to be called in to quell the riots and to disperse those malcontents who dared publicly to protest at poverty and unemployment; but on the whole, as the year moved on, most people's minds were much more exercised by the coming Golden Jubilee on the 22nd of June, than by those subversive elements who muttered disruptively of social reform and radical change. Most people in fact, if asked, would argue that things had changed quite enough already. After all, was it not true that even working-class children were now being educated? Most of them, anyway. And had not working men's conditions improved? If they behaved themselves and spent their time working instead of foolishly and contentiously trying to form unions to challenge their betters, the majority of them could earn a decent living — and if there were those to ask what happened to working men and women when their useful lives were over or were blighted by sickness or by injury and they were thrown on to the charity of an uncharitable world, self-righteous words like thrift and prudence came easily to most middle-class tongues.

In the Rose household there were few committed political attitudes. Josef was concerned only with his family and his business — in that past life of which he never spoke and tried not to think, politics had already cost him too dear. Grace, in this as in all things, dutifully took her cue from her husband. In her view, which was the prevailing one of the time, politics were, anyway, man's business; the running of the home and the dispensing of charity woman's, and so with her dear friend, Hermione Smithson, despite her own still far from perfect health, she spent a considerable amount of time and energy collecting money, food and clothes for distribution to her 'deserving poor' and helping at an East End refuge which catered for those whose only crime was destitution but whose sentence, too often, amounted to a slow death. She took it as God's will that these inequalities existed — the idea of an egalitarian society where such injustice might be eradicated simply never occurred to her. Even her own close brush with disaster, before she had met Josef, had taught her nothing. In common with most of her age her concept of social justice was simple, and based upon the paternalistic principles of charity.

The enthusiasm in the Rose household for the coming Jubilee was intense and shared by everyone from the smallest housemaid to Josef himself — who, in the way of most converts, had become in the twelve years he had lived in England more English, as Grace was fond of saying, than the English themselves. Grace and Josef — the Piccadilly shop shut for the day — planned to take the children to see the procession which promised to be a spectacle the like of which had only rarely been seen before in the streets of the city. New clothes were ordered, patriotic flags and favours purchased. The day itself dawned with all the excitement of Christmas, a birthday or a wedding. Very early in the bright June morning, decked in their finery, the happy party set off for their chosen spot not far from St Paul's, where the Queen was to give thanks for her long and prosperous reign. With Grace, Josef and the children went Tanya, Boris, Joss, Trudy, the little maid Sally — the latter twittering with excitement and totally unable to stop talking — a dozen flags and enough refreshments, as Trudy exclaimed, to feed the Queen's Guard.

"Oh, just look, Ma'am — Trudy — do see! How handsome the soldiers look! And the Jack Tars! Oh, my — I do love the sailor boys —" Sally was fairly jumping up and down with excitement, her usual discreet good behaviour entirely abandoned for the occasion.

Josef shepherded his flock to a good vantage point. The boys, like Sally but for different reasons, were greatly impressed by the gallant uniforms of the men who lined the processional route. Anna was enthralled by the crowds in their gay Sunday best, the wide skirts of the women like great upturned bell-flowers in the sunshine, their hats perched like pretty butterflies on their heads. They waited with growing anticipation, watching the slightest occurrence with the minutest of interest — a stray dog parading down the centre of the road got the biggest applause of the morning — and commenting upon their neighbours. Grace, even her usual calm disrupted by the atmosphere, and resolutely ignoring the tiredness that seemed recently to be with her always, held tightly to her husband's arm, a buffer against the surge of the crowd, and kept a sharp and slightly anxious eye on the rest of the party. Even so they nearly lost a member—James, lured by a barrel organ man and his mischievous monkey, wandered into the crowd and might well have been mislaid had not Boris scooped him up and with an easy movement swung the child up on his broad shoulders, where he sat happily and proudly, hanging on to a handful of bright, curly hair and looking out over the sea of bonnets, bowlers and waving flags.

"See the soldiers, Boris! Just see them! Aren't they splendid? Aren't they fine? I'm going to be a soldier when I grow up. A soldier in a fine red uniform!" He waved, wobbling precariously, at a nearby, impassive guardsman.

Boris reached a hand to steady the boy upon his shoulders, laughing, a glint in his hilariously brilliant eyes too bright to be explained simply by the excitement of the day. Joss, standing nearby, glanced at him suspiciously. He had seen that look before —

"They're coming! They're coming! Hear them!" Above the roar of the crowd came the compulsive sound of martial music. James wriggled excitedly, almost unbalancing the laughing Boris. "I see them! Oh, look — the horses — and the splendid carriage!"

The progress of the monarch could be charted by the rising tumult of sound that accompanied her coming. Dumpy, plain, bolt upright beneath her lace parasol, her determined mourning black lightened by silver, her black bonnet trimmed with white flowers, the old lady rode through the streets of her capital upon a frenzied wave of cheering. She had been criticized bitterly in the past for her withdrawal from public life following the death of her beloved Albert more than twenty-five years before, had believed herself — at times with good reason — to be unpopular with her subjects. Yet here, on this occasion, the affection of a nation for a queen who had presided over fifty unprecedentedly eventful years was fervent and undisguised. Her people roared for her. The old Widow of Windsor might be a bit dull with her mourning black and her prim and proper ways — but by God she was theirs, and the old country wouldn't be the same without her.

The Roses cheered with the rest — Alex so hard that he nearly choked and had to have his back banged by Trudy. Anna watched the wonderful procession in utter, breath-held silence. She had never seen such colour, such splendour. She wanted to draw it. The curve of a horse's neck, the lift of a hand — it was like one of Joss's stories of the magical splendours of the past. As the procession passed at last, leaving in its wake a residue of wild, emotional excitement that demanded release, someone in the crowd struck up the National Anthem, "God save our gracious Queen." In no time the whole throng was roaring the patriotic words, tears streaming down flushed faces. Small Michael, safe in Trudy's arms, put his fingers in his ears, knocking awry his sailor's cap which was decorated with a red, white and blue ribbon. Ralph, enthusiastically conducting with his Union Jack, caught Alex on the nose with it and received a buffet for his trouble.

It was a day of pride and pageantry, of friendliness and good-tempered excitement. A day never to be forgotten — for more reasons than one.

It was Joss who noticed, after the procession had returned in another boiling swell of excitement and people were rolling up flags, brushing down skirts and straightening headgear in preparation for leaving, that his brother Boris was missing.

"Where is he? Did anyone see him go?"

"I did." James, together with his wilting flag, clutched a scrap of paper. He was almost bursting with excitement and self-importance. "He told me to count to two hundred and then give this to you. I'd only reached a hundred and eighty-three —"

Joss, who still managed, despite the heat and the crowds, to look dapper in his check trousers and well-cut grey jacket, took the note and read it, his dark brows drawing together, the austere line of his mouth hardening.

"What's the matter? Joss — what is it?" Josef reached a hand to Joss's shoulder, "Is something wrong?"

"Boris is gone."

"Gone? How can he be gone? He was here a minute ago." Vaguely Josef looked around, as if expecting to see the bright head and laughing eyes bob out of the thinning crowd.

Joss shook his head. "He's gone." As so often in moments of emotion, his voice was absolutely expressionless, his accent strong. The rest of the party, puzzled, looked at him and waited. Joss stood for a long time staring at the note he held in his hand.

"Well?" prompted Josef uneasily, at last.

Joss lifted his head. His face was sharp with anger. "I have to apologize for my ungrateful brother. He has chosen to leave us."

"Leave us?" Grace echoed blankly. "Whatever can you mean?"

In reply Joss lifted the note. " 'I thank you all for your kindness and care,' " he read evenly, " 'and I apologize if I distress you in this. Uncle Josef, I know a desk and a pen are not for me. Give them to Josef. I go to be a soldier. I ask you not to be angry. Pray God for me. Yours in affection and thanks. Boris.' "

There was a moment's unbelieving silence.

"The whippersnapper!" Josef said, more in amazement than anger.

"Deary me!" said Sally, a scandalized hand to her mouth. "Well, deary me! There's a thing!" Trudy nudged her, hard, to silence.

"The little devil!" Josef said, and then, suddenly and surprisingly, laughed. He turned to Joss, slapped him on the shoulder. "Well, Joss my boy — it's just you and me, eh? Since your brother it seems is willing — anxious indeed — to exchange a place in Rose and Company for a dashing red coat —"

"If he wished to do this he should not have done it so. It shows ingratitude and thoughtlessness. Again I apologize for him." Josef's voice was still grim, but his anger was more for the manner of the action than for the action itself.

"Well I'll say one thing for Mr Boris," Sally's stage whisper, intended for Trudy's ear alone, reached them all in an unexpected lull in the noise around them, "he's goin' to look a treat in one o' them uniforms. A real treat!" And as tension broke into laughter the martial drums and trumpets that had lured the restless Boris sounded again in the distance, a faint, challenging call to arms.

CHAPTER SEVEN

Sally was right — Boris did indeed make a striking figure in his uniform. On the day he came to Bayswater to tell the family of his regiment's posting to India, the boys were goggle-eyed with envious admiration and the females of the household, one and all, were more than favourably impressed. Even Joss softened towards this scapegrace brother of his.

"I'll have a stripe soon," said Boris, confident as ever in his own abilities.

"You'll be a brigadier in no time." Joss's voice was sardonic, but his expression softened as it did for few others.

"Oh, Boris — India! You'll be careful?" Tanya's lovely face was worried. "You'll take care of yourself?"

Boris laughed and settled his plumed shako upon his head at a particularly rakish angle. "Of course I will! And if I can't —" he saluted her with a light kiss upon her cheek "— I'll get some lovely lady to do it for me. Who can resist the romantic, exiled son of a Russian Count?" He cocked his head on one side, "Even if he is only a lowly private."

He was gone before Christmas. In the spring they heard from him, a rambling, almost illegible letter, the grammar atrocious, full of jokes about the army, the officers, the heat and the lice — Boris Anatov had obviously — at least for the time being — found his niche in life.

So, indeed, had his brother. Early in 1888 Joss had persuaded Josef to allow him to visit South Africa, to make personal contact with some of the smaller suppliers. Whilst a power struggle raged in the diamond fields between the two giants, Cecil Rhodes and 'Barney' Barnato, there was little or no control over the price of diamonds and, as uncertainty reigned and prices fluctuated wildly, Joss knew that there was a place for a shrewd businessman and his money. A man on the spot could take advantage of the situation, and Joss acquired some very good stones at rock bottom prices. These he shipped to London, some to be sold at a profit, others to be used in the Hatton Garden workshops. Whilst in South Africa he also, on his own initiative, invested some of the company's money in shares in a small, unproductive and unquestionably ill-run claim near the Kimberley mine. The claim was difficult to work and was making little or no money. Three months later the shares were at a premium as Rhodes and Barnato fought for control of Kimberley. Josef, whose first reaction when he had heard of Joss's purchase of the apparently worthless shares had verged on the volcanic, now found himself the possessor of an unexpected and handsome profit and the recipient of congratulations on his shrewdness. Over a celebration lunch in the snug, discreetly opulent dining room where the more favoured clients of Rose and Company were sometimes entertained, he beamed with proprietary pride at the young man he was coming to regard almost as a son of his own blood. They had been examining the batch of stones that Joss had had shipped from South Africa, and the clouded, glass-like gems gleamed dully in the heavy-shaded light. Josef smiled. "More champagne, I think." He nodded, smiling, to the waiter who stood attentively beside his chair. "Another magnum, Thomas, if you please. And then you may leave us. I'll ring if I need you."

"Yes, Sir. Thank you, Sir." The white-gloved Thomas took a second bottle of champagne from the great ice-filled bucket, opened it with a flourish.

Josef took it from him. He leaned across the table to refill Joss's glass, and both men watched the silver-gold wine stream, sparkling, into the tall, elegant glass. As the door shut quietly behind the manservant Josef filled his own glass, picked it up and lifted it in toast towards Joss. "To a very successful trip."

Joss acknowledged the words with a small, graceful smile, and sipped his drink.

Josef's eyes were glinting with mischief. "And here," he added, innocently, lifting the glass again, "here's to Rose and Company's new Financial Director. Let's hope we can all work with him without too much trouble."

Joss's narrow hand had stilled utterly, half-way to an answering salute. "I beg your pardon?" he asked of the silence, carefully polite. "A new Financial Director? I didn't know —"

"But yes. Of course. The company is expanding. We need someone — don't you agree?" He could not keep up the joke. He had drunk the better part of the first bottle of champagne — and that after several generous glasses of the dry Madeira that he so loved — and was now feeling expansively and happily relaxed. He laughed. "To Mr Josef Anatov," he said, "new and very highly regarded Financial Director of Rose and Company."

Joss did not move, nor, for a moment, did his expression change. Then, within his dark eyes, a sudden gleam of excitement kindled. "I?"

"But of course, you! Who else? You're just what this company needs, my boy. Just what *I* need — young, energetic, astute —"

"I — don't know what to say or how to thank you." Joss's voice was very quiet.

"Then don't bother. It's actually simple selfishness, and in fairness I shouldn't be thanked for that." Josef laughed again, pleased, and downed his glass of wine. "You know better than most what a donkey I am when it comes to matters of finance. It was fate, my boy, that sent you to me. Fate and nothing less! Now I will have more time for the things that I really enjoy —" He reached again for the champagne bottle.

Joss, absently, covered the top of his glass with his spread hand and shook his head a little. "No more, thank you." His eyes, despite the small spark of excitement, were distant, veiled windows practised at disguising the subtleties behind them. Then, suddenly, as the full import of what Josef had said registered in his mind, he smiled brilliantly and his expression was more warmly happy than Josef had ever seen it. "Thank you, Josef. Thank you." The simple words were heartfelt.

Josef brushed the thanks aside with a waved hand. "I tell you — it's pure selfishness. To give me more time to spend in the workshops —" With the success that the company had achieved as the Rose name in jewellery design became better and better known in the exclusive circle that comprised their customers, the Hatton Garden workshops had long since been expanded to include those rooms where Josef and Grace had spent the early years of their married life.

Joss reached for the paper of uncut diamonds that lay between them, picked up a particularly fine, large, pebble-like stone and held it to the light between long, thin fingers. Josef's hand lay upon the snow-white tablecloth, the thumb darkly marked.

"Would you never consider practising again your old craft?" the younger man asked, idly curious, half his mind still busy about its own affairs, his eyes still upon the caged light of the stone. "Doesn't a gem like this ever make your fingers itch? I should have thought it must."

The silence that followed the words had about it the quality of shock. Puzzled, Joss glanced at Josef. The older man's face was suddenly closed, like a door slammed shut and latched against intrusion. "No," he said.

Joss lifted a shoulder. "What — never? Alone you cut and polished the stone upon which this company is founded, did you not?"

"Where did you hear that?"

The harsh tone raised the younger man's eyebrows in astonishment. "But Josef — everyone knows. Well," he paused, his sharp brain, as always and almost without volition weighing fact and figure, possibility and probability, "that's the story most tell, anyway. Why Josef, you know how our small world gossips!"

"Yes. I know." Josef, slowly, lifted his glass to his lips. The laughter had gone entirely from his face. "And what else do they say of me?" he asked, softly.

Joss, alerted, considered carefully. "They say," he said at last, "that you — as so many of us — escaped from persecution in Russia — and that you brought with you —" he paused "— rough goods of enormous value. One stone, they say. There is, of course, speculation as to its origin —" He left a small, enquiring silence, to which Josef responded not at all, then half-shrugged. "It is said too that you carried with you into exile the tools of your trade. Indeed, we have all seen them, have we not — displayed there in the workshop? And that with these and with your skill and courage you created a wonderful stone. A stone that, ironically perhaps, then travelled back to Russia."

He paused, waiting for a moment before, his rare curiosity aroused by the expression on the other man's face, he asked, "Is this not, then, the truth?"

Across Josef's face passed a spasm of pain so acute that the younger man made an instinctive, swift, conciliatory gesture with his hand, quickly stilled. "It's — true, yes." Josef said at last, his voice grating in the sombre quiet, "At least —" For how long had he needed to speak of it? To excuse, explain, placate that pain of conscience that each sight of Tanya inflicted? His eyes were upon the unremarkable-looking diamonds, in the lines of his face an anguish that gave pause even to his companion who knew more than most of pain. "In Amsterdam," he said, very quietly, "I —" He stopped. Closed his eyes. "Amsterdam." The very tonelessness of the word bespoke an intolerable pain.

"What? What happened in Amsterdam?" Joss asked very gently.

There was a long, long silence. Josef sat with bowed head, his gaze unblinking upon the diamonds.

"Josef? What happened in Amsterdam?"

The older man lifted his head. His face was shuttered. He shook his head. "Nothing. Of course. Nothing happened in Amsterdam. Except that your damned relatives turned your sister and me away —"

"As they did us. Yes. I know the story."

Josef's face was haggard even in the shaded lights. "Their fault," he said, softly and violently, as if to himself. "All of it. Their fault."

"All of what?"

Josef poured more champagne, drank it with no enjoyment, like a man dying of thirst. Then he picked up one of the stones and held it in the hardened palm of his hand, rocking it a little. "Poor Tanya," he said. "My poor little Tanya."

Dark brows lowered in puzzlement. "It wasn't your fault that the family wouldn't help you."

The quiet, sympathetic tone brought a bitter smile. "No. Of course not. Not my fault. But — other things —"

"What other things?"

The temptation to confess at last was all but overwhelming —

to share his pain and guilt with another, to receive absolution from the young man with whom he felt such affinity. He lifted his head. "Joss, do you believe that good can ever come out of evil?"

Joss shrugged in his characteristic way. "I suppose — yes — sometimes." He waited.

"Sacrifices have to be made, do they not? Sometimes." Josef's face was intense, his consonants a little slurred.

Joss shook his head. "Josef. You must know that I don't know what you're talking about."

"Tanya," Josef said, very low. "That accursed stone. All this —" He gestured at the expensively appointed room.

A faint, puzzled frown had appeared on the younger man's dark face. "Are you saying," he asked, slowly, "that there's some sort of connection? Between my sister and — the Shuvenski?"

Sudden alarm bells rang, loudly and very clearly in Josef's slightly befuddled brain. What in God's name had he been about to do? He laughed unconvincingly, a sound that did little to ease the odd tension that had unexpectedly grown between them. "Connection? Of course not. How could there be? Truly, I shouldn't drink champagne at lunch time. It makes me maudlin!" The bluffness of his manner was almost convincing. Joss watched him, the intent frown still creasing his brow. Josef stood up, swaying a very little. "Well — back to work, eh?" He pulled his gold watch from his pocket and consulted it. "Good Lord! Is that the time? Grace and little Anna will be here any minute. The child has pestered me into taking her to the workshops. Funny little thing she is — I can't think what she believes she'll find to interest her there."

Joss said nothing. The level gaze had not faltered, neither had he smiled. Now, however, he stirred, stood and smiled and the peculiar tension was gone. "I'll see you later then?"

"Yes, yes. Come to my office at four. We'll all take tea together."

For a long moment after the young man had left the room Josef stood, his hands white-knuckled upon the back of the high chair behind which he stood, gazing into the void into which he had so nearly thrown himself. He was sweating. Never again.

Never, never again would he ever think of Amsterdam, let alone allow himself to mention it. To think that he had almost — he closed his eyes, took a long, shaking breath. In his mind's eye, Joss's dark, intelligent, guarded face watched him, a dawning and potentially terrifying question in the eyes. Josef shook his head sharply, reached for his jacket. Not a young man, that, to find forgiveness easy. And who could blame him? Josef strode to the door. "You may clear away now, Thomas."

"Yes, Sir. Thank you, Sir."

Heavily Josef mounted the shallow polished marble stairs that led to his office. The conversation with Joss still nagged in his head. *Fool*, he told himself savagely. To have roused his curiosity. To have invited him to make the connection between — he opened his office door.

"Papa! Papa! Where have you been? We've been waiting for absolutely *ages*, and the cab's waiting —" Anna launched herself at him, velvet ribbons flying. "Can we go to the workshops? Can we go now?"

"Anna! Where did you leave your manners today?" Grace, however was smiling, her tone indulgent.

Anna swung on her father's hand. He ruffled her hair. "Of course, my dear. Come along."

"I want to see it all — absolutely all. Can I see them make a necklace? And can I see the enamellers?"

" 'May', Anna." Grace's voice was sharper this time. " 'May I see —' "

Josef held up his hand to forestall another torrent. "You may see everything that we can pack into an hour. So — come along. My dear —" he offered his arm to his wife.

Ten minutes later they arrived in the busy thoroughfare of Hatton Garden. Anna, to her mother's exasperation and her father's somewhat abstracted amusement, had hardly stopped talking long enough to draw breath. "— and most of all I want to see the man that draws —" she finished as she tumbled from the cab.

"And so you shall." Josef escorted them into the workshops. Grace's face softened as she looked around her. These rooms — so familiar still despite their different use — held many memories.

"Here we are —" Josef pushed open a door. "We'll start here, where the work starts." He smiled down at Anna. " 'The man who draws', as you so rightly called him, my dear. Good afternoon, Thompson."

"Afternoon, Sir." The young man so addressed made to scramble from his stool and was waved back to it by a smiling Josef. "No, no my boy. Don't let us disturb you. This is my daughter, Anna. Would you mind if she watched you for a while?"

The young man grinned engagingly at the bright-eyed Anna. "Not a bit, sir."

Anna very nearly got no further on her tour, so bewitched was she by the sure, delicate draughtsmanship, the intricate fragility of the design upon which the young man was working. But at last she allowed her father to tear her away, and was soon being instructed in the mysteries of the issues office, with its stores of precious materials, its little nondescript white paper packs of beautifully cut and polished gems. They then moved on to the scalloped workbench of the chief mounter, his leather apron spread across his knees to catch any valuable scraps that might fall. He was working, surrounded by the tools of his trade — tools so apt to their task that they had not been improved upon for centuries — upon a heavy gold bracelet which was, Josef told Anna, to be set with rubies, the rarest stones in the world.

"Even rarer than diamonds?" the child asked, wide-eyed.

"Even rarer than that." Josef was finding it hard to devote his mind entirely to the child's eager questions. Damn his wine-induced indiscretion! What had he said to Joss that had brought to the boy's face that odd, disturbingly intent expression that he, Josef, was finding so hard to dismiss from his mind? The conversation in the dining room was a little muddled in his head. What had he said?

Anna's small finger was poking amongst the mounter's tools; handsaw, drill, file, and others with more exotic and esoteric names. "This is a scooper, isn't it? And that's — a graver. And *that's* a swage block." Jerked from his preoccupation Josef looked at her in surprise. "How on earth do you know that?"

"I saw them all in the book in your study."

The mounter, an elderly man with thinning hair and a deeply

lined face looked up at Josef with exasperated eyes. "Am I to get on with my work, Sir?"

Anna jumped at his tone and snatched the obviously offending hand from the precious tools.

"Yes, yes. Of course. We're sorry to have troubled you. Anna, come —"

"But — I wanted to ask him about the solder. How he does it without melting the —"

"Anna!"

They visited the polishing shop, with its distinctive, tangy smell where Anna, mollified, was made much of and allowed to help polish with pumice a small silver brooch into which a carved cameo was to be set, and from there moved on to the well-lit room where the setters worked, painstakingly and delicately, bent over their benches, their concentration such that the visitors might not have entered the room at all.

Anna watched in commendable and absolute silence for a while. At last, his task done, the man she was watching sat back, straightening his bent frame, rubbing his back and eyeing the piece he had completed. Small diamonds glinted with their own distinctive fire.

"What happens next?" Anna asked very softly, even she was impressed by the almost church-like atmosphere of concentration.

"It goes back to be polished again," Josef said. "And you, young lady, have seen quite enough for one day, I think —"

"Oh! But, Papa — we haven't seen the enamellers! Or the —"

"Anna!"

The one word, in that tone, from her mother subdued her. Her father took pity on the disappointed little face. "Another time, my darling. We really do have to go now, for I promised Joss we'd meet him for tea. And then, if you'd like, Mr Simpson shall show you around the showrooms. I know you enjoy that."

"Oh, yes! That would be lovely. But," Anna glanced around again, "you do promise you'll let me come back? Soon?"

Her father smiled. "I promise."

*

That summer of 1888 Josef for the first time took a house by the sea for the summer months. Since her own illness and the death of the baby, Grace's health had been a source of constant worry to him. So, together with their close friends the Smithsons, they rented a large family villa in a small seaside town on the south coast, the women and children moving there for the whole of the summer, the men joining their families whenever the pressure of business allowed, taking the train to the coast and finishing the journey in some style in the smart pony and trap that the stationmaster kept for just such contingencies. It was a happy time — a summer that Anna never forgot, and one that was to change her life and that of almost every other member of the family.

For Tanya, too, the temporary move to the seaside was a happy one. The house stood, gabled and verandahed, in its own small garden from which a small wicket gate gave on to a narrow, sanded road which led directly down to the quiet beach. She loved the sea. It did not threaten — was indeed one of the few things in life of which she was not faintly afraid. The hypnotic movement fascinated her, the incessant sound overcame as did nothing else those small, still, distant voices that murmured so often in her mind. She would sit, pensive, for hours, her knees drawn to her chin, watching the breakers roll in to wash the shingled sand, smooth and glistening, scoured fresh and clean in the sunshine, whilst around her the children played and squabbled, paddled, rode donkeys, built sand castles. Even Alex, thirteen now, home from school and considering himself very much a man of the world, enjoyed the beach games they all played with such gusto. With the Smithson boys to augment their numbers, there were games of cricket, of Kick the Can, and of beach croquet, where almost everyone cheated. The days were long, the weather on the whole kind, though often breezy. Grace and Hermione passed their time in happy companionship embroidering, watercolour painting, and helping the children with their scrapbooks. Tanya watched them all in quiet contentment — they were her world, she wanted nothing else: if they were happy, then so was she. The world beyond this closed circle terrified her, she wanted nothing of it — though the reasons for this were hazy in her mind, unnamed, confused, vaguely associated with the pain and darkness and dread that sometimes haunted her dreams. Faced with an intruder from this other, threatening world she withdrew like a snail into its shell, bewildered and made next to witless by a paralysis of nerves that she simply could not control. Even the proximity of the boisterous Smithson family, whom she knew so well, disturbed her a little, especially when bluff Obadiah visited the house with his loud voice and rumbustious laughter. It was then a shock when, seated upon the sand one day a little removed from the younger folk who were busy constructing a spectacularly intricate sand castle, her abstracted contemplation of the glittering waves was interrupted by a shadow which fell suddenly across her. Startled, she looked up and discovered a young man standing beside her, a bowler hat clutched a little awkwardly in his hand, the trouser legs of his neat suit dusted with sand. For that first moment he appeared as tongue-tied as she was herself. He had a boyish, fresh face with large, blue, innocent eyes and a soft mouth that was in no way disguised by the young and less than luxuriant moustache that decorated the upper lip. The blue eyes were fixed upon her face in something she could only interpret as an astonishment that amounted almost to shock — though why he should look so Tanya, the least vain of people, could not conceive. She felt blood rising to her cheeks, experienced that dreadful breathless thumping of her heart that any unexpected situation inflicted upon her.

The young man cleared his throat uncomfortably. "Er — Miss Anatov?"

Tanya's voice had deserted her entirely. She glanced, quickly and anxiously, to where the children were playing under the comforting gaze of Trudy, then looked down at her hands, which, clasped around her knees, looked tense even in their little white lace gloves.

"You are Miss Anatov?" The young man's voice was more confident.

Tanya nodded, not looking at him.

"I'm sorry — I startled you." He was looking a little puzzled now, clearly unsure of what he had done to produce this rather strange reaction to his presence. "My name is Smithson. Matthew Smithson. I'm looking for my young cousins. Aunt

Hermione said —"

"Cousin Matthew! Cousin Matthew!" Charles, the youngest Smithson, scampered across the sand towards them, "Mama didn't tell us you were coming!"

Matthew Smithson, regardless of his London clothes, swept the youngster up into the air. "Didn't know myself, young Charlie! Bashed off to the station and came down on the off chance —"

"Will you stay? Oh *will* you stay?" Charlie clung to him like a limpet and would not be put down.

The castle-building party had broken up as, shouting excitedly, the other Smithson boys joined their younger brother, plump Christopher panting in the wake of the younger Arthur. "Hello, Matthew!"

"Hello, you two." Matthew smiled past his cousins to Anna and her brothers. "And you must be the Roses."

"That's right." Anna liked the young man on sight. "I'm Anna. How do you do? This is Alex, Ralph and James. The little one's Michael."

"I'm not little!"

"Don't be silly. Of course you are."

"I'm not!"

Cousin Matthew hunkered down beside the child. "How old are you?"

"I'm six." Michael cast a wary glance at his sister and added, "nearly."

"Well! Six, eh? I'd certainly have said you were older than that. Six-and-a-half — seven, even."

Well pleased, Michael beamed. Matthew stood up, turned again to Tanya. He was puzzled by her obvious and — it seemed to him — excessive agitation. He was also, for the first time in a fairly uneventful life, spellbound. Here, in pale silk and muslin, her lovely, anxious face shaded by a wide-brimmed, flower-trimmed straw hat was, quite simply, the most beautiful human being he had ever seen. Matthew Smithson was an extremely well brought up young man. He tried, unsuccessfully, not to stare, tried — equally ineffectively — to control the idiotic hammering of his heart. "Aunt Hermione and Mrs Rose sent me to find you all. They thought perhaps a stroll down into the town for tea."

"Oh, lovely!" With no further ado, Anna began gathering buckets, spades and towels. "Come on, everyone, hurry. Oh, Alex! Do be careful. It took me all morning to collect those."

Alex, in his haste, had kicked over a bucketful of small shells and pretty stones. "Oh, for goodness' sake, Anna," he said crossly, "not *more* of them? Your room's full of the beastly things already. I can't think how Tanya puts up with it. What with them, and the smelly seaweed — ugh!" He made to roll the bucket over with his foot.

"Don't! You pig!" Anna flew at him.

Tanya, her voice trembling very slightly, said sharply, "Anna! Alex! Stop this at once. Alexis — help your sister pick up the things you spilled. Trudy — please help the boys to gather their things." She stood up, apparently not seeing the hand that Matthew Smithson offered to steady her. The young stranger was watching her in a way that disturbed her intensely. Flustered, she busied herself with the younger children, gathered together her own book and parasol.

"Please, let me —" Refusing this time to be ignored, the young man determinedly took her small burden from her, smiling reassuringly.

"But, really, I —" she stopped. She could not meet his eyes.

Trudy, occupied with tidying young Michael's disordered attire, glanced sideways at her with a glimmer of a smile: S'truth, Miss Tanya certainly blushed easy. And as for the young man — plain Trudy had never had a follower, though she lived in hope, but if she had she knew she'd be lucky if he ever looked at her the way this handsome Smithson cousin was looking at Tanya Anatov.

The precious stones and shells safely stowed, Anna straightened, swinging the heavy bucket.

"What on earth *are* you doing with all those things?" Christopher asked in honest mystification. "As Alex said — you're always off collecting them. You must have *millions*."

Anna tapped a thin little nose with a thin little finger. "You wait and see. It's a secret."

"Something to do with the mothers' birthdays?" Christopher was more astute than he looked.

Anna pulled a distinctly unladylike face. "Wait and see," she said again.

"I say, that's a pretty one." Matthew reached into the bucket and took out a small, cone-shaped, pale pearly shell.

"It's a top-shell," Anna said eagerly. "I've got some lovely ones —"

"See, Miss Anatov — isn't it pretty?" As if enticing some highly-strung small animal, he held the shell towards Tanya on the palm of his outstretched hand. If only she would look at him —

Tanya did — a fluttering, nervous glance that netted his heart as surely as if she had been the most practised coquette in the land. "Is it not pretty?" he urged again.

"It — yes, indeed it is. Very pretty."

He watched her, gently insistent, willing her to smile.

"We're ready. Come on, Ralphy, get a move on. Oh, I do hope Mama will take us to Brown's — they do the most scrumptious teacakes —" Anna, ever-restless, was dancing round them. Tanya did smile then, not at Matthew, but at the eager child. It was enough.

"*Are* you staying, Cousin Matthew?" Little Charles caught his hand and swung upon it like a little monkey.

Matthew laughed, and lifted him high. "Just for the day this time, young Charlie. But," he glanced at Tanya, who was over-busy trying to tidy Anna's flying hair, "I'll come back. If you'll have me?"

"Oh, good! Often? You'll come often?"

Tanya straightened. A small swirl of wind gusted from the sea and her full, soft skirts billowed. With a quiet exclamation she put up a hand to secure her wide-brimmed hat.

"Oh, yes," Matthew Smithson said, a little abstractedly, "quite often, I should think."

He was — to all the children's delight, for he soon became a firm favourite with them all — as good as his word and in no time had become a welcome and familiar figure at the house. There being no spare rooms — the house, big as it was, was already filled to capacity by the two families and their servants — he found a room not far from them in a fisherman's cottage, close to the beach. He joined his aunt and cousins and their friends for all meals except breakfast, with pleasure squired the ladies when they required an escort, played with the children with gusto and good humour, graced the social evenings of music and games that they all so much enjoyed and daily and very obviously fell further and further beneath Tanya's spell.

She herself was truly unconscious of this, although the situation was charmingly obvious to the older members of the party. So inexperienced was she that the simple possibility that Matthew might be courting her never entered her head. She was aware of how often he would come and find his young cousins on the beach and how often on those occasions he would, after a short and boisterous game, settle quietly beside her, talking or not as her mood dictated, until she grew quite used to his company. It seemed also remarkably frequently she would find him sitting next to her at the table, or in the evening as they played charades or sang around the painfully tuneless little piano that stood in the cluttered parlour. Certainly her diffidence and acute nervousness eased considerably as his easy companionship became more familiar — she came, almost without realizing it, to look for his coming when he was away. It took Trudy, however, to open her eyes to the astonishing fact that the young man was pursuing more than her friendship.

Tanya had washed her hair, and Trudy, with brush and towel, was drying and attempting to tame it — a task which Tanya herself found almost impossible. It was Grace's birthday — coincidentally in the same week as Hermione's — and tonight was to be a double celebration. Josef, Obadiah and Joss were expected at any moment, the children, bathed, brushed and shining-clean, were watching impatiently from the open windows downstairs, appetizing smells wafting from the kitchen. All over the house prettily-wrapped, long-guarded presents were being brought out of hiding. On the dressing table of this, the room that Tanya shared with Anna, stood two beautifully decorated boxes, patterned intricately with tiny shells and stones. On the lid of each, picked out in pale, translucent colours, a dragonfly swooped, elegant wings outstretched. Trudy stilled her movements for a moment, looked at the boxes.

" 'Oever'd a' thought Miss Anna 'ad it in 'er to do something like that? They're as good as anything Mr Josef's got in 'is shop, I'll be bound."

"They're certainly very beautiful. And she drew all the designs herself." Tanya smiled. She had watched with admiration and affection the painstaking hours Anna had spent on the boxes and their contents. "Anna sometimes sees things, I think, with different eyes than others."

Trudy resumed her brushing. "Well, I don't know about that. I just wish I 'ad that way with me 'ands meself. Must be lovely to be able to make things like that."

"Yes."

The smell and sound of the sea came to them through the open window, mingled with the sound of the children's voices, calling to each other. A gull cried, oddly desolate in the softly pleasant evening. Tanya looked to where the bird wheeled gracefully in the sky, drifting and swooping on the gentle breeze.

"There." With her fingers Trudy arranged the fashionable tiny curls upon Tanya's forehead, teased the fair, still damp tendrils on her neck. The girl's thick hair was swept up and coiled on the top of her head, perfectly setting off the spectacular bone structure and pearly skin of her face. Trudy surveyed the effect of her labours in the dressing table mirror with a mixture of satisfaction and mild envy. "You wearing the yellow?"

"I thought I might, yes."

Trudy nodded sagely. "Look a treat, that will, with your 'air all shining. 'E'll like that. I 'eard 'im say just the other day that yellow was the colour suited you best." She stopped as she caught Tanya's astonished, lifted eyes in the mirror.

"He?" Tanya asked.

Trudy began to gather the paraphernalia of hairdressing from the dressing table. "Why, Mr Matthew, of course."

"Mr Matthew? Why should it concern Mr Matthew what I wear?"

Trudy gave a small, disbelieving puff of laughter. Miss Tanya might have a bit of a screw loose, but surely — not even she could be that daft? "Why indeed, Miss Tanya. No fault of yours if 'e's sweet on you, eh? None of 'is business what you wear. That's what I like to 'ear. Keep 'em dangling, say I —"

Flaming colour was possessing Tanya's face. Her hand fluttered nervously at the neck ribbons of her flowered cotton robe. "Trudy? What do you mean?"

Trudy had had enough of such pussy-footing affectation. "Lord 'ave mercy. You aren't trying to tell me it's escaped your notice that the poor young man's 'ead over 'eels in love with you?"

Tanya stared. "Don't be silly." Her voice was small, childlike, her long fingers clutched again at the ribbons at her throat. "Trudy, you mustn't joke about such things. It isn't right."

There was a short, offended silence. Then, "Sorry I spoke, Miss." The nursemaid's voice was huffy. "Sorry I spoke I'm sure." She brushed down her apron busily. "Well, if you don't mind I'd better be off. I've to see to Miss Anna yet. She's bound to be in a pickle —"

"I — yes — thank you for doing my hair, Trudy. It was very kind of you. No one does it quite like you."

Mollified, Trudy smiled. "Want me to lace you before I go?"

Tanya shook her head. "No. Thank you. I can manage."

As the door closed behind the other girl Tanya stared at her own reflection in the mirror. Recollections flitted through her mind like small birds through the branches of a tree. A smile here. A word, an expression there. The brief touch of a hand. Blue and gentle eyes upon her. And — suddenly — Grace and Hermione smiling, exchanging glances. "Why don't you two go ahead with Trudy and the children? We'll be along later —"

Inexplicably in the warm evening, she shivered.

Outside the window the clatter of hooves, the racket of ironshod wheels, the joyous sounds of arrival.

She crossed her arms over her breasts, wrapping her fingers about her upper arms, holding herself still. She felt a little giddy. Panic fought with a strange mixture of fear and excitement.

Fear. Why fear?

Upon the bed lay starched petticoats, drawers, chemise, corset and the yellow dress that had prompted Trudy's comment. With odd, stiff movements she stood and began to dress. The house was humming with activity now — voices called, doors slammed, there was laughter and a snatch of song.

Tanya herself, in this quiet little room, was walled into an all too familiar cell of silence. She did not herself know why the possibility of Matthew's devotion to her should arouse such a sudden and disturbing storm of confusion and dread — she only knew, with no reason, that somewhere in the love of that kindly soft-spoken young man there was a terrible threat. A threat that stopped her breath in her throat and keened in her mind like a distant scream.

Half dressed she stood, looking into darkness, trying to remember.

"Tanya! Oh, Tanya, do hurry! Papa is here, and Joss and Mr Smithson. Papa has brought Mama the most *enormous* present. And he's teasing her terribly — he won't let her open it until we're all there — *Tanya!*" Anna's voice rose in exasperation, "You aren't even *dressed!* Here — let me help you with your laces — and oh, do hurry. There. One petticoat will do. That's it. Now the dress —". As the lemon muslin fluttered and settled softly about Tanya's white-stockinged ankles Anna stood back, hushed. "Oh, Tanya, you look truly beautiful. Honest you do. I'll never be able to look like that —" Her voice was perfectly matter of fact.

Tanya, with an effort, focused upon the child. "Don't be silly, little one. Of course you will." She slipped her feet into soft kid slippers.

Anna shook her head just a little glumly. "No. I'm not pretty now — growing up isn't going to make much difference, is it?"

"What nonsense." Tanya took her by the shoulders and marched her to the mirror. "Now, see," she pulled the tow hair up and back softly from the child's face, "how lovely your eyes are. And how straight and fine your mouth."

"I'm miles too thin. And I've got big hands and feet. They seem to be getting bigger every day."

"No, not big." Tanya took the girl's hand, straightened the fingers on the palm of her own. "Long. Artistic. Dear Anna — there are many kinds of beauty — you of all people should know that. You show it in your art. You have a beauty of your own."

Anna shrugged, unimpressed.

"And talent. The boxes are truly beautiful."

The words brought them both back to the urgency of the

moment. "Will you help me carry one?" asked Anna, a little nervously — she would die, just die, if the mothers did not like them. "I can't manage both on my own."

From downstairs a voice called. "Miss Anatov? Anna? Are you there? Everyone's waiting —"

"That's Matthew! I didn't know he'd arrived!" Anna picked up one of the precious boxes and flew from the room.

Tanya followed much more slowly.

Matthew Smithson's official courtship of Tanya Anatov began that very day, the day of the double birthday party. The dinner was an enormous success, the high spot undoubtedly being the presentation of the various gifts and in particular, to Anna's delighted embarrassment, of her own efforts — the two shell boxes and their contents. Hermione, on discovering the butterfly brooch that hers held was unfeignedly charmed. "My dear, where ever did you get such a pretty thing? You must have emptied your money box."

Anna blushed to the roots of her hair. "I made it. From shells and things, like the boxes." Her eyes were upon her mother who was sitting, her own box on her lap unopened, watching her friend's delight with undisguised pleasure of her own.

"Made it? But — my goodness — Mr Rose, just look at this! The child's a true artist." She held out a pudgy hand. The butterfly perched like a living thing.

Josef took it, studied it, looked at Anna. "It's lovely, darling. Well done."

"Papa got me the pin from the workshop," Anna explained. "But I wouldn't let him see what I wanted it for. I wanted it to be a real surprise. Didn't I, Papa?" Josef nodded thoughtfully and handed the pretty thing back. Anna looked expectantly at her mother, "Mama?"

Grace looked up questioningly, then exclaimed, "Why, surely not one for me too?" She opened the box, stilled for a moment, then reached a careful hand into it. "Anna!" she said softly. "It's truly beautiful."

"I wanted to make it into a brooch, like Aunt Hermione's. But I couldn't. I couldn't make it fit on to the pin. It turned out too big. Does it matter?" Anna's voice trailed off. Her eyes were anxious.

"Of course it doesn't matter. It's lovely just as it is." In Grace's small hand nestled a dragonfly a few inches long, fashioned of silver wire, gossamer material and tiny, shimmering glass beads.

"I made it before we came. It took all spring. Papa gave me the bits and pieces. And then he looked after it, so that you wouldn't see it till today —"

"All these secrets," jovial Obadiah laughed.

Joss reached for the glittering insect. "Why, Anna — it's one of the prettiest things I've ever seen." He was not looking at the child, did not see the depth of colour that rose in her face at his praise.

Grace opened her arms to her daughter. "They're quite the nicest presents that I've ever seen. See, Josef, we have a little jeweller in the family."

Anna, within the circle of her mother's arms, watched her father inspect the glittering insect and held her breath. Would he remember? Would he? The promise had been made, casually, months ago —

Josef looked up. "It seems, little one, that you have certainly earned another visit to the workshop."

Delighted, she flew to him. "Oh Papa! When? When can I go?"

He laughed. "As soon as you're back home, if you'd like."

"Oh, yes! Yes, please! You won't forget? Promise you won't forget?"

He shook his head, amused. "I won't forget."

Grace stood up. "Hermione, my dear. Children — shall we take a stroll in the garden and leave the gentlemen to their port?"

It was later that same evening as twilight dimmed the sky that a strangely tense Matthew cornered Josef and Joss and asked, awkwardly formal, for a private word. They gathered in the small room that was designated the parlour. The others were still in the garden, their voices lifting above the evening birdsong and the distant shingled whispering of the sea. Matthew cleared his throat. "I do apologize if this seems a little clumsy. The truth is that I wasn't certain which one of you I should speak to — and so decided that the proper thing might be to speak to both." The stilted words fell into a silence that on Josef's side was mildly amused, on Joss's surprised. Two pairs of dark eyes watched Matthew. He struggled on. "You, Mr Rose are, I believe, Miss Anatov's guardian. You, Joss, her brother —"

Josef smiled. Joss's brow furrowed.

"I wish — to ask — that is, to ascertain — if either of you would have any objection to my — to my addressing my attentions to Miss Anatov, with a view —" He had, in nervous preparation for this moment, partaken rather more liberally than usual of Josef's port. To his horror his mind had become suddenly and disconcertingly empty and his carefully prepared speech slipped from it like water from a holed bucket. He looked helplessly from one to the other, "with a view to persuading her — to become my wife."

Josef, sitting in an inappropriately small floral armchair, steepled his fingers. "Well, now —" he paused, looked at Joss, a twinkle in his eye. He, too, had drunk well of the port and — primed by the astute Grace — had been awaiting this interview all evening. Had Matthew but known it, all enquiries regarding his character and his prospects had already been made, discreetly, via the ladies. "I daresay that we might see our way clear to allowing that — providing Miss Anatov has no great objections of her own. Joss?"

Joss grunted half-heartedly. His expression was still notably unimpressed, his eyes piercing.

Matthew was a little unbalanced by the unexpected ease of it. "I, oh, I say. That's wonderful. Thank you, Mr Rose. Joss —"

"Don't thank me yet, lad," Josef said, smiling. "We've only given you permission to engage in the battle — we don't guarantee the outcome, eh, Joss?" Not for the first time that day he pushed determinedly aside an absurd worm of doubt. How many times must he tell himself that yesterday was yesterday, and its nightmare best forgotten? For indeed sometimes, when recollections of a shambled room, a terrified, bleeding child, the slumped, bloody body of a man, invaded his mind it seemed to him that it must be just that — a dreadful dream, best forgotten, something that had happened to other people in another life, that could have nothing to do with them now. He stood up, slapped Matthew jovially on the shoulder. "And now — before the ladies begin to suspect another round of the port bottle — shall we join them?"

And so it began, the quiet, gentle courtship. Through that long holiday summer, slowly as a flower in the sunshine, Tanya bloomed in the warmth of Matthew's love. His wooing was a graceful combination of determination and restraint, of courteous persistence and tender care that would have done credit to one much older than he. He did not rush her, yet neither did he allow her to escape his diligent attentions. Where she was, there was he, attentive and entertaining, anticipating her every whim, her servant in all things but one — he would not allow her to dismiss him. They were hardly ever actually alone together — the tenets of middle-class society saw to that — but in company with the children and Trudy — who was often ready to conspire in setting them a little apart — they walked the country lanes, ran barefoot on the tide-wet sands, laughed at Punch and Judy, rode in the pony and trap across the wide, windswept Southern downs and slowly, slowly, his gentle and devoted friendship began to succeed where a more passionate assault would most certainly have failed. He made her laugh. He teased and pampered her. Nothing was too much trouble if Tanya's happiness or comfort were at stake. He had loved her from the first sight of her lifted, lovely face; having found such treasure, having, incredibly, been given the chance to possess it, he had no intention of letting it slip through his fingers. To his love-struck eyes Tanya's strangeness, that distanced her from others, was an added spur — if it were harder to make her laugh, to draw her from herself, to gain admittance to that shuttered private place to which she still too often retired, then so much the more rewarding was success.

Grace watched the progress of the courtship with a lively interest that amounted to undisguised if tacit encouragement. At twenty-one Tanya was, in those days of early wedlock, well on the way to old-maidship — a terrible fate in the eyes of that society. That her first and only admirer should be a young man of such character and standing as the young Matthew Smithson

— nephew of Obadiah Smithson, M.P., son of a merchant banker whose interests ranged from railway companies in the United States to sheep farming in Australia — was a bonus indeed. Grace was honestly surprised that such a young man should show such interest in her foster daughter, despite her beauty, and was more than ready to encourage his hopes at every opportunity. Tanya herself, as the weeks passed, changed visibly. She became less tense, less withdrawn. She smiled more often. Her laughter, so rare before, rang through the house like a peal of bells. Matthew demanded little of her, sensing still beneath this outward change that tense timidity that reminded him of the wild deer he had encountered on a trip to Scotland — lovely, timorous, ready to flee at the slightest threatening movement.

"When I grow up," Anna said one afternoon, a little wistfully to Alex, "I don't suppose anyone'll run around after me like that."

Alex snorted. "I should jolly think not!" In Alex's thirteen-year-old masculine eyes Matthew Smithson was letting the side down badly with all this dilly-dallying.

It was a quiet Saturday afternoon, very late in August. Most of the adults were resting, the younger children had gone to the beach with Trudy. Tanya and Matthew were in the garden below the window where Anna sat drawing. Tanya, her skirts spread around her in a pastel cloud, was swaying gently to and fro on the swing that Josef had fixed from the apple tree for the children. Matthew sat on the grass, a long-stemmed flower in his hand, watching her.

Anna smiled.

"What tommy rot!" Alex turned from the window in disgust.

The garden gate clicked. Through the bushes Anna saw Joss coming up the path. She slipped from her chair.

"Where are you going?"

"Out," she said with sisterly brusqueness.

Joss was standing talking to Tanya and Matthew when she caught up with him. He smiled at her, absently, in mid sentence, and tweaked her hair. She took his hand. "Joss, do come for a walk? I haven't seen you for ages —"

Joss glanced towards the house. "Well —"

"Oh, *please*. Just across the cliff and back? It'll be the last chance you get. You know you like the view, and we'll all be home next week."

He smiled. "All right, then, little one. Why not?"

They walked down the lane and along the quiet seafront to where the track lifted over low, chalky cliffs. A light, chill wind blew from the sea, capping the waves with white. Bathing machines were lined like defensive weapons along the seashore. Parasols fluttered in the wind, small figures dashed about the beach below. Two donkeys plodded back and forth, heads down, their small, excited burdens clinging like limpets.

"Oh, look, there's Trudy and Michael! I'm sure it's them — he's having a donkey ride! Coo-ee!" Anna danced up and down, waving her arms.

Joss was amused. "They'll never see you."

"I suppose not." She subsided, fell happily again into step beside him, glancing up at the dark, hawk-like face as she spoke. "What do you think of Matthew?"

"Think of him?" His voice gave nothing away.

She tugged at his hand. "You know — Matthew and Tanya."

He shrugged slightly.

"Don't you like him?" she persisted, surprise in her voice. How on earth could someone not like Matthew?

"Yes, I like him." Others of his acquaintance might have stopped there, taking into consideration that particular tone of voice.

"Well, you don't sound as if you do."

He did not reply.

"Joss?"

Exasperated, he stopped and looked down at her. She looked back at him, wide-eyed for a moment before an almost comical look of understanding came over her face. "Ah." She nodded sagely, totally baffled: honestly, grown-ups could be peculiar at times, even this one. "You don't want to talk about it."

He nodded. "That's right."

"Why not?"

"Anna!"

"Sorry," she said hastily, and took his hand again, tugging him along the path. "Come down here. It's a lovely quiet bit of beach. It's my favourite — it's where I collected my stones and shells."

He glanced back the way they had come. "Truly, Anna, I think perhaps —"

"Oh, please! Please! It's my favourite place — and you've never seen it —"

He shrugged. "All right." He followed her down the steep, crumbling path, watched as she scuttled across the sand, looking for shells. "Will you be sorry to go home?"

She lifted a surprised face. Her skin was golden brown, despite the dubious protection of the floppy sunbonnet that she was supposed to wear, but that spent most of its time, as now, dangling by its strings untidily down her back. There was a streak of sandy mud on her white cotton skirt. "Oh, no. Of course not."

He raised surprised brows. "But I would have thought —"

"No! I've enjoyed it, of course. Very much. But when we get home Papa is going to let me visit the workshop again — don't you remember? And —" her eyes were aglow, her face alight with anticipation "— Papa has promised to let me have some bits and pieces to make Christmas presents for Mama and Tanya. Proper things, from the workshop. He really liked the things I made. He says that if I want to I can learn how to do things properly."

"And do you?"

"Oh, yes! More than anything in the world." She glanced at him, slyly, "Well, almost anything." She blushed at her own daring. He did not notice the look, nor did he for a moment suspect the signficance of the words.

A wave broke, ran up the sand almost to their feet. Joss stood up. "Time to go, little one."

"Just a minute. There's a pretty piece of seaweed over there." She ran and picked it up, and folded its smelly length carefully into her pocket. "Joss?"

"Mmm?"

"Do you think — one day — that you might get married?"

He looked at her in astonishment. "What a question! What brought that on?"

"I — just wondered. Will you?"

Another wave swept almost to their feet. They sprinted for the path. Joss lifted her over a chalky outcrop, smiled into her face.

"Will you?" she persisted. "Get married?"

"Oh — I shouldn't think so."

"Why not?"

He laughed. "What an exasperating young lady you can be once you set your mind on something! I won't get married because —" he thought for a moment, then, uncharacteristically impulsive, he leaned to her and touched her nose with his finger "— because I'll never find anyone as pretty as you."

He was taken aback by the effect of his words. Colour flared in the thin cheeks, anger sparked in her eyes. "I think you're horrible," she said flatly, and turning, marched straight-backed away from him.

Puzzled — as he often was — by the perversity of female nature, Joss followed.

CHAPTER EIGHT

Anna's visit to her father's workshop was both as exciting and as pleasurable as she had hoped it would be. Eagerly she begged to be allowed to go again and her father, with growing pride and enthusiasm at his daughter's interest, readily agreed. So it was that the one visit turned into two, three, four — until by that winter of 1888 Anna was a familiar figure in the Hatton Garden rooms as, absorbed, she watched the — to her — magical and fascinating processes that produced the lovely objects that glimmered upon velvet in the Piccadilly showrooms. The goldsmith and the silversmith, the enamellers and the workers in precious stones, she got to know them all; and most of them, at first amused or ready to be irritated by the child's precocious interest in their work, came genuinely to enjoy her company, her unfeigned admiration for their skills and her avid eagerness to learn. For her part Anna — hardly until then known for her brilliance or application in the schoolroom, where she had often been the absolute despair of Miss Spencer as she stumbled through times tables and mental arithmetic — showed a quite remarkable grasp and understanding when it came to this, the subject that had fascinated her for as long as she could remember. Very soon she knew at a glance the cut of a stone, could discuss intelligently and informedly the pros and cons of a particular cut for an individual jewel. Time and again she would beg her father to tell her of his work on the Shuvenski Diamond, the stone upon which Rose and Company was founded; of all things she longed to see the fabulous thing, and her pride in her father's skill and courage in attempting such a task in such conditions both touched and pleased him. The process of enamelling particularly fascinated her — the glowing colours laid, layer upon layer, fired and lovingly polished to brilliance. She spoke knowingly of *cloisonné*, of *champlevé* and of *guilloché* — to her mother's quiet disapproval, for Grace, whilst gratified at her daughter's unexpected talent, nevertheless did not consider such knowledge either desirable or ladylike, since she could see no possible application for it in the future and was concerned that in pursuing this eccentric interest the girl was neglecting those accomplishments so dear to Grace's own heart that might recommend her in the future to a young man looking for a wife. Heaven knew, the child had little enough to offer in the way of looks — a few ladylike and practical accomplishments would take her a lot further in Grace's opinion than a superfluous knowledge of brilliant cuts and the method of achieving oyster enamel. In this, however, happily for her daughter, as in everything else, she recognized her husband's authority and accepted his rulings, though not without private reservations; and so Anna continued to spend hours at the workshops, mostly watching her father's chief enameller, Tom Logan, experiment with the subtle shades and colours that were so popular with Rose's clients, occasionally helping to polish some of the minor pieces with the wooden wheel and wash-leather used for that purpose. The alloys, too, of the silversmith and goldsmith pleased her colour-conscious eye — rose-gold, green-gold, white-gold.

"Father, the snowdrop pin for Lady Masham — don't you think green-gold would be better? The white is harsh, I think, with pearl."

"Anna," Grace looked up from her plate and fixed her daughter with a severe eye, "I hardly think that your father needs to be told his own business at his own dinner table."

Anna subsided, but not before she had caught the conspiratorial half-wink that her father sent her way.

In her room she would sit for absorbed hours, pencil in hand, drawing those flowing, stylized designs that she so loved; delicate flowers, curving leaves, fairy-winged butterflies and — most frequently and in all shapes, sizes and colours — her beloved dragonflies. For her mother at Christmas she had designed a graceful spray of moonstone bluebells with a narrow knotted ribbon of gold flowing through the slender, green-gold leaves. The conception was entirely her own, the execution of it was left in the hands of her father's craftsmen. She thought it quite the most exciting thing that had ever happened to her. She took the finished brooch to her father, watched him anxiously as he held it for a long time before commenting.

"Don't you like it?"

"I like it very much indeed." He studied the spray. "It might well have come from Paris, or from Liberty's — the style is modern, yet somehow distinctive." She stood before him, her breath held — he was talking to her as he might to Tom, or to one of the others. He lifted his head. "It occurs to me — would you mind if we made another — perhaps a little bigger — using sapphires, maybe? The Countess was looking for —" He stopped, seeing the expression on her face "No?"

"Well, I —" She wanted more than anything in the world to please him — but this was her mother's and she wanted no one else to have it. "Might I try to do something else for you? A little different? I've tons of ideas —"

"Of course. Of course. Do another by all means."

"Tomorrow. I could do it tomorrow —" She stopped as something he had said registered in her mind. "Sapphires? You'd have it set with sapphires?"

"That's what she wants. And Anna —"

She looked at him enquiringly.

"Don't you think it's time you stopped working for nothing? A workman, I believe they say, is worthy of his hire. You make me a design that I like — I'll pay you for it."

She laughed delightedly. "Oh, Papa — you are the loveliest father in the world — and I'm the luckiest, luckiest girl!" The agonies of rejection she had suffered a couple of years earlier seemed now a bad dream. She had never been happier, and it showed in her face, radiated from her like sunshine.

"I declare, child," her mother said one day in some astonishment, "I do believe that your fairy godmother has waved her magic wand at last! You're growing. And you've actually got some colour in your cheeks." She, Tanya and Anna were gathered in the stone-flagged lobby of the Bayswater house, a miscellaneous and unlikely collection of blankets and bundles of clothes about their feet. Grace handed the covered basket she was holding to her daughter. "Carry this for me, will you? And do be careful — Cook's junket never seems to set really well. Tanya and I can bring the blankets. The cabbie will help us with the clothes —"

"Oh, Mama — must I come today? Tom says he might find time to look at my drawings for the little decorated box today — he'll be waiting."

Her mother marched briskly to the door. "Then I'm very much afraid that he'll have to wait. The Refuge needs these things and extra hands far more than Mr Logan needs you to keep him from his workbench. Come along."

Anna knew when not to argue. Reluctantly, she went. These trips to the East End with her mother and Aunt Hermione were the one thing she truly detested. She knew it was wrong, knew it her Christian duty, as her mother so often informed her, to help those less fortunate than herself, but try as she might she could not bring herself to do anything but hate that part of the city with its filthy, over-crowded streets, its soot-darkened brick-work and reeking gutters. Even more was she repelled by the ragged, sallow, undernourished and spiritless people who came to the Refuge for shelter and hand-outs. She hated having to know that such people, such an environment, even existed. The squalor and the ugliness repulsed her, and no amount of self-castigation could stop that. She huddled now in the corner seat of the cab, her head turned from the distinctive, unpleasantly musty smell of the heap of clothes beside her, staring out of the window — seeing not the passing dingy streets but emerald dewdrops upon a leaf-comb, diamond raindrops upon an enamelled flower — why not? Tomorrow she'd go to the workshop with Papa — she'd talk to Tom about it.

It was spring when Matthew Smithson asked, at last, for Tanya's hand in marriage — a spring when industrial unrest was stirring in London's docklands, when the troublesome and recurring Irish Question split the country's politicians and when, in far-off South Africa, Cecil Rhodes, with the resources of de Beers Consolidated Mines behind him signed the largest cheque that had ever been written — for more than five million pounds — and with the stroke of a pen achieved his dream of gaining control of the greater part of the world's output of diamonds. The marriage proposal — long looked-for by most of the Rose household — was finally prompted by the fact that Matthew was required to go abroad for several months on business for his father's bank. Rather than leave his still, as he saw it, far from certain prospects to cool for five or six months' absence, the young man took his courage in both hands and, one cool April evening, gambled upon Tanya's growing trust in and undisguised fondness for him and asked at last the question upon which he had no doubt all of his future happiness rested.

Tanya stood quite still, eyes downcast, her hands in his.

He waited, heart thumping like a frightened schoolboy's. "My love?" he prompted at last, unable to bear a moment longer such suspense.

She lifted her eyes. Within them was a light of desperate uncertainty. His heart sank. Fool! After all his patience, all his restraint, he had misread her heart and her fears — he would lose her.

"I — yes, Matthew. I'll marry you."

The words were so low that he could barely hear them — barely credit what he heard.

She half-smiled, fearfully.

He clutched her hands. "I'll make you happy. I swear it. There's a little house just around the corner from here. Father says he'll buy it for us as a wedding gift. So — you shan't be far from Mr and Mrs Rose and your brother —"

"I should like that."

They stood, absurdly awkward, their tight-clasped hands between them, breast-high. He had never kissed her — had never even attempted to do so, daunted as much by Tanya's reserve as by the conventions. He kissed her now, however, lightly and tenderly upon her closed, cool mouth and wondered at the tremor that shook her as he did so. She drew back quickly, ducked her head so that her fair hair brushed his cheek and its fragrance mingled with the soft perfumes of the spring garden. He exercised every ounce of restraint he possessed and let her go.

"September," he said, softly. "We'll be married at the end of September. Does that suit you, my love? The house should be ready by then."

She nodded, not looking at him. He reached a finger to her

chin and turned her face towards him. Serious, trusting as a child, yet apprehensive she watched him. He kissed her again, then, long and gently, feeling her tremble again, unable in his inexperience to tell desire from fear, knowing only that within himself was a fire lit and raging that only her nearness could quench. He stepped back, formally offered her his crooked arm. "Shall we go and tell the others?"

No one in the household was unaffected by the announcement. Josef, resolutely dismissing fears with which he had lived for so long that they had almost ceased to threaten, was openly delighted. Joss, won over at last by Matthew's obvious and tender devotion to his sister, offered gruff congratulations. Anna almost at once begged her father to be allowed to design the wedding present and Grace — as delighted as if Tanya had truly been her own daughter — found herself reflecting upon the duties of a surrogate mother to an inexperienced girl about to marry.

Not for a couple of months, as it happened, did a suitable opportunity arise to broach the delicate subject that demanded discussion. By that time the wedding preparations were well under way. It was after a fitting of the all-important wedding gown — a marvellous creation of ivory silk with a fall of lace at throat and wrist and a train that swept the floor a full three feet behind its wearer, an extravagance that was a personal present from Joss to his sister — that Grace decided that, embarrassing or no, the effort must be made. She took a deep breath. "My dear —"

Tanya looked up, smiling, paused in the rebuttoning of her day dress. It was June. The weather, sultry all day, looked ready to break at any moment. Heavy clouds threatened and a distant murmur of thunder silenced the birds in the garden.

Grace cleared her throat. "I feel — that perhaps we should — that is that I should — speak to you. Regarding —"

Tanya buttoned the last of her buttons and waited obediently, her face puzzled.

"— regarding the — delicate subject of marriage. Of the duties of a woman with regard to her husband's — needs." Uncharacteristically nervous, she avoided the girl's eyes and looked into the garden. Brief storm-wind tossed the branches of the trees and turned the leaves. The room fell to silence for a moment. Tanya waited, her pale face expressionless now.

Grace struggled on, heartily wishing she had never started. She could just as easily have let well alone, as her own mother sensibly had. "You understand, of course, that there are — certain differences between man and woman. Physical differences. And differences of —" She stopped again. She knew she was making a wretched job of this. Her one desire now was to finish. "That is to say — within married life — within the marriage bed — there are certain demands that a man is entitled to make of his wife and to which she must submit obediently and with grace." Beyond the window a flash of lightning split the summer darkness. Moments later the thunder cracked above their heads. Inside the room the silence lengthened. Grace, on sudden impulse, leaned to the girl and touched her arm. "I'm sorry. I'm not very good at this. Don't be afraid, Tanya dear. Your Matthew is a truly gentle man. He'll teach you the way of these things. It isn't something that I find easy to talk of."

Tanya nodded and attempted a smile. Her long fingers fiddled restlessly with a narrow velvet ribbon at her throat.

"Well, now," relief was tangible in Grace's voice, now that the awkward and undeniably unsatisfactory interview was over, "I'll have to leave you, I'm afraid — cook's waiting for next week's menus."

As the other woman hurried from the darkening room Tanya turned to the window. Outside great spots of rain had started to fall, rustling restlessly in the leaves, splashing upon roof and paving stone. Lightning and thunder crashed together. The girl did not even blink. The rain fell faster, quickening to a torrent, drowning the beaten earth, beating down grass and flower.

Somewhere in memory a child screamed.

Tanya Anatov, still as an alabaster statue, stared into the streaming curtain of rain and tried to remember.

That summer was one when the increasing restlessness of a working population, whose conditions and wages had in no way kept pace with the wealth that their sweated toil had produced for others, became focused upon London's docks. Dock work was hard and dangerous, the pay meagre, the conditions often atrocious. The indignity of the infamous 'calling on' system — the men caged, queueing, begging for work at dawn and noon, fighting, often literally, for a chance for survival for themselves and their dependents — was a matter of bitter resentment. For years a discontent had been bred that culminated, at the end of those summer months, in an angry demand for improved conditions and a decent living wage; sixpence an hour — the 'Dockers' Tanner' as it came universally to be called. In August 1889, just a few days after Matthew Smithson's return from America, the dockers — united, determined, pushed to outraged and, some considered, outrageous action — went on strike. Not a crane moved, not a ship docked. Stevedores, carpenters, lightermen, dockers; the action was solid. With bands and banners, men, women and children marched the streets of London. Cargoes rotted at the waterside, nothing moved on the wharves or in the great warehouses, and the capital almost at once began to feel the pinch. Yet, oddly, support for the strike was widespread and by no means confined to the working-classes. When the action started the union had in its coffers the far from princely sum of seven shillings and sixpence — no work meant no money and families, already undernourished, might easily have starved. Yet, astonishingly, the money rolled in and the strike held. For a month Londoners sweltered, the shortages grew, yet still the pennies, the shillings and the pounds were donated — by other unions, some from as far away as Australia, by individual workers, by people of comfortable means who were beginning to be sickened at the exploitation that had been condoned and encouraged by generations of profit-takers in the docks.

By early September, Grace declared herself truly worried — not, as might have been expected, by the threat to the established order posed by a rabble of working men, nor yet by the issues that had sparked the action — but by the fact that the wedding was fast approaching and the caterers were complaining that nowhere at any price could they obtain the supplies they needed. The happy occasion was but three weeks off; surely, surely, the wretched dockers could not hold out so long?

They did not have to. On the 14th of September the dockworkers' demands — incredibly to some — were almost all met, a paralysed London began to move again and, to Grace's relief, disaster was averted.

Matthew it was who brought the news of the return to work to Bayswater — a Matthew mildly amused by the heartfelt relief with which Grace received it. In his opinion, it mattered not a jot that there might have been nothing to offer the guests at the wedding breakfast. If the strike had gone on for ever — if the sun had fallen from the sky and the world stopped turning — what did it matter? Tanya would be his. Nothing and no one could spoil that. He watched her, that afternoon, across the tea table. Everything she did, her every expression and movement held him spellbound. It seemed to him that he would never tire of the sight of her. He turned to find Grace's eyes upon him, amused and affectionate. God, he'd been gawping like a lovestruck schoolboy! He blushed fiercely.

Grace moved her chair back from the table and reached for the small silver handbell to summon the maid. "Well now, why don't you two young people take a walk in the garden before the sun goes? I know you've a lot to talk about."

Anna jumped to her feet. "May I come?"

Tanya opened her mouth to answer, smiling. Grace, taking pity on Matthew's disappointed face — he had not had a moment alone with Tanya since his return from America — said sharply, "No, you may not. With all this gallivanting off to the workshop you've sadly neglected your piano practice. If you're to play that piece at the Smithsons' on Sunday evening, then an hour's practice now wouldn't come amiss. Or you'll disgrace us all."

'Oh, but —"

"Anna!"

Anna subsided, her face rebellious.

Matthew escorted Tanya on to the verandah and down into the garden. She was dressed in rustling sapphire silk trimmed with heavy Brussels lace. He was certain that no one in the world could possibly look lovelier. In companionable silence they strolled through the small shrubbery to the little pool. Sun glinted golden on the dark surface of the water. From beyond the high wall came the familiar street sounds — vendors called their wares, wheels creaked and rattled, horses' hooves clattered upon cobblestones. Yet here, within this enclosed green refuge, even the house hidden by the trees, they might have been alone in the world. Matthew took Tanya's hand in his.

"Two weeks. Just two weeks and you'll be Mrs Matthew Smithson. I still don't dare to believe it."

She smiled. Her hair was spun gold in the sun.

"Have you been to see the house lately? It's looking very smart. It's small of course — but it will do for a start, won't it?" His voice was a little anxious.

"It's lovely. I like it very much."

"And you don't mind that my wretched mother's insisted on interviewing all the servants?" Matthew's mother was a forceful lady of great authority and little tact.

She laughed a little. "Of course not. I should not have known where to start."

He tugged at her hand, drew her to the small grassy bank that was Anna's favourite place in the garden. "Let's sit for a moment. It's quite dry. Here —" He took off his jacket and laid it upon the ground for her to sit on. She settled herself beside him, straight-backed, her hands loose in her lap, her head turned from him as she watched the insects skimming the surface of the water. Matthew leaned on one elbow, studying her sun-gilded profile, aware of a rising need to touch her, to feel her warmth, her nearness. He had been away for a very long time; each day of his absence he had thought of this girl, dreamed of her, imagined what it would be to take her to wife —

"Tanya," he said suddenly, and she turned at the strangeness of his voice, straight into his arms and his seeking mouth.

She froze.

"Tanya," he said again. "Dearest love." His hard-held self-control was no match for the desire that flooded his body, burning him, blinding him to the panic in her eyes. His mouth was at her neck, his breath hot. His hand brushed her breast, constricted beneath its layers of clothing. Eyes closed he sought her mouth with his own, his weight, awkwardly unbalanced as he was, bearing her over beneath him. She lay rigid as a lifeless doll. He opened his eyes. She looked at him in horror and in fear.

He drew back. "Tanya —"

She slid away from him, levering herself with her arms, her terrified eyes not leaving his face. She looked at him as she might have looked at a fearful, threatening stranger. "No," she whispered. "No. No. No!"

"Tanya — please — darling, I'm sorry." Concerned, he reached a hand to her. She shrank from him. She was shaking her head now, jerkily, from side to side, rubbing her open palms against the fine material of her skirt in a strange, compulsive movement, as if to clean them. "No," she said again, and this time her voice was lifted and threaded with unmistakable hysteria. It seemed to him that she looked through him to some horror that lay beyond. "Oh God!" she said then and, trembling violently, buried her face in her hands.

He was frantic now. "Tanya, please, I didn't mean to hurt you — to frighten you — you know I wouldn't —" He tried to put an arm about her.

With the most violent movement he had ever known her make she turned from him. Between her fingers he saw the glint of tears.

"Don't touch me! Don't!" She began to rock, to and fro, like a desolate child. "Oh, God!" she said again, and the terrible tone of her voice struck him to stillness and to silence. He drew back, watching her, helpless. She sat for a long time so, rocking, face covered, shoulders hunched as if she were protecting herself from blows. When at last she lifted her head the sun had gone and dark shadow had invaded the garden like an enemy. Her face was a still, cold blur of white in the twilight.

From the house Grace's voice called. "Tanya? Matthew? Are you there?"

"Please go," Tanya said.

"Go? I can't go and leave you like this. You know I can't. Darling, I'm sorry, truly sorry, but I don't understand. If you are to be my wife —"

She shook her head. "No."

"What?"

"No. Matthew, I can't be your wife. Not yours, not anyone's. Please don't ask me why. If you love me, please don't ask. Just go. Now." Her low, trembling voice still sounded to be on the very verge of hysteria.

"Can't marry me? Tanya, for heaven's sake — what is this? I'm sorry if I frightened you — if I was clumsy — , shouldn't have kissed you like that — but —"

She scrambled to her feet, eluding his hand, and began to walk fast through the trees, back towards the house.

"Tanya — wait!" He ran after her, caught her arm.

She wrenched away with surprising strength. "Don't touch me. You mustn't touch me. I'm —" She stopped. "I love you. You mustn't touch me. I'm — dirty. Filthy! You don't understand." She picked up her skirts and flew through the gathering dusk, tears streaming down her face.

"Why, Tanya? What on earth —" Grace stood on the terrace, waiting. The girl fled past her and into the house.

From the garden Matthew called, tears in his voice. "Tanya? Tanya!"

Within the house a door slammed and there was silence.

She would not leave her room. Food left outside the door remained there, untouched. One after another they tried to speak to her through the door; to no avail. For twenty-four hours she spoke to no one, nor was there any sign or sound of movement. Indeed the only evidence that she was there at all was in the door being firmly locked on the inside.

"But — what can be wrong? What's got into her?" Grace was terribly distressed. A distraught Matthew had stumblingly attempted to explain what had happened before, his presence an obvious embarrassment, he had left. "Matthew swears he didn't hurt her — he wouldn't, we all know that. Do you have any idea? She seems finally to have taken leave of her senses."

Standing by the window, his back to her, her husband shook his head. He could not bear to turn and meet her eyes, could not indeed meet the eyes of any of them. His fault. All his fault. Be sure your sins will find you out. Josef Rosenberg knew as surely as if he had entered her skin what ailed Tanya Anatov. If she would just let him in — just let him speak to her — explain — reassure —

Upstairs, Tanya sat as one struck deaf and dumb, tearless now, and comfortless; remembering, hating herself and the had done this to her. But most of all herself; defiled,

Joss who finally, that second night, gained admittance, shouting, nor by begging and pleading as Josef had done, but by the simple expedient of sitting down in the corridor, his back against her closed door and informing the silence that he, as stubborn an Anatov as any, could remain so for as long as it took her to open the door. For hours he sat, unmoving, speaking occasionally to the closed door, inconsequential things, sometimes in his still heavily-accented English, more often as the night wore on in his own strange, quiet tongue; the tongue of Tanya's forgotten childhood. At last, in a house exhausted and sleeping, long past midnight he heard the key click softly in the lock above his head. Wordless he stood, and entered the room.

Hours later he emerged. Behind him a kind of peace had descended after the storm. A wraith moved on the dark landing; Grace came to him, candle in hand, hair streaming down her back, her voluminous nightgown billowing as she moved. Unconsciously he noted how frail she looked so, in contrast to her carefully groomed daytime self, how much older than she had just a year or so before. She voiced no question, but stood looking at him, anxiety in every drawn line of her face. Joss's own face, by the light of her candle, was perilous, bone-white and cruel with pain. "She'll sleep now, I think," was all he said, and with that Grace had to be satisfied.

But Joss was terribly wrong. His haunted sister did not sleep. Just before dawn saw the end of an endless night she rose, dressed, and left the house. As the pearl-glow of sunrise touched the eastern sky she stood above the dark waters of the Thames and remembered the sea, beside which she had first met Matthew; the cool, rushing, cleansing sea of which she had never been afraid.

They recovered her body the following afternoon, at the turn of the tide. The boatman shook his head as he disentangled his hook from the unfeeling, dead flesh. Another of them. What made them do it? And this one — Lord she'd been a looker all right. Amazing how many of them were. What a waste.

INTERLUDE

1889–1898

Joss Anatov was nothing if not a man of patience; he had learned to be so in the hardest of schools — learned too that to leave vengeance to God was to leave it to chance and that was something Joss would never accept with regard to the man he implacably blamed for the death of the sister he now found himself mourning for a second time. In the moment that he stood, dry-eyed, beside Tanya's bloated, waterlogged corpse, the Josef Anatov who had seen his parents murdered, who had survived the slums of Kiev, Budapest and Vienna resurfaced; embittered, inimical, coldly determined to exact retribution, no matter how long it might take. Hard as diamond itself he vowed that, sooner or later, he would see tears on the face of the man he had been deceived into loving as a father, and upon whose shoulders in Joss's eyes clearly rested the blame for Tanya's death. Not for an instant did he betray his knowledge or his feelings — not from the moment that he stood by his sister's new-filled grave to the time, nine years later, in September 1898 when he stood before the altar with Josef's daughter — the man's pride and joy, his only true comfort since Grace's death two years before, and his hope for the future of Rose and Company — beside him. By then the business was relying heavily upon Anna's fast-burgeoning reputation as a designer of distinctive jewellery in what was coming to be known as the style of 'Art Nouveau'. Working with Tom Logan and her father's other craftsmen, she had succeeded in creating a style that was both fashionable and unique to Rose and Company; and the books that Joss still handled so adroitly told their own story of a growing prosperity based more and more upon her talent.

Not that Joss had seen Anna immediately as the instrument of his revenge upon Josef — indeed, it was her single-minded pursuit of him that ended in sowing the seeds that were to bear such bitter fruit for both of them. She had adored him steadfastly since childhood — in her eyes he had never ceased to be her handsome prince, the subject of all her dreams. Resolutely she resisted family plans to marry her off to Christopher Smithson — "Can you *imagine* being married to *that*!" — and through her growing years her devotion to Joss, despite the change they had all sensed in him after his sister's tragic death, far from faltering became stronger. Indeed, as she grew older and came to recognize the disturbing, strangely sombre attraction of the man, her infatuation grew. Both her father and her mother — before Grace's death from fever in the winter of 1895 when a constitution more fragile than it would admit finally gave out — tried gently and for their own separate reasons to guide the girl's affections elsewhere, both only too aware that Joss was unlikely to make her happy, but to no avail. She followed him, when she could, like a small, patient puppy, looked for his homecoming when he went away, gloomed through his absences like a lovesick child. While the world went about its business — linking London to Paris by telephone, tunnelling underground railways beneath city streets upon which people rode with eager pleasure in dirt and discomfort, exchanging its oil lamps first for gas mantles and later, if it were lucky, for electricity, granting Mr Marconi the first patent for a system of wireless telegraphy that would eventually revolutionize communications — Anna and her brothers grew up. Alex — spurning 'trade', however high-class, opted to go into law; Ralph, to everyone's astonishment, expressed a quiet but utterly determined wish to enter God's ministry; James — to his father's initial indignation — kept faith with the resolution he had made the day that Boris had visited them before leaving for India and stood out for a commission in the Guards. As Anna irreverently pointed out, with a soldier, a lawyer and a priest in the family they had most of their options covered. Michael, the baby, trailed lightheartedly — and lightmindedly — behind the others, an easy-going and happy go lucky scamp whose main aim in life was comfort, if possible at someone else's expense.

The loss of Grace in December 1895 was a terrible blow to

them all, and to Josef in particular. So great, in fact, was their introspective grief at this time that the significance of a well-publicized event in the Transvaal at the turn of the year — the Jameson Raid, ominous portent of trouble to come — all but escaped them. Even Joss tended to dismiss the affair as the hot-headedness of a crazy Scot. But while at home preparations were soon under way for the Queen's Diamond Jubilee the following year, tempers and patience were running short in South Africa as the Boer settlers' resentment of British insensitivity and high-handedness became a groundswell of rebellion.

Nothing, however, could have been farther from most minds on that day in 1897 when the city, the country and what seemed like half the world acclaimed Victoria's sixty years as queen in a jingoistic extravagance of patriotic fervour. In common with many other of the city's merchants, Rose and Company made its own small contribution in the form of a gold pin surmounted by a small, diamond-studded crown, which offering Her Majesty was pleased to accept along with thousands upon thousands of other gifts presented by her wildly enthusiastic subjects.

That year of 1897 gave the Rose family cause for double celebration — the public one of the Jubilee and the private one of Alex's advantageous marriage to Alice Peabody, a young woman blessed not only with looks and breeding, but with — as Anna noted with a cynicism beyond her years — an exceedingly rich father who possessed no other offspring. Anna, unfortunately, disliked her prospective sister-in-law on sight — but since she did not care greatly for Alex either, lost little sleep over the fact. Within a week of Alex's elaborate nuptials, news of another wedding was received — news which was undeniably more startling. Boris, it seemed, now stationed with his regiment in troubled Egypt, also had acquired a wife — daughter to a Sergeant Major with a strong right arm and a high regard for the proprieties. The idea of feckless, attractive Boris as a husband was a novel one; the situation, however was a little clarified six months later by the laconic announcement of the birth of a child, a daughter, Sophie Anne. Alex and Alice, as was to be expected, were rather more conventional, and, "typical of

Alex", as Anna was heard disgustedly to remark, even more successful. In the summer of 1898 Alice was brought to bed of not one son but two, Rupert and Richard, twins as like as two peas in a pod.

Through all this Anna pursued zealously the butterfly of artistic success and watched Joss, waiting — whilst Joss, unknown to her or to anyone, brooded, the gall of his hatred for Josef corrosive within him. He had put his own harsh interpretation upon the story that Tanya had told him the night she had died, and everything that Josef was or did Joss now saw through the distortion of his own bitterness. The means of his revenge, however, came to hand in a form that, blind to the last, he least expected. At the celebrations that followed the baptism of the twins Anna, ever impulsive, ever unconventional, followed Joss on to the darkened verandah and stood beside him looking over the starlit garden. At twenty she was taller than might earlier have been expected, was indeed almost as tall as he, but she was still willow-slender, in an age that preferred its women well-rounded, almost breastless, waif-like. Joss had had far too much champagne. His thoughts had turned to the little whore in Whitechapel who — for a price — served his needs with avid pleasure. He turned and leaned against the wrought iron balustrade, studying the young woman beside him, saw her blush at his openly appraising regard. Yet she stood her ground. Half-amused, he kept his eyes steadily upon her; astonishingly then it was she who stepped to him and lifted her mouth to his. Without thought or tenderness he kissed her, hard and hurtfully, forgetting the child for which he had felt such affection, knowing only the grown daughter of a man he secretly and bitterly hated. Her reaction astounded him. After the first, shocked recoil from him she kissed him back with a wildness that more than matched his own, her thin body tensed against his, her teeth sharp and fierce. If he had not been utterly certain of her virtue he might have thought he held a practised young harlot in his arms. Half-drunk he made no gentlemanly effort to control his own easily aroused passions. He turned her into the shadows of the verandah, trapped her body with his own against the railings and handled her as he might have handled his whore in Whitechapel, his hard hands at her buttocks and in her bodice, seeking the bare, rigid nipples. But she did not try to break away. At last, more than half-disgusted with himself he drew back, turned away from her.

"Joss?" Her young voice shook forlornly.

He did not answer.

"Joss, I love you. I truly do. I always have. I'll never love anyone but you."

He shook his head, trapped by hatred and by love.

She caught his hand. "I do! I do! And — oh, Joss — you love me too — don't you? You wouldn't have — kissed me like that — if you didn't. Would you?" The words were desperately uncertain. He tried to move away from her. She caught his hand, clutched it to her meagre breast. "Don't go. Please — don't go. I'll do anything, Joss. Anything you want." She was whispering, desperate, tears in her voice. She had rehearsed this moment, or one like it, a thousand times in her dreams. She knew, instinctively, it would not come again.

He looked at her, expressionless in the glimmering dark. Light streamed from the windows behind them. Voices were lifted in song.

She watched him, wide-eyed, frightened but stubborn. "Anything you want," she said again.

Revenge waited, smiling. A favourite only daughter, ruined, disgraced — then another thought, more subtle, obscurely more satisfying and of a lifetime's duration. Deliberately he reached for her, kissed her again, felt once more the unexpected wildness of her. "Anything?"

"Yes."

"Would you marry me?"

She froze, looked up at him, mouth open.

"Well?" Already he was half-regretting it.

"You aren't joking? Oh, Joss — you aren't teasing me?"

"No."

Her face lit like a lamp. "Then yes! And yes, and yes, and yes! Oh, Joss!" She clung to him, laughing and crying.

He looked over her head, into darkness.

So it was that, in the same week that his brother Boris stormed into Omdurman with his comrades behind Lord Kitchener to seal yet another victory for Empire, Josef Anatov took to wife Anna Amelia Rose, till death should them part. As they came from church on that bright September day a group of children playing nearby stopped to watch the spectacle, and then, as the last of the brightly decorated carriages bowled off down the street, took up their game again:

> In and out the dusty bluebells,
> In and out the dusty bluebells,
> In and out the dusty bluebells,
> Who will be my master?

PART THREE

1898–1901

CHAPTER NINE

It was within a few short hours of her marriage that Anna Anatov began to suspect that her husband did not love her as she loved him; understandably, it took much longer than that for her truly to believe it. The wedding itself was a family event, with none of the grandness of occasion that had characterized the splendid marriage of Alex and Alice the year before — but Josef nevertheless was determined not to stint upon the celebration and the wedding breakfast, though a comparatively small affair, was lavish; too lavish, indeed, it seemed for the groom who quite clearly had not recovered from the pre-nuptial celebrations that had kept him from his bed for best part of the night and had served to dull his senses and his conscience about equally. He sat beside his wife at the head of the table, the aftermath of last night's vodka warring grimly with the glittering, heady wine, toying with his food, monosyllabic, hardly smiling. Yet it seemed to Anna's lovestruck eyes that he had never looked so fascinating; the set of his head, the high slant of cheekbone, the firm, straight mouth — each time she looked at him, which was often, if covertly, a small shock of excitement stirred within her. The dream that had been hers since childhood had magically come true. She had married her handsome prince and — of course — all that was left to do was to live happily ever after. In a short while they would leave her father's house and drive to the rooms that Joss had rented for them a few miles away across the river at Kew. These rooms, Joss himself had been living in for the past few weeks and Anna, to be truthful, on the only occasion she had visited them, had not greatly cared for them. As for many a bride, however, such considerations seemed for the moment secondary; once their married life had started she would persuade Joss to find something a little larger, a little more convenient.

Their married life.

Once again that half-fearful frisson of excitement stirred. Motherless and innocent she had no idea whatsoever of what might be demanded of her by her husband: she had only her own inexperienced emotions and instincts to guide her. Since the abrupt announcement of their engagement on the day of the twins' christening — an announcement that she was aware had come as a shock to friends and family alike, though she had confessed to no one that it had been an equal astonishment to her — Joss had, to her surprise and unspoken chagrin, not once touched her or tried to spend a moment alone with her. The decision made, he appeared simply to be intent upon implementing it as soon as possible. Remembering Matthew and poor, beautiful Tanya, Anna had sometimes wondered and worried about that — but then impatiently reassured herself, scolding herself for her doubts; whoever would expect Joss Anatov to act as others did? And always, to set against her uncertainties, she had the memory of those fiercely arousing moments that had preceded his proposal, a memory that in turn excited and half-frightened her. In the dark, quiet moments of night she would find herself feeling again the demanding pressure of his man's body against hers, the mystifying reaction of her own body to his. More than half-shamed by the feelings such memories aroused, she had no one to confide in, nor anyone to explain. It had, of course, been out of the question for her to approach her father on such a question; kindly and devoted though he was, for such a subject to be broached between father and daughter was unthinkable. Even during their last, strangely sad evening together, as they had talked before the study fire, it had not once occurred to her to ask the questions to which she most longed to know the answers. Remembering now she glanced at Josef, sitting to her left, and a small furrow of worry appeared between her brows. Since Grace's death her father had aged visibly; he now looked more than his age — in two years he would be sixty. She suspected that his health was not all it should be, though he stubbornly refused to see a doctor. He still worked harder than anyone she knew — the company he had built and was still building, its reputation for excellence, its firm financial establishment had become, since his wife's death and the growing up of his children, his whole life. New workshops had been purchased adjoining the old, the shop had been extended and refurbished; new and valuable stock had been bought in; and Anna suspected that her father worried rather more than he admitted about the loans that Joss had persuaded him to take on to pay for these ventures. Also with Joss's encouragement he had begun to speculate on the stock market, hoping to increase his capital, an activity that Anna felt to be not truly in character for her father who, unlike Joss, was no natural gambler. But it was not so much the remote spectre of possible — if unlikely — financial worries that concerned her: her fear was more nebulous than that, simply a disquieting and possibly unfounded daughterly feeling that all was not right with him, that something troubled him badly. As the years passed he, the most apparently outgoing of men, had become prey to occasional depressions, to moments of introspection in which his face assumed an expression so melancholy, so haunted, that it cut Anna to the heart to see it. Last night she had come upon him by the fireside in his darkened study, his chin sunk upon his chest, a glass and a half-filled bottle of brandy by his elbow.

"Papa?"

He stirred at her voice, lifted a hand to her. She moved swiftly to him, settled herself upon the floor by his feet, as she had come so often before and as they both knew she was unlikely to do again.

"Don't be sad," she said. "Please don't be sad. I won't be so very far away. And we'll see each other often — almost as much as we do now."

He half-smiled, ruefully, said nothing. Firelight flickered upon a face that looked almost a stranger's, lined and old and far from happy. In the silence a coal tumbled and sparks flew.

"Is it — is it Mama?" Anna asked at last, timidly. "Is it that she can't be with us tomorrow?"

For a long, odd moment she thought that he was not going to answer at all, wondered indeed if he had even heard the words. Then he stirred. "That — and other things —" He fell to silence again.

She could not believe it. "Other things? What other things? Papa — please — what's wrong?"

Avoiding her questioning eyes, he moved to stir the fire, then leaned back tiredly in his chair. "Wrong." He spoke the word on a breath so quiet his daughter hardly heard it. He seemed only half-aware of her presence. He reached for his glass, sipped it, tilted his head to the back of the chair and closed his eyes, speaking softly and disjointedly into the darkness. "The things a man does," he said, "he can never be free of them. He gives up his God — because he cannot believe in Him — and thinks perhaps that at least then he cannot be haunted." He took a long, slow breath. "But this I know now. In time He will find you. Whoever — whatever — He is."

Anna lifted a surprised face, questioning. The movement seemed to bring him back to the moment, to her presence. Suddenly and urgently he leaned forward and caught her hand. "Take care what you do, Anna. Take care that the things you want are worth what you may have to pay for them. What others may have to pay. And remember that the cost is not always immediately apparent."

"I don't understand."

"No." He exhaled, long and slowly, and the hurtful pressure on her hand eased. "How should you? Why should you? Take no notice, my dear — the ramblings of an old man."

"You aren't old."

"Oh, yes, I'm old. But you — you're young. Your life is before you." With an undisguised effort he attempted to throw off his melancholy abstraction, and a false note of jocularity entered his voice. "What it is to be young, eh? Even I remember it, though it sometimes seems another life."

She caught eagerly at his hand again, eager to change the subject. "Oh, tell me about it, Papa, please do. What was it like when you were young — in Russia?" Her voice was pleading. Her own and Joss's Russian backgrounds about which she knew so astonishingly little had always fascinated her. It had been a source of constant disappointment to her that her father would never speak of his childhood. Joss's bitterness she could understand and accept, but not her father — he had been a grown man before tragedy had overtaken him. There must, surely, have been some happy times?

He shook his head, the strain back in his face.

She did not notice it. "Please?" She leaned eagerly upon his knee, her chin upon her hand. "Your family — Joss's family — what were they like? Where did they live? How did they live?"

He moved uneasily. "Questions, questions!"

"But, Papa — shouldn't I know? Aren't they all a part of me too? Aren't they?"

In the dying light of the fire he bent to her, kissed her head lightly then tucked a finger beneath her chin and lifted her face from the shadows. She returned his regard gravely. The clear pain in his face struck her to the heart. Suddenly from her soul she wished she had left well alone. "I had another little girl once," he said, very quietly. "And two little boys. Natasha, Sergei and baby —" He stopped. "God in heaven," he said, anguished, "I have forgotten the child's name."

She caught her breath. "Papa — please don't! I'm sorry — sorry I made you think of it." Anna was appalled. Neither she, nor as far as she knew, any other member of the family had had any idea that her father had been married before. The thought did not occur until later that Joss, surely, must have known. Strange indication of the uncommunicative character of the man that he had never mentioned it, even in passing.

"The Cossacks came. And the innocents died — my wife Anna — the children. And in my own innocence I thought it must be the worst thing that could happen."

She pressed her face into his hand, instinctively knowing that only silence would serve.

He fell silent for a long time, then sighed, a long, shaking, gathering of breath. "But that was yesterday," he said. "A yesterday for which we can mourn, but about which we can do nothing. Tomorrow my daughter Anna marries — in an English church, dressed in English lace and with English flowers in her hair. Which is as it should be."

Anna laughed a little. "But she isn't marrying an Englishman."

"Yes you are!" The words were very sharp. "Joss is a naturalized Englishman. As I am. He can never go back. He wouldn't want to. Anna, this country has been good to us, very good. Don't doubt it. And don't waste your dreams on something that is part of the past, something you can never have. My own true parents I never knew." She lifted startled eyes. This, too, she had not known. "From the start it made me rootless. I belonged nowhere. Until I came here. Until I met your mother. But you — you belong here. Your children will belong here. Be satisfied with that. Be happy with your respectable English wedding —"

She tried to distract him, disturbed by his unexpected intensity. "Will it be so different, then? From a wedding in Kiev?"

For the first time and despite himself, he laughed. "In Kiev, my dear, the whole street would be dancing." He laughed again. "By midday the whole street would be drunk!"

She smiled, eased by his laughter. "Perhaps then we should bring some old Russian customs to Bayswater?"

He shook his head, smiling. For a moment neither of them spoke. In the silence he squeezed the hand he still held. "You're sure you're happy?"

She laughed up at him, relieved at the change of subject. "That must be at least the dozenth time you've asked! Yes, Papa, I'm happy."

"Then that is all that counts."

"There's just one thing that would make tomorrow absolutely perfect —" She grinned, quickly and mischievously, like the child he remembered so well. "What a terror I am for wanting things I can't have!"

"What? What can't you have?"

"The diamond. The stone they call the Shuvenski. I've always wanted to see it. When I was little I used to dream that you might become very rich and buy it for me! Now there would be a thing — to be wed with that on my finger!" She stopped, aware of the sudden, almost violent stiffening of his body. "Papa? What is it?"

He withdrew his hand abruptly from hers, picked up his glass. "It's nothing. Of course not. It's just —"

"What?"

"An old man's whim." His voice was strangely grim. "It isn't a good omen to have mentioned that stone."

She stared at him astonished, more than half-inclined to laugh. "What on earth? A bad omen? Oh, Papa — are you joking? You surely can't be serious?"

He shrugged.

"But Papa! How can you possibly believe such a thing?" Such an aberration in her usually down to earth father astounded Anna. "A diamond — that diamond — unlucky? The stone that you guarded for a thousand miles? That our business — our prosperity — our lives! — are founded upon?" She laughed. "You're joking. Teasing me. Aren't you?"

His hesitation was barely noticeable. "Yes, little one, of course. I'm teasing you. A father may tease his very grown-up daughter on the night before she marries, may he not?"

She came up on to her knees and threw her arms about his neck. "Of course, oh, of course."

She remembered that conversation now, watching him beside her, wondering at the things she knew of him and the things that she did not. This man, the father whom she had always accepted, without thought, as the very soul of propriety, who dressed so soberly and worked so hard, who was so totally dedicated to his determination to become the very model of a respectable Englishman of comfortable means, who throughout her childhood had been taken for granted as a pillar of established thought and behaviour, had seen murder and worse, had in his journey from one world to another suffered privations and perils at which she could hardly guess. And — what else? What in that conversation last night had left her with the impression that something — something apart from the massacre of his family and the terrible trek westwards — haunted him still, after twenty-three years? The thought disturbed her, and was followed sharply by another. Joss. Did he know? He knew so much, gave away so little. She turned to him now. His sardonic eye, surveying the company with its usual dispassion, caught hers and she thought — she hoped — softened a little in private acknowledgement. Again that unnerving lift of excitement. She loved him more than life. She always had, from that first moment she had seen him, thin-faced, shabby, defensive, walking across the lawn on her eighth birthday. Every line of his face, every movement he made, fascinated her — she surely, she thought, must be the envy of every woman in the room.

Not so. Alice Rose, née Peabody, for one, had no time for such dark and brooding affectations. She leaned to Alex, her well-bred nose wrinkled in faint distaste. "Is he always so boorish? Really — Anna may not be much to look at but I should have thought — with your father's money — she might have done better." Her voice was clear and piercing in the hubbub around them. She leaned back, dabbing delicately at her fine-drawn, pretty face with a scrap of lace handkerchief.

"Though I do suppose that no gentleman would be happy to take a working woman to wife." There was no love lost whatsoever between Anna and her sister-in-law.

Alex shrugged, his mind elsewhere. He had just this morning returned from the town of Saffron Walden in Essex, where he had been in close consultation with the best solicitors in the county about a legal wrangle concerning the northern boundary of Alice's father's country home, Bissetts Manor, just a few miles from the town. Mr Peabody was always generously grateful to those who worked in his service. And anyway Bissetts, one day, would come to Alice. Alex had no intention of inheriting a legal dispute with the property. He picked at the meal before him. Honestly, Pa had really gone too far — there was enough to feed an army — to say nothing of the drink. Surreptitiously he felt in his pocket for the elegant solid gold watch that had been a present from his father-in-law on the day twin sons had been born; he had promised to be at the club by early afternoon. How long, he wondered, before he could decently slip away? "I'm sorry?"

His wife made a small, irritated movement with her head, "Really, Alexis, I sometimes wonder if you listen to a word I say. I asked where they are to live?"

"Who?"

"Why Anna and Joss of course."

"Oh — rented rooms I believe. Somewhere in Kew. As a matter of fact I think that father's a bit put out that Joss doesn't want to buy a house near here. Joss says they can't afford it yet, though I must say I find that a bit hard to take. He's a close-mouthed fellow, but from what I've been picking up in the City lately, he's been doing very well for himself on the quiet — to say nothing of what he's taking from the firm." He waved away the hired footman who hovered at his elbow waiting to refill his glass. Joss on the other hand, at the end of the table, did not wait to be helped but took the bottle from the tray and filled his own glass brim-full. Alice and Alex exchanged pained, meaningful glances, and Alice's elegant eyebrows lifted slightly.

Further down the table someone else noticed the action also. James, resplendent in his subaltern's uniform, buttons and buckles gleaming, caught Joss's eye, grinned, and lifted his own glass in admiring salute. In his opinion his new brother-in-law had drunk enough already this afternoon to put the toughest fusilier under the table. His eyes moved to Anna. With her hectically flushed cheeks and bright eyes, hair piled upon her head and prettily threaded with fresh flowers, she looked as striking, he thought, as he had ever seen her. In fact — he made a valiant effort to focus eyes that were a little blurred by his father's lavish hospitality — with her pale eyes and sharp cheekbones accentuated by her high colour, her upswept hair revealing a grace of bone that was not usually immediately apparent, his sister came close to the beauty for which he knew she had always yearned. She looked up at that moment and found his eyes upon her. He lifted his glass again and winked brotherly admiration. She smiled, brilliantly, answered his salute with her own glass but did not drink. James looked back at Joss's dark, unsmiling face. He hardly looked the eager groom. James, with more than a suspicion of the way that Joss may have spent the previous night, was not altogether surprised. He wondered, briefly and with a flash of perturbing sobriety, if his sister knew what she was taking on: then dismissed the uncomfortable thought. What a gentleman did with his wife obviously could have no connection at all with those activities in which he, James, and Joss had indulged one riotous night in Whitechapel a few months before. That surely was the service that the ladies of the night offered their more respectable sisters — to satisfy a man's carnal needs so that his relationship with his wife should be pure, unsullied — his drink-befuddled mind gave up the hunt for the right word — well, different, anyway. Who could possibly imagine Anna, or

Alice, or shy, simpering Dulcie who sat beside him now, giggling and fluttering her eyelashes, engaging in the lewd antics of the strumpets in the Whitechapel house? The mere thought brought embarrassed colour to his cheeks. He took another steadying mouthful of champagne. Dulcie pouted, charmingly reproving, her eyes sharp.

"Ladies and Gentlemen. Pray silence for Mr Josef Rose, the father of the bride —" The gavel rose and fell. Josef stood and cleared his throat painfully. Anna sighed and, beneath the starched tablecloth, slipped her lace-gloved hand over Joss's. How much longer?

The towering confection of a cake gleamed in the light. From the far end of the second table she caught a glimpse of Christopher Smithson's face. He watched her glumly, looked away when she caught his eyes upon her. Poor Christopher. He really wasn't so bad. And much better looking now he'd grown a bit and slimmed down. Not that he was or ever could be any competition to her Joss — guiltily she tried to concentrate on what her father was saying. The problem with champagne was that it was so wretchedly easy to drink — really, her head felt positively light. She suppressed a giggle at the thought. Joss quirked an enquiring eyebrow at her and she almost laughed aloud with happiness. Soon, soon they could go. She imagined a darkened room, the fire lit, supper for two — herself and Joss alone at last — suddenly and unexpectedly she found herself to have difficulty in breathing evenly. And the thumping in her heart — surely that could be seen beneath the pale, fragile silk of her gown by everyone in the room? She felt herself flushing at the thought. Heavens — now Michael, in his capacity as Joss's best man had come, a little unsteadily, to his feet. Would they never stop?

It came to an end at last, and with Anna changed into her going-away suit of dark blue linen with puffed sleeves, wide reveres and crisp white blouse, a ribboned and plumed blue straw hat upon her piled hair, they left in a flurry of rice and rose petals, a bustle of kisses and hugs and good wishes. The chimney sweep who had been hired for luck — and who had irritated Alice almost into a seizure by planting a large black handprint upon her pale blue silk — deposited a last sooty kiss on Anna's cheek. "Good luck, Missis. An' may all yer troubles be little 'uns."

"And so say all of us." James hugged her, squeezing the breath from her body. "Be happy, love."

"I will."

Alex saluted her soberly upon her cheek. "Goobye, Anna."

Anna suppressed an urgent desire to explain kindly to him that this was a wedding, not a funeral, but with considerable strength of will resisted. Since his marriage to the — in Anna's opinion — appalling Alice, Alex had irritated her more than ever.

"Bye, Sis. Have fun." Young Michael, much the worse for an uncounted number of glasses of champagne, thrust the unopened bottle that he carried into her arms. "Take this for luck!"

She laughed, and hugged him hard. Ralph too had a warm goodbye for her and then she was in her father's arms and for the first time inexplicably close to tears. Joss stood by, watching, waiting, his hand on the carriage door. Anna and Josef stood wordless for a moment in each other's arms. The sparkle of tears was in Josef's eyes. Then he stepped back and Anna allowed herself to be handed into the waiting hansom. Moments later they were bowling away, the lifted voices fading behind them. September sunshine, evening-gold, slanted through the window. Anna reached a hand to Joss's arm. He looked, she thought suddenly, tired to exhaustion. His expression was unreadable.

"Mrs Anna Anatov," she said, softly. "That's who I am. Mrs Anna Anatov."

He half-smiled, that slight downward twist to his lips that she loved so much. "As a matter of fact," he said, and despite herself she registered the precision with which he pronounced the words, a sure sign she had already come to know, that he had been drinking heavily, "the Countess Anatov. Had you forgotten?"

She stared at him in delight. "Goodness! Why, yes — yes, I had! It always seemed so odd — that you should be a Count —"

He shook his head. "Don't take it too seriously. In Russia such titles are two a penny. And an unlanded and outlawed Count is no catch at all."

"I think he's a catch." The new Countess snuggled close, lifted her face to his.

His lips were quiet, cool, entirely passionless. She held at bay her disappointment. He was tired. It had been an exhausting day. "Are we nearly there?" They were trotting now across Kew Bridge, the river swirling below, metallic with light.

"Nearly."

The sun was setting as they drew up outside an unprepossessing block of apartments in a street that was a turning off the main, busy thoroughfare of Kew Road. Anna stoically ignored the faint sinking of her heart. It would have been so nice to have had their own little house in a quiet square somewhere —

Joss paid off the grinning cabby. Passers-by glanced, smiling at the now-grubby ribbons that had been tied by mischievous fingers to any protruding part of the hansom. Feeling horribly conspicuous in her so obviously new outfit, the bottle of champagne she still clutched as great a give-away as a written notice, Anna fidgeted self-consciously on the pavement.

"Good luck, Guv'nor." The cabby touched his whip to his greasy hat, watched with a sly smile as his passengers walked the narrow path to the door.

"Second floor," Joss said.

"Yes. I remember." Their words were stilted. A strange and awkward embarrassment seemed to have stiffened Anna's joints. Twice she nearly fell up the steep stairs. Her chagrin at her own, inexplicable clumsiness was, however, eliminated entirely by the shock she received when Joss opened the door of the apartment. She stared, speechless.

"Damnation!" Joss said, grimly.

"But — Joss! What's happened? It looks as if — as if —" Anna stopped as various particulars of the chaos struck her numbed brain.

Angrily Joss strode into the disordered room. "Mrs Avery? *Mrs Avery!* Damn and blast it, where is the woman? She was supposed to have cleared this lot up —"

Empty bottles and glasses cluttered every surface. The curtains were half-shut. The air was heavy and acrid as poison. A woman's red stocking draped the back of an armchair. Joss snatched at it, but not before Anna's shocked eyes had taken it in.

"Mrs Avery!"

"There's no one here," Anna said. Her voice sounded odd in her own ears. The stale air and the reek of liquor turned her stomach queasily.

Joss strode to the window, flung back the curtains and threw the window up with a crash to demolish the building. "I'll murder the woman when I see her."

"Who?"

"Mrs Avery. The woman who's been looking after me while I've been living here. I thought it best to keep her on at least until you've hired staff of your own. She's a passable cook, if nothing else. She was supposed to have come in today and —" He stopped as they both heard the sound of the key in the lock.

"Mr Anatov? That you, Mr Anatov? I saw you from across the road. My, my — what you doin' here?" The thin, slatternly woman who came through the door stopped short at sight of Anna. Her hand went to her mouth. "Oh, Lordy me! Don't tell me — it wasn't today? I was sure you said termorrer —"

"No, Mrs Avery. Today." Joss's voice was exceptionally quiet. "Today. You were supposed to have cleared up this mess and cooked us a meal."

"I r-really don't want anything to eat." Anna hated the tearful trembling of her own voice. She bit her lip, hard.

Neither Joss nor the woman paid the slightest attention to her. She stood like an abandoned child, hands clasped incongruously around the champagne bottle, trying not to look at the appalling mess about her, trying even harder not to draw the obvious conclusions from the disordered room.

"I'm really sorry, Mr Anatov. Wouldn't have had this fer the world. Tell you what — why don't you take the young — that is, yer wife — fer a nice little walk — the Gardens are a treat at this time of year — an' I'll have the place ready in a trice."

"I don't want to go for a walk." Anna's voice was firmer this time and not to be ignored. "I'm tired. I want to change, and to rest." She looked at Joss. "There surely must be a bedroom I can use?"

Joss hesitated. With a knowing smirk Mrs Avery bustled to his rescue. "Two shakes of a lamb's tail, dearie. You just wait here. I'll see to it." She slipped through a door and into a dark, narrow hall in which were stacked the trunks, unopened, that Anna had had delivered to the apartment a couple of days before. A door beyond stood ajar. Anna turned away. The bedroom, it seemed, certainly needed Mrs Avery's attentions. She fought fiercely the rising, miserable tears, looked at Joss.

"I'm sorry," he said, stiffly. "Believe me, I didn't intend this to happen."

She gestured helplessly at the wrecked room. "But — Joss — what happened? How did it get like this?"

"Some friends came. Last night." He shrugged. "The party got — a little out of hand."

She stirred an empty vodka bottle with her foot. "Yes."

He watched her, on his face, had she seen it, a strange mixture of exasperation, near anger and something close to sympathy. "Poor Anna," he said, very softly.

Her head came up sharply at that. "What do you mean, 'poor Anna'? Is that any way to speak on our wedding day?"

The shutters closed upon his face once more. He did not reply.

"Joss — please — what's wrong? Why are you acting so strangely? You haven't even — haven't even," the imminence of tears was now evident in her voice, "kissed me," she finished, desolately.

"Mrs Avery must be nearly finished in the bedroom," he said brusquely. "Go and unpack your trunks. I'll clear up in here and get the fire going. Here, give me that." He took the bottle of champagne that she had all but forgotten that she was clutching from her unresisting hands.

She turned from him, head high, and walked through the dingy hall to the bedroom. Mrs Avery, smoothing the counterpane of the freshly-made bed, looked up with bird-like, inquisitive eyes, straightened and watched as Anna, with slightly shaking hands, carefully withdrew her long hatpin, then took off her blue hat. "Not much of a homecomin', dearie," she commiserated with over-familiar solicitousness.

Anna's misery snapped into temper. "Mrs Avery, my homecoming is none of your business. And I'll thank you during the short term of your working here to call me Ma'am."

The thin lips tightened. "Yes — Ma'am." The woman stalked past her.

Anna slammed the door behind her and leaned against it, trying to control her trembling and surveying the dreary room. Iron bedstead, old, battered pine washstand with a line of sickly green cracked tiles, and a chipped discoloured jug and basin, curtains that looked as if they had not been washed since the day they had been hung, threadbare, colourless carpet — the place was even worse than she remembered it. And there, tossed into a corner and missed — by accident or by design? — in Mrs Avery's hurried attentions to the room, was the partner to the scarlet stocking that had been in the sitting room. The tears that rose this time were not to be resisted. They ran down her cheeks as if of their own volition, dripped from her chin to the wide, starched collar of her blouse. She sat ramrod stiff on the edge of the lumpy, uncomfortable bed and stared in blank wretchedness at the rapidly blurring, dirty wall.

It was more than an hour before she felt composed enough to face Joss, and in that time, despite her not unreasonable hopes, he made no attempt to approach her. When at last, her clothes unpacked and tidied away, her swollen face bathed in the awful basin, her hair loosened about the shoulders of her red velvet wrap, the chill of evening and a desperate certainty that Joss had forgotten her existence drove her back into the now comparatively tidy sitting room, she found him sitting in darkness before the small fireplace. Of Mrs Avery there was, thankfully, no sign. The champagne bottle was open, and emptied. On the small table by his side stood a bottle of vodka and a glass. She took a deep breath, trying to control her shaking and to banish the emotional tears that she knew were very close to the surface and which she sensed would do nothing but make a bad situation worse.

"Joss?"

This time he did move, turning his head from the light and from her.

"Joss — I'm sorry I got upset. It wasn't your fault that that odious little woman had got the days wrong. It just —" She swallowed. He neither moved nor looked at her. "It just isn't quite what I expected."

"No. I don't suppose it is."

She waited. He said no more, but lifted a hand to his face, pressing the heels of his hands for one short moment hard into his forehead. Something in the movement, some sense of desperate tiredness or confusion, wrenched her heart. The room was very still. The sound of traffic from the main road had died. Somewhere in the building a dog yapped. Impulsively Anna dropped to her knees beside Joss's chair and took his cold hand in hers, laying her hot cheek against it, her aching tear-stained eyes upon his shadowed face. "Joss — please — what is it? Are you — angry with me?"

"No."

"Then — what?" Her voice sounded small, wretched, almost childlike. Unhappy tears were close.

He looked at her sombrely. "Go to bed, Anna."

She swallowed. In truth the thought of laying her aching head upon a pillow was more than attractive. "I — aren't you coming?" She blushed, fiercely.

"Later."

She did not know how to argue, had no means within her experience to deal with the awful, inexplicable breach that she felt yawned between them. Helplessly her hands dropped from his. She stumbled to her feet, her toe catching in her skirt, almost tripping her. She walked blindly to the door and towards that bedroom that had so recently shown signs of riotous occupation. By comparison now the silence in the apartment was like the grave. The door clicked shut behind her.

Joss Anatov stared into a sullenly glowing cave of coal and tried to recall the bitter satisfaction afforded him by Josef's farewell to his daughter that afternoon. His enemy was isolated. His punishment was begun. That was enough. To the devil with anyone else's suffering. He stretched a hand to the glass.

From the bedroom came the sound of a dry, instantly stifled sob.

Joss's eyes flinched closed for a second. Then he reached again for the vodka bottle.

CHAPTER TEN

Anna had never spent a more miserable night. Despite her exhaustion she slept badly and woke when, at some time in the dark hours of morning, Joss climbed heavily into bed beside her. She stiffened, her heart suddenly pounding suffocatingly, though whether in fear or in relief that he had finally remembered her existence she did not herself know. She lay rigid with apprehension, but he did not touch her; instead he settled himself with his back to her and apparently slipped immediately into what she supposed to be an alcohol-induced sleep. She lay for hours then, staring into darkness, reliving every moment of what should have been — what indeed had begun as — the happiest day of her life and had ended in fiasco and misunderstanding. Lying still as death beside the sleeping man she swung back and forth upon a pendulum of emotion from anger and self-pity to self-chastisement — had she herself been in some way to blame? Had she acted childishly? Demanded too much? Perhaps so. His body was warm against her back. She let herself relax at last. Tomorrow they must make a new start. She would not think of today. Of his surly behaviour. Of the red stockings. Most of all of the red stockings. She would show him that her love was not so frail as to be daunted so easily — that at last he had someone to care just for him and against whom he need raise no defences — upon this more comforting thought, with the grey light of a rainy dawn seeping through the threadbare curtains she slept at last.

She woke to the instinctive certainty that he was already awake beside her. She moved her head upon the pillow to find him resting upon his elbow, his dark eyes fixed upon her face. Still sleep-bemused, his oddly unexpected nearness alarmed and disturbed her. Infinitesimally she drew back into the pillow, watching him, wide-eyed and silent. His skin was very dark against the white of his nightshirt. Everything about him looked suddenly unfamiliar and frightening. She had woken up beside a stranger in a room whose drabness and lack of comfort was so alien to anything she had ever known that it combined with the circumstances to make her feel lost, afraid and utterly alone. She lay tensely, fighting a surge of sheer panic. Her husband leaned to her, wordless, and his mouth sought hers. Real terror rose, choking her. She felt his hands upon her body; in her fear could neither respond nor resist. Her flesh might have been clay, so chill and unresponsive was it. His mouth and his body were still hot from sleep. She felt his tongue upon her clenched teeth and, suddenly and strongly, revulsion rose. Yet this was her husband and this was his right and she knew nothing but to submit. She lay frozen beneath the weight of his body, deaf and blind to anything but shame, discomfort and final, unbelievable pain. Her single, stifled moan was the only sound she made. He drew away from her, upon his face a bafflement that was quick to turn to a faint exasperation. He dropped abruptly on to the mattress, lay on his back staring at the ceiling. Silence stretched intolerably. Anna felt cold tears slide into her hair. The wetness between her legs shamed and frightened her: she was afraid to move. Surely — surely — it couldn't always be like this?

Beside her, Joss took one long, deep breath, released it slowly. Neither of them, still, had said one word. He sat up abruptly and threw back the bedclothes. "I have to see someone this morning, at ten o'clock. I'm not sure when I'll be back. Mrs Avery will be in to help you."

"I don't want her."

He stopped in the act of pulling on a sock, turned a sardonic eye upon her. "You think you could manage without her?"

She bit her lip. He knew as well as she did herself that she had never so much as lit a fire, let alone cooked a meal.

"She'll be here at eleven."

"No!" Anna was surprised herself at the flat contradiction of the word. "I tell you I won't have her here." She sat up, clutching the sheet to her as if it were some kind of protection, glaring at him fiercely. "I won't."

He shrugged, reached for his other sock. "Perhaps I should eat out tonight."

It was calculatedly cruel. She blinked, caught her breath painfully, and rallied. "If that's what you'd rather do." Her head was up, her eyes suddenly blazing.

He turned and looked at her in silence for what seemed to be a long time. For a moment she was absolutely certain that he was going to apologize. "I'll be back sometime later this afternoon," he said, quietly. "I prefer to eat early, as you know."

It was not until she had wasted almost an hour in panic and near desperation that the simple answer to her self-inflicted problem occurred to her. Of course: Aunt Hermione. Since Grace's death Hermione Smithson had often taken on a mother's guiding role. She would help — of course she would. Anna flew to the cupboard for her coat and hat. She'd show him. She'd shown him that she was no child, that she did not need him and the odious Mrs Avery to manage her life for her — the bitterness and anger that she had been fighting all morning welled again, and stubbornly again she stamped it down. She loved him. No matter what he did, no matter how difficult he might be — and in honesty she could only admit that she had always known him not to be the easiest of men — she loved him. The shock of their lovemaking, if it could be truly termed that, had worn off a little. She could live with that, she told herself determinedly, if that was what he wanted of her. The unkindness that she felt that he had shown was another matter, but one that would have to wait until she discovered the means to counter it. Her father's words, the night before her wedding, echoed in her head: Take care that the things that you want are worth what you will have to pay for them. She would make it work. She would. And meanwhile there was enough in her of her mother to make her first determined to solve the practical problems and to prove to him — and to herself — that he had married no weak and whimpering female fit for nothing but faints and defeated by the first obstacle.

"Of course, my dear. Nothing simpler." Hermione Smithson poured another cup of tea, handed the delicate china cup to her young guest, her kindly eyes upon the pale, peaky face and reddened eyes. "I'll send Thomas round to the agency I use. They're really excellent people. I can recommend them. What would you be looking for? A live-in maid and a cook, to start with?"

Anna fidgeted with her teaspoon. "The apartment isn't really big enough for a live-in maid. I was thinking more of a — a kind of general housekeeper — who might come in each day."

"Of course. I'm sure they'll fix you up." Hermione reached for the bell pull, "You'll be ready to interview — when? — tomorrow? The next day?"

"As soon as possible, please."

"Nothing easier, my dear. Ah — Thomas," she bustled to a small writing desk, scribbled a quick note, "I want you to take this round to Mullins', please. At once. Tell them that the matter is urgent."

"Yes, Ma'am." The serving man took the note and left. Hermione looked back at Anna. "Now, is there anything else I can do?" If she found it in the least strange that a wife of only a day's standing should be visiting alone and in the throes of such an early domestic crisis she gave no sign, except for perhaps the gleam of sympathy in her eye. Yet despite that sympathy — which was perfectly genuine — there was still a certain satisfaction in being proved right. Hermione Smithson had never believed this poor child to be capable of coping with such a man as Joss Anatov, moody and ungentlemanly foreigner that he was. Anna and Christopher would have been so much better matched, though to be sure she had always suspected a headstrong streak in the girl — a streak that had indeed been confirmed by this sudden and unsuitable marriage.

"I — well, yes —"

"What is it?"

Anna spread helpless hands. "Today — and tomorrow — until I find someone suitable —"

"Tch, tch. Don't worry about that. You shall borrow our Harriet for a few days. She's a passable cook, and there really isn't enough for her to do nowadays, with the boys grown up —"

"Oh, Aunt Hermione! Are you sure?" Anna's relief was so great that she almost leapt up and hugged the other woman. The awful tears that seemed to have been dogging her for the past twenty-four hours were close again, but this time through sheer thankfulness. She stood up and moved to Hermione, bent and dropped a kiss on her plump cheek. "Thank you. Thank you so much."

Hermione, when all was said and done, was very fond indeed of Anna. She trapped her small hand, held it lightly. "Anna? Are you sure you're all right?"

The girl stood for a moment, fighting the urge to let her unhappiness flood out to a sympathetic ear. "Quite all right," she said brightly. "Of course."

"Of course." Hermione patted her hand. At least she had tried. And Anna, the older woman thought with a kindly cynicism that was more part of her nature than most people knew, was not the first romantic-minded young woman to find the reality of marriage a little more than she had bargained for. Still, she thought, with a totally unexpected touch of something close to envy, life with Joss Anatov, beastly man that he quite obviously was, would never be dull, whatever else it was. She stood up briskly. "Now, I've something to show you. You've saved me a journey by coming to see me. You know I've found this *wonderful* little dressmaker — I'm sure I told you?" Chattering lightly, she sailed from the room towing Anna behind her like a small dinghy behind a man o' war. In the sewing room she began to rummage in a drawer, still talking.

Anna was only barely listening. If Harriet could come back with her now, between them they could surely make something of that horrible apartment before Joss came home? She'd give him the surprise of his life, just see if she wouldn't. Scrubbed and cleaned, and with the furniture rearranged.

"Ah. Here it is."

"Sorry?"

"What I wanted to show you. I thought of you at once. See. Isn't it marvellous? So tiny — so perfect — one would have to look with a magnifying glass to see the stitches."

Anna took the scrap of material she was offered and all thoughts of homemaking fled her mind. "It's exquisite!"

"Isn't it?" Hermione Smithson smiled, pleased.

Anna studied the tiny embroidered flower — a rose upon a delicately thorned stem, with a dainty spray of leaves. "It's perfect! The stitches are almost invisible."

"Look at this one." She handed Anna another scrap, upon

which was embroidered on a pale background a miniature spray of dark, spiky holly, the leaves subtly coloured, the berries a sumptuous red.

"But — they're absolutely marvellous!"

"I thought you'd like them. I knew you cared for such things."

Anna's eyes were bright with the delight of a new discovery.

"Aunt Hermione — you're an absolute godsend!"

"Thank you, dear." Hermione said, equably, "I just wish the rest of the world would recognize that!"

This time Anna did hug her. The colour had returned to her cheeks and her voice, until now subdued, was firm and excited. "Can't you just see how perfectly I could use these? In boxes — brooches — lockets — they're so fine, so perfect! There's no end to the possibilities. Aunt Hermione — I must meet this wonder. At once!"

Hermione's face dropped a little. "Ah, now that, I'm afraid, will be a little difficult for a while. She's visiting her mother in the north somewhere."

"When will she be back?"

"Now that I don't know. A month or so she said."

"There's no way I can get in touch with her?" Reluctantly, Anna offered the sprig of holly to the other woman.

"Oh, keep it, dear, if you like. And, no, I'm afraid you can't. But she'll certainly let me know the minute she gets back." She leaned a little closer, her voice confidential. "Such a nice young woman — good breeding, you know. Though what she's doing mixed up with arts and crafts and students and such I can't imagine. But she'll certainly be in touch. She needs the money, you see. The money that the dressmaking brings in —"

"Is dressmaking, then, not all she does?"

"Dear me, no. She teaches a little, I believe. And —" she waved a vague hand "— and exhibits things."

"Exhibits things?" Something Aunt Hermione had said earlier now made sense to Anna. "Arts and crafts you said. You mean the Society? The Arts and Crafts Exhibition Society?"

"Oh — something of that sort, yes."

Anna's eyes were thoughtful. "Will you promise to tell me the minute you hear she's back?"

"Why, of course, dear." Hermione was amused and more than a little relieved to find that something so trivial had raised the girl's spirits so. The problem then can't have been too bad. "I promise. The minute she comes back."

By the time that moment came, however, Anna had other things to think about, for she was at the difficult start of what was to prove a difficult pregnancy, and her mind as well as her body was fully occupied with that.

Anna always thought — or perhaps simply hoped — that she could pinpoint exactly the moment of the child's conception. Those first few weeks of married life were perhaps the most difficult that she had ever lived through, as she struggled to adjust to living with a man who had, it seemed, as many moods as there were shadows in woodland. Unaware of the underlying emotional struggle that influenced his attitude to her she battled on, learning as she went, confused as much by his occasional gentleness as his more frequent uncaring lack of kindness. Conditioned by the age, she sincerely believed it to be her duty to love, honour and obey her husband whatever his temper, whatever the temptation to rebel, as had her mother her father. Such social mores, however, ran absolutely counter to a fiercely independent temperament. For a kindly word she would do anything; antagonized, the desire to strike back, to wound as she had been wounded, was not easily controlled. That Joss was as unhappy in his way as she was in hers never once occurred to her. Why should it? She had no inkling of the oft-regretted impulse upon which her strange marriage was founded, could therefore have no idea of the warring emotions within her husband that made a normally difficult temperament next to impossible. There were times when he saw in her the child he had loved, times which could soften his heart to tears, but when he could no more have made love to her or spoken the love words that she so needed to hear, than he could have violated that same child. Equally, there were times when he saw her simply as her father's daughter, spawn of the man who had traded his sister's sanity and finally her life for worldly gain — and at those times he could use her like a whore, knowing she hated it, and think no regret. Confusingly, however, more and more often as time wore on, he came to see her in moments of clarity simply as herself — an individual, stubborn, infuriating, talented, intelligent — if to his analytical mind often hopelessly illogical. And it was this individual that, disturbingly, he discovered to be a threat to his peace of mind and to his implacable determination to break and ruin her father. She loved him. They both knew it, for she did not attempt to hide it. That he loved her was a secret from them both.

Their everyday life, as is the way of such things, soon settled into a workable routine. Joss was out most of the day — where and doing what Anna did not always know. For herself, she set up a small desk in the bow window of the sitting room, having with some pleasure removed the grimy lace curtains, and there she worked for happy, self-forgetful hours with paper, pencil and paint. The daily help obtained with Hermione Smithson's help turned out to be a true 'treasure' — Mrs Lacey was a motherly person of ample physical proportions and a heart to match. Left free to pursue her own interest, Anna found herself spending more and more time at galleries, museums and exhibitions, her eager mind open to the welcoming artistic stimulation of others' work, past and present. Together with her father's craftsmen she produced a few pieces with which even she was tolerably pleased — a nephrite box of delicate hue upon which the huntress Diana discarded her bow and fed from her outstretched hands birds of fable and legend; the combs she had once as a child dreamed of creating, leaves of the lily in jade adorned with crystallized dewdrops of diamond. She began to study the designs of the Egyptians, the Romans, the Celts, designs of the East and of the West. Her sketchbook went everywhere with her and her passion for the flowing line, the precision of pattern and the translation into precious stone and metal of the beauty of living things grew and flowered.

She was intent, late one October afternoon at her desk, upon trying to capture on paper the veined, skeletal structure of a decayed leaf when she heard the click of Joss's key in the lock. She had been studying with her father's goldsmith at the workshops and was keen to try her hand at producing this, the lovely cobweb structure of autumn in precious metal. A moment later she sensed movement as Joss came up behind her and stood looking over her shoulder.

She neither paused nor looked up. He watched the moving pencil in silence for a while.

She straightened, narrowing her eyes.

"It's excellent," he said.

"No. It's too heavy. Not — fragile enough." She stood surveying her work, her bottom lip sucked between her teeth. The sky, having been bright all day, had become overcast and the light was fading. The fire was unlit and the air a little chill.

He leaned across her and pointed with a sharp brown finger. "Perhaps there? A little less strong?"

"Yes." She rubbed at the pencil marks with the heel of her hand. "Yes. That's better, isn't it?" She turned her head, smiling, and finding her face just inches from his stopped, the smile gradually fading. He straightened. They stood so for a moment, looking at each other in total silence. Then, shyly and very slowly, she lifted a hand, loosely curled, and placed the backs of her fingers and her knuckles upon the uncompromising line of his cheek. It was an odd little gesture, of love and sorrow. After a single second's stillness almost imperceptibly he turned his head, pressing his cheek against her hand. The movement generated within her an unexpected, almost unbearable excitement. She caught her breath, seeing that same excitement, half-puzzled, reflected in his eyes. Then slowly, slowly he lifted a hand to cup her breast. As she often did when she was working, she was wearing a loose smock over her blue serge skirt. Never taking her eyes from his she unbuttoned it, slipped it from her shoulders. Her movements were somnolent, strangely dreamlike in the quiet half-darkness. For the first time since that far-off day on the verandah of her father's house true desire stirred and she wanted him; simply, fiercely, wanted him.

He caught her to him. She lifted her face to the leaden skies above his bowed dark head, arched her back to offer her breasts. Pain and pleasure were inseparable. He bore her to the floor, took her as she lay, with urgency and an oddly gentle strength. They lay afterwards together in silence, their clothing in disarray, arms and legs still entangled, neither quite certain of the cause of the unexpected storm that had swept them. Anna slowly to herself. He moved away from her. She became denly aware of her bared skin, of her shameful posture. She sat up quickly, ducking her head, rearranging her clothes. The room had darkened further; she could hardly see him.

Say it. Please say it. Tell me you love me.

"I'll light the lamp," he said, and his voice was soft but the words were wrong.

Her pregnancy was a discomfort from the start. She lost weight, was constantly sick, her energy seemed to desert her. She struggled through the winter months cossetted by Mrs Lacey, lectured to and organized by Hermione Smithson, counselled upon every subject under the sun by her grandmother who, though physically frail, had lost none of her strength of mind. Indeed, a distracted Anna discovered, the whole world seemed to have at its fingertips advice for a pregnant woman, and the whole world insisted upon giving it. Nobody but Anna seemed to regard it as an invasion of her privacy for near-strangers to be kept informed of her slightest physical problem or discomfort. She did not bloom, as some women do: on the contrary she found the whole business little to her liking, from the bulky, cumbersome body that seemed no longer to be entirely her own, to the feelings of resentment that she discovered herself to harbour for the small intruder who now shared that body and her life at considerable cost to herself in pain and discomfort. A large part of this resentment undoubtedly stemmed from the fact that the unborn child, she felt, came between herself and Joss just as they were beginning to find some kind of understanding. From that October afternoon when they had first truly made love to the time when her pregnancy began physically to affect her was the happiest time of her life; everything she had hoped for seemed to be almost within her grasp. Then the sickness began and the debilitation, and the time had been too brief, and nothing had been established between them. She knew herself to be short-tempered and mortifyingly and constantly tearful. She could not bear Joss to touch her swollen and painful breasts: from there it was a simple step for him not to touch her at all. She was permanently exhausted. The idyll — such as it was — had passed. Her irritability, which she seemed incapable of controlling, caused quarrels about the most insignificant things. February she caught influenza. Hermione Smithson, contacted by an anxious Mrs Lacey, made short work of packing Anna, her small case and her medicine into a cab.

"But — Aunt Hermione — what about Joss? He'll —"

"He's more than capable of taking care of himself. Besides, he has Mrs Lacey, doesn't he? It's you we have to look after, my dear — you and the baby. Just look at you! Skin and bone!"

Anna felt too wretched to argue. With some relief she allowed herself to be put to bed with a warming pan and a cup of comforting lemon and honey, and drifted into a feverish sleep. It was not until her illness was over and her head finally cleared that she realized that in ten days Joss had visited her only twice and seemed in no great hurry to persuade her home. She tried, unsuccessfully, not to think of a pair of red stockings.

Yet it could not be said that Joss was not pleased about the baby. Indeed, on occasion he would fuss about Anna almost as much as Mrs Lacey did — yet even this could not please her, for she felt strongly that his attentions were not those she desired from him — the attentions of a man for the woman he loved — but those of a conscientious doctor for a valued patient. His thoughts were always for the coming child, and her resentment grew. She knew she was being perverse, disliked herself for her own moodiness and quarrelsome touchiness. She began to look forward to June and the birth of the child with a passionate intensity that had nothing to do with a longing for motherhood. She wanted the business over and done with. She wanted her body to herself again. She wanted to be normal, to get back to her own life. Her work suffered badly during those months — she could not concentrate, her drawings and designs seemed to her to be as heavy and as dull as her own body felt. When Hermione, thinking to distract her, offered to introduce her to the needlewoman she had been so keen to meet she made an excuse and refused. Her mind seemed incapable of its normal enthusiasms. Even the stirrings and rumours of more trouble in South Africa hardly seemed to pierce the self-centred and peevish veil with which pregnancy had invested her. The Boers wouldn't take on the might of the British Army; they wouldn't dare. Crossly, she dismissed the war talk. April. May. The agged on. Her distended belly was sore and uncom-. She could neither sit nor lie comfortably. She cried James came to see her to tell her that his regiment was ed to South Africa, but her tears were more of self-pity than for him. Nothing would happen to James. But she — she was beginning to be very frightened indeed. In the last weeks she was haunted by the memory of her mother's ordeal when Margaret Jane was born.

Oh, God — would it never happen? Would she never be free?

The birth, on a warm June night with thunder rumbling in the distance and the heaviness of storm in the air was slow, painful, and utterly exhausting. Anna never herself knew where she acquired the strength to fight the fight of all mothers to bring a new life into the world. At last, after inconceivable effort, it was done and the bawling scrap was laid in the crook of her tired mother's arm.

A daughter. Blue-eyed, fair-skinned, the downy hair already thick, curly and glinting silver-gold.

Joss stared at his daughter, his eyes sombre, lifted his gaze to Josef who stood on the other side of the bed.

"She'll be beautiful," Josef said, painfully, his eyes tormented.

"Yes. She'll be beautiful." Joss's voice was even.

Josef bent to the child, offered a slightly unsteady finger. He looked old. There was an unhealthy tinge of grey to his skin. Anna smiled, sleepily. "A little granddaughter, Papa."

"Yes."

"She looks like —" she stopped suddenly, frowned a little, "— like Boris," she finished.

Joss bent and scooped his daughter from her mother's side. Above the small, vulnerable fair head his eyes upon the older man were totally unforgiving.

CHAPTER ELEVEN

Whilst through the temperate days of an English summer Anna fought an often losing battle to adjust to motherhood and to a marriage that she was coming to understand was going to be anything but easy at the best of times, in the cool of the South African winter the gulf between high-handed British and stubborn Boer widened inexorably. As the inevitable end drew near both sides prepared for it as best they could, then settled to wait — the one for reinforcements from home, the other for the fresh grass of spring that would feed the horses and oxen of their commandos. In the event, perhaps predictably, the grass grew before the reinforcements arrived. When Paul Kruger demanded that the British give up their claim to the Transvaal and issued an ultimatum that expired late in the afternoon of October 11th 1899, 47,000 men under the command of Sir Redvers Buller were still en route for South Africa. Within a month and before the desperately needed extra men had arrived, the towns of Ladysmith, Kimberley and Mafeking were under siege. In Britain war fever flickered, flared, then flamed through the country as it had not for a century in a wave of jingoistic excitement. Headlines screamed, bands played and young men queued to enlist. National pride was outraged; it simply was not possible that an army that had built and defended an empire could be held at bay — more, could be beaten into retreat — by a rabble of Bible-thumping Dutch farmers. The recruiting sergeants banged their drums and spoke to eager ears. The troopships sailed, bravely, amidst fluttering handkerchieves and the tears of women. Then reports began to filter back, blacker by the day and the tears for many were shed in earnest, no longer simply the sad tokens of parting but the bitter gall of final loss. Those that commanded the British Army were slow to learn that scarlet-coated, rigidly-ranked discipline and courage were simple lunacy when pitted against a handful of crack shots and rough riders whose home and hunting ground that wide, wild country was. Columns marched to relieve the besieged towns, and one by one the marchers died, picked off like wooden soldiers in a fairground shooting gallery by marksmen who had learned to handle a rifle and a pony in the same year that they had learned to walk. In just such a way Subaltern James Rose died, marching to Kimberley where was imprisoned Cecil Rhodes, certainly the most important Englishman in South Africa and, so it was said, the richest Englishman in the world. James never saw the man who shot him, did not feel the mortal blow of the bullet that scattered his brains on the dusty soil. In this, at least, he was lucky; more than half of those who marched with him died harder under the African sun in the defeat that followed as officers too blinded by regulations to see that their enemies were fighting a different kind of war, led charge after desperate charge against a hail of viciously accurate bullets and an enemy who simply refused to stand still to be charged. Hundreds of men died that day, and for nothing; the lessons so painfully offered were not learned and the columns kept marching.

The news of his son's death was a blow from which Josef was slow to recover, and one which further confirmed his growing conviction that those malicious fates from whom he had imagined he had escaped had found him once more. Despite his efforts, his hard work, his success and his repentance for sins past, the things and the people that he loved were not, after all, safe. Tanya, Grace and now young James — all dead. Alex, his eldest son, hardly a son at all now and scarcely recognizable as the boy he had been as he ruthlessly pursued his own life and ambitions separately from his family's. And Anna — his pride, his special child — what of Anna? That she was not happy was clear to anyone who cared to look beneath the brittle veneer she always assumed in company. Since the baby he hardly saw her. She had done little or no design work, rarely came to the shop or the workshop, almost never visited the Bayswater house except at direct invitation. When she did come he was always taken aback by her appearance. A beauty she had never been, but always she had had her own slightly eccentric charm and never had her dress or toilette been less than meticulous; since the birth of little Victoria she had become lackadaisical, her hair scraped unbecomingly back, her clothes crumpled and sometimes stained. Each time he saw her it seemed to him that her eyes were reddened as if by recent tears. Yet she would not confide in him, as once she might have done, and though he grieved for her he could see no way to help. She and Joss must work things out between them.

Joss.

If anyone could be said to personify Josef's worry and confusion it must be Joss. Entirely gone was the boy, bitter to be sure and always difficult yet eager in his own way to please, to care and to be cared for — and in his place a man that Josef, no matter how hard he tried, could not come to know. Some part of Joss was closed to him, and he did not know why, though sometimes in his darkest moments a terrible suspicion assailed him. How often, oh how often, as the years passed did the memory of those last long hours that Tanya and Joss had spent together before she had taken her life nag at his mind like a toothache that would not be soothed? What had she remembered? What had she told him? He could not bring himself to ask. Nothing, said his common sense stoutly — for surely no man could smile and be civil and keep such a secret? And yet through long nights the thought of Joss's sister haunted him and he knew that atonement must still be made, somehow, by someone. He found himself plagued too by thoughts of the tainted stone upon which all their lives were based. More and more, as he tried to tell Anna on the night before her marriage, he had come almost superstitiously to see the diamond as the root cause of the trouble that seemed to dog him and those he loved; the cursed thing had been nothing but bad luck for anyone who had had anything to do with it. And now, as if to confirm that belief, he was beginning to suspect that the very business in which he had worked so hard and which was founded upon that unlucky stone was no longer as secure as it had been. Still grieving for the son cut down in South Africa, aware sometimes fearfully of growing ill-health, he found himself now for the first time in years uncertain of the financial status of the business. Joss guardedly assured him that the setbacks were temporary — the shortage of diamonds and of gold caused by the South African war, a slight change in fashion, to which Rose and Company had not been quick enough to adjust, the now not so propitious situation of the shop — times were changing, Rose's now found themselves in a popular rather than prestigious premises; the rich and titled demanded to be wooed — new premises were called for. In Conduit Street perhaps, or New Bond Street — to Josef the idea of spending more money to improve their apparently failing profits was more than a little confusing, but he was getting old and for so long now he had trusted Joss to take care of the financial side of the business that to take his advice, especially since Grace's death, had become second nature, to question it a departure from the norm. He hoped that Joss did not know of his own personal recent failures in the Stock Market; when the tide of fortune turned against a man it turned, it seemed, with a vengeance.

"Do we actually have the money for this new venture?" he asked his son-in-law one day in December, the last month of the nineteenth century. The day was dark and dreary, the news matched it. The names Magersfontein, Stormberg, Colenso were on every tongue, there were rumours of incompetence, of massive casualties, of defeat and humiliation.

"We'll make a profit on the Piccadilly premises. The rest we'll borrow."

"Borrow?" Josef's voice shook a little. The wearying breathlessness was upon him again.

"Of course. As you know our capital is rather tied up at the moment."

"But, Joss —"

Joss looked up from the ledger he was studying. Waited with polite, barely veiled impatience. "Yes?"

Josef hesitated, his troublesome breath catching in his chest. Suddenly he was aware as never before of the younger man's vitality, of the power and restlessness so severely penned in the slight frame. All at once Josef felt very tired. "Nothing. Of course, you know best. We'll borrow."

Christmas was a subdued affair that year. Alex, busy as it seemed he more often than not was with his other and in his eyes more prestigious family, did not manage to put in an appearance at all. Ralph, home from his seminary but wrapped up in his own religious observances of the season, was like a vague and gentle shadow in the house. Michael, home early from his first term at university and strangely subdued, spent much of his time uncharacteristically quiet in his room. Joss, Anna and the baby visited on Christmas day, but the laughing ghost of James was too evidently present for them all and the occasion was a mockery of those other, happy festivals when they had all been children and Grace had presided at the Christmas table.

After dinner Anna found herself sitting with her father before the dying fire in the parlour. Ralph had gone again to church. Victoria lay, mouth milky, fast asleep upon the couch next to her mother. At six months she was a pretty robust child, even-tempered and well-behaved.

"Where are Michael and Joss?"

Anna lifted her head from her silent contemplation of the flames. "Still in the dining room. Michael wanted to talk to Joss about something. It's odd, I think, that they should get on as they do."

"Why odd?"

She shrugged. "I don't know. Joss doesn't make friends easily. He has very few," — that I know of anyway; she did not speak the thought. "And Michael's so much younger." She leaned back and added, tartly tired, "Perhaps it's just that Joss knows that Michael thinks he's first cousin to God Almighty. He'd appreciate that."

Her father looked up sharply at her tone, but curbed his tongue and refrained from comment. "Anna?" he said, gently, after a short silence.

"Yes?"

"We haven't seen much of you lately. Here. At the workshop. Tom was asking the other day — the design he spoke to you about — for the silver box for the Marquis — have you done it?"

Anna turned her head. "No. Not yet."

"Tom's waiting."

"Yes. Yes, I know. But —" she sighed a little, helplessly "— I'm sorry, Papa, I just can't seem to —" She stopped. In the lamplight he thought he saw the sudden gleam of tears.

"Anna! Anna, my pet, it's nothing to cry for! I just promised Tom that I'd ask —" Josef was concerned.

She blinked rapidly, fussed with the sleeping child. "I'm not crying." She was crying. Again. She hated it. Hated herself.

"Anna?" His voice was quiet, questioning.

She glanced at him. She had noticed over dinner how ill he looked. Even in this flattering half-light his face had in it an unhealthy tinge of grey, the eye sockets shadowed. He was grieving still for James, she knew, as indeed were they all. How could she add to his burdens with her own silly worries? How could she even put into words the things she could not explain to herself; the depressions, the tears, the inability to cope with the smallest thing that seemed to have overwhelmed her since Victoria's birth. A spoiled dinner, the baby crying, a broken bootlace — everything assumed the proportions of a disaster. No wonder Joss was hardly ever at home — if those odious rooms in Kew could be described as such. She remained silent. The baby beside her stirred, settled back into sleep again. Absently Anna adjusted the shawl that covered her. She and Josef sat for a long time unspeaking, with too much to be said and no way of saying it.

In the cab going home Joss said, with no preamble, "Michael's been sent down from university."

She looked at him blankly. "What do you mean?"

"He can't go back. He's been expelled."

"Oh, no!" She waited. Joss said nothing. "Wh — what did he do?"

Joss shrugged. "An unsavoury business involving a girl. The dean's daughter, I believe."

"How bad?"

"Very bad. The girl procured an abortion and very nearly died."

"God!"

"They're hushing it up, of course. But — obviously — he can't go back. And no one else will take him."

Sudden anger stirred. "Of all the stupid, irresponsible, half-witted fools! What in God's name is the matter with Michael? Is he never going to grow up? Doesn't he ever think of anyone else but himself? Papa — What will this do to Papa? Has Michael even considered that? Hasn't Papa enough to worry him without this?" She paused, then added firmly, "He'll have to tell him. He can't skulk in his room for the rest of his life." It seemed all at once as if all the frustrations, all the self-contempt of the past months at her own weakness crystallized into a determination to face this, a real crisis, in a positive and constructive way. "It could kill him. Doesn't Michael understand that?"

Joss turned his head from her to look out into the dark, gaslit streets. "It won't kill him."

So intent was she upon her own anger and concern she missed the oddly intense note in his voice. "It could! Oh, I could murder Michael myself!" She wriggled in her seat, the sleeping child clutched to her. "When is Michael going to tell him? Did he say?"

"I don't know. Some time soon, he said. He keeps putting it off."

She sat suddenly bolt upright. "Well, he's got a nasty shock coming. I'll go and see him tomorrow. Both of them. I'll make Michael tell Papa while I'm there. At least it might help a little." For the first time in months she felt the stirring of real energy, of an interest outside her own four prisoning walls of a demanding child, depression and easy tears.

He said nothing. But loudly as if he had spoken she knew his thoughts. The old Anna might have done such a thing. But the new one? She pressed her lips tightly together. Enough was enough. She could not — must not — be content to let the world move on without her. Her father needed her.

The incident, unpleasant as it was, had a strangely efficacious effect upon Anna. That initial spurt of anger and energy carried her through the next couple of distressing days, and her presence did, as she hoped it might, help her father to face the fact of his youngest son's disgrace so soon after the blow of James's death. Michael she left in no doubt at all as to her opinion of his behaviour. He was, predictably, repentant and eager to make amends and accepted with a grateful humility that Anna suspected could not last long Joss's suggestion that he start work with no time lost in the most menial of capacities in the offices of Rose and Company. The storm passed — but to Josef it was another calamitous stroke of bad fortune and one he found very hard to take.

For Anna, however, the web of listlessness and depression that had bound her for the past months had been at last torn away and determinedly she set about ensuring that it should not enmesh her again.

The new year that saw in also the new century was a troubled one for a country at war with the casualty lists inexplicably rising and as yet no good news to cheer the nation, yet still it was after all a once in a lifetime event, and there were many celebrations despite the gloomy war news. Anna's resolution for the new year and for the new century was simple; she would get back to work, get back to life. She would find someone to help with the baby and she would — she must! — persuade Joss that now they were a family they needed a proper home. In this last she had in fact less difficulty than she had anticipated, for Joss, although still strangely loth to spend money, did not himself care for cramped living quarters when one of the occupants was a lively and noisy six-month-old. He was, however, adamant that they could afford nothing too big nor in a fashionable area. To Anna's expressed surprise at their apparent lack of capital he replied shortly and to the point. Their financial affairs were his concern. He would make what decisions he felt necessary — and at this time, though he agreed that they needed a home, he refused to invest capital and buy one but agreed to rent a small house by the river not far from Kew Gardens, and with this for the time being Anna had to be content. At least it meant that the invaluable Mrs Lacey could remain with them and in addition she was able to employ a live-in maid to help with the baby and with the household chores. If she had hoped, however, that the move might encourage Joss to spend more time at home she was disappointed. Since the birth of the baby Joss had shown little or no interest in his wife — and Anna, to be strictly fair, accepted that in the circumstances the blame was not entirely his. She had let herself go. She had not bothered to buy new clothes, had become slipshod about her appearance. This too she became determined to change, and in this she was unexpectedly helped by a new acquaintance.

Elizabeth Brown was the needlewoman whose work Anna had so admired at Hermione Smithson's house before her pregnancy. When finally they became acquainted, during the month of February when the tide of the South African war was turning at last in Britain's favour as first Kimberley and then Ladysmith were relieved, this admiration was augmented by a genuine liking for the girl. She was a lively young woman with an infectious laugh and Anna thought her one of the most striking-looking people she had ever encountered. Her mass of dark hair she left loose, flying from her head in a vivid halo that framed a pale face in which greenish eyes were set wide apart above a mouth too generously wide for beauty. Her neck, however, was long and elegant, her skin alabaster white and fine. It was perhaps a strange rather than pretty face, but her constant flashing smile and animated expression lent to it an illusion of beauty. Her clothes, too, were out of the ordinary; not for Elizabeth the imprisonment of stays and corsets and tight bombazine. She dressed with a gypsy-like freedom, her skirt bright and gaily swirling, blouse and shawl wonderfully embroidered in jewel colours. The effect was truly arresting, and fascinated Anna, who felt beside her like a sparrow beside a bird of paradise. They met by arrangement at Hermione Smithson's house, and though Beth made no secret of her initial scepticism that anything could possibly come of it, she brought with her some samples of her work. Anna was enchanted all over again.

"Would you accept some commissions from me? If I drew what I wanted you to embroider?"

The girl nibbled her lip doubtfully. "We–ell —"

Anna whisked a stub of pencil from her small reticule, reached for an envelope that lay upon the table, "May, I, Aunt Hermione?" Without waiting for reply she sketched swiftly upon the back. In a few flowing lines a winged insect appeared, wings poised as if for flight, "See — like that? Or —" the pencil moved again and a shadowed pattern of leaves and flowers with curled, fairy-like tendrils flowed about the letter 'A' "— like that?" She stopped, looking up into silence. The girl was staring at her. "Is something wrong?"

Beth, as many people had discovered to their cost, was a girl of instant decision. "No, Mrs Anatov. Nothing's wrong. I'd be delighted to accept your commissions." She grinned her sudden, infectious smile. "I was obviously wrong. I thought you'd want me to embroider 'Mother' wreathed with violets."

The significance of the remark did not at that moment strike Anna, absorbed as she was. "Wonderful! You must come to the house. Tomorrow. Could you come tomorrow?"

Beth Brown stood up, laughing. "Lordy, Mrs Anatov, give a girl a chance to catch her breath —"

"Oh, I'm sorry. I'm just so excited — so keen to start. I can see so many things we could do together. Marvellous things. And, please — call me Anna, won't you?"

The other girl smiled. "I can't manage tomorrow, I'm afraid — Anna — I do have a living to earn you know. The next day, though — would that do?"

"Perfect. I'll have some ideas ready by then. And I'll get together a few pieces so that you can see some of the work I've done."

Anna could not remember being so excited or so stimulated for a very long time. In the cab going home, her fingers itched for a pencil. Light glittered on the river and in her mind's eye she saw the glimmer of silver and the gleam of gold. When she reached Kew the house was empty but for Mrs Lacey, who sang amongst the clattering pots of the kitchen. Anna took off her hat and coat then, as she was turning from the full-length mirror stopped suddenly and turned back, her swiftly busy movements slowing. For the first time in months she really looked at her own reflection, studying herself from the crown of her unflatteringly scraped-back hair through her drab and conventional clothes to her scuffed, dull boots. For the first time the significance of Beth's remark about the kind of work she had expected to be asked to do struck her. She stood still for a long time, studying the dowdy figure of the stranger in the mirror. Beside that image she saw Beth, stylishly flamboyant, striking. With sudden impatient movements she put her hands to her hair, pulling out the pins and shaking her head sharply. Her light brown hair tumbled into her eyes and down on to her shoulders. She fluffed it out, coiled it more softly and becomingly at the nape of her neck. She leaned to the mirror, pinched her pale cheeks hard and watched the flush of colour that brightened her eyes and shaped her face. Beside her stood a small table with its peacock-shaded fringed tablecloth almost touching the floor, upon which rested a small vase of flowers. On impulse she plucked a flower from the vase and tucked it into her hair, then, smiling at her own absurdity, pulled the tablecloth from the table and draped it dashingly about her shoulders. The effect was startling. The uninteresting figure in the mirror was all at once a gypsy. Anna lifted her chin, set her head at a haughty angle. Nothing would ever make her beautiful — but then Beth Brown was not beautiful in the true sense of the word. Suddenly she remembered a sunny room, the sound of the sea, two decorated boxes, a birthday dinner. What had Tanya — beautiful Tanya — said that day? "How lovely your eyes are. And how fine and straight your mouth." She studied herself with narrowed, critical eyes. Her face was a good, interesting shape — she had her father's high, Slavic cheekbones and her mother's short well-shaped nose. If her colouring were a little nondescript, and her mouth a little thin? That same mouth set in a familiar determined line. She did not have to look plain. Dowdy. Dull. And facing herself now, fairly and squarely, she had to admit that these were the words that came quickest to mind. What had she been doing all these months? No wonder Joss had barely looked at her since Victoria's birth.

Spring was coming. The dead earth, the bare, stark trees would soon be dressed for lovely summer. And so, she resolved, would she. Perhaps Beth would help her. She hoped so. For Beth obviously had a secret, and Anna, here and now, decided she would discover what it was.

Beth Brown's secret, as it happened, was called Arabella Dawson. Anna met her a couple of months later in Beth's slap-happily cluttered and overcrowded little room in Bloomsbury, from whose windows stretched an unbroken vista of roofs, chimneys and spires. By the time she actually met Arabella Anna was well used to this muddle of a room where there was never a clear square inch in which to sit that was not covered in material, patterns, clothes, embroidery silks or one of Beth's stray cats. In those two months the girls had grown very fond of each other and Anna had discovered almost for the first time the joys of fast friendship with a member of her own sex. Their relationship was based in the first instance on mutual admiration for each other's work. Anna had already recognized Beth's mastery — Beth had been thunderstruck at Anna's craftsmanship.

"But — Anna! You must exhibit with us! You can't just *sell* this stuff! It's marvellous! How come I've never heard of you?"

"Heard of me?" Anna laughed, self-consciously, "Why should you have heard of me?"

"Have you never thought of exhibiting?"

Anna shook her head.

"Well, we'll soon change that. Our — that is the Arts and Crafts Exhibition Society's — next shindig is in the summer. I'll eat my hat, and yours too, if you aren't in it."

"But —" Anna stopped.

"But what?" The other girl looked sharply at her.

"I'm not sure if — well, my husband, my father — they might not think it right."

Beth straightened, on her face a look of almost comic disbelief. "Are you joking?"

"No. Of course not."

"Then let's have no more of that. You're a grown woman and this is the twentieth century, not the tenth. We'll do something together, perhaps. We've a few months before we have to submit it."

"Submit it?" Anna's voice was a little faint.

Beth giggled. "Do you know you've taken to repeating everything I say? Of course submit it. They don't take just anything, you know. The Exhibition is the equivalent of —" she spread eloquent hands "— of being hung in the Royal Academy."

"Have you been accepted before?"

Beth waved an airy hand. "Once or twice. Now — what about colours for the Unicorn Box? I thought silver thread at first, but I'm not sure now —"

Anna was instantly absorbed. "Oh, no. Too sharp, I think, with mother of pearl. I had more in mind an oyster colour —"

Both Joss and Josef showed real interest in the new designs Anna was producing together with Beth. The girl's exquisitely embroidered miniatures in Anna's settings made unusual and beautiful jewellery — brooches, lockets, bracelets, even finger and earrings. Her work was set into panels for boxes and other ornaments. She worked decorated monograms and name-brooches.

"Perhaps we should retain her?" Joss suggested soon after his first meeting with the dark-haired and eccentrically impressive Miss Brown.

Anna shook her head. "She wouldn't. I've already asked. She won't tie herself down to working for one person, no matter how much we offered her. She likes things the way they are."

But if Beth's free spirit could not be bought with money, her friendship was given freely and without stint. She it was who suggested one day when Anna shyly asked her advice about buying some new clothes that Anna might like to be introduced to Arabella Dawson. "If she wants to she'll do wonders for you. Mind you if she doesn't like you you'll get nothing from her. You think *I'm* independent?" Beth rolled her eyes. "Friend Arabella is out on her own. She had a husband once. Jut upped and walked out on him. Now she's involved with the Suffragist movement — the Pankhursts and all, you know? She'll lecture you till you're blue."

"What exactly does she do?"

Beth shrugged and grinned. "Exactly what she likes. But when she isn't heckling politicians or holding meetings she is — mainly — a stage designer. She dresses a few people privately as well — I often make the clothes up — but mostly it's stage stuff. Ballet, opera —"

"How fascinating!"

"It would be if she'd give herself half a chance!" Beth bit through a thread, grimaced. "She's brilliant. But she's an idiot. If it comes to a choice between a paying job and addressing half a dozen down-at-heel mill girls in Manchester, the mill girls win every time. And you can only let people down just so often. Arabella has —" she pulled a funny, wry face "— a very strong mind."

Anna laughed with her, a little nervously. "Then perhaps we'd better not bother? I can't see someone like that wanting anything to do with me."

Beth put down the work she was holding and straightened, her face serious. "Anna, Anna, Anna!"

Anna said nothing.

"You really do need taking in hand, don't you?" Beth said. And she still was not smiling.

"Stand still." Arabella Dawson's every word was brusque. She was tall, thin, angular, her features sharp and uncompromising. Yet her presence was undeniable, her poise and style something that Anna could only helplessly admire. She did as she was bid and stood still. A bony finger lifted her chin roughly. Blue, piercing eyes studied her face dispassionately. She felt blood rising in her cheeks.

"Yes. That's what you need. A bit of colour. Turn round."

Bemused, half-resentful, Anna turned. Beth was sitting cross-legged upon the bed, a cat in her lap, her laughter stifled and her eyes hilarious.

"You aren't standing up straight. Here." Arabella grabbed a heavy book and balanced it on the astonished Anna's head. "Walk to the door and back. Right. And again. Can't you feel it? You're two full inches taller. Can't abide a woman who creeps around like a mouse. Beth — where's that blue?"

"Behind you."

Arabella turned, picked up the bolt of blue silk, unrolled it with a smooth, flamboyant gesture so that it glimmered like sapphires in the light. She lifted it, looked consideringly at poor Anna who still stood embarrassedly with the book poised precariously upon her head. "Sit down," ordered Arabella.

Anna put a hand up to take the book from her head. "No, no, no! Book and all. Sit down. That's it. Can't you feel the difference? The world, my dear, is out there —" she swept an arm, almost knocking a cup and saucer from the table "— if you want to see it, and more importantly if you would have it see you — you have to keep your head up!"

Anna all at once had had enough of being spoken to like a recalcitrant child. "Yes," she said, "I expect you're right," and composedly and determinedly took the book off her head. Unexpectedly she caught a gleam of amusement in the other woman's eye; and she was aware that despite her feeble gesture of defiance her back had remained straight and her chin up. She laughed.

Arabella smiled a spare, satisfied smile. "Blue and green,"

she said. "Let's see what we can do with that."

When Anna arrived home, a little later than usual, the odd exhilaration of the afternoon still with her it was to find Joss, unusually, already in the house.

He did not turn from the window from which he had evidently watched her arrival. "Where have you been?"

"To see Beth. I met a friend of hers. A quite extraordinary young woman. A Suffragist of all things. Passionately political. She lectured me all afternoon on the rights of women. Or rather the lack of them. Did you know —" Anna stopped, struck suddenly by his stance. "Joss? Is something wrong?"

He turned. His face was set, his mouth a grim line. "It's Boris." The words were flat.

She stared at him, white suddenly to the lips. "Boris? Oh, Joss — no!"

He moved a hand in a sharp little negative gesture. "Not dead."

Her heart resumed its beating. "Thank God for that. But — what then?"

For one moment pain flickered upon the impassive face. "He's lost an arm. His right arm."

Anna's hand was at her mouth. "Oh, God."

For a fraction of a second his head went down, his eyes closed. She was across the room in a flash, catching his hand in hers. Still figures caught in the web of light that streamed through the window they remained so, silently, for a full minute.

"He's coming home?" Anna asked at last.

Joss, entirely in control of himself again, lifted his head and nodded. "Yes. He'll be here quite soon as a matter of fact. The letter was — delayed."

Anna nodded. Who could blame Boris for communicating such news at the last possible moment? "I'm sorry," she said, helplessly; in her mind as clearly as it had been yesterday was the picture of two young, shabby figures as they walked across the lawn at a little girl's birthday party. "Poor Boris."

"They'll be home in a week or so —"

"They? Why of course, I had quite forgotten — his family."

"They're hoping to stay with your father until they can find somewhere of their own to live."

"I'm sure that will be all right. Papa will be pleased. It'll be company for him." Anna turned away. "Poor Boris," she said again, softly.

"Anna?" The question in his voice stopped her. She turned back. He put a finger to her chin and turned her face to the light. "What have you been doing to yourself?"

She smiled, pleased that he had noticed. "Arabella — the girl I was talking about — did my hair for me. Do you like it?"

"It's very becoming." His expression had not changed.

"She's — she's designing some clothes for me. Something — a little different —" Anna stopped at his frown.

His hand dropped. "That sounds very expensive."

She suppressed a twinge of irritation. She could not for the life of her understand why he should act as if they were paupers. What did he do with their money? For what was he saving it? "No. As a matter of fact it isn't. She's a friend of Beth's. She only works for people she — well, likes or is interested in. I can easily afford what she's charging from the money that I've earned from —" she stopped suddenly, flushing "— that is, of course, if you agree? If you don't think the money better spent elsewhere?"

He turned from her abruptly. "The money that is yours you must do with as you think best. I want none of it for my purposes."

The door closed behind him. She stared at it, all the exhilaration of the exciting afternoon drained from her, and not simply by the news about Boris. "I want none of it —"

What, she wondered bleakly, did he want? From her or from anyone else?

When she found out it was to both their cost.

CHAPTER TWELVE

Mafeking Night in London, the eighteenth of May 1900, and never had there been such a spontaneously jubilant night of celebration. After two hundred and seventeen days of siege the garrison of Mafeking was relieved and when the news was received London went wild. The hansom in which Joss and Anna were trying to make their way to Bayswater was held up again and again by the rejoicing crowd.

"Ma-fe-king! Ma-fe-king!" There had been so little to celebrate during the first months of the war: now here at last the people sensed the turning of the tide and were openly exultant.

"God bless Baden-Powell!" A man leaned through the carriage window and, grinning, thrust a small Union Jack into Anna's hand.

Laughing she accepted it. "God bless him!"

Joss sat beside her, his head turned from her as he looked out of the window.

"I've never seen anything like it!" Anna said excitedly, clutching the little flag, and leaning to the window. A man toasted the passing cab with a bottle, wiped the neck with his sleeve and drank deeply. "Mafeking!" he roared then, waving the bottle. Laughing, Anna saluted him with her flag. "Do you think everyone in London has come out into the streets?"

Joss did not reply.

She turned. "Joss?"

His face was blank. "I'm sorry? I was thinking of something else."

"I said — oh, never mind. It doesn't matter." She smiled, her gaiety now a little forced. "Though I do think you might try to listen to at least half of what I say. You seem to have been in a dream all afternoon. Is anything wrong?"

"No. Nothing's wrong." He turned back to the window.

Anna sighed, absently smoothed the blue silk folds of her skirt. She had taken a very great deal of trouble about her appearance tonight, the evening of the celebration dinner that her father was giving to welcome Boris and his wife home. Beth had managed to finish for the occasion the outfit that Arabella had designed especially for Anna, and the end result, Anna knew, could not have been bettered in her wildest dreams. Arabella had cleverly combined the conventional with the exotic to produce an ensemble that was outstanding without being outrageous. The colour combination of the peacock blue and softest green flattered Anna's pale colouring and light eyes. The pastel green blouse was loose, the sleeves flowing, the exquisite embroidery exactly matching the striking blue of the shimmering skirt. The shawl which kept the chill spring air from her shoulders was of shot silk in the same combination of colours, its silken fringe almost a foot long, upon it embroidered in silver Anna's favourite dragonflies. A jewelled dragonfly of her own design glimmered in her softly-coiled hair. The faint blush of colour on her cheeks daringly owed a little less to nature than she would have cared openly to admit. She knew beyond doubt that she looked more attractive than she ever had in her life before.

And Joss had said not a word.

He had come home late, held up he said by the celebrating crowds, and had hurried straight upstairs to change. Anna, dressed for hours, had waited in the parlour, moving restlessly about the room, anticipation and excitement churning in her stomach. The electric jubilation in the air at the long-awaited news of victory combined with her own anticipation to make her tremble like an excited child. Several times she stopped her restless wanderings to peer anxiously into the mirror, tweaking a whisp of hair here, re-arranging the set of the shawl, fussing with the neck of the blouse — then Joss had hurried into the room, dapper and handsome in his dinner suit. He had stopped short, looking at her. She had waited, breath held. Then, "We'd better go," he had said. "Half of London's on the move and the roads are jam-packed." She had been so disappointed she could hardly speak. Remembering it now some of her excitement seeped from her. She sat in silence, the little flag still upon her lap. The hansom lurched to a stop, the driver yelled something and they started slowly off again. A noisy crowd on the pavement were singing. She pitched her voice against the din. "How was Boris when you saw him this morning?"

"As always." He half-shrugged and his expression softened. "Laughing."

She nodded. "I suppose we shouldn't be surprised that he's taken it so well. I do admire him."

"Yes."

"And Louisa. I was so afraid — well, we didn't know what she was going to be like did we? We might have known that Boris would have married a winner."

He raised one sardonic eyebrow. "It's a shame that everyone in the family doesn't think so."

"Oh, take no notice of Alex and Alice. Anything less than a Lord's daughter might as well be a washerwoman as far as they're concerned, snobs that they are. I'm surprised they talk to us. Sometimes," she added a little sourly and only half joking, "I wish they wouldn't."

Joss, unexpectedly, laughed at that, a quiet unforced chuckle of amusement. Anna smiled, pleased. Joss's eyes remained on her. "I don't believe that I told you how very pretty you look this evening."

She stared at him. "No. You didn't."

He seemed for a moment to be struggling for words. "Anna —"

"Yes?"

"'Ere we are, at last, Guv. Cor blimey, what a night, eh?" The cab driver's beaming face appeared in the opening above them.

Anna, accepting Joss's outstretched hand with good grace, swallowed her exasperation at the ill-timing of life and braced herself for the evening ahead.

Anna had been speaking the truth when she declared her real liking for Boris's wife. Louisa was a small, extremely pretty woman, forthright, practical and sharp as a razor — all attributes invaluable when dealing with her dashing, handsome and totally impractical husband. Her vowels and her quick wits betrayed about equally her East End origins that so pained Alex and Alice. Indeed, anyone more different from Alex's well-bred wife would have been hard to find, and Alice for one was at no pains to disguise the fact. Boris, whose cheerfully courageous acceptance of his own mutilation had won the admiration of all of them, obviously adored Louisa. He had, upon first introducing her to Anna and Joss, described her easily and with no bitterness as 'my right arm'. Together they made an attractive and touching pair, and Anna had made no secret of her delighted approval of her new sister-in-law. As she entered her father's drawing room now Louisa waved cheerfully from where she stood by the fireplace talking to an attentive Michael. Anna waved back.

"Anna, my dear — how perfectly lovely you look —" Her father hurried to her, beaming, kissed her cheeks. Over his shoulder Anna saw with a small, unworthy but entirely enjoyable feeling of satisfaction the look, quickly suppressed, of blank astonishment on Alice's face as her quick, sharp eyes took in Anna's changed appearance. Alice herself was dressed, as always, expensively and in the height of fashion, her silk dress with its draped bodice and sweeping skirt decorated a little fussily with chiffon frills and bows, a small cream satin cape edged with sable about her slim shoulders. At her neck and in her hair she wore pearls. Her eyes uncharitable, she gestured graciously, inviting Anna to join her. Anna took the glass of sherry that a servant offered upon a tray and made her way across the room, pausing to greet other members of the family and guests on the way, enjoying to the full their expressed admiration of her changed appearance. She finally joined Alice, Alex and Obadiah Smithson in time to hear Alex say " — best damned army in the world and I don't care who hears me say so. It may take time to rouse the old British Lion — but when he's roused, just watch the monkeys run, eh?"

Alice, whose sharp eyes had not left Anna since she had entered the room affected a look of superior feminine boredom. "Anna, my dear — do come and rescue me from all this war talk! Your brother has taken us through the siege, blow by blow, at least three times since we got here —"

"Can't expect women to understand such things." Alex's face was a little red. He held an empty glass. With a brusque gesture he called a tray-carrying servant near and replaced it with a full one.

"Possibly not." Alice's voice was tart, her eyes repressive. "All the more reason I should think, to change the subject. Tell Anna about the work you've been supervising at Bissetts —"

It was not lost upon Anna that her sister-in-law had studiously avoided mention of the peacock-and-green outfit. She suppressed a smile, letting Alex's voice drone on, half-lost in the murmur of general conversation as he spoke of stabling and conservatories and replanted parkland and the small fortune it cost to renovate these country houses.

From across the room Louisa's eyes were drolly sympathetic.

"— and what's all this Papa tells me about your thinking of exhibiting in the summer?" With a jolt she realized that her brother had changed the subject.

She jumped. "I'm sorry?"

"Exhibiting." Alex's voice was rather more than faintly disapproving. "You surely aren't serious?"

"As a matter of fact I'm very serious indeed." The words were short. "The exhibition is next month. I've had a silver inkstand accepted, and a couple of pieces of jewellery. I'm also designing a silver frame for something that Beth's doing." Despite the irritant of his patent and patronizing disapproval, she kept her voice bright. Beside her she was aware of Alice, unusually quiet, her eyes still taking in every detail of Anna's appearance. Anna resisted the strong temptation to offer to turn around so that her sister-in-law could make a more thorough inspection, and kept her attention upon her brother.

He cleared his throat. "Well — do you think it — quite the thing?"

She half-laughed, exasperated. "Oh, Alex — what can you mean? Of course it's 'quite the thing'! I'm not thinking of exhibiting on a market stall in Whitechapel, you know! The Arts and Crafts Exhibition Society is an extremely prestigious organization. It's a privilege to be exhibited by them."

"Really."

"Yes. Really." Anna's tone was short.

Across the room Joss, Boris and Josef stood talking. Michael and Louisa were still engaged in their animated conversation beside the big marble fireplace. Louisa gurgled with sudden laughter, and finding herself attracting smiling glances she blushed a little and ducked her head. Only Anna noticed the tightening of Alice's lips as Alex's wife in her own inimitably autocratic way cut across the conversation to ask bluntly, "What do you think of Boris's wife?"

"I like her very much." Anna's voice was utterly uncompromising, the words as near a challenge as good manners would allow. Her eyes strayed again to her husband and her father. Joss was talking rapidly and earnestly. Her father, she thought suddenly, looked a little worried as he listened.

The pause that followed her words to Alice was, as she had intended it to be, undeniably awkward. The glance that Alice threw her husband was graphic as words. Anna, suddenly, lost patience with them both. "If you'll excuse me," she said, coolly.

"Anna, darling! You're looking absolutely spiffing! You old dark horse!" Michael kissed her warmly as she joined them, and Louisa smiled.

Anna laughed, her incipient bad humour evaporating. "Thank you."

Louisa turned to Michael. "Michael, you really mustn't let me keep you all to myself, you know — there must be ever so many people that you want to talk to."

He grinned happily, cocked a cheeky blond head. "Oh, I don't know —" He lifted a long finger, wagged it at Louisa, "You wouldn't be trying to get rid of me, would you?"

"Would I do that?"

He grinned, shook his head at Anna, "Cut you to the heart these women —" he said, sorrowfully, and wandered cheerfully off.

Louisa laughed. "He's such a dear. But your sister-in-law has been watching us like daggers for the past ten minutes. I thought perhaps —"

Anna pulled an unladylike face. Her third glass of sherry and the knowledge that she was drawing, for the first time in her life, admiring glances from every corner of the room, had conspired to produce a happy glow that blurred discretion. "Don't worry about her. If you're going to worry about what Alice thinks you'll make your life a misery for nothing."

"P'raps. But I really don't want to get off on the wrong foot —"

Anna sensed suddenly the insecurity behind the bright smile. "It must be awfully difficult for you," she said gently, "being thrown in at the deep end like this — I mean you couldn't have expected —" She stopped, awkwardly.

Louisa smiled. "No. We didn't expect. But here we are, and here we'll stay, I reckon. I just —" her eyes flickered to Alice and back again "— just don't want to step on anyone's toes that's all."

Impulsively Anna reached a hand to her. "Of course you won't." She pulled a funny little face. "No one that matters anyway! And if you do — don't worry about it. And if there's anything I can do to help — to make things easier for you —"

"That's kind. In fact — there is something — that you could tell me."

"Of course."

Louisa fiddled with the finely twisted stem of her empty glass. "It's going to sound daft, I know — but I never know when Boris is kidding me — and you just can't get him to be serious — and — well, I didn't like to ask anyone else —"

Anna waited.

"Is it — is it true that his father was a — duke or something?" She lifted her head, her pretty face half-defiant, obviously expecting Anna to laugh.

"A count," Anna said.

"Ah." She considered this for a moment. "And now — your husband, Joss —"

"Yes. He's a count too, I'm afraid." On Anna's face was an expression of half-comic wry apology. "And before you ask, that makes me —"

"A Russian countess," supplied Louisa solemnly. "Blimey. Sergeant-Major Bentall's little girl's gone up in the world, hasn't she? Hobnobbing with countesses and things?"

"Oh, please don't —" Anna stopped, catching the twinkle in the bright eyes. She grinned happily.

Louisa rolled her eyes. "The kids'll never believe it. A countess for an aunt! Wait till I tell them!"

"I'm looking forward to meeting them."

"How much?"

Anna looked a question.

Louisa stood her glass upon the mantelshelf. "I promised Sophie I'd pop in about now, just to check they were all right. Want to come?"

"Nothing I'd like better." Over Louisa's shoulder Anna caught Alice's cold eyes upon her. Mischievously she sent her her sweetest smile. "I'll just tell Papa and Joss where we're going."

She approached the three men, Joss, Josef and Boris, quietly. None of them noticed her coming. Joss was speaking, Josef and Boris both listening intently. Boris stood easily, the cruelly empty sleeve tucked into his pocket, nothing in his stance encouraging sentiment or sympathy. Anna watched him for a moment. He caught her eye and smiled a little.

"— always utterly unpredictable in time of war," Joss was saying. "Consolidated are about to drop like a stone, or so I hear. Yet — strictly between ourselves — the new S.A. Mines look to be set to shoot up. And of course with today's news and rumours of peace —" He stopped suddenly and looked sharply at Josef. "Josef — before we eat — might I take advantage of your new toy? I've just remembered that I shall be busy all day tomorrow — there's someone I should like to contact."

Josef seemed to shake himself from some abstraction. "My new — oh, the telephone. Yes, of course."

Anna laid a hand upon her father's arm. "Louisa and I should like to pop upstairs and take a peek at the children. Have we time? Papa," her voice changed a little, in some consternation, "are you all right?"

He regained his breath, forced a smile. "Yes, my dear. Of course I am. By all means visit the girls. We have five minutes to the dinner gong."

Upstairs on the nursery floor the sounds of the party could still be faintly heard. Anna paused for a moment, remembering. Then they entered the night nursery and were engulfed in a breathless flood of excited words.

"Have you seen the fireworks? Aren't they wonderful? Is it eight o'clock yet? Isn't Grandpa clever to give Daddy a party on a night when there are fireworks? Did he know there would be?

can you hear the people singing? Are you going to sing? Grandpa has a piano and he says I may learn to play it. Doesn't he, Mama? I can sing, too —" Sophie, bright and pretty as her mother and woefully over-excited opened her mouth. Her mother shut it for her with a small spread hand.

"No, thank you dear. Your little sister is asleep."

"She's always asleep. Singing doesn't wake her."

"Well, don't let's take the chance, eh? Come on — say hello to this nice new aunty and then snuggle down to sleep like a good girl."

"Hello," Sophie said.

"Hello."

The child lifted a small, soft face and Anna kissed her rosy cheek. Sophie held out a tattered rag doll. "Say hello to Podge."

"Hello, Podge."

The little girl beamed. "Can I have some blancmange?" she asked, beguilingly.

Louisa came to the rescue. "No you certainly may not." From downstairs, faint against the continuing sounds of festival from outside came the sound of the dinner gong. "Off you go to sleep!" She tucked the child in then followed the smiling Anna out of the room. "She can be an absolute terror! Boris says she ought to go on the stage. I don't know where she gets it —" She stopped as from behind the closed door a high little voice called.

"Mummy?"

"Yes?"

"Is Daddy all right?"

"Of course."

"Does his poor arm hurt him?"

Louisa's hesitation was fractional. "Of course not." She did not look at Anna, and her smile had faded.

"Are you sure?"

"Of course I'm sure." Louisa's reply was much too quick, and if the child did not notice it Anna did.

"Oh, good. Will he come to see me?"

"No, Sophie, he won't. He's busy. Now — be a good girl and go to sleep. Good night. God bless."

"Good night." There was a moment's silence. Louisa started to creep away from the door.

A small, extremely piercing voice was raised in song. "Baa, baa, black sheep —"

"Oh, Lord!" Louisa put a hand to her head in mock despair. "I'll have to get her settled down or we'll get no peace all night. You go on. I'll be down in a minute."

Anna smiled and started alone, quietly down the carpeted stairs. How marvellous that Boris should have — she stopped. Beneath her in the hall her father stood outside the half-open study door. Something in his attitude, a furtive, listening stance, took her attention sharply. She could hear Joss's voice echoing faintly up the stairwell "— yes, that's right. All we can lay our hands on, before the news gets out and the rush starts —" Her husband was speaking on the telephone. And Papa — Anna's heart took up a slow, disturbing beat — Papa was listening. Eavesdropping. She stood for what seemed an endless moment, staring, trying — and failing — not to believe the evidence of her own eyes.

Above her a door closed noisily. "Shut up and go to sleep," Louisa ordered in a peremptory fashion that could only have come directly from Sergeant Major Bentall.

In the hall below, Josef heard. He jerked his head, guiltily, looked up. Anna shrank into the shadows.

"Anna — are you there?" Louisa ran lightly down the stairs. Anna smiled very brightly, held out her hand to the other girl.

When she looked down into the hall her father had gone.

Anna was never able to decide whether Alice Rose's snubbing of Louisa Anatov that evening at the dinner table was a calculated attempt on Alice's part to establish once and for all what she saw as her own natural superiority over the other girl or if it were sheer mischief provoked by Louisa's bright and burgeoning self-confidence, which Alice undoubtedly took as a personal affront. That a newly created baronet's daughter should be asked to rub shoulders with the offspring of a Sergeant Major from Bow was bad enough; that that young woman should be bold enough to attract attention to herself was clearly too much. Whatever the reason, however no one could be in any doubt that the small unfortunate incident paved the way for what followed.

insult so blatantly offered had passed.

Anna watched her, willing her to look up so that she could offer at least the moral support of a sympathetic smile, but the other girl sat as if struck, head bowed, unmoving.

"Alexis, darling," Alice was sparkling, "do tell everyone about that *awful* little man who came to do the drains at Bissetts —"

Anna leaned across the table. "Lou?" It was the first time she had used the diminutive that she had heard only Boris use.

Louisa lifted her head. Her eyes were unfocused and bright with mortification.

Anna could think of no words that would not simply aggravate the hurt. "Have some mustard sauce," she said with a subversively bright smile. "It's much nicer than the onion. Mrs Acton calls it 'her special'." She was rewarded with at least the shadow of a smile.

Beyond the heavy, drawn curtains London revelled still. Beside Anna, Boris unobtrusively leaned his left elbow upon the table and wrapped his forearm across his body. Anna was reminded suddenly of Sophie's concern for her father. She leaned to him. "Does it hurt?" she asked, with direct sympathy.

He shook his head in an automatic negative. "The shoulder? No."

She persevered. "But —"

He half-laughed. "You won't believe me."

"Try."

"The arm. The hand. They hurt." He saw the look she could not suppress, and laughed wryly. "Sounds absurd, doesn't it?"

"You mean — the arm and hand that you don't have — actually hurt?"

"Just that. Hurt. And itch like the devil. It's the nerves, so the surgeon said. There's nothing to be done —" His eyes, watchful and worried, were upon his wife's subdued face. Every now and again they flicked briefly to the end of the table, where Alice held court.

"I'm sorry," Anna said.

He shook his head, smiling.

"Will it ever get any better?"

"The doctor said —"

Alex's voice from further down the table lifted suddenly and drowned what he was about to say. "— and good riddance! Hang the lot of 'em, I say. In front of their wives if necessary. P'raps that'd teach 'em — damned bunch of rebellious Dutchmen!"

In the brief moment's silence that followed Boris turned and surveyed the other man, a dangerous gleam of dislike in his eyes. "It's been done," he said, quietly. "And I'm sure you'll be surprised to know that the effect was not a salutary one. For every man we hanged another picked up his gun and mounted his pony. For every farm we burned a woman urged her son to fight us —"

Alex, a little red-faced, waved his dessert spoon belligerently in the air. "So we hang every last one and burn every last farm. See what they make of that!"

"You think that's the way to make war?" Boris's voice was still quiet. Louisa glanced at him, sharply and with concern in her eyes.

"Of course it isn't — but whose fault's that? Who started the damned war? Who didn't have the decency to stand and fight? Who adopted the damned nigger tactics of hitting and running — of shooting from ambush?"

Anna saw the look of pain that flickered upon her father's face. "Alex — for Heaven's sake —"

But Alex had the bit between his teeth and was not to be stopped. Was he not simply repeating the views that had received such admiration, approbation at his club just last week? "If a bunch of bigoted, bull-headed foreigners think they can get away with ignoring the decent, civilized rules of war —"

Boris shifted in his chair, shook his head in clear disbelief at what he was hearing.

"— then they'll damned well have to take the consequences and not scream 'foul' if our own boys step over the boundaries a bit."

Louisa's faced paled. She glanced at her husband, opened her mouth. Shut it again.

Anna, disturbed, said, "Alex — really — I don't think —"

"The damned cowards need to be taught a lesson."

Boris shook his head. He was making an obvious and valiant

attempt to keep his temper. "You're wrong, Alex. Bigoted, yes. Stiff-necked. Pig-headed. But cowardly? No. No one who had been in South Africa would call the Boers cowardly."

The pinprick did not even scratch Alex's thick skin. "What else would you call them? They snap and run like curs. Why don't they stand and fight like men?"

"Because they are not an army. They are not professional soldiers, drilled and regimented. They are individuals. Brave, obstinate individuals who are defending their homes —"

"Defending their homes? Defending their homes against whom? I'll tell you — against the properly constituted authority that —"

"Oh, for God's sake, Alex!" Boris's restraint snapped. "You don't really believe that — that nonsense?" He leaned across the table. "What do you and those armchair soldiers you spend so much time with at your club think this war is about?"

Alex opened his mouth.

Boris's one hand crashed down on to the table so that the silver jumped and rattled. "I'll tell you. Greed. Pure and simple. It's about gold. It's about diamonds. Don't be fooled by all this talk of national pride, of honour and glory. There's precious little honour in what's going on in South Africa. And no glory at all. The Boers are a people for whom, as individuals, I have very little sympathy. Their religion is harsh and humourless, they treat the natives worse — much worse — than they treat their dogs. But it cannot be denied that they are a people who have fought a living from a hard a hostile land for years, only to find that despite their efforts to avoid confrontation and the arrogance of British rule that land is being arbitrarily taken from them because of the riches that have been discovered beneath it —"

"Boris —" Louisa's voice was miserable.

"Are you saying they're *right*?" Alex was outraged.

Boris leaned back. He looked suddenly tired. "Right? Who knows who's right? What right have we to be there? What right have they to be there? Perhaps everyone's right. Perhaps no one is. But one thing's certain — it is always the innocent that suffer most, and to turn angry men loose upon a stubborn civilian population is no way to fight a war."

"What are you suggesting?" Alex's voice was cold. "Are you inferring that our men are in any way acting improperly towards the civilian population?"

Boris looked at him for a long moment. "Yes, Alex, I am. I am suggesting that to send men out to burn the roofs over the heads of the families of the men that are away is acting improperly. I'm suggesting that in such circumstances incidents happen of which no nation could be proud."

"It seems to me, Boris," Alex snapped, contempt in his voice, "that you lost more than your arm in South Africa."

"Alex!"

Boris, pale to the lips, lifted his head, but said nothing. Into Louisa's face, slowly, rose the bright blood of anger.

"Alex — that's enough," Josef said.

"No," Alex said, stiffly, "I'm sorry, father, to distress you; but I've had enough of listening to Boris's treasonable views. Are we not allowed to question what he says? Must we remain still and hear him denigrate our country and its fighting men?"

"Boris did not start this conversation." It was Joss, speaking for the first time, his eyes sharp and hard upon Alex's face. "He did not force his views upon you."

Alice, delicately, eyes lowered, nibbled at a tiny spoonful of dessert. She was the only one still eating.

"It's a damned bad show," Alex said heavily, "when a man can sit at the table of the house that's lost a son to this war and talk treasonably and cowardly rubbish and not be contradicted —"

"For God's sake, Alex, everyone doesn't have to agree with you," Anna's irritation at her brother was clear in the words.

Louisa, very slowly, stood up, her eyes fixed upon Alex. "What's the matter with you?" she asked quietly, her voice shaking. "Are you really as stupid as you sound? Do you really believe that you know better than everyone else about everything? Can you really be so self-centred? So blind? What do you know? Have you been there? Have you seen what's happening? When your fine soldiers march to burn a farm that is occupied only by women and children, what do you think they do? Tip their hats and ask them nicely to leave? A handful of men has held to ransom these past few months the greatest army the world has seen in centuries. How do you think that army reacts to that now it is no longer losing? Many of them are bent upon vengeance — and no one is trying particularly hard to stop them." She paused. Alex was looking at her in utter astonishment, as if some inanimate object had suddenly given offensive tongue. "Do you want to know how Boris lost his arm?" she asked, quietly.

"Louisa, no. Stop it." Boris reached his hand to her. She did not look at him.

For a moment, uncertain silence reigned.

Then, "Tell us," Alice said, very softly, her spoon poised an inch from her mouth. "Tell us how Boris lost his arm."

Anna could have killed her, cheerfully, there and then.

Louisa's chin went up. "He lost it defending a Boer woman and her baby against a bunch of drunken Highlanders. Their officer was puking in a ditch. Two kids had already been cut to pieces in front of their mother. The woman had been raped. She'd hidden the baby in a barn. The soldiers had just found it when Boris came up with them. They were making her —" For the first time she looked at her husband, and at the sight of his bone-white face her voice lost its strength and faltered to a stop as tears filled her eyes. "I'm proud of him," she said. "I don't care what any of you say, I'm so proud of him." She sat down suddenly and buried her face in her hands.

"James was not like that," Josef said, very clearly and precisely, looking at no one.

"Of course he wasn't! Most of them are not." Boris's voice was raw. "Uncle Josef, no one would suggest —"

"I should damned well think not!" Alex snapped, glaring belligerently at Boris.

Boris stood up, and awkwardly with his one hand shifted his chair back from the table. "I think it best perhaps if I leave."

Alex, embarrassed at last, grunted. Alice applied herself demurely to her plate.

"Boris, please — there's no need —" Josef was close to tears.

But Louisa was there now standing beside her husband, her hand upon his left arm, her chin high. In deepest silence they left the room.

"That beastly Alice engineered the whole thing! Did you *see*? Oh, what an *odious* woman she is!" Anna stormed about the bedroom, the temper she had been fighting to control finally defeating her. "The way she egged Alex on! And after snubbing poor Louisa like that! I should truly like to wring her neck like a chicken's!" She flung her shawl upon a chair, kicked off her pale satin slippers with such force that one of them somersaulted in the air and landed on the bed. "I'll never speak to her again. I swear, I won't! Oh, wretched thing!" She was fiddling furiously with the buttons at the back of her blouse, "Joss — would you help me? My fingers are all thumbs."

Joss, having already methodically discarded his own clothes and put them neatly away, had been seated upon the bed in his dressing gown watching her. His own anger at Alice's bad manners and Alex's treatment of Boris had been tempered by ten minutes of quiet talk with his brother before they had left the house that evening.

"Boris doesn't want that," he said now, walking to her and with surprising gentleness disengaging her fidgeting fingers from the offending buttons. "He said it particularly. He doesn't want a rift in the family. People taking sides. Stand still, now. There."

"But it was unforgivable!" Anna began to wriggle out of the blouse.

"Perhaps."

She became aware suddenly that, his small task done, he had remained there behind her, his hands lightly upon her shoulders. She stood absolutely still, something more now than righteous anger making her heart thump. In the mirror of the dressing table she could see his face; dark, intent, strangely tender. She watched as gently he lifted his hands and unpinned the jewelled insect from her hair. Then one by one, inexpertly, he removed the pins that secured the coils. She was trembling a little. He leaned his face upon her loosened hair and murmured something.

She shook her head a little, sucking her lip. "You'll have to translate," and turned into his arms. They stood so for a moment before she felt his body harden against hers, and anger and distress forgotten for the moment she lifted her lips to him.

Always he could trigger in her that surge of dark almost destructive excitement. The silken skirt slid, whispering, to the floor, and he laughed softly, reaching for her mouth again, his teeth sharp, his hands strong.

Some time later she lay, staring into darkness, his breathing soft and even beside her. Small waves of excitement lifted and ebbed still in her aroused body. She reached a hand to touch his hair, and he moved a little in his sleep. Would she ever truly come to know this strange, unpredictable man in whom cruelty and callousness seemed inextricably mixed with a tenderness and vulnerability that defeated her will and enslaved her heart?

Outside the window a late reveller staggered past, singing. Anna smiled into the darkness, content, and slept.

The exhibition in which Anna took part was an enormous success and for her something of a personal triumph. Her work was noted and discussed with enthusiasm, and she found herself to her own astonishment the centre of some very flattering attention. So sheltered had she been in the comparatively small world of her father's workshop that it had never occurred to her that the wider world of artists and of craftsmen might be interested in her work. The biggest surprise of all, however, came upon the last day, when she had accompanied Beth, who had also done well and gained several commissions, to the exhibition rooms to take a last look at some of the lovely and inspiring pieces. Anna was inspecting a fascinatingly beautiful piece of stained glass when Beth bounced up to her. "Mr Spencer's looking for you. He's got someone with him who wants to meet you. Awfully impressive gentleman." She rolled her eyes irrepressibly.

"Oh?"

"A Russian no less. And a prince to boot. Aren't they all?" She waved an airy hand. "Shuvoski or Shuveski or some such —"

Anna stared. "Shuvenski? Prince Shuvenski? Surely not?"

"You know him?"

"Why no — but the name — Papa once cut and polished a wonderful diamond that was bought by a family of that name. But — surely — it can't be the same man?"

Beth grinned. "Only one way to find out —" She waved a hand in the direction from which she had come.

Prince Vassili Shuvenski was a man of distinguished middle age, moustachioed, handsome, autocratic, and with the assurance of wealth and position charmingly disguised by perfect and attractive good manners. To Anna's astonishment, she soon discovered that he knew a good deal more about her than she did about him, and he openly admitted to having inspected not only her pieces in the exhibition but many examples of her work that were in private hands. "I hope you are not offended." His English accent was impeccable, better in fact, she noticed with wry amusement, then either her husband's or her father's. "I intended of course to contact your father and introduce myself formally, but when Mr Spencer informed me that you were here — well, it seemed absurd not to take advantage of a fortuitous situation. May I offer my congratulations. Your work is exquisite."

Anna blushed with pleasure at the forthright compliment. "Thank you."

Shuvenski watched her in pensive silence for a moment, one long finger stroking his luxuriant moustache. "I am right, am I not, in believing you to be the daughter of Josef Rose?"

"Yes."

"And you know of the connection that exists between our two families?"

"You mean – the stone? The diamond my father cut twenty-five years ago?"

"Exactly. It is of the stone that I wish to speak to you. And to your father, of course."

She waited.

"The stone — the Shuvenski diamond — is to be reset. I have never cared for the present piece — the Princess's tastes were —" he paused, delicately "— not my own. However, now my only son is to marry the daughter of my very good friend and as a present to my new daughter I wish a necklace designed with the stone as a centrepiece."

A strange combination of excitement and trepidation had robbed Anna of her voice. She cleared her throat. "Are you suggesting that I — that I might —" She faltered to a stop.

"Indeed I am. The thought was in my mind from the start that I should seek the advice of the man who cut the stone so finely. There are, of course, many excellent craftsmen in St Petersburg — my wife is much addicted to Monsieur Fabergé's pieces —"

"Fabergé," Anna repeated, faintly.

"— but since I was coming to London anyway, and since I had always harboured the hope that I might meet the man who created that wonderful stone, I waited. And now I am very glad that I did. There is no doubt in my mind whatever, Madame, but that Josef Rose's daughter should design the necklace," he smiled his warm, attractive smile. "Always providing of course that she is willing —"

"I — why yes! Of course! — if you really think I could. I'd be honoured. You say that you have always wanted to meet the man who cut the stone." She smiled. "I love the man dearly and have always wanted to see the stone he cut —" She paused. Somewhere in her mind a small voice spoke, when had he said it? I shouldn't like you ever to have anything to do with it. What nonsense. "Do you have the stone here in London with you?"

His eyebrows lifted, half-amused. "Why no. Of course not. The stone never leaves Russia."

She stared. "Then —"

He waited, faint surprise in his eyes.

She swallowed. You would want me to visit Russia to design the necklace?"

"But of course."

"But — I assumed the piece would be made in my father's workshop."

He spread sorrowful hands. "To my great regret, no. You must understand, Madame. The stone is worth a very great deal of money. I simply could not take the risk —"

Disappointment was sharp as pain. She shook her head. "Then I'm sorry. I don't think it will be possible. I couldn't possibly travel so far alone. My husband would never hear of it."

"Would he not accompany you? I had assumed —"

"No." The sharpness of the word raised his eyebrows again, but he did not comment. "My husband would not be able to accompany me." Anna continued more quietly, "And it would be quite impossible for me to travel alone. I'm terribly sorry."

"What a pity. What a very great pity." He picked up gloves and a silver-topped walking cane from the table, smiled the quiet smile of a man more used to getting his own way than not. "I suppose I must simply hope that you might change your mind."

"Agreed? Joss, what can you mean? You *can't* have agreed!" Anna stared in dismay at her husband. "I can't go to *Russia*! You can't have told him that I'd go — without telling me." The volatile temper bubbled in her voice. "On my own? Are you mad?"

"You won't be on your own."

She lifted her head. "You'll come?"

He moved abruptly. "No, Anna — you know I can't do that —"

"Then what do you mean, that I won't be alone?"

He meticulously re-arranged the papers on his desk. "I've asked Michael to accompany you."

She stared at him in disbelief. "You've *asked*! — Joss, what is going on? What other arrangements have you made behind my back? And *Michael*? What good would Michael be? He'd be a liability. *I'd* have to look after *him*." In her agitation, unable to keep still, she was striding back and forth in front of his desk, her hands clasped tightly before her, as if to prevent herself from some physical action, which in her present state of mind was not so far from the truth. Now she whirled on him, threw her hands up in exasperated anger. "Joss — I can't. I just can't. I'd be terrified! How would I get there?"

"By train, of course." His voice was patient. "You think I'd ask you to walk?"

"You appear," she said, dangerously quiet, "to have omitted to ask me anything."

He leaned forward. "Anna, listen to me. Don't you see how important this could be to us? It's the opportunity of a lifetime — for you, for Rose and Company. The Prince could have had anyone — literally anyone in the world — design that necklace. He has asked for you. He has the ear of the Russian Imperial family. He is related to half the royalty of Russia. If you make a good job of this —"

"— and suppose I don't? Has that even occurred to you? Suppose I make an absolute fool of myself?" A compound of anger and panic had brought her close to tears. "I've never worked with anything like the Shuvenski before! Supposing I can't —"

"Of course you can." The interruption was quiet, but emphatic.

"You don't know that. And anyway — that isn't the only thing, and you know it. Joss — how *could* you have been so high-handed about it all? Agreeing — making the arrangements — asking Michael — without telling — without *asking* me."

"Anna, do please stop shouting."

"I've every right to shout!" Nevertheless she lowered her voice, took a deep breath, watched him for a long moment. Shook her head. "I will never as long as I live understand you," she said at last, flatly. "These last weeks — we've been happy, haven't we? Really happy, perhaps for the first time since we were married. I began to feel that we were coming together at last. What was it Joss?" Her voice was bitter. "A whim? A game? 'Let's play being a good husband for a while?'" She had never spoken to him so before. He steepled his fingers, elbows on the desk, and watched her. "And now — a click of your fingers and you send me away."

"Don't be so melodramatic. I'm not sending you away." He was impatient.

She ignored him. "And what of Victoria? What of our daughter? Have you made plans for her as well?"

He did not reply. She stared at him in utter disbelief. "You have. Haven't you? *Haven't you?*"

"Mrs Lacey has kindly agreed to stay for as long as she might be needed."

There was a long silence. "Well, good," Anna said at last, very quietly. "I'm really pleased to hear that. So you'll be well looked after. And Victoria will be cared for. And I'll have nothing to worry about at all. Thank you Joss."

"Is there need for sarcasm?"

"Is there need for any of this? I had already told the Prince that I would not go to Russia. I told him — heaven help me! — that you would not allow it. What a joke! Joss — why didn't you speak to me? Why?"

He stood up. "Because it never crossed my mind that you would do anything but accept the offer." His voice was brisk. "Because I thought better of you than that you would whimper about being alone, about being afraid. Because I'm not as stupid or as insensitive as you believe me to be, and I know that the life of wife and mother is not enough for you —"

She opened her mouth. He waved a brusque, impatient hand and continued talking.

"— you talk of Victoria? How much do you see of her now? How long since you walked her yourself in the park? Chose a dress for her to wear? Oh — I'm not criticizing. We are not good parents, you and I. We never will be. We are too involved with our own lives. I ask you simply to see the truth, and not to lie to yourself." He reached into the drawer of his desk and drew out a long envelope. "I have here two first class tickets to St Petersburg. The train leaves Victoria Station next Tuesday morning. The journey will take a little over two days. You will be met on its arrival. Now. If you are afraid to take this opportunity — afraid of the challenge — say so now and we'll speak no more of it. But never repeat to me again the nonsense with which your precious Arabella fills your head. Independence, my dear Anna, is not something that anyone will hand you, prettily wrapped, upon a plate —" He extended his hand, the envelope held between two fingers.

The silence that followed his words was like a blade drawn between them.

Wordlessly then she snatched the envelope from his hand, turned on her heel and stalked from the office.

CHAPTER THIRTEEN

Her anger at her husband's high-handed action did not leave Anna through all the whirlwind preparation for the trip, though Joss himself acted as if nothing untoward had occurred. In one thing, however, Anna could find no fault; the journey agreed, nothing it seemed was too good for her and Joss's usual protestations of penury were completely forsworn. When finally she settled herself, in a state of nervous excitement and apprehension that verged upon panic, into the comfortable window seat of their reserved carriage, and the train set out from Victoria Station and steamed powerfully southward towards the Channel, she carried with her in her new and smartly matching leather suitcases everything she could possibly require for her comfort, convenience and well-being. The Prince, Joss pointed out, had made it quite clear that the Countess Anatov, whatever her husband's situation, was to consider herself an honoured guest as well as an admired artist. He had apparently failed to see that the thought filled Anna with more trepidation than she cared to admit even to herself.

"Well," Michael settled himself opposite her, grinning, "here we go, then. Next stop, St Petersburg."

She smiled back. "Hardly that."

"I say, there was a spiffing girl. Did you see her? Baby blue eyes and lots of fluffy hair. She's travelling with her mother. They're in the carriage next door." He winked and laughed at his sister's expression. "I helped them with their luggage. See what a gentleman you have for a brother? They're travelling all the way through to St P as well. Her father's something in the Embassy there. They've been home for a holiday."

Anna watched the green, familiar countryside flow past the window and tried to feel a little less than wretched. "You seem to have found out an awful lot in a short time."

He lifted one shoulder and smiled the charming, self-deprecating smile that caused too many hearts to flutter for his own good. "It's a talent," he said modestly.

To add to Anna's misery, the Channel crossing was terrible, and a prey to seasickness she spent the cheerless hours, cold and shivering at the ship's rail, whilst Michael entertained his new acquaintances, Effie Bishop and her mother, in a fair degree of warmth and comfort below. He could not, he pointed out reasonably, do anything to help his sister, and there seemed no advantage in their both being miserable.

"Lord!" Anna said to her brother as she crawled into her berth as the train left Ostend, "Can you imagine what it must be like in *winter*!" Having, however, slept the afternoon and Belgium away she regained her appetite if not her spirits and was more than ready for dinner that evening as the train sped in the failing light through the neat and busy towns and villages of Germany.

"I say — I hope you don't mind," Michael smiled his most engaging smile, "I sort of invited Effie and Mrs Bishop to dine with us. Thought it might be fun. Interesting too. They've lived in St P for three years. Thought they might sort of fill you in —"

"Do I — sort of — have any say in the matter?" Anna asked mildly, re-adjusting a row of coral beads about her neck.

"Not really." Michael stood in the doorway for a moment, watching her. "I say. That outfit. It's not half bad, you know. A bit Isadora Duncan if you ask me. Terribly *outré*. This Isabella —"

"Arabella."

"Arabella. She's worked wonders, hasn't she?"

Anna lifted exasperated eyes. "You mean like making a silk purse out of a sow's ear? Honestly, Michael — would you be so rude to anyone else?"

He grinned at her in the small mirror, dropped a quick kiss on to the top of her head from his superior height. "'Course not. What are sisters for? There's no other female in the world I can be that honest with!"

Effie Bishop and her vague and nervous mother Anna found about equally painful, but in fairness she knew that to be not entirely their fault. Within her mind she was battling a longing for safe yesterday and a sick nervousness about unknown tomorrow, and she found it hard to concentrate upon the social pleasantries of travelling acquaintanceship. But about one thing Michael was certainly right; Effie and her mother knew St Petersburg well.

"Such a pity that you won't see it in winter." Effie's remarks, accompanied by a good deal of — to Anna — irritating eyelash fluttering, were addressed almost exclusively to Michael. "Piter is *such* good fun in the winter — the balls, the parties, the troika rides — have you ever ridden in a troika? Oh, it's just *wonderful*. But in the summer — well, the place just *dies* if you ask me."

Mrs Bishop leaned close to Anna, confidentially. "The thing one finds about St Petersburg," she said, "is that it is so awfully big. Overwhelmingly so. I mean —" she fluttered ineffectual hands "— not big in area, but in scale, if you understand me. It makes one feel quite like an ant. Quite like an ant. I've never really liked it, to tell the truth."

"Oh, Mama, what nonsense!" scolded her daughter. "It's a wonderful city, you know it is! And really very friendly." She turned back to Michael. "Do you know that as a general rule, if a foreigner is invited as a guest to dinner everyone around the table — twenty or thirty guests — will spend the whole evening conversing in his language — English, French, German — isn't that so, Mama!" Mrs Bishop nodded. "And as for feeling at home — why we've even got our own English shop on the Nevsky Prospekt, did you know that? Stilton cheese, and good old English bacon —" She paused and cast a sideways, inquisitive look at Anna. "Where did you say you were staying?"

Anna had not said. "The Shuvenski Palace."

"Good Lord." The eyes this time were wide and openly impressed. "But — aren't the Shuvenskis away in the country at the moment? They have a dacha up near the Finnish border, don't they? One hears the most fascinating stories — of the Princess baking her own bread and suchlike. The Russians are the most extraordinary people — they do so love to play-act —"

"I don't know anything about that. But yes, the family are in the country. Michael and I are to stay in St Petersburg for a few days with the Prince, and then we're to join the rest of the family in the country, I believe."

"Well, well," Effie laughed gaily, "lucky you! There are a lot of people in Piter who'd give their eyeteeth to be invited to Lemorsk." She paused, then added, delicately persistent, "The Prince you said. Would that be the young Prince or the old one?"

Anna was tired of the catechism. "Prince Vassili."

"Ah." Effie rested a small pointed fingernail upon her pouted red lower lip. "And Nicolai? His son? Have you met him yet?"

"No."

Effie smiled a very small smile. "A treat you have to come."

"Effie!" Her mother was truly outraged.

Effie lifted innocent eyebrows.

"In my day young ladies would not dream of speaking of a gentleman in such terms."

Effie all but shrugged, rolled her eyes at Michael, who nearly choked on his coffee.

"He is soon to be married, I believe?" Anna asked, bored by the conversation and by the silly byplay.

"Yes. To some distant cousin or other." Effie said lightly, her eyes still on Michael. "The match was arranged when they were children." She pulled a face. "Wouldn't care for that myself. Hardly seems the start of a perfect marriage, does it? I thought people were supposed to fall in love, or something," she giggled coquettishly.

Anna turned her head to the window. A perfect marriage, she thought, bleakly — was there truly any such thing? In the window beside her she saw reflected the small, red-shaded table lamp, the glittering cutlery, the faces of the people about her. All unreal, as this journey was unreal and the place to which she was going was unreal. The train's echoing whistle screeched emptily back along the iron ribbon of track that led back to normality. To home. She stood up abruptly. "I do hope you'll excuse me. I'm very tired."

Düsseldorf, Magdeburg, Berlin, Poznan, Warsaw — where they changed trains and began the long pull northward — names on a map. And to Anna, unable to shake off that sense of unreality, they remained so. Cocooned in the comfort of the train, the stations, the cities, the changing countryside had little or no reality. She ate and slept and held conversations and the wheels beneath her gobbled the miles at terrifying speed. The train hurtled northward, through Poland, Lithuania, Latvia — and as it did the prospect of the task she had taken on assumed an aspect of threat that she could neither rationalize nor control, and her sense of being on the edge of panic increased. Somewhere ahead, in an unknown city full of strangers the Shuvenski diamond waited. Time and time again she took out her small sketch pad and sat, sometimes for as long as an hour, staring at the blank white page. And time and time again the little book was put back, untouched and unmarked. The most that she could hope was that this journey, this strange suspension of time and space between a known and an unknown world, would somehow go on forever. It came as a positive shock, therefore, when Michael looked at his watch, stood up and stretched, straightened his tie.

"Nearly there. If you don't mind, I'll pop next door. Got a couple of arrangements to make."

Nearly there. Anna sat rigid with dismay. They couldn't be nearly there. She wasn't ready to be nearly there. What in the world was she doing in this idiotic situation anyway? Why wasn't she sketching at her desk in the bedroom window at Kew, or sitting cross-legged upon Beth's bed listening to Arabella's passionate account of Mrs Pankhurst's latest speech? What had Joss been thinking of, to manoeuvre her into this corner?

The dusty countryside had given way to buildings — shacks, small houses, dirt-track streets, the occasional onion-domed church, odd to Western eyes. There were farm carts drawn by oxen or by shambling horses. The train slowed a little. Intrigued despite her own self-centred anxiety, Anna leaned to the window, rubbed away the film of her breath. For the first time real interest stirred; this after all, was the land of her father, and of her husband. The people were dark, the cast and slant of their features distinctive, their dress, to Anna's eyes, strange and outlandish; the men in skirted coats or blouses and baggy trousers and dusty boots, the women, stockily built, in voluminous skirts, aprons and colourful shawls, their hair usually covered with a bright headscarf.

"Well," Michael's voice brought her back to herself, "this is it. Piter, as Effie will insist upon calling it, awaits."

Anna stood up, patted her hair, adjusted her hat. Despite a good night's sleep and the luxury of a private toilet and washbasin she felt tired, untidy and at less than her best. She followed Michael into the corridor. The train, puffing long, thankful sighs of steam, was clattering into a vast station. Upon the platform crowds of people waited — servants, peasant women, men in bright, dashingly unfamiliar uniforms. Amidst a pandemonium of slammed doors and pushing people they stepped on to the platform. "This way," Michael said. "Hey, Porter! Drat that man — hold on a minute. I'd better see that Effie and her mother are all right."

"Michael!"

But Michael, with a brief wave was gone, back into the crowd, his bare fair head bobbing above caps and headscarves and military caps, and Anna found herself and her suitcases stranded in a stream of hurrying humanity. Blast Michael! And blast Joss for getting her into this in the first place. She'd told him what an irresponsible idiot her brother could be.

"Madame Anatov?" The voice behind her was young, and very pleasant. She turned to find herself looking into a pair of the brightest and most arresting blue eyes she had ever encountered. The young man was about her own age, tall and slightly built. His smile was warm and lit those striking eyes with laughter.

"Yes." It had been agreed in London that while it was safe to use her married name, it might be best not publicly to declare her title.

With grace and utter unselfconsciousness he bowed a little, inclining his shining brown head, the attractive smile widening. "Nicolai Shuvenski. My father asked me to meet you. The carriage is waiting. I trust the journey was not too arduous?"

She shook her head.

He snapped his fingers and two men came forward to take Anna's luggage. Nicolai Shuvenski looked around. "You are surely not alone? I understood that your brother would be travelling with you?"

To Anna's utter consternation something inexplicably strange had happened to the rhythm of her breathing in that first moment and she was having some trouble in correcting it. "I — yes — he's here somewhere. He made a friend on the train and he went back to — I'm afraid he can't always be called the most reliable of people — ah, there he is — see, the tall, fair young man —" She was gabbling dreadfully. She pressed her lips tight shut and forced her stupidly fluttering hands to stillness. God in heaven — she sounded like that awful Mrs Bishop! What had got into her?

Michael joined them, beaming. "They're all right. Someone's here from the Embassy. Hello, who's this?"

Nicolai's grin matched his own. He extended his hand. "Nicolai Shuvenski."

"Michael Rose." They shook hands.

Nicolai spoke in rapid Russian to the men who held the cases, then turned back to Anna and offered his arm. "Madame."

Gingerly she laid her gloved hand upon his sleeve, barely touching it. Yet still there was a small shock of excitement at the slight contact. She glanced up at him, and he smiled. She looked away. He led her through the crowds and handed her with careful courtesy into the splendid open carriage which awaited them outside the station. Their host saw to the stowing of their luggage, climbed into the carriage and they set off at a spanking pace through the wide, impressive streets and boulevards of the Imperial capital. Anna sat bolt upright upon her leather seat, her head turned, watching the splendid buildings. In one thing Mrs Bishop had certainly been right — the grandeur and scale of the city was overawing. The carriage, big as it was, seemed like a matchbox in the vast streets and squares, in which few people walked or drove, though the weather was clement.

"It is your first visit to our city, I believe?"

She turned her head. The blue eyes were watching her attentively. "Yes, it is."

"It's a little overwhelming at first I think — and very unlike London."

"You know London?"

"Very well."

Anna glanced around her. "It's very — grand."

He laughed. His laughter, like his voice, was warm and attractive. "A good word for it. One gets used to the scale of the place eventually, but it does take time. See — the river —" The wide, glimmering Neva flowed smooth and bright as metal in the warm sunshine, its great breadth nature's complement to the monumental palaces, public buildings and churches that lined its banks. "For many months of the year, of course, it is frozen over. Like a great frozen road through the heart of the city. Then in spring the ice breaks and the river flows again. It is one of the most spectacular sights in the world."

"I should like to see it."

"You must visit us again, and perhaps you will." His words, like her own, were the merest politeness, a pretty exchange between host and guest. Yet it seemed to Anna, as when she had touched his arm, that something warm and unspoken had passed between them, and that those eyes held more interest than the occasion warranted as he studied her face. She looked down at her clasped hands, furious with herself. The wretched journey must have unhinged her mind! A handsome face, a softly spoken word and here she was all but swooning like a schoolgirl!

"I'm very much looking forward to seeing your work. My father spoke very highly of it. And I very much liked the things he brought back from London with him. The inkstand is particularly fine."

She blushed. "Thank you."

"I was in Paris last year. I saw nothing there any better —"

She looked up, startled, shook her head, "Prince Nicolai, I —"

"Nicolai. Please. Just Nicolai."

"I think you're exaggerating just a little."

"Not at all. The jewelled insects — they're exquisite — my mother loved them."

"I'm glad."

"We have some wonderful jewellers in St Petersburg —"

"You have Monsieur Fabergé!"

"Quite. We have Monsieur Fabergé, and his work, quite rightly, is famous throughout the world. I, however, happen to share my father's view that it is a little too opulent. My tastes are simpler. An elegance of line, the —" he paused, his face serious "— the symmetry of nature. These things are true beauty, are they not?"

"Yes. I think so." Alarmingly, she was having some difficulty with her breath again. She turned to Michael, saying gaily, "Michael, do look — a pair of Sphinxes! One would think oneself in Egypt rather than Russia!"

As Anna had more than half come to suspect during the ride from the station, the Shuvenski Palace was breathtaking; an immense and spacious building with the sweeping staircase, the marble floors and columns, the glittering chandeliers that spoke of a confident and opulent age. Yet it was not, as she had certainly expected, overawing. For the size of it and the treasures it held it might have been a museum: but the great bunches of flowers that adorned the tables and the summer-empty fireplaces, the lovely Oriental rugs, the soft colours of furnishings and fabrics, the comfortable furniture, all proclaimed it the family home that it was. To Anna the most intimidating thing was the enormous number of servants. They seemed to be everywhere, resplendently uniformed, ready with positively oppressive attentiveness to anticipate her every need. She found herself installed in a suite of rooms that might have done service for a princess — indeed, she thought, gazing at the velvet-draped bed and the great, gilded mirrors — probably had. She dressed for dinner carefully — amazed to discover that every item of clothing had been removed from her trunk, sponged, pressed and hung in the enormous wardrobe or laid in the sweet-smelling drawers — and swept down the magnificent staircase, a glimmer of amusement in her eyes at her own charade of confidence when only she knew the effort it took to swallow a mouthful of food, or to answer politely the questions that were put to her across the glittering crystal and silver of the flower-decked table. She escaped as soon as she decently could, pleading a perfectly excusable tiredness and fled to the sanctuary of the enormous, wonderfully comfortable bed where she lay staring at the ornate ceiling in the long twilight, facing a confusion at whose roots undeniably lay a pair of bright, attentive eyes and a smile as warm as summer itself.

The next day, after a night of fitful sleep that was only partly due to the unfamiliarly light northern night, Anna saw at last the object of her journey, the creation of her father, the stone known now to the world as the Shuvenski Diamond. It had been taken already from its old setting and rested now in a box lined with black velvet. It was, beyond argument, the most beautiful thing she had ever seen. As she held it upon the palm of her hand she could feel Josef at her shoulder. Predictably, he had been much against her coming to Russia, and even more against her having anything to do with this stone. Was it possible, she thought, that he had forgotten its magic? If he could see it now, hold it as she held it, his fears — whatever they were — surely could not possibly withstand the sheer lustrous beauty of the thing? A beauty that he himself had created. For the first time she wondered at her father's skill, and wondered more that he had forsaken it; for since the cutting of this stone he had never to her knowledge touched his tools again. It had never until now occurred to her to question that.

"Well, my dear," Nicolai's father smiled at her across the glittering stone, "what do you think now of the Shuvenski Diamond?"

"It's wonderful." She paused, and shrugged helplessly, "And terrifying. As I knew it would be."

"Nonsense." He shook his head, patted her hand. "Don't be afraid. You know you have the skill. And such a thing, surely, speaks to you? It is fitting that you should provide the setting for the stone. Remember — your father had the courage to bring it to life — your task is not, I think, as frightening as that?"

She lifted her head. "No. Of course not."

For most of the day, absorbed, she studied the stone, alone, in an opulent room of high ceilings and tall windows that overlooked the shining river. At a desk by one of the windows she sketched, and frowned, and threw away the paper, and sketched again, drank tea, refused lunch and was startled late in the afternoon by a shadow that fell across the paper.

"We did not," Nicolai said, his face drolly serious, "intend to take you prisoner. Nor to make of you a slave. Won't you leave your labours awhile?" He smiled suddenly. "Your industry makes us all feel guilty."

She looked to where the shadows lengthened in the city.

"What's the time?"

"Five o'clock."

"*Five?*" She shook her head. "I'd no idea." She riffled the sheets of paper abstractedly.

"My father commands —" he tilted his head, smiling that warm smile "— in the politest possible way! — that you join us. Unless, he said, you are so bewitched by the stone that you prefer its company to ours."

"Oh — of course not. How very rude I must seem." Anna was flustered.

He shook his head. "No. If the truth be known we are simply jealous. How hard it is for unaccomplished men to see a talent at work so absorbed and so absorbing." He picked up a discarded piece of paper, studied it. She found herself waiting with strangely bated breath. "You have a fine hand," he said softly.

She made a small, dismissive gesture. "I came with some preconceived ideas. But they simply won't do. None of them." She picked up the box, tilted the diamond so that it caught the slanting rays of the sun. "It's like a teardrop," she said quietly.

He was at her shoulder, silent, caught as she was in the web of the stone's brilliance.

"A tear of sorrow, do you think?" he asked at last. "Or of joy?"

"I don't know." The moment was suddenly strangely intimate. Had he physically touched her it could not have been more so. She stood quite still, unable or unwilling to put a name to the emotion that his proximity brought, knowing only instinctively and with absolute certainty that he shared it. She moved, then, breaking the spell. "I won't come down just yet, if you don't mind," she said collectedly, "I'd like to work a little longer."

"You'll be down for dinner?"

"Of course." She had the strangest feeling that they were each hearing words the other was not actually speaking.

"I leave for the country tomorrow," he said.

"Oh?" Ridiculously, the thought of his going jolted her like a blow.

"My mother and sisters are expecting me. But — you are to join us, are you not? In a few days?"

"I believe so."

He moved to the window, stood with his back to her, arms stretched to either side of the frame, looking out across the city. "You'll love Lemorsk. I know you will. It isn't far. Thirty miles or so, near the Finnish border. There's a lake. And forests. Do you ride?"

"Not well, I'm afraid." She was studying his silhouette against the light.

"Then we'll walk." The pronoun was naturally and easily used. She made no comment, but watched the strong profile, lined in red-gold against the light sky. How could a stranger become so rapidly a part of one's thoughts? A part of one's being? Her love for Joss had grown with her own growing over the years. Standing here in this unfamiliar room in an unknown city she knew that if she allowed it love for this young man could strike like lightning. And be as savagely painful.

"The house is quite small," he was saying, laughter in his voice. "It's absurd really — we live like peasants. Well — what mother conceives as the way that peasants live. Which means simply putting up with about half the number of servants as we have in the city. And mother plays at housewives in the kitchen, which means that meals aren't always what they should be. But it's the most enormous fun. There are always dozens of us. And it's all wonderfully informal. Just family, and friends. We have picnics. And swim in the lake. And play silly games —" He turned, smiling. "My sisters and I and our cousins have holidayed at the dacha ever since any of us can remember. Katarina — my eldest sister — swears we revert to childhood the minute we set foot across the boundary. I think she may be right."

"And your future wife?" Anna found herself asking, very lightly, "Will she be at Lemorsk too?"

His hands dropped to his sides. "No. She is with her parents in the Crimea. She finds the north — not to her taste." His tone matched hers, but it seemed to Anna that a shadow darkened his face.

"Oh?" She picked up a pencil and spun it idly between her fingers. "And shan't you miss her very much?"

"Of course."

In the silence she stopped playing with the pencil, laid it with careful precision on the desk at exact right angles to the paper. She lifted her head. He was watching her, waiting.

"And your husband, Madame? You will miss him?"

"Of course."

He moved abruptly. "I'll leave you to your work."

She watched him to the door. Once there, he turned. "Do you know of the white nights, here in the north?"

"The light? I found it hard to sleep last night, yes."

He said no more. The tall, elegant doors clicked shut quietly behind him. Anna turned back to the desk, swept aside the paper she had used, picked up her pencil. Very quickly she worked, the pencil held loosely, her face absorbed. A ray of sunshine struck redly a tall mirror, and reflected like blood across the room. She leaned back, smoothed the paper. The diamond was to be a love-gift to a bride. She lifted the stone from its box, looked at it for a moment, then laid it gently in its place upon the design she had sketched. White gold, she would stipulate, and the only other stones, tiny, perfect, brilliant-cut diamonds for the eyes of the doves. And beneath their touching breasts and entwined necks the diamond depended, a blazing teardrop.

She knew in her heart that once the basic design was finished and enthusiastically endorsed by Prince Vassili, the craftsmen carefully instructed and the work under way she should, Michael's disappointment notwithstanding, sensibly have refused the invitation to the country and boarded the train for London.

But she did not.

Five days after her arrival in St Petersburg she did indeed board a train, but it carried her north, towards Finland with its age-old lakes and pine forests. She, Michael and Prince Vassili were met at a tiny halt in a woodland glade by a pony and trap, which delighted her. The Prince laughed. "Of course, you are right — it is from England. We bought it many years ago for the children." The little trap carried them smartly along the forest tracks, their luggage following behind at a more sedate pace in an enormous old farm waggon. The small hooves raised clouds of dust and pine needles, and the resinous scent of the trees was heady. Anna lifted her face to the sun that flickered through the tall trees and fell across their path in banded spears of light. A few days. That was all. Just a few days out of life — a once in a lifetime opportunity she would have been a fool to refuse. Hadn't Joss himself urged her to accept the opportunity to make friends of this influential family?

And all the while the little pony's hooves clipped out the name — "Ni-co-lai, Ni-co-lai."

"I say! Look at that!"

Anna followed the direction of Michael's pointing finger. Water sparkled through the trees, glittering gemstone-bright against the darkness of pine. The track narrowed and wound down to the shores of a tiny lake across which could be seen a rambling wooden house with a wide verandah.

"Lemorsk." The Prince said, his voice soft.

Many people were gathered upon the verandah to greet the new arrivals — the Princess Maria, her daughters Katarina, Elena and little Nadia, several servants and a host of small children. They were all dressed simply and colourfully in peasant style, though Anna's artist's eye noted that the embroidery upon the full-sleeved blouses and the pretty aprons was far superior to any she had seen upon a true peasant's dress, as was the quality of the material. The princess's desire to play-act was obviously tempered by her aristocratic tastes. At the sounds of arrival Nicolai and another young man came running round the corner of the house, in open-necked shirts and slacks, tennis racquets in hand. The young man was introduced as a cousin, a Grand Duke with a name which Anna did not catch but which was as long as any she had ever heard, who was called by everyone 'Mitka'.

"There are more cousins around," Nicolai waved an airy hand, "but it's best you meet them bit by bit — you'll never remember them all anyway."

"How do you do?" Mitka's English was not quite as perfect as his hosts'. He muttered something in Russian. The Princess lifted an imperious finger. "No, no, Mitka! We agreed — English only while our guests are with us. Anna and Michael do not speak our language."

"Oh, please —" Anna was embarrassed. Michael had hardly heard, he was smiling his most beguiling smile at Elena, Nicolai's middle sister. He had quite obviously already decided that language — or the lack of it — was going to be no hindrance.

The Princess waved her hand. "But of course. It is simple courtesy. And very good for the young people to speak your language. They all grow lazy in the summer! Ah — here comes the luggage. Elena — show Anna to her room, please. And Nicolai — Michael will be sharing with young Igor. I do hope you don't mind?" she asked Michael, a little anxiously. "We are rather pressed for space —" She bustled away, the very image of a prosperous farmer's wife making disposal for her weekend guests. Anna shook a bemused head.

Elena laughed. "Mama just loves it here. She was brought up in the country — her family rarely came to court. Now all winter she has to cope with protocol and society and hordes of servants, and balls and dinners and parties and politicians —" she wagged her pretty head back and forth like a small clockwork toy "— and she simply *hates* it. Here we live the simple life and the only rules and regulations — as Mama is always telling us — are those of good manners and hospitality. If your Queen came to stay Mama would install her in the attic bedroom and go off to supervise her jam! There —" They had climbed several sets of stairs and had come to a small wooden door which she threw open. It led into a tiny, charming room, white painted and with a sloping ceiling. A bunch of wild flowers graced the windowsill, the only furniture was a narrow bed, a pine washstand and a chest. "It isn't our most luxurious accommodation, I'm afraid."

"It's absolutely lovely! It truly is!"

"We hope very much you will enjoy your stay with us." The other girl smiled a flashing, attractive smile very much like her brother's.

"I'm sure I will."

Elena paused at the door. "Do you and your brother play tennis?"

"A little. Not well, I'm afraid."

The other girl's smile flashed again. "Oh, la! That's all right. None of us play well. Perhaps we could make up a foursome later, with Nico? He said earlier that he thought it would be a nice idea. I'll lend you something to play in if you haven't brought anything?"

"That — would be fun," Anna's voice was unsure.

In a swirl of brilliant material Elena left the room. Left alone Anna wandered to the window. The sky arched to blue infinity above the dark, fronded trees. The small lake gleamed in the light. Someone called in the clear, summer air, there was a splash and the sound of laughter. Someone in the house was singing, a haunting, lilting melody that rose and fell like wind in the forest. Five days. Five long days in this idyllic spot and then it would be back to St Petersburg, and thence home to London. Home. It seemed — it was — a world away. She tilted her head back, breathed the sparkling, pine-scented air. Voices still called from the lake. A group of children scampered, laughing around the side of the house and streamed into the woods.

She turned from the window, smiling, and began to unbutton the jacket of her travelling suit.

That evening after dinner the company played an acting game very like charades at which Michael with what appeared to be a roomful of young ladies to impress, excelled despite the obvious language difficulties — for with the best will in the world and for all the Princess's insistence not all the company spoke English as excellently as did the Shuvenskis.

Anna sat upon a window seat, watching, smiling, taking no part, the long, strange northern twilight haloing her head.

"Your brother is enjoying himself."

Startled, she turned and looked into the bright blue eyes she had been avoiding all evening. "Yes."

"And you?"

"I — beg your pardon?"

"You also are enjoying yourself?"

She had stayed well away from him all afternoon and evening. She smiled brightly. "Yes, thank you. Very much."

"And the design of the necklace? You are pleased with what you have done? Papa says it is charming."

"I'm glad he likes it."

He looked down at her, frowning a little. "Elena says she asked you to play tennis with us this afternoon. Yet you would not."

She looked down at her hands. "I really play very badly. I didn't want to spoil your game."

Laughter rose from the other end of the room. Michael, draped in what looked like an old curtain was on one dramatic knee. "Marry me! Or I will die of love —" Her brother, Anna thought wryly, predictably was making the most of every opportunity. She became aware of silence. She looked up, Nicolai was watching her, waiting for her to look at him. Inexplicably she felt colour rising in her cheeks.

"There is a picnic tomorrow. At the other lake." He bent his brown head to her. "You'll come?"

"I — I haven't anything to wear."

He regarded her for a very long time, and for the first time there was a hint of coolness in his gaze. "I think, Madame," he said, softly and clearly, "that you are avoiding me. There is no need, I assure you."

That brought true colour to her face.

He left her.

That night she stood at her window staring into the hauntingly beautiful pale night. Down by the lake two figures moved, and merged into shadow. She wondered who they were. Two lovers keeping secret tryst? Her heart ached dully. She should not have come.

She would not go on the picnic.

Joss had sent her here, high-handed and arrogant. So sure of her. Of course. Why should he not be?

She leaned against the windowframe, tilted her head back against the wooden frame. The light night made her restless. Cool air moved against her throat. From out of nowhere came suddenly the memory of that night on the verandah of her father's house, the night when Joss had so unexpectedly, so astonishingly, asked her to marry him. She remembered the fierce pain of his mouth against hers, the strength of his body.

And then it came to her that it was not really of Joss that she was thinking.

She pulled the curtains with a sharp, angry movement, climbed into the cool, narrow bed.

She most certainly would not go to the picnic tomorrow.

CHAPTER FOURTEEN

In the event she was given no choice: by the Princess's command everyone was to go on the picnic and nothing short of a broken leg would have been accepted as an excuse to stay behind. Probably not even that, Anna told herself wryly, as she climbed with Elena into the straw-filled farm cart. Yet she could not bring herself to regret having the choice taken from her. The day was glorious, the air like wine, the company enormously entertaining. In convoys the two huge carts and the pony and trap set off from the house and wound up the track into the sun-dappled forest. In the first cart the young men rode, and their voices rang through the stilled woodland as they sang, led by one full-blooded bass, all the music of the Russias in the harmonies.

"That's Mitka," Elena told Anna. "You'd never guess it, would you? He sings magnificently." She giggled infectiously, "It's the only thing he can do, actually!"

They rode for an hour or so at a leisurely pace until they reached the shores of another lake, slightly larger than the one at Lemorsk. Standing out from the shore, its banks lapped by sun-gilded water was a large wooded island upon which movement could aready be seen, and the unspoken question that had been in Anna's mind — how anyone could go on a picnic without apparently taking any food — was answered. Fragrant smoke lifted from charcoal fires, laden tables were spread ready beneath the trees. When the Shuvenskis picnicked they did it in style, the servants were there before them. She smiled to herself, not for the first time, at the Princess's idea of a simple life.

They were ferried in relays to the island amidst much hilarity in four large rowing boats which were then moored by the small tumbledown jetty on the island. The children, obviously familiar with the place, scattered, calling, into the woods, while the Prince, Princess and their contemporaries settled themselves in the shade with glasses of lemon tea and the young people who fell between those two extremes took themselves off, singly, in pairs or in groups to explore the island, to fish, to laze in the sun, to coquet and to flirt.

Michael bounced up to Anna. "I say — Elena sort of wants to show me the island —" His eyes were upon the group of young people to whom Elena was talking animatedly. He was obviously dying to get away. "Do you mind? Will you be all right on your own?"

Anna was amused. "For heaven's sake — I'm a grown woman, not a child! Of course I'll be all right. I've brought my sketch pad — I'm going to do some sketches, for a Commonplace Book, like we used when we were children — remember? Off you go. But Michael —" he paused, in the act of turning away and she brandished an admonishing finger "— behave yourself!"

Laughing, he left her.

Anna spread the blanket she carried beneath a tree and settled herself upon it, her back against the gnarled trunk, her pad upon her knee. The dark, decayed wood of the jetty stood stark against the glittering water; engrossed she worked, her pencil busy, long finger rubbing at the swiftly drawn lines, shadowing. A little way away the samovars were steaming. Her sketch completed she watched in fascination as a manservant placed his high Russian boot upon the funnel of the vessel and pumped it vigorously, making the charcoal glow. She drew a man's face, wrinkled, ageless, good-natured.

Katarina, the eldest of Nicolai's sisters, approached her. Not far away one of the distant cousins watched, his eyes not leaving the slim figure in its bright peasant's dress. "Papa is worried that you sit alone," the girl began shyly.

"Oh, please — no — I'm very happy." Anna indicated her pad. "There's so very much to see —"

Katarina clapped her hands in delight, "But — look at Sergei!" She pointed to the sketch of the serving man, "It is his very image! No wonder Nico speaks so highly of your work!"

By the water's edge a little way away Nicolai and Mitka fished, Mitka hunkered down on his haunches upon the bank,

Nicolai leaning indolently against the straight trunk of a pine, his profile sharp against the glittering water.

Katarina fidgeted self-consciously with her apron, her eyes flicking to where her young man stood. "So — would you think it terribly ill-mannered of me if I left you for a while? Pierre and I thought — perhaps a row on the lake —"

Anna brought her attention back to the girl, smiled. "But of course. I promise you — I'm very happy alone."

She sketched for the rest of the morning. The sun rose high, coaxing from the trees their resinous perfume and the woodland shadows foreshortened. So absorbed was Anna in her work that the ringing gong, struck to bring the wanderers back to eat, startled her.

They ate with the ravenous appetite of the outdoors; zakouski — the wonderfully varied open sandwiches Anna had already come to love, fish balls, meat cutlets and patties, followed by the inevitable rich, sweet cakes and fruit. The fragrant lemon tea that washed it all down was strong and refreshing. As the servants set about dismantling the tables and rowing them back to shore, Anna made her excuses, picked up her pad again and declining with a smile several well-meant offers of company set off into the quiet interior of the island. From the shore she had noticed the slope of a small intricately tiled roof; following a narrow but fairly well-trodden path she discovered the little building to which it belonged — a charming rustic summer-house, decayed but still whole, perched upon a tiny knoll beneath the tall trees. She sketched it swiftly. This too would be a part of her Commonplace Book. She was glad she had remembered those happy, childish books of recollection. She sketched, too, the view from the small shaded porch across the lake. Then she lifted her face to the sun and closed her eyes letting the flickering light make rainbows through the curtain of her lashes. For a few timeless, magically disembodied moments she allowed herself to drift, thoughtless, upon the warm, pine-scented air.

She did not hear Nicolai's approach. The first she knew of his presence was the shadow that fell across her face and the gentle removal of the sketch pad from her lax fingers. She opened her eyes, but did not move. He stood above her, leafing through the pad. The sun gilded brown hair and skin to bronze. In his white open-necked peasant shirt and loose corduroy trousers he looked a young gypsy.

"Most people ask," she said, but her voice was gentle.

He smiled a little. "May I?"

She shrugged. Let him see it. Why not? "Of course."

She knew when he had come to the page. He studied it for a long time. Then he knelt down beside her, laid the open pad on the ground between them. "Do I really look like that?"

On one half of the open page two figures were silhouetted against shimmering water, the one crouched on his heels, the other, tall and graceful, leaning against a tree. From the space beside the picture Nicolai's own face looked out, handsome, laughing, head tilted in a distinctive and lifelike way. He tilted it so now, watching her.

"Today you do," she said collectedly.

"May I have it?"

She shook her head. "No."

The look of surprise that crossed his face verged upon shock, and the thought occurred to Anna that here was a young man who was not too used to hearing that word. She picked up the pad and leafed through it. "I'll do you another, if you like. As a memento. But this one belongs here, in my book. When I get back to England I plan to make a scrap book — a book of memories —"

"I see." He picked up the book again, studying it, looked at her slyly, "And this is a memory you want to keep?"

"Yes." She twitched the pad from his fingers. "It's part of the day. When I look at it I shall remember this island — the smell of the pines — the sound of children playing —"

He nodded, smiled a little. "And I? May I not have a memento of the day also?"

No man, not even Joss, had ever so affected her simply by his physical presence. He lay, relaxed and smiling, gently teasing, watching her. A small, sudden breath of wind stirred through the trees above them. Anna smoothed the paper and sketched swiftly. Within moments the picture was complete; beneath a stand of pine two figures sat, the one reclined easily upon one elbow, the other sitting as she herself was at this moment sitting, knees drawn up beneath her skirt, pencil in hand. "There." She tore the page out and handed it to him.

He took it, studied it, lifted his head, smiling. "That's wonderful. Thank you." Very carefully he folded the paper and stowed it in the pocket of his shirt. Then he stood, extending a hand to her. "And now — I'm afraid we must go. They sent me to find you."

She took his hand without thought or hesitation. He pulled her swiftly to her feet. And then he kissed her, very lightly, upon her mouth, a mere brushing of sun-warmed lips as natural as the greeting of a child. Startled, she drew back from him, their hands still linked. He laughed then, a warm, infectious sound that echoed through the woodland like a song. "A small memory, Anna," he said, "that you cannot bind into your scrapbook."

She could not help but laugh with him. Then their laughter died and they stood for a moment in absolute silence, looking at each other, shimmering sunlight spinning their hair to gold and glimmering in Anna's pale eyes as if in water, lining the delicate serious lines of her face in light. He dropped her hand and turned away. "It's truly time to go."

They rode back to Lemorsk, singing, in the carts, Mitka's wonderful bass leading the other voices. The songs Anna did not know, and the words were meaningless to her, yet the sound, the very soul of Russia, brought the sting of tears to her eyes and she thought of the words that Nicolai had used — A small memory, Anna, that you cannot bind into your scrapbook — and in thinking it she felt again that light brushing of his lips against hers, and could feel nothing but happiness at the recollection. Michael sat upon the tailgate of the wagon ahead, legs swinging, face bright with enjoyment as with uplifted arms he conducted the singing, making eyes at Elena who nestled next to Anna in the straw. Catching Anna's eyes upon him he grinned and raised a hand. She waved back. Behind Michael Nicolai sat, his back propped against the side of the cart, singing at the top of his voice, his eyes unwavering upon Anna's face. Bracing herself against the jolting of the cart, for a moment Anna returned his look, and in a strange, suspended moment of clarity knew how much she loved him. Not in the way that she loved Joss, but love nevertheless — a sudden, free, lightning-strike of love that sang in her veins with her blood. She loved his bright eyes, the set of his head upon his slim shoulders, the sound of his voice. And, too, she knew that in three days she would leave him and that as time went on memory must fade and he would lose the vivid warmth of reality and become a loved shadow, a face and a figure in her sketchbook. Knowing, however, that she would not be able to hold on to this passion in no way devalued it: on the contrary the bitter-sweetness of that knowledge served to sharpen her senses and her emotions to a degree of almost painful happiness. She did not wonder if he shared her feelings; in a strange way it hardly mattered — his feelings for her were irrelevant to her own emotions. Of Joss she was always asking — does he love me; does he care — for in her relationship with Joss his caring for her was the root need upon which her feelings for him were based. But this, this was different. How could you ask the sunshine, or the mountains, or the forests, if they loved you? They were, and that was all that mattered.

Elena touched her arm. "Have you enjoyed the day?"

"Oh, yes. Truly I have. It's been wonderful."

"It's a pity you can't stay longer. There'll be other picnics. But still — there's tomorrow — perhaps we'll go walking."

"That sounds lovely."

"And then the party — you'll be here for that —"

"Party?"

Elena looked surprised. "Did Papa not tell you? We have a party every year. Many of our friends holiday round about — it's wonderful fun to get them all together. Each year we have —" she stopped, a thoughtful frown upon her face "— I'm sorry. I don't know the word. A party when we dress as — something other —" she faltered to a stop.

"A fancy dress?" Anna supplied.

"Ah. Yes. A fancy dress party —"

"But, Elena — I don't have anything to wear to a fancy dress party."

"Oh, this is not a problem." Elena waved an airy hand, "It's not like the winter parties, when everyone must be —" she kissed her fingers, laughing "— just so. There's a trunk in the attic — our parents, grandparents, their parents — all, when something becomes —" she thought for a moment about the word "— outmoded," she said, triumphantly "— put it in this trunk for the children to play. Every year we choose something from the trunk. There is certainly something left for you — and for Michael too."

The carts rattled and jolted back to Lemorsk, the sun-flushed faces of the company testament in themselves of a happy day. But the fun was by no means over, for spirits were high and refused to be damped. After dinner Anna found herself sitting with the Princess Maria in the half-darkness of the verandah when Elena dressed in an old and somewhat shabby riding skirt and shirt tumbled through the door and grabbed her hand. "So there you are! I've been looking for you everywhere! I wouldn't let the others start without you! We're going to play Cossacks and Turks —" she suddenly caught sight of her mother and stopped, flushing. "I'm sorry, Mama. Am I interrupting?"

Her mother raised severely quizzical eyebrows. "What do you think?"

Elena was appealingly contrite. "Yes, of course I am. And I am sorry. But, please — may Anna come and play?"

Her mother could not help but laugh at the childish phrase. "Come and play?" She turned to Anna, "Did you ever hear such a thing? You must think us mad! How it is that my sensible, almost adult offspring become children again in this place I'll never know! Cossacks and Turks, indeed!"

"But, Mama, it's such fun!"

"Perhaps Anna doesn't want to crawl around in the undergrowth being chased from pillar to post by Cossacks. Has that occurred to you? Whatever she must think of us I cannot imagine —"

Anna laughed. "It sounds very much like what we used to call French and English, but rather more exciting. I'd love to join you Elena — but I'm not exactly dressed for it."

"Oh, that's all right. I'll lend you something. Come on," Elena held out a hand, laughing.

Anna turned, apologetic, to the Princess, who, smiling, made a small shooing motion with her hands. "Off you go. Enjoy yourself."

The shaded, bright-darkness of the pinewoods was a perfect

setting for the game. Most of the young company were 'Turks', whose task was to slip from a small hut about half a mile into the forest to a point on the lake shore without being caught by those young men elected 'Cossacks', of which one was Nicolai. Anna, knowing the absurdity of the thing, yet still was caught up in the breathless excitement of the game as she slipped through the shadows, crouching to the ground at the slightest movement. A laughing shriek in the night told of a 'Turk' captured. She flattened to a wide tree trunk, waiting for the sounds to die down, then moved on into the milky, sky-bright darkness. Behind her something moved. She gathered her skirts and fled. A triumphant call and a reaching hand; Michael's voice, "Got you!"

But he spoke too soon. With a small, childish squeal of excitement she dodged the reaching hand and ran, flying through the trees regardless of danger. She heard a crash behind her and a muttered, very English curse as her brother caught his foot and fell. She ran until she was breathless, half laughing, half in earnest. When she stopped all was still. Far in the distance a voice called and then was quiet. She sat upon a fallen tree to regain her breath. And to wait. Below her she could see the lights of the dacha gleaming on the lake. Her legs were trembling with the effort of her flight.

She did not have long to wait.

"Well, my little Turk. Do you surrender without a fight?"

She knew who it was without turning.

"I followed you," he said simply.

She nodded. She had known it, had seen the glint of his shirt in the trees behind Michael in that instant before she had fled.

He sat beside her upon the log. In silence they watched the fitful gleam of light below them, listened to the hilarious sounds of the game in the distance.

"You leave in three days," Nicolai said at last. It was almost, but not quite, a question.

"Yes."

"Three days. Such a little time."

"Yes."

He had neither touched her nor looked at her. Now he turned his head, his face a blur in the shadows. "This afternoon – at the summer house on the island —"

She waited.

"I wanted to say —" he stopped, leaned forward, his elbows on his knees, and ducked his head into his hands to ruffle his hair distractedly, "I wanted to say — so many things, and I said nothing."

Her heart was beating very fast. "What kind of things?" she asked softly, her voice commendably steady.

He looked at her. In the strange light his face was troubled as a boy's. "There is something that I don't understand," he said softly. "Since first I saw you — standing on the station — it's as if somehow you speak to me. Without words. Speak to my heart. How do you do that?"

She shook her head, unable to speak.

"You feel it too?" he asked, after a moment, quietly.

"Yes."

"It should not happen."

"No."

"We are not free. You are a wife, and a mother. I am soon to be married. We don't know each other."

She said nothing, knowing now what must happen. Accepting it. Wanting it.

"And yet — you are Anna and I am Nicolai and we know each other as we know ourselves —"

"Yes."

A laughing shout echoed through the trees. Michael's voice. "Look out! There she goes!"

"It's a kind of love," Anna said. "A different kind of love. Nothing to do with our other loves, our other duties. I thought it this afternoon, watching you. You're right, we don't know each other. We don't have time to know each other. And yet we love each other. For this little time."

"For this little time," he repeated, quietly into the silence and held out his hand to her. She it was, then, who moved to him.

They made love on the softly scented carpet of pine needles and to Anna nothing had been more natural nor so full of giving. They came together in loving hunger, simple, direct, a relief of their need for one another. Their loving was gentle and warm as the night itself. And in the act of love with this man — this stranger — Anna found the tender communication that she had always known to be missing with Joss, whom she had loved as long as she could remember. In those few, snatched, dangerous moments they shared something, told each other something, that might have taken a lifetime to put into words.

Afterwards they lay quietly for the precious space of perhaps two dozen breaths. Then, very gently, she disentangled herself from him and began to straighten her disarranged clothing.

He caught her hand. "Anna! Tomorrow!"

She shook her head. "No. Not tomorrow. Not ever."

"But —"

"No, my love. Don't you see what that would mean? This evening was right, natural, perfect. Tomorrow it would be planned. It would be deceit. It would be spoiled."

He drew back. "I'm sorry. You're right, of course."

She kissed him, long and tenderly, her love and her sadness in her soft, undemanding mouth.

Sounds of laughter echoed from the lakeside.

"We have to go. It sounds as though they are going home. They'll miss us."

"Wait —" He caught her hand, drew her back to him. "One more moment. I know a quicker way back. We'll get there before them —"

"Separately," she said.

He hesitated, and she saw the sorrow in his face as he accepted the necessity of the words. "Separately."

The next day they went walking, a group of them, along the forest tracks. The day was fine but cool with fair weather cloud scudding high across the sun and a chill in the breeze that filtered from the north. Anna enjoyed the day, hard though it was to be close to Nicolai without touching him, without speaking those words of endearment that hovered treacherously upon her tongue, and ironically made harder by Michael's outrageous flirtation with Elena — open, friendly and of no substance whatsoever. As the evening chilled they made their way back to the dacha. After dinner a group of them retired to the attics to deck Anna and Michael for the party the next day. Michael, characteristically easily suited, made a dashing

Cossack, strutting around the dusty attic swishing his genuine and lethally curved blade through the air.

"But there'll be so *many* Cossacks," Elena demurred.

Katarina laughed. "But how many will be blond and handsome?"

"And how many," Anna asked a little tartly, "will be in danger of decapitating half of the guests at one stroke?"

For herself she chose a charmingly old-fashioned soft pink ball gown, long outdated with its swaying crinoline skirt and deep, scooped neckline, signs of wear in its stretched seams and worn hem.

"That was Mama's, years ago." Katarina said. "I wore it two years ago as Catherine the Great. Not a very authentic Catherine the Great," she added with a giggle.

"But — who are you to be?" Elena asked of Anna. "The dress suits you beautifully, but you must be someone —"

"Something." Anna's head was buried in a trunk. "Ah — there," she emerged triumphantly waving a leaf-green, slightly tattered shawl. "Perfect." She held the dress to her, draped the shawl about her shoulders. "An English rose!" she said.

It took a moment or two to sink in. Then Katarina clapped her hands. "How very clever! Of course! We must raid Mama's garden and find some roses for your hair —"

"And green slippers! I have some green slippers you can borrow —"

Over the heads of the laughing girls Anna's eyes met Nicolai's. His no longer smiled. She coaxed him with a little, tender smile of her own and was rewarded by the sudden brightening of his sombre face.

That night she pondered, standing by her open window, on the events of the past few days. Forty-eight hours from now she would be on the train and heading home. Towards Joss. Away from Nicolai. She could feel his presence, close to her, within the house. She looked to where water glimmered and the darkness of the forest began. Easily — oh, so easily — she could have been meeting him there, now. She turned from the window.

No.

She would not have it spoiled.

The next two days passed in a whirl of activity that gave her scarcely time to draw breath, and no matter how she tried to hold the time, it flew on treacherous wings. The party was a kaleidoscope of faces and names that her benumbed brain refused to register, and a number of struggling, well-meaning conversations with people whose words she never came close to understanding and whose polite smiles and bemused eyes indicated the self-same problem in reverse. She danced with a great many young men and noticed only one of them; Nicolai's brilliant eyes held hers as he swept her around the lawn in a gay polka, the silks and satins of his Eastern costume gleaming in the light of the lamps that were strung from the trees and from the verandah. "Later," he said, his voice brooking no argument, "I will see you. We must talk."

But they did not. When they met in the dark shadow of the barn beside the house they clung and they kissed, but they could not find the words. On the lawn in front of the house Mitka was singing now, the deep bell-tone of his voice ringing through the night with no accompaniment but the sighing of the wind in the trees. Anna stood with her face buried in Nicolai's shoulder, listening, the moment crystallized in her memory like a precious stone. Like the glittering teardrop of the Shuvenski diamond.

"You leave tomorrow?" Nicolai asked.

"Yes."

"Will you write?"

"No. I don't think so."

He put a finger beneath her chin, tilted her face to him. "I'll never forget you," he said.

She stood on tiptoe, wound her arms about his neck and drew his face down to hers. "Neither of us," she said softly, "will ever forget."

They gathered on the verandah to see them off: all of the family, including the cousins, some of whose names Anna had never actually managed to register in her memory. That odd and slightly discomfiting distance that always develops at the start of a journey between those staying and those leaving was already apparent. Anna shook hands, touched cheeks, made promises — to write, to come again, to entertain them all in

London — and wished, simply and fervently that the goodbyes be over and they should be on their way. When she found herself by the pony and trap with Nicolai she could barely look at him. In front of them all they could do nothing, say nothing. The pain in his eyes she knew reflected her own. He took her hand, raised it to his mouth, lightly and courteously. Over his bright, bent, head the sun blurred and she blinked rapidly.

"Goodbye, Anna."

"Goodbye."

"I shall be in London again, perhaps, one day. Might I presume to call?"

"Of course. We'd be delighted to see you." She hated to use that hurtful pronoun, needed now simply to leave. To run away.

He handed her into the trap and stood back. The pony pawed the gravel, the little vehicle turned in a sweep in front of the house, the assembled company waved and called.

Nicolai stood like a statue, his face in shadow, and watched them go.

CHAPTER FIFTEEN

To Anna the first part of the journey home seemed entirely unreal, an interlude, of melancholic adjustment in which her confusion and dawning guilt wrapped her like a veil which little penetrated. She sat for hours, unspeaking, watching sightlessly the passing countryside, trying hard to forget that one face, that one voice, the feel of that one body. At first it seemed an impossibility. A train thundered by her window, streaming northward, and her heart went with it, back to the lighthearted laughter of Lemorsk. Back to Nicolai. But then, against expectations, her common sense exerted itself. What good to dream if the dream were totally impossible? And, even if it had been offered, which she knew it could never be, a life with Nicolai would be unthinkable: she could never leave her family, her country, her work. Victoria. Joss. Above all, she suddenly found herself thinking, Joss. Despite what had happened that she still truly loved her husband was undeniable. As they sped towards the Channel she forced herself to think of their life, of their relationship. How much of her disappointment was her own fault? She demanded too much; he gave too little. But if that were in the nature of the man now it always had been, and she must have known it. So, she must either learn to live with it or show him by example the satisfaction and joy of giving. Stoically she ignored the pang of physical pain that brought, remembering Nicolai and those brief moments that had shown her so much. Joss. She loved Joss, her husband. She would remember that. She would cling to it. And when she saw him, the very first moment, she would begin again. She must have learned something? She must use it constructively. Use it to build a future with Joss. During the blessedly calm crossing of the Channel she studied that thought, leaning on the ship's rail watching the misty, smudged horizon that was England as it took firm shape, and colour and reality. Joss would be waiting for them at the station. Then and there she would begin anew. She would make it work.

But Joss was not at the station to meet them. It was Boris who stood at the barrier, his bright head unmistakable in the crowds, his face uncharacteristically and unconcealedly sombre.

After the greeting, Anna looked around, still half-expecting to see her husband. "Where's Joss? Isn't he here?"

"No. He was — detained —"

"But — I told him the train we were coming on —" She looked sharply at Boris. "What is it? Boris — what is it? Has something happened to Joss?"

He shook his head. "No. I promise you. Joss is all right."

"Then what? Something's wrong. What is it?"

Boris took her hand in his. "It's your father, Anna. A heart attack."

"What? Oh, God! Why didn't someone tell us? Send for us?"

"Please — calm yourself. It was on Josef's specific instructions that you were not informed. He's ill, yes, but the doctor assures us that he will be all right. It was a mild attack."

"I want to see him. Now. At once. Is that where Joss is? Why didn't you tell us at once? Michael — quickly — find a cab —"

"There's one waiting," Boris said. "I guessed you'd want to go straight to your father. But — Anna —"

Anna, looking round distractedly for a porter, turned sharply at his tone. Michael appeared to have been struck dumb by the news.

"Joss is not at Bayswater," Boris said.

"Then where is he?"

"I don't know. At work perhaps —"

She stared at him. "Something has happened to Joss, " she said flatly. "Hasn't it? *Hasn't it?* You're keeping something back."

Michael found his voice at last. "Oh, for Heaven's sake, Anna — he's already told you Joss is all right. It's Papa we should be thinking of — we have to go —" Michael raised his voice. "Porter! Here, please! Boris — where's the cab?"

The journey to Bayswater, spent mostly in an awkward silence that was broken only by Boris's stiltedly polite enquiry as to the trip and Anna's equally stilted reply, was thankfully short. When the vehicle stopped outside the house Michael tumbled from it and took the steps to the front door two at a time. Anna about to follow him, found herself restrained by Boris's hand. She stilled, and looked at him. "Tell me," she said. "What's happened to Joss."

"It's as I said. Nothing's happened to him. It's what he —" he hesitated "— what he appears to have done."

"Done? What do you mean?"

"Anna, I can't let you go in there — face them — without telling you —"

"What? Telling me what?" Her voice was sharp with apprehension.

"Joss — Joss seems — indirectly — to be the cause of your father's illness."

"*What?*"

"We can't altogether discover what happened — your father absolutely refused to discuss it — but the facts —"

"What facts?" Anna's voice was suddenly calm. The front door of the house had opened and Michael had disappeared inside. A figure appeared at the top of the steps — Alex, his face like the crack of doom. "*What facts, Boris?*" she asked, urgently.

Boris shook a helpless head. "You'll have to come inside, Anna. Everyone's there. They'll explain."

"Tell me something first. Are you saying that you believe that Joss — deliberately —" she stopped.

"No." He could not hold her eyes. "That is — I don't know, Anna. Joss won't say anything. Neither will your father. Joss refuses to defend himself. And on appearances, I have to say —"

Alex was beside them. "Anna." His voice was heavy, and held no greeting. "You'd better come in. Father heard the cab. He's asking for you."

Everyone was gathered in the drawing room — Alex and Alice, Boris and Louisa, Ralph and Michael — waiting for Anna when she came downstairs from seeing her father. As she entered the room the heavy silence of antagonism rang in her ears. Boris stood by the window, his back to the room. Alex, feet astride, hands behind his back, stood before the fireplace. He was putting on weight, Anna noticed, and his face was florid. Alice and Louisa sat one each end of the long sofa, as far from each other as possible. The two had not spoken unless absolutely forced to it by social necessity since the quarrel some months before, as indeed neither had Boris and Alex. Ralph sat in an armchair upon whose high back Michael leaned, his usually carefree face dark with worry. He it was who broke the silence. "May I go up now?"

Anna shook her head. "I'm sorry. He's gone to sleep. The nurse said perhaps in half an hour or so."

Michael turned away abruptly. Ralph put out a gentle hand. "He's going to be all right, Michael. It wasn't a bad heart attack."

Anna surveyed the room, sensing the hostility, hurt and confused by it. "How did it happen?" she asked flatly.

"Father didn't tell you?" Ralph asked.

She shook her head. "He absolutely refused to speak of it. Simply said he'd guessed it was coming and should have taken more care of himself." She looked to where Boris stood. "He didn't mention Joss." Her eyes moved then to Alex, sensing that it was from him that the greatest hostility emanated. "Will someone please explain?"

Boris turned from the window. Alex stepped forward. "Are you telling us that you truly have no idea?"

She made an impatient movement. "I? How should I have? It may have escaped your notice, Alex, but I have been away. A very long way away. For nearly three weeks. Hardly a lifetime, I know – but long enough."

"Long enough for your husband to ruin our father and bring him to death's door."

Anna could not have been more shocked had he struck her. "No," she said, her voice shaking.

"And do you really expect us to believe that you knew nothing of what was going on? That you didn't connive with Joss to inveigle Michael away from father so that he'd have no one to turn to?"

"What are you talking about? No!"

"Alex, that's enough!" Boris lifted his head sharply. "You're jumping to conclusions. We've no proof of anything —"

"Proof? How much proof do you need? My father is lying up there, his business — my sons' inheritance — gone, the very roof above his head gone — and you talk of proof?"

"*Will someone tell me what is going on!*" Anna's control was all but gone. Tears were rising. She swallowed them fiercely. Louisa's eyes were sympathetic, Alice's totally hostile.

Alex lifted a finger and stabbed it at his sister like a prosecuting counsel. "I'll tell you. In words of one syllable. Father had seemingly got himself into some financial difficulty — God knows how, or why, but that apparently was the case. To recoup he borrowed heavily on the house and the business. From Joss. He then invested the money he had borrowed in some dud shares that Joss advised him to buy —"

"Joss did not advise him. I keep telling you that." Boris's voice was sharp with anger. "Josef himself insists on that. Joss did not advise him. Josef overheard something that Joss said to someone else, and thought to use the information to recoup his losses. He must have misinterpreted what he heard. You can hardly blame Joss for that."

"Overheard?" Anna's voice was faint. She saw again that scene in the hall, her father's stealth, Joss's voice, unusually loud — something stirred uncomfortably in the pit of her stomach. "Boris is right. I don't see how you can blame Joss for that."

"You can blame him for foreclosing on the loan when the shares crashed," Alex said, grimly. "For that's what he's doing."

"I don't believe it!" Anna was stone-white. She looked at Boris in desperation. "There must be some mistake. Joss wouldn't —"

Boris shrugged helplessly. "I'm afraid so. The house — the business — Joss, quite legitimately, is claiming them both. Then — Josef became ill —"

Alex turned on him. "You speak of it as if it were an act of God — instead of the direct result of your brother's dastardly underhand actions —"

"That's not fair!" Louisa snapped. "How was Joss to know what might happen?"

"The same way we all would." It was Alice, her sweet, cultured voice vitriolic. "Father-in-law had been unwell for years and we all know it. What would you expect to happen?"

"Please, please!" Anna put a hand to her head. "I'm sorry." She was battling hard to hold her composure. "I still can't believe what you're saying. You're trying to tell me that Joss lent Father money, accepting Rose and Company and this house as surety? And that — oh, no — it simply isn't possible. There's some mistake."

Ralph shook his head. "There's no mistake, Anna."

"What we want to know —" It was Alex again, aggressively quiet, "is how much you knew about all this before you packed Michael off to Russia with you, leaving the old man alone —"

Anna stared. "What are you saying?"

"That's a bit thick, Alex." Michael made a dismissive gesture. "What on earth makes you think —"

Anna interrupted him, turning fiercely upon her older brother, "And what of you? Where were you whilst all this was happening? This hasn't blown up over three weeks! Couldn't you have helped Papa? Lent him the money? Why did he go to Joss in the first place? Why did he accept the terms?"

Ralph stood up. "That's one of the things none of us can understand, Anna. Father didn't approach any of us. He didn't tell anyone. Didn't ask anyone's advice. We didn't know what was happening until it was too late. You saw yourself — he won't speak of it, won't explain. He appears simply ready to accept what Joss has done with no argument and no attempt to defend himself. The business he's spent a lifetime building up — the house —" Ralph made a small, defeated gesture, "it seems to mean nothing to him that Joss has taken them."

Anna shook her head. "I knew nothing of this." Her voice was intense. "I swear it. I never would have gone away if I had guessed —" Small, sharp images pricked like nettle stings in her mind. Joss's unexpected determination that she should go to St Petersburg. His challenge to her, that he knew her pride would force her to accept. His unusual generosity. His choice of Michael as her escort. "What does Joss have to say about it all?"

"Absolutely nothing." Boris turned from her, avoiding her eyes. "He refused to speak of it."

"There's nothing he can say," Alice said. "What can excuse what he's done?"

In the silence that followed the words children's voices called from the garden. Down by the little pool Anna could see two sturdy, handsome small boys, Alex's twin sons, with their nanny. Not far from them Louisa's Sophie stood, a little apart, watching, her thumb in her mouth.

"Someone tell Nanny to keep those boys quiet," Alex's voice was brusque.

Wordlessly obedient, Alice stood up, brushed down her skirt and left the room.

"I think," Anna said, very quietly, "that I'd better go home."

He was waiting for her, as she had expected. With unfeigned delight she greeted her daughter with hugs and kisses and watched her open the presents she had brought her, then sent the child into the garden with Mary and followed Joss into the small parlour. They faced each other across the room, unsmiling. "Well?" Anna said.

"You've been to Bayswater?"

"I have. Boris was at the station."

"I thought he would be."

"And you were not."

"No."

"Joss — I want to know what's been happening."

He almost shrugged. "I suspect you've been told."

"I've been told something, yes. Something that I can't — won't believe. I've been told that you're trying to ruin my father. Trying to take away from him everything he has, everything he cares for —"

Joss remained silent.

"Well? Aren't you going to say anything? Explain anything?"

"No." The word was brutally blunt.

The sudden rise of temper almost choked her. "You can't mean that! You can't mean that you aren't even going to try to explain what you've done and why you've done it."

He took a short, impatient-seeming breath. "What I've done is more or less what you've been told I've done. Why I'm doing it is between me and Josef. Ask him."

Anna was looking at him as if at a stranger. "I did. He won't talk about it."

"That's his choice then, isn't it? It's a pity a few others don't follow his lead."

She looked at him for a long moment, suspicions crystallizing in her mind with a terrible clarity. "Tell me something," she said quietly. "How long have you been planning this? And how much responsibility do you bear for Papa's difficulties in the first place? You've been advising him for years — he trusts you implicitly — yet you've made money and he has apparently lost it. How is that? You've been saving every penny you've made. What for? To do what you've now done? To take over the business? To take, God preserve us, the very roof from over his head?" Her voice was rising. "He told Boris he overheard a conversation about some shares. Was that all a part of it? Did you know he was listening? Did you trick him into believing what you were saying? Did you?"

Her husband said nothing. His dark eyes were implacable and totally without warmth. She hated him. Hated him. The memory of her father's face, grey upon the white pillow, skeletal, defeated, rose in her mind.

She stared at Joss. "They're right, aren't they? Alice and Alex — they're right! You manipulated the whole thing. You did want to ruin Papa. To take from him everything he had. Joss — in heaven's name — why? And why has he let you do it — with no protest, no attempt to defend himself?"

He turned from her, took a cigar from a box on the table, applied himself to the task of cutting it. "I told you. You must ask him that. If he wants you to know then I suppose he'll tell you." His voice was perfectly contained; they might have been discussing the weather.

She shook her head dazedly. "I think I must be going mad. I just don't believe any of this. I can't."

"Believe it. It's happening." He did not look at her.

She took a breath, trying to calm herself. "And what of me?" she asked quietly. "Have you thought at all of me? Do you know that half the family suspects that I've had a hand in all this?"

He lifted his eyes to hers. "I'm sorry for that," he said.

"But nothing else?"

He shook his head.

"Why, Joss? Why?" she asked again.

"Ask your father."

She looked at him for a long moment. "You want him to tell me," she said at last, slowly. "You won't tell me because you want to force him to do it. Because whatever it is — it will hurt him to tell me. And you haven't had enough yet, have you? You *want* to hurt him, don't you? You must really hate him. But how can that be? He gave you everything — you, your brother, your sister — he treated you all as his own sons and daughter. You above all. What can he possibly have done that is bad enough to deserve your hatred?"

The dark eyes did not falter. Joss lit the cigar. Fragrant smoke drifted in a cloud between them.

"Don't expect me," Anna said then, when it became clear that he was not going to answer her, "to live with you in the house that you've taken from my father."

"I suppose you must please yourself in that."

She stared at him, sick at heart. "You don't care. You don't care if I stay or go. Live or die. Or anyone else either for that matter. Do you?"

He looked directly at her through the drifting cigar smoke. "Would you believe me if I denied it?"

She had to hurt him somehow, make some kind of point no matter how small. "No," she said, flatly.

He gestured with his free hand. "Then there's little point in a denial, is there?" His voice was soft.

She watched him for a long time. "You're detestable," she said, slowly. "Absolutely detestable. And I hate you for what you're doing. For what you are."

That barb went home and he flinched at it, but she did not see it. She turned from him to the door.

"Anna." His voice was sharp.

She stopped, her back to him.

"If you went. Where would you go?"

"I don't know. With Papa, perhaps — wherever that might be."

"Think carefully," he said. "A mother's bond with her child is hard to break. You'd miss Victoria."

She turned slowly. "You'd do that?" She knew as she said it that she had lost.

"I would," he said, the words tranquil.

She stared at him in silence, pale eyes silvered with impotent rage before she turned and left the room, shutting the door very quietly behind her.

A couple of weeks later Josef himself, his health much improved, still absolutely refusing to discuss what had passed between him and Joss, urged her against rash action.

"Leave? Leave your husband, your daughter — oh no, child. Don't think it. Where would you go? What would you do? Rose and Company is your life —"

"As it was yours."

He sighed, shifting in his chair.

"I thought I might come with you," she said, stubborn to the end. "Help you. Try to make up for what Joss has done." She knew how absurdly childish it sounded.

He shook his head. "I shall be perfectly all right. I promise you. In the end it would have come to something like this anyway — with my health so frail I should have had to give up the business."

"And your home?" Her voice was bitter as his was not.

"Anna, Anna —"

"Why did he do it Papa? Why?"

Josef looked down to the hands that were clasped in his lap. Upon his thumb still could be seen the brand of his trade. Half-unconsciously he folded the thumb into his hand, hiding it.

She dropped to her knees beside him. "You know, don't you, you know why he did it." Her voice was urgent.

He took her hands. "Anna. Child. Please listen to me. Believe me when I say that the best thing you can do for me is to stop questioning me so. Joss did what he did and it is done. I have told the others and I tell you — I don't want trouble in the family because of it. To have seen you turned one against the other would have broken your dear mother's heart. Joss has what he wanted — the business. And that means that Rose and Company is in good hands and your work can go on. If I can find satisfaction in that, can't you? As for this house — it's far too big for an old man alone. Boris and Louisa are leaving, Michael is hardly ever here. I should so have hated to see it go to strangers."

"Michael's staying with us," Anna said, her voice subdued. She had hardly spoken to her husband since that first evening except upon this one matter of her young brother. His ready capitulation had been the last thing she had expected, giving as it did the impression that Joss, for all his implacability regarding her father, had already decided in his own mind to offer Michael a home. "I spoke to Alex yesterday," she continued. "He said you're going to Bissetts —"

"That's right. To a cottage on the estate. You see how well it's all worked out? I shall have a little home in the country, and you will all come to visit me —"

"But — how will you live?"

"I have enough. Enough to live comfortably, if quietly. He left me that." His face was suddenly, sombrely intense. "Remember that, Anna. He could have taken everything. But he did not."

She stared at him in bafflement.

He reached a hand to her. "I say it again, Anna. I have told the others — and I tell you — there is no place for bitterness. I want no rift in the family. I want no one digging and prying. If my family is destroyed — and Joss, and his brother are still part of that family in my eyes, no matter what has happened — then I truly have nothing left. And whatever I deserve, I don't believe that I deserve that."

"Deserve? Papa — what are you saying? After all you've done for us all — all you've given us — you deserve nothing but love and respect!"

"Anna —"

She rushed on. "And most especially from Joss. You took him and Boris in when they had nothing. You cared for Tanya as if she had been your own —"

"Anna!"

The tone of his voice stopped her. She got to her feet, a little shakily, put a hand to her head. "I don't understand."

He looked at her in quick concern. "Anna — are you all right?"

She shook her head. "I — no — I've been a little unwell lately. If you would please excuse me, Papa? I think a little air —" She left the room on unsteady legs and fled to the bathroom where she was extremely sick. For the fourth time in three days.

Her pregnancy seemed, to Anna, to crown a misery that just a few short weeks before would have seemed inconceivable. There was, she knew, no possibility that the child could be Joss's. She plodded through the days, wretchedly sick, haunted by anxiety. At last and in near despair she confided in Arabella Dawson one late September afternoon when a wind that skittered coldly through the London streets, presaging autumn made it chill enough to light the first fire of the season. Arabella looked at her with sympathy. "I suspected that something was wrong."

Anna took a long breath. "I'm at my wits' end. I don't know what to do. I have to tell Joss. I can't keep it secret for much longer. And I've no idea — absolutely no idea — what he'll do. He seems not to care — but this —" She lifted helpless hands and let them drop to her side. She looked pale and thin and her eyes were shadowed. "He might — he could — turn me out."

"It couldn't be his?"

Anna shook her head.

"And you couldn't —" Arabella paused, delicately "— arrange it? Make it look as if —"

"No." The word was flat.

"I see." Arabella tapped her teeth throughtfully with a long polished fingernail. "If you'd like," she said after a moment, "I might be able to put you in touch with — someone who might be willing to help."

It took a moment for the meaning of the words to sink in. Anna looked up in shock. "No! Oh, no, Arabella — I couldn't! Don't you see? This is a child — Nicolai's child! Whatever happens — whatever Joss does — I couldn't kill it! I couldn't!"

"Then you're just going to have to face it out," the other girl said simply. "And soon. It isn't going to get any easier —"

The confrontation with Joss, though he neither ranted nor raved nor threw her from the house was, if anything, worse than Anna had anticipated and she had expected it to be bad. The news itself he greeted with no trace of surprise. She stared at him. "You knew?"

"My dear Anna —" his voice was cold, slightly impatient "— your pregnancies being what they are I should imagine that the whole world knows. You look like death."

"And — you haven't said anything?"

He lifted scathing eyes. "Should I have? Is it any of my business?"

She flushed, painfully, to the roots of her hair. "I'm sorry." she whispered, stammering with mortification. "I — it was —"

"No!" He held up a sudden, imperative hand, "Spare me that. I don't want to know who, or where. Or why."

She stood dumb with mortified humiliation. "What — what will you do?" she asked at last, quietly; and none of her efforts could keep the miserable trepidation from her voice.

He kept her waiting for the space of a dozen hammered heartbeats. "Do?" he asked at last. "What would you expect me to do? Throw you from my house?"

"I — thought you might — yes — I — suppose you could not be blamed —"

He stood and walked to her, his step light, his face hard. With enormous effort she stood her ground and did not shrink from him. In the clear second before he struck her it came to her that since he had guessed at her pregnancy he had had time to plan this scene, and her humiliation and punishment, in advance. Beneath her guilt pride and fury stirred and she lifted her head. His hand caught her sharply high on her cheekbone — not with the full force of his strength, as in anger, but crisply and stinging; a chastisement and a gesture of contempt.

"Have your bastard, Anna," he said, softly, "I wish you joy of it." And in the moment that she registered the savage pain deep in his eyes he turned and left her alone.

INTERLUDE

1901–1909

On January 22nd 1901 an era ended with the death of the old lady who had ruled an empire from Windsor for an incredible sixty- four years. Her subjects genuinely mourned her passing — for most of the population she was the only monarch they had known and her reign had been crowned by national prosperity, prestige and success in arms. Dressed in deepest mourning, they lined the black-draped streets to bid her farewell. And yet, despite the sadness, there was too a new stirring of excitement. Bluff Edward was King at last, a new day was dawning, and the hope abroad was that it might perhaps be a day a little less sober, a little more amusing.

Anna named the child that was born just four months after the Queen's death, Nicholas; and she doted upon him from the first moment that he opened his brilliant, unfocused eyes. Joss's unexpected willingness to protect her and to accept the child as his own, at least publicly, still mystified her. On just one occasion, a few weeks after the birth of the child, she swallowed her pride and attempted to thank him — but he dismissed her and her thanks with an acidity that stopped the words in her throat. She saw little of him in the weeks that followed. When forced into one another's company they were civil but distant and their conversation was confined to impersonal matters. Surprisingly, though, Anna could not have said that she was entirely unhappy. She suffered none of the depression after the birth of Nicholas that had so plagued her when she had borne Victoria. Under Joss's astute management Rose and Company flourished, and with it flourished Anna's reputation as a designer. Encouraged by Arabella, whose ideas and free spirit inspired her, she designed some exotic and adventurous pieces especially to complement Arabella's flamboyant clothes, whose clients, most of whom were part of the esoteric world of dance and the theatre, a world of art in which Anna found herself more and more at home, greeted them with rapture, but which served to widen the gulf between herself and Joss — who considered her new friends affected and sybaritic — even further. Of Alex and Alice and their twin sons they saw little at this time. Despite Josef's pleas, the attitude of Anna's brother to her husband was understandably one of frigid hostility, though in deference to his father's wishes Alex did to his credit make the effort to avoid an open break. However, Boris, Louisa and their daughters were frequent visitors to Bayswater. They had taken a small, inexpensive house in Plaistow, a respectable working-class area to the east of London. To supplement his meagre pension Boris, despite his handicap, obtained a job with the proprietor of a public house in Green Street, his tasks ranging from handling the accounts to serving on a busy evening in the public bar, where his good humour and quick wit made him very popular. In vain Joss railed at him — Boris would accept from his brother neither employment nor charity. He had made his decision and left the company: while there was breath in his body he would stand by his choice and support his own family. And still he found time for laughter.

In her son more than in anything Anna found delight. She had always in the past been more than happy to hand Victoria to whatsoever waiting arms would take her; Nicholas she guarded jealously. No one was to be allowed to take her place with him. She cossetted and cuddled him, would give up anything — her work, her friends — to be with him. All this was not lost upon two-year-old Victoria, young as she was. Yet Anna's daughter was a docile child and her vague unhappiness at the obvious favouritism that her adored mother displayed for the new baby did not evince itself in tantrums or bad behaviour, as it had in Anna herself those many years before. On the contrary, it had the effect of making the little girl almost painfully well behaved: in her eagerness to placate the mother she was afraid of losing altogether her sweetly docile nature, so much like Tanya's, led her to meek biddability which, if not exactly having the desired effect, at least would sometimes draw from Anna a word of absent-minded praise, a word that the child would hug to her for days, basking in her mother's casual and insubstantial approval. Like her Aunt Tanya, too, she had a pretty cloud of fair hair and the wide violet eyes. Not unnaturally, it never occurred to Anna to connect this circumstance with Joss's absolute insistence that she take her daughter with her every time she made the trip into the country to see her father: neither did she ever perceive the pain that the sight of the child afforded her father, despite the fact that he dearly loved her.

It was not, however, and to her own detriment, only in the case of her father and Victoria that Anna lacked perception; she did not see — it did not remotely occur to her — that by that late summer of 1901 her daughter was not the only one who resented her absolute devotion to her son. Her husband had expected her to be as little interested in this child once it had been born as she had been in the last. He watched her now with Nicholas, his face apparently impassive but within his eyes a perilous gleam of surprising and bitter anger. It seemed that what her act of unfaithfulness had failed to do, the constant sight of her adoration of the child, the fruit of her adultery, did. The sight of her besotted love for the child offended his manhood and his pride. A just retribution had not been exacted. Anna, thinking herself safe from him since he had not touched her, in desire or in violence, since the day he had struck her, did not notice the danger signs. They shared neither bed nor bedroom. He had made no attempt to claim or enforce his conjugal rights since Nicholas's birth. She assumed that he, like herself, found their mutual estrangement the only satisfactory way to face their unsatisfactory marriage.

She discovered her mistake one warm August evening, when the children in bed and believing Joss to be from home, alone in her bedroom she reached into the drawer of her dressing table and, with a feeling of secret, unshared pleasure that the action never failed to produce, drew out the much-handled, dog-eared sketch pad. Standing by the open window, with the speed of familiarity she flicked through it to the page that she wanted. Beyond the window a song thrush sang its tribute to the summer's evening. She lifted the precious picture to the light of the fading sun. She could almost smell the scent of pine and the fragrant woodsmoke. Nicolai's face, young, unchanging, smiled up at her.

She did not hear the door open. The first she knew of Joss's presence was the shadow that fell across the paper she held. Frozen, she stood as he reached and tweaked it from her hand. He looked at it, head bent, in silence. In a long agony of apprehension she watched him. Nicholai's smiling face trembled as the paper quivered almost imperceptibly in Joss's apparently steady hands. Then, lifting his head to look at her, very precisely he tore the page from the book, the paper from one side to the other, put the pieces together and tore again. The small sound Anna made was like a gasp of physical pain. Joss lifted his head. His voice was cold, perfectly steady. "However you may have convinced yourself, Anna, you are still my wife."

She said nothing, her eyes riveted to the paper he still held.

"And I think it not too extreme of me to expect you to act so. If you are ready to accept my protection for your son it seems to me that the least you might do is to try to keep your side of the dishonoured bargain of our marriage."

"I — I tried to thank you. For Nicholas —"

"I don't want your thanks."

"Then — what do you want?" Her voice was faint.

"I want what any man might reasonably require of his wife." The words were quiet. "I want what you have already given another. I want a son."

She stared at him struck utterly dumb. Then, "No," she said. "Joss — please —"

"A son," he said implacably. "Is that not a fair price to pay, Anna? And then your life is your own."

Benjamin Anatov was born on the very day in May 1902 that the stubborn, brave and bigoted commandos finally capitulated and the peace treaty was signed that brought to an end the South African war — a war that had seen a small guerilla force for a while hold at bay the might of an empire and had seen also an innovation in warfare ominous to any enemy civilian population, the concentration camp.

From conception to birth Anna's feelings for the child were ruled by absolute distaste: the only warmth upon seeing the tiny squalling scrap came from her heartfelt thanks that here was the boy that Joss had demanded and the loveless act that had led to the conception of this child need not be repeated. As for Joss himself, the child born and his pride appeased, he paid little attention to his new son. Indeed, to Anna's relief he paid little attention to any of them. His interests outside the home were expanding and prospering. He had put Michael — courting now and showing some signs of settling down — in charge of the fashionable new premises in New Bond Street that had more than once been patronized by the new King in search of baubles for his doting female 'friends', whilst he took offices in Piccadilly from which to run independently his growing financial empire. Tea in Ceylon, railways in the United States, gold in South Africa, silk and jade from China — it seemed to Anna that her husband had a finger in every financial pie in the City. Privately, as the years passed, the open acrimony between husband and wife was slowly overlaid by the everyday commonplace exchanges of a marriage in which, by mutual consent, contact between them was minimal and governed on the whole not by the fierce intimacies of a close relationship but by the more general rules of civilized behaviour. There were times when, bitterly, Anna found herself regretting the childhood infatuation that had tied her forever to this man, times when she could convince herself that the light of her love for him had died when he had with malice ruined her father, the man who had given him everything he had. And yet it was not always so, and there were occasions when, alone and lonely in her bed, she listened for his returning footsteps, could not sleep until his presence in the house reassured her that at least in that he was constant; whatever the reason, it seemed that he would not leave her. She knew that there were other women — told herself indeed that she felt nothing but relief that they kept him from her. She supposed that in the eyes of the world she had little to complain of: she had money, position, and a creative life both interesting and fulfilling. Victoria was a pretty, amiable child, a favourite of everyone. Nicholas was growing into an extravagantly handsome boy, the light of her life — and if there were those she knew who were ready to mutter words such as over-indulged and spoiled — she assured herself that it was sheer jealousy occasioned by the child's good looks and lively personality. As for Benjamin — who from the time he could toddle followed his older brother about like a small, devoted slave — he was a nice enough child, if quiet, and if Nanny were to be believed possessed of a reasonable brain, though for herself she could not feel the slightest warmth for the boy. Many women would, she knew, with good reason envy her. And if she yearned, she yearned in secret, loving in place of the reality that was denied her, a shadow, a memory with little substance except in her son's brilliant eyes. Many times, especially at first, she dreamed of presenting the son to the father. Of seeing the happiness in those warm, remembered eyes. Of a future, together, somewhere away from the eyes and the problems of the world — and then she would wake and know her dream for what it was: the fantasy of a child who loved always the stories that finished "— and they lived happily ever after". Life was not like that. Life rushed on, regardless, like a river in flood and one fought, and swam, and survived, or one allowed oneself to be overwhelmed, and drowned. So, tenderly, the pretty dreams were hidden in a treasured corner of her mind and she set about surviving the currents and pace of a world that was moving so fast that there were many to ask where it was heading in such a hurry.

Motor taxi cabs appeared on the streets of London, and in America Henry Ford watched the first car roll off the first assembly line in the world, and a machine that was heavier than air flew — this last piece of news greeted with downright scepticism as a hoax by many. Arabella, with great enthusiasm, joined the new Women's Social and Political Union that had been formed by Mrs Emmeline Pankhurst and threw herself predictably into the campaign for Votes for Women. Beth, laughing, refused to have anything to do with it, declaring herself entirely unable to tell one politician from the other, let alone vote for him. Anna, though she attended some meetings, found the feverish single-mindedness of most of the active members not to her taste and despite Arabella's stern disappointment, kept her distance. From Russia, during the year of 1904, came the first faint but persistent rumours of the stirrings of a revolt. Anna, more concerned that the great Fabergé had opened a branch office in London, paid scant attention to the reports. When she thought of Nicolai and the others she thought of them always in the idyllic safety of their northern retreat beside the lake — what had they to do with politics? Elena had written twice, her letters a year apart, and Anna had answered neither, her good sense telling her it was better so, for a wound constantly aggravated would never heal. It was therefore a surprise and something of a shock to receive unexpectedly another letter in Elena's distinctive writing in the February of 1905. She opened it with a strange feeling of trepidation. No one could have been unaware that since the infamous 'Bloody Sunday' a month before, when the wide streets and squares of St Petersburg had run with the blood of demonstrating workers cut down where they stood by the Tsar's troops, the city had been in a terrible state of unrest. Anna had stubbornly reassured herself then, and did so again now: nothing could have happened to Nicolai. She would have known. She would.

From the envelope as she opened it fell a piece of paper. She picked it up. Stared at it. It was the sketch that she had done of herself and Nicolai beneath the pine tree, that she had given him as a memento of the day. On the back of the picture, in Nicolai's hand, was the single word 'Anna' and the date 'August 1900'. She stared at it for a long time before she could bring herself to open the brief, sad letter.

"— trying to get home to his wife and baby — cut down by rioters in the Nevsky Prospekt — this sketch among his possessions — a memento of a happier day in a happier time — God rest his dear soul."

How long she sat, the paper clenched in icy, trembling hands Anna never knew. At last she stood. The cold shock was ebbing, the pain was making itself felt. Knife sharp. Agonizing. Blindly and with limbs stiffened as if by a stroke she climbed the stairs to the nursery.

"Mama! Mama! See what I've made!" Nicholas, always the first to greet her, bounded across the room and into her arms. She clenched the surprised child to her, bending her face to his bright head, tears shining on her cheeks. Victoria, face solemn and puzzled, walked to them and stood, worried and wondering, at the sight of her mother's distress. Ben, sitting amongst the building blocks discarded by Nicholas and already, with baby fingers, constructing a more complex contraption than his brother's, sat blinking and did not move. Mama would not want him to touch her, the child knew that already. Phlegmatically he went back to his intricate creation.

Outside the window the cold wind of winter, symbol of and brother to the wind of revolt that eddied and scurried in the corners of other cities than tragic St Petersburg, bent bare branches and blew tears of rain against the glass.

That wind of dissent — dissent against unemployment, against exploitation, against the denial of the basic right of the working man to have some say in his own destiny — blew, a year later, a Liberal Government into power in Britain, gave the newborn Labour Party its first significant electoral victories and sent a chill of foreboding through the ranks of the Establishment that had never believed such political changes possible. Unfortunately, however, for that other passionately embattled section of the population, the Suffragists, now coming universally to be known as the Suffragettes, the Liberals were no more interested in women's votes than were their Tory counterparts and so now the battle commenced in earnest, with Arabella in the thick of it. To Anna these larger events meant little. In 1905, the year of Nicolai's violent death, she designed for the Arts and Crafts Exhibition a casket of nephrite and rose gold. Red-gold leaves of ivy wreathed it. Hidden within that gleaming foliage a blood-red ruby, heart-shaped, nestled. The exhibit won interest and praise, but she would not sell it. The Exhibition over, the casket was placed upon a small table in her bedroom, within it the sketch that Elena had returned to her and that other picture, lovingly and skilfully repaired, that Joss had ripped. With strange delicacy Joss, who had his own sure sources of information, neither questioned nor commented on the box or its contents; but if Anna noticed this odd and gentle courtesy she was too shocked and sick at heart truly to appreciate it.

For the next two years the Liberal Government fought against an Opposition of almost all entrenched wealth and privilege to redress the wrongs that too fast and too uncontrolled a change in British society had wrought over the past century.

The Roses and the Anatovs, through it all, thanks to Joss's acumen, prospered greatly. In 1908, with the first introduction from America of comparatively cheap Ford motor cars, the price of rubber, essential for the comfortable motoring afforded by inflatable tyres, soared. Joss, always, it seemed, uncannily aware of the needs of tomorrow, had invested heavily in the fledgling Malayan rubber industry and in one day without moving from his office made a small fortune.

Josef, closeted within his small cottage in Essex and more at peace than he had been for years, watched them all and kept his own counsel. He felt little rancour at what Joss had done, for though it still had never been put into words he knew why it had been done, and felt that in allowing Joss his revenge his own sin had been at least in some part expiated. His every effort had been bent to minimizing the destructive effect that Joss's actions might have had upon the two interconnecting families, for that — the destruction of those family ties that had survived so much — would have been a punishment impossible to bear and one he was sure that Tanya herself would never have exacted, whatever Joss in his blind bitterness might believe. Joss himself would certainly have been astonished to know of the concern that the man he had ruined, the man who had been foster father to him, still felt. In exacting such vengeance, Josef wondered, and in tearing in anger from a reluctant world a success from which it would in time no doubt demand exacting payment, what debts was Joss incurring? And how would he be forced to pay them? Josef pottered in his garden and pondered these things, an old man whose greatest joys were the visits of his family, especially the younger members, even that one who reminded him so vividly of past tragedy — and watched with relief the world and its troubles pass him by.

About the same time that Joss made his killing on the rubber market, Michael married his Jane, a young lady he had pursued single-mindedly for a year until she had him — as Louisa put it — well and truly caught and nailed to the floor. Two months later, Louisa and Boris themselves came into a small bequest. Louisa's Sergeant Major father, still in India, fell victim at last to that continent's patient malice and succumbed to dysentery. His bequest to his only daughter — a handsome five hundred pounds — came as a surprise to both of them. Boris, to the varying degrees of exasperation of both the Anatovs and the Roses, needed little thought as to how to use this gift from heaven. Laughing still he invested it in the business he had come to know best, and Louisa found herself installed as hostess in the public house known as the Red Lion close by Plaistow Station. Of both families, only Alice Rose took any satisfaction from the move. For did it not simply confirm her long-held and unshakable opinion of the Boris Anatovs. They had found at last their proper level; and in Alice's opinion they should be left by their betters severely alone, to enjoy it.

PART FOUR

1910–1918

CHAPTER SIXTEEN

On the sixth of May 1910, the man who had waited so long to become King died after nine short years on the throne and both Britain and an unquiet Europe lost a valuable and virtually irreplaceable worker in the cause of European peace. The following week the peace of the living accommodation above the Red Lion was also disturbed, for Sophie Anatov, inevitably as she was herself coming to believe, was in disgrace again.

"You wrote this?" The words were barely a question. Her father lifted the piece of paper that he held, covered unmistakably in the ungainly scrawl that no effort by Sophie seemed able to discipline.

She all but shrugged, then, taking note of the dangerous gleam in his blue eyes, thought better of it. "Yes."

Boris studied the paper for a moment and then read from it: "In a so-called civilized country where half the population is female, half the work force is female and all of the mothers are female —" He paused, looked at Sophie, unsmiling, "Isn't that just a little heavy-handed?"

Unable to believe that he could truly stay angry with her, she grinned, swiftly and coaxingly, and then was sober again.

"— it is surely an outrage that intelligent, responsible people should be barred from the political life of their country simply because of their sex." He lifted his eyes.

Sophie flinched. "Miss Bantry didn't like that word either," she conceded, and rubbed her knuckles surreptitiously, remembering still the sharp cut of the ruler.

Her father sighed. "Sophie, as you well know, Miss Bantry didn't like any of it. Any more than she liked last week's effort on the iniquities of the calling-on system down at the docks, or your lecture last month on the recognition of Trades Unions. She knows you're simply repeating what you hear here in the bar. And — not unreasonably — it doesn't impress her. If you're told to write a composition on 'A Day At The Seaside' she doesn't expect you to get on your ill-informed soap-box and shout about the conditions on the docks."

Sophie did shrug this time, her lower lip set rebelliously.

"And this one —" he held up the offending composition "— 'My Hobbies,'" he said. "'My hobbies'?"

"I don't have any hobbies", Sophie said, perfectly and pertly truthful, "so I couldn't write about keeping guinea pigs, or embroidering handkerchiefs, could I?"

"So you decided to repeat what you heard at your Aunt Anna's last week?"

"I didn't repeat it!" His daughter's dark eyes met his own. He raised his brows and said nothing. The indignation in her strong-boned face gave way suddenly to that glint of mischief that was his delight and his bane. "I sort of rephrased it," she said.

Boris laid the composition on the table, turned for a moment to the window. In the busy street below, cartwheels clattered, a fish vendor called raucously, an electric tram clanged noisily by. When he turned, his face was still serious. For the first time his daughter eyed him with a trace of nervousness. "Papa. You aren't taking all this seriously, are you? Miss Bantry's punished me already —" she rubbed her knuckles again, ruefully "— I've got the bruises to show for that. It's only the same as the other times, isn't it? All right — I suppose it's a bit soon after the calling-on row — but, Papa — you *know* how beastly Miss Bantry can be — I don't believe you like her yourself. And once she's got it in for you," she shook her head, "you could be the Virgin Mary and she'd —"

"Sophie!"

"Well, it's true," Sophie muttered. "All this silly fuss about a stupid old composition. She's not satisfied with making my life a misery at school — she wants to get me into trouble here too. Pretending she's going to expel me so that we all go up there again and crawl around her." She stopped. Her father was shaking his bright, handsome head very slowly, and the faint sympathy in his eyes was alarming. "You can't mean — that she seriously wants me to leave?"

"This time — yes, I'm afraid so."

Sophie's face hardened defiantly. "Then good riddance to bad rubbish, I say. If the silly old bat's going to get the stupid vapours about *one word* —"

"Sophie!" her father said again, and this time the reprimand brooked no argument. Sophie frowned ferociously. Her lower lip was trembling treacherously. "I'm sorry," she muttered.

With commendable patience Boris kept his voice level. "It isn't one word, and you know it. And it isn't just what Miss Bantry sees as subversive or deliberately provocative compositions — yes, Sophie, deliberately provocative —" He held up a quick hand as his daughter made to intervene. "You may believe you can fool the rest of the world, but — please! — don't think you can fool me. I know what you do. I can't say I always understand why you do it —" He paused. Sophie said nothing. He strode to the bureau that stood in the corner and picking up a letter that lay there he read from it "— troublemaker, undisciplined and self-willed —"

Sophie blinked and bit her shaking lip hard.

"— incites misbehaviour in other pupils, is defiant and insolent when chastised —"

"I'm not!"

Boris ignored the indignant interruption, read grimly on. "I very much regret having to tell you that I find Sophie a disobedient and unbiddable child and as such she can have no place in our small and happy establishment —"

"Hah!"

"— to which she contributes nothing but discontent and disorder." Boris laid the letter down, looked at his scarlet-faced daughter. "Sophie", he said, his voice gentle, "you know the trouble we had getting you and Maria into Miss Bantry's in the first place —"

"Yes. And why? Because you run a public house! So what? Amy Brenton's father runs a grocery shop, Annie Howard's family are coal merchants! What's so special about them? How *dare* she — how dare anyone — look down on you because you run a pub! It isn't fair! It isn't right!" The tears that were stinging her eyes lit them to angry brilliance. Her fair hair, always untidy, tumbled across her wide forehead. Boris had to resist the urge to reach and gently brush it away. He kept his voice stern.

"And what of Maria? Do you ever think of her in your mischief-making? How hard it makes it for her to be the younger sister of someone who's always in trouble?"

Sophie hung her head. "She doesn't care," she muttered defiantly.

"Don't be absurd — of course she cares! Do you think she enjoys seeing you constantly punished, constantly and publicly held up as a bad example to her and her friends? Oh, yes," Sophie's head had lifted at that, "we know what's been going on. And not from Maria, either — she'd die before she'd tell on you. No — your mother has heard the stories from Mrs Howard, Mrs Brenton, Mrs Spencer! How do you think that makes her feel?"

There was a long, miserable silence. "But Papa," Sophie said at last, "I don't mean to be a trouble to you. Or to anyone. I don't mean to be naughty. Honestly I don't. It's just — oh, I can't bear it — all those silly rules and regulations — they're not *for* anything, are they? They're just for the sake of it, most of them: don't do this, don't say that — don't *think* anything, because that's bound to break a rule! And the girls, simpering and giggling and having crushes on the teachers, oh, it's all so unbearably *stupid!*"

"You mean that everyone is out of step but you?"

"No, of course not —"

"Or that you think you can go through life obeying only those rules that you agree with?"

"No! But — Papa, you always say we should think for ourselves, don't you? So I do — at least I try to. And then they cane me for it. They don't talk about it, or explain anything — they just beat me and tell me I must do as I'm told.". She stuck out a rebellious lip. "Miss Bantry believes a young lady should be 'mild, obedient, well-tempered and accomplished in those arts that will stand her in a good stead in her future home'. I ask you! Well, if that's what being a young lady means then —" she paused, dramatically "— then I'd rather die!"

"Well, now," her father's voice was quiet and not terribly

impressed by the threat, "from what I can gather since you are nowhere near approaching that state, I think we can say that your life is safe for now. What isn't safe, however, is your immediate future. When you are grown up and able to take your own decisions, then of course you may do as you wish. But for now, Sophie, you are our responsibility and we must fulfil our obligations to the best of our ability. With or without your approval."

At the tone of his voice Sophie had stilled and was watching him, wide-eyed. "What do you mean?" she asked bluntly, trepidation undisguised in the question.

"Miss Bantry, I fear, has made it quite clear that she has made absolutely certain not only that you lose your place in her establishment, but that you do not gain a place in any other of the same kind in the area."

"But I don't *want* —"

"Hold your tongue for a moment, will you?" The sharp edge of anger in his tone, brought on had she known it as much by his own distaste for this task as by anything else, made her jump. She clamped her mouth shut. "Try for a moment to consider what others want and need. You have disrupted not only your own education but your sister's. You have caused distress to your mother and to me. You're thirteen years old; you aren't old enough yet to know what is best for you. Of course you are right — we have no desire to see you turned into an empty-headed little doll. But neither do we want a hoyden for a daughter. It is time your learned the virtues of obedience, modesty and — above all — self-control." He paused, cleared his throat. She watched him, dawning horror in her eyes. "To that end," he said, folding the letter he still held very precisely into quarters, and not looking at her, "we have applied to a school in Essex, near Saffron Walden, not far from where Uncle Josef lives —"

She was staring at him, aghast. "You're sending me away?" she asked faintly.

He still could not look at her. "No! No, of couse not! You make it sound as if we're putting you in prison —"

"You might as well." The tears that the child had until now stubbornly resisted were pouring down her cheeks. "Papa — please don't send me away! I'll be good, I promise I will, I'll apologize to Miss Bantry. I'll get on my bended knees to her — I'll do anything you want —" She ran to him. He caught her to him, strongly, with his one arm, rocked her gently, this brave, headstrong, vital child that he loved and suffered for so much.

But the die was cast, and he knew it. They had given in once too often. "Too late, little one, I'm afraid. Miss Bantry has made it perfectly plain that she would not take you back under any circumstances. We have also verified the fact that no other private establishment around here will take you. Miss Bantry has a long arm, I fear."

She lifted her head, her eyes pleading. "But there's St Michael's just around the corner — why couldn't I go there?"

"No. I'll not have you attending that place."

"But why not? It wouldn't cost you anything — other people round here don't pay for their children to go to places like stupid Miss B's. Why should we be different?" In the miserable uncertainty of the question, had Boris had the ears to hear it, lay the core of his daughter's frustration and confusion.

He moved from her, turned her gently to face him, lifted her chin with his finger. Her tear-streaked face was woebegone in the May sunshine that filtered through Louisa's well-laundered lace curtains. "Listen to me, Sophie, with your undoubtedly clever little head, not just with your ears. We're only trying to do what we believe to be best for you. You must trust us. You must try to —" he paused, searching for words "— to have patience with the world. To see it, and to see yourself, as others do, at least sometimes."

"I will! I promise! But please don't sent me away!"

"We aren't 'sending you away'. St Hilary's is a fine school — it isn't too big —" he tried to smile, not very successfully "— nor too expensive. Just think — it will be an adventure. A chance to prove yourself."

"I shall hate it."

"Well, of course you will if you don't give yourself a chance to do anything else."

Unhappily the girl looked down at the hands that were clasped, twisted, before her and again the untidy, heavy fair hair fell across her eyes. She tossed it back, eyed her father with faint defiance. "When do I have to go?"

"They'll take you in October, after you're fourteen."
"I see," she said, very quietly. "It's all arranged then?"
"I'm afraid so," her father said gently.
She nodded briefly, her lips tight.
In the silence Louisa called from another room and Maria answered. A door opened and the noise from the bar drifted up the stairs, died again as the door closed with a bang. "You'll be able to visit Uncle Josef sometimes from the school. I know he'd love to have you. Which reminds me — he asked if you'd like to stay for a few days, you and Maria, after his birthday party. Your mother and I can only make it overnight, of course — with the business to care for — but if you like, we could leave you —" His voice, despite himself, was coaxing.
Stonily she ignored the tacit appeal. "That would be nice." The high colour had receded from her face and her mouth was set. Her father knew the expression well. He sighed. She looked him in the eye, open provocation in the lift of her head. "Papa?"
"Yes?"
"Why are we to stay in the cottage for Uncle Josef's party, when everyone else is staying in the big house?"
"Because," Boris said with quiet patience, refusing to rise to the bait, "Uncle Josef invited us to. It is his seventieth birthday after all, and we are to be his guests."
She watched him unblinking. Waiting.
"Besides," his gaze was unruffled, "as you well know, Aunt Anna's brother Alex and I don't get on well. He has every right to have — or not — whoever he likes to stay at Bissetts. It's his house."
"Only because his beastly wife's father made a fortune out of other people, then died and left it to him."
"Sophie, I will not have you speak so —"
"Well it's true. She is beastly. And so's he. I can't imagine how Aunt Anna managed to have such a horrid brother! The airs and graces they put on you'd think they were royalty at least."
"That — is — enough."
Knowing herself to have pushed him far enough, she subsided.
Boris, his face stern, perched on the edge of the table and held

out his hand. "Sophie. Come here."

Reluctantly she walked to him.

"Look at me."

She lifted her reddened eyes.

He looked at her for a long time. "Whose fault is it that you're having to be sent away to school?"

She opened her mouth, hesitated. Then, "Mine," she said.

"Exactly. Now — be my brave girl. Make the best of it. A new start. Make up your mind to make a success of it. You know you could if you really tried. Perhaps in a couple of years, when she's old enough, we'll be able to get together enough money for Maria to join you. Let her be proud of you if she does." He paused. "Let us all be proud of you."

She nodded. Stubbornly she was biting back tears again.

"And Sophie?"

His voice had changed a little — the stern note was ebbing, the warmth that usually so characterized it and that his daughter so loved was back. "Yes?"

"The party. At Bissetts. Best behaviour? Please?"

She made a sudden, funny, rueful face and sniffed. "Yes."

"Promise?"

"Promise."

The old bricks of Bissetts glowed with a mellow warmth in the June sun as Josef walked slowly up the winding lift of wooded drive that led from the stables and his cottage to the big house. Seventy years old. No matter how often it was said, how often he told himself, it was still almost impossible to believe. Seventy years, that stretched from one life to another, that encompassed happiness and misery, striving and achievement. That held at its core a shame he could not obliterate no matter how hard he tried. Each time he saw his grandchild, Victoria, so like that other, docile, lovely child, the knife turned in his heart. Ah, Joss — should that not be enough? He stopped for a moment, leaning on his stout walking stick surveying the peaceful scene of house, and lawns, of ancient trees, herbaceous borders and the solid tile-crowned walls of the enclosed garden and small orchard. The sweep of gravel in front of the house was freshly cleaned and raked, as was the main drive which curved from where he stood past the house and on to the road. On the lawns that were planted here and there with magnificent specimen trees, tables and chairs were set, the white cloths blowing a little in the light breeze that whispered too in the leaves. Soon the place would be full of people, most of whom he would not know, despite the fact that this was supposed to be his party. The chairs and music stands of the musicians were already set up near the little thatched summerhouse in the shade of a great stand of flowering rhododendrons. He stood quietly for a moment, to let his breathing ease.

Joss would not be here.

His refusal had been polite, his excuse perfectly acceptable. Josef sighed. This party had not been his own idea, but Alice's — ready always to show off to the family her own social expertise and connections. And yet he had been happy at the thought; amongst the strangers that his daughter-in-law would invite — to impress them or to impress others — would be his own family, Grace's family, all together again for the first time in years. And he had hoped an old man's hope: that Joss would find it in himself to forget twelve years of bitterness and would come. A man of seventy could surely hope to be forgiven by others — if not by himself — for the sins committed by a young man he had almost forgotten what it had been like to be.

A small dog, a King Charles spaniel, appeared on the top of the wide, shallow steps that led from the porticoed front doors, which stood open to the sunwarmed air. It sniffed the breeze excitedly, then, spying Josef, went into an ecstasy of yelping greeting and scampered to him, flag tail waving. He bent, smiling, to stroke the long, soft coat and to quieten the little animal.

"Father-in-law! Why, look at you! — you aren't dressed!" Alice had followed the dog out on to the steps. She was dressed exquisitely in pastel grey and white, the narrow hobble skirt and high waistline of her dress emphasizing with elegance her slight build. Upon her softly swept-up hair was perched a very wide-brimmed dove grey hat that was crowned with roses of pink and white. She looked, Josef told himself with the irreverence that he often, in self-defence, found himself employing against his domineering daughter-in-law, like nothing so much as an extremely elegant, flower-trimmed mushroom. "Everyone will be here in no time at all. Alex!" She turned to her husband who stood in the shadows behind her, did not bother to lower her voice, her tone sharp with annoyance. "For heaven's sake! He's wandering around out there as if he's got all day! He looks like the gardener! Alex — do something —"

Alex, splendid and portly in his formal day dress and black top hat came down the steps towards Josef. "Come along, Father." He was jovial, man of the world. "Let's get you home and changed. Can't have a party y'know, without the guest of honour, what?"

Alice tapped a small, grey-kid-shod foot impatiently as she watched Alex shepherd his father back towards the cottage. Honestly the old man could be utterly impossible. And after all the trouble she had taken to arrange this celebration for him! Such a pity that the twins were away — it would have been nice to show them off, her two tall, enviable sons, to the rest of the family. She knew that she looked well flanked by her handsome, impeccably mannered boys. She turned back into the house, stopped in front of a large mirror, leaned to it for a moment regarding her reflection critically. Then she tucked a charmingly stray hair back beneath her hat, smiled a little and lifted her voice. "Hetty? Hetty — here at once! The hall mirror has not been polished."

Boris, Louisa and the girls, despite their best efforts, were late. By the time they arrived the manicured lawns were crowded, the string ensemble was in full flight and all but being drowned out by the clatter of cups and saucers and the hum of conversation and laughter. Louisa climbed out of the hired trap that had brought them from the station, nervously smoothed down her last-year's dark blue serge that was much too hot for the day, and put an anxious hand to her small straw boater. A strong, long-fingered hand stopped her fidgeting. She looked up into her husband's smiling face. "Leave it. You look wonderful." She thought he looked pretty dashing himself in his borrowed striped trousers and black frock coat, despite the empty sleeve, and did not miss the covert glances thrown in his direction by a young lady in fashionable lemon and leaf-green who stood not far from them. Little Maria, sweet in Sophie's cut-down white muslin, was guarding her father's top hat with as much care as if it had been made of solid gold.

"Here — give it to me," Sophie tweaked the hat from her sister's grasp. "There. Now — you get out, and I'll hand it down." This exercise safely accomplished, she herself jumped lightly from the trap and stood looking around her with interest. The lawns of Bissetts looked exactly like the picture of a fashionable race meeting that she had seen last week in the *Illustrated London News*. The elegant, slim-skirted, high-waisted and softly coloured ensembles of the ladies with their enormously wide-brimmed miraculously trimmed hats contrasted picturesquely with the sober and formal dress of their partners. On the other side of the lawn she could see Aunt Anna, talking animatedly to a flamboyantly dressed young man, her daughter Victoria demure and still by her side. Anna, as always, was dressed more strikingly than any other woman in the gathering. Sophie had never seen anything like the slim, layered, tunic-like costume that her aunt was wearing, in a deep rust colour that stood out like flame against the green of the trees; and upon her head, totally in contrast to what looked to Sophie like every other woman's attempt to carry the entire contents of a fruit and vegetable barrow upon a hat whose breadth in many cases encompassed its wearer's shoulders and made a kiss of greeting all but impossible, was a creation in matching colour that hugged her head and looked like nothing so much as a turban. Victoria, all fluffy hair and wide violet eyes, was dressed in white and navy blue that was simple, charming and utterly appropriate. Sophie, in the fussy gingham that hadn't looked bad in Mr Burns' Drapery Shop, smiled brightly at her father. "Looks as if the bunfight's started."

"Boris! Louisa!" Ralph, tall and quiet-faced, excused by the attire of his calling from the elegant uniform of the other men, detached himself from the crowd and as the trap wheeled and pulled away, hurried towards them, hand outstretched. "How marvellous to see you. Father's around somewhere. He was asking after you —"

He ushered them through the crowds. Sophie hung back, eyes and ears eager, unashamedly eavesdropping as they moved from group to group.

"— nine times out of ten the damned — excuse the language my dear — the damned so-called working man doesn't know when he's well off! Unions my foot! What good are they?"

"— the Kaiser? All talk, old boy, all talk. He wouldn't dare —"

They paused beside their hostess. "— such a shame the boys couldn't make it. No, the South of France. The Bateleys — do you know them? They have a big place in Yorkshire. Such charming people. And so well-connected. Really too good an opportunity to miss, and they did so want to go. I couldn't bear to say no, even though it was their grandfather's seventieth. It's all Richard's fault, of course. He's off like a runaway at the first chance to do anything, and nothing will do but that Rupert must be everywhere with him. They're positively *inseparable* —" Alice, in midstream of conversation, barely bothered to pause, but nodded coolly at Louisa and Boris, and turned back to her listeners. Sophie valiantly resisted the almost overwhelming impulse to pull an extremely rude and childish face at the slim, dove-grey back.

"Boris! Louisa! Topping that you could make it!" Michael erupted into their path, shook Boris's hand, grabbed the smiling Louisa and gave her a smacking kiss, then stood back to survey the two girls. "Good God, how you've *grown*! This *can't* be little Sophie?"

Sophie indicated with a small, philosophically restrained smile that indeed it was, and reflected that it was likely that this would not be the only time today that she heard those words. She knew she was growing like a weed, regretted it bitterly, since her now patently unachievable hope had always been to be petite and trim as her mother. She found herself wondering, in one of those inconsequentially irreverent moments to which she was, according to Miss Bantry, so unnaturally prone, how adults would react if she greeted them with a phrase such as, "Golly, Uncle Alex — haven't you got fat?" Remembering her promise to her father, however, she resolved not to try it. Not today, anyway.

"Michael —" The cool, firm voice of Michael's young wife Jane cut through the general hubbub like a silver knife through butter. "The Russells are asking for you. Bertie wants to hear about the new motor car. Why Boris, Louisa, how nice to see you." She greeted the newcomers with genuine pleasure, offered them each a small, slim hand then, smiling and firm, said, "You don't mind if I steal Michael from you? There are some people waiting to meet him —" Like a lamb, Michael followed her into the crowd. Louisa and Boris exchanged smiling glances.

They found Josef with Anna, Victoria and the picturesque young man that Sophie had noticed earlier, who appeared to be hanging upon Anna's every word as if on a sacred utterance. Anna introduced him as Carl Latimer, a rising young actor of whom even Sophie had heard. She looked him up and down in open interest which, since his entire attention was once again focused upon Anna disturbed him not at all. One of the most fascinating things about her altogether fascinating aunt, Sophie had long ago decided, was her exciting and unusual circle of friends. Not for Aunt Anna the orthodox middle-class acquaintanceships occasioned by church, or children, or husband's occupation. Artists and actors, dancers and designers were more frequently to be found at the Bayswater house than the sharp-eyed, sharper-tonged, tea-drinking neighbours with little on their mind other than the more scurrilous current gossip whom Louisa tolerated for convention's sake and Sophie unreservedly detested. Though she knew that the rest of the family sometimes eyed Anna's friends with reservation, she herself both envied and admired her aunt's ease and vivacity in their company. So too, quite obviously, did the almost-famous Mr Latimer, since he seemed unable to keep his eyes off her.

"Anna's been gallivanting again," Josef said, after greetings and congratulations had been exchanged.

"Where to this time?" Sophie heard the tiny note of envy in Louisa's voice, and looking at her father knew that he too had recognized it.

Anna smiled. "Paris again. I had something in an exhibition — so Arabella and I took a couple of days off and went. There was a ballet we wanted to see, at the Theatre National de l'Opera —"

"Another Bakst?" Louisa was rather proud of herself to have remembered the somewhat odd name. No one could have been in contact with Anna over these past months without hearing her ecstatic reports of the costumes and decor designed by Leon Bakst, a Russian Jew newly launched upon Europe for the ballet *Cléopatre*, in Paris the year before. "Was it as good?"

"Good?" Anna made a sweeping gesture with both hands. "It was unbelievable! The man is an undoubted genius. An innovative genius —"

Sophie, bored with the adult conversation, smiled a little half-heartedly at Victoria. The cousins, though much the same age, were divided by temperament and environment and had never been particularly close. Sophie found Victoria dull to the point of tedium; had she but known it she, on occasion, terrified her older and quieter cousin almost speechless with her restless energy and quick mischief.

Victoria, as ever the soul of good manners, felt bound to react to the obviously well-meant overture. "Nicholas and Benjamin have gone to play in the orchard. Shall we go and find them?"

Anna, taking the question to be addressed to her, smiled absently at her daughter. "Oh, please do, darling. Nico is *bound* to be doing something outrageous. I'd feel happier if you'd keep an eye on him —"

Sophie, whose idea of a party was not to keep an eye on other people's small boys, opened her mouth, then caught her father's eye. He winked and jerked his head a little. A little less than graciously she extended a hand to Maria. "Come on, then. We might as well."

Before they trailed off after Victoria, however, Josef — who had also noticed the small byplay — bent to her ear. "I've some special marzipan in the cottage. I stole it from the kitchen, right from under Mrs Brown's nose! I saved it for you."

Impulsively she kissed his lined cheek. "We'll share it." There was a very special friendship between these two, even though there were no ties of blood.

The young people skirted the new deserted tennis court, followed the high old brick wall to the small gate that led into the garden and orchard. Within the walls it was shaded, warm, and comparatively quiet. At the foot of a gnarled old apple tree a small, bespectacled boy sat, snivelling.

"Oh, dear," Victoria said, a combination of vague distress and timidity in her voice that produced in Sophie a quick rise of what she knew to be unreasonable irritation. "Benjamin? Oh dear — Benji —"

The boy sniffed and hiccoughed.

"What's up?" Sophie asked.

"I can't find Nicholas. He ran away from me. He won't come back —"

"Oh dear," Victoria said again, and looked round vaguely, as if expecting to see her brother pop up from the ground. "Nico? Nicholas — where are you?"

"He won't come," sniffed the desolate Benjamin. "He said he was going to run away to sea and never come back."

"How silly," Sophie said.

"Nicholas!" Victoria shouted again.

Silence.

Maria tugged at Sophie's hand.

"Ni-cho-las!"

Sophie looked down at her sister. The smaller girl pointed. Sophie crouched down. Dangling amongst the thick foliage of a tree perhaps a dozen yards from where they stood was a small, woollen-stockinged foot in a shiny black leather shoe.

Sophie dropped her sister's hand, put her finger to her lips and crept forward. With a sudden movement she grabbed the foot and jerked. There was a shriek and a crackling of branches, and Nicholas Anatov, red-faced and absolutely furious, was deposited at their feet in a sprawling heap.

"Beastly thing! What do you think you're doing?" He leapt to his feet, fists at the ready, then subsided a little upon finding himself face to face with a girl. "Oh. It's you," he said.

"Yes, it is," Sophie snapped back brusquely. "And never mind about what I'm doing — what about you? Poor little Ben was in tears —"

"It doesn't matter." Small Benjamin had taken off his glasses to wipe his eyes. Now he replaced them, carefully, and blinked owlishly, "It really doesn't matter. Nico was only playing," he said anxiously.

"Funny sort of play that makes people cry."

"Silly sort of idiots that cry at a game," Nicholas clipped back, his eyes repressive upon his brother.

"I wasn't really crying."

Victoria, always the peacemaker, broke in hastily. "Why — why don't we go and find some lemonade or something? It's most frightfully hot and Mrs Brown does make the most lovely lemonade — I'm sure there must be some somewhere —"

They sat in the shadow of the wall, Sophie, Nicholas and Ben — Ben sitting as close to his brother as he could and still sniffing — Victoria and Maria discussing with well-informed interests the ladies' dresses and hats. Sophie, losing interest at last in the unproductive business of swapping mild insults with Nicholas stood up. "I'm going to find Uncle Josef —"

She discovered him sitting alone at a table beneath the magnificent spread of a cedar tree, a cup of tea and a large plate of cream cakes untouched before him. "Fancy sitting all by yourself at your own birthday party!" She dropped with inelegant force into the chair beside him.

He smiled. "It is one of the privileges of age, my dear. To choose one's company. Even at one's own birthday party."

She giggled. "Do you want me to leave?"

"Good Lord, of course not!"

"I say —" she pointed to the cakes "— can you spare one of those?"

"I can spare them all. Help yourself."

She laughed, hunted through the plate of cakes for the one that looked biggest and most interesting. "Are you enjoying it?" she asked through an unladylike mouthful. "The party, I mean?"

A small, open trap carrying one passenger had turned in at the drive and was approaching the house. Josef watched it, idly. "Yes. Very much. It's nice to —"

Sophie looked up from her cake at the sudden dying of his voice. The trap had stopped not far from them and its single occupant was stepping from it. Joss Anatov, slight, unruffled, paused to pay the driver. "Good heavens. Isn't that Uncle Joss? I thought he wasn't coming?" Sophie took another bite of cake. "I say, these are awfully good. Are you sure you won't have one?"

"No — thank you."

Sophie took her attention away from the cake again. "Uncle Josef? Is something wrong?"

"No, my dear. Nothing." Josef was watching the newcomer, a strangely apprehensive look upon his face. Anna too had seen Joss and was hurrying to him through the crowds. As she spoke to him he shrugged, shook his head, looked round.

Josef stood up.

Sophie, pondering the advisability of another cream cake, glanced up as Joss and Anna joined them and smiled her sudden, brilliant smile. She rather liked her Uncle Joss, though it had not escaped her attention that some others did not. She thought him handsome, rather exciting and always interesting. Like now, for instance. From the look on Aunt Anna's and Uncle Josef's face they neither expected him nor knew what to expect now that he had arrived — Sophie took another cake and watched with interest.

"Papa — look who's here —" Anna's face was flushed, her voice over-bright.

"Joss," Josef said quietly, "I thought — I understood — that you would not be coming."

"The business I had to attend to finished sooner than I thought. There was a train —" Joss made a small, sparely graceful gesture with his hand. Sophie nearly smiled; one of the things she liked most about Uncle Joss was that, like her father, no matter how English he might think himself there was always about him a spectacular 'foreignness' that in her eyes added splendidly to his attraction. "— so I caught it." His voice was even. In his hand he held a small parcel. Oddly abrupt, he held it out to Josef. "I found this. I thought — a small gift —"

Josef took the package with hands that trembled a little. Anna was watching her husband with eyes in which astonishment, exasperation and disbelief warred. Sophie turned her attention back to the cake, which was lamentably leaking cream on to the tablecloth.

"I found it in a secondhand bookshop," Joss said. "The illustrations were very beautiful, I thought. As you see, it was bound in St Petersburg."

Josef held the little book in hands that were now truly shaking. "Thank you."

"Sit down, Papa." Anna was at his side, her hand gentle upon his arm. "You mustn't overtire yourself." She settled him in his chair, straightened and looked at her husband. Her unpredictable, infuriating, unfathomable husband.

"I wish a word with Boris," he said, coolly polite, and left them. She watched him through the crowd. How was it that after all this time, all the bitterness, he could still stir her so unexpectedly? Why, when she had seen him arrive, had she left her young and attentive escort and hurried to him? He had greeted her politely, of course, congratulated her with faultless good manners on her appearance. What else had she expected? Nothing, of course. Nothing.

Sophie stood up, licked the last of the cream from her long index finger. "I'd better go and find Maria and the others. May I take these — if you don't want them?"

"Of course."

"Thanks, Uncle Josef." She kissed him again, smiled at Aunt Anna, who did not notice because her eyes were still fixed upon Uncle Joss, who was talking to Papa, and, plate precariously balanced, made her way back to the shadow of the wall. "Your Papa has arrived," she told Victoria. "He's over there — see? Have a cake —"

"Gosh — thanks," Ben said.

"I thought he wasn't coming." Victoria's sweet face was puzzled.

"Well, he has. Here — tuck in before they all go —"

It was later, as the crowds began to thin and a steady stream of carriages crunched through the gate and up the gravel drive to pick up their passengers, that Sophie finally gave in to her own desires and slipped off alone.

"Where's Sophie?" Victoria asked Maria.

Maria shrugged. "Don't know. Gone off somewhere. I say — just look at that carriage — isn't it grand? Must belong to a Lord or something, mustn't it?"

With the final guests seen at last on their way, most of the family gathered at a table beneath an enormous oak tree, bottles of champagne open before them. The sun slanted through the branches, not yet in their full leaf, and the air rang with bird song. Jane and Michael had changed from their finery and were playing tennis, their laughing voices and the singing of the ball from the racquet echoing from the sun-warmed walls of the old house.

Anna and Louisa, escaping from Alice by mutual and silent agreement, strolled beneath the trees.

Louisa turned her head. "I — wanted to ask you a favour."

"Of course," Anna said, instantly, "what is it?" These two, though not often in each other's company and necessarily divided, as were their daughters, by interests and environment, were still fast friends.

"It's Sophie. We're having a little trouble with her again. She's been — well, I'm afraid she's been expelled from school. We're sending her to a boarding establishment not far from here. In October. It's a very nice school. It really is. I found the headmistress most charming — most understanding —" She trailed off. Anna waited. "But Sophie — oh, dear, she does so hate the idea. And has simply made up her mind to be miserable. I wondered — if you perhaps had a word. She does admire you — she might listen to you."

Their feet rustled in the fresh and fragile grass of early summer. "I'll try. If you think it will help."

"I'd be very grateful."

Anna looked around. Maria and Victoria were still sitting by the wall, their skirts spread prettily around them, their attention taken by the tennis players. Nicholas and Benjamin were playing fivestones on the path not far away. Of Sophie there was no sign. "Where is she?"

"Maria." Louisa lifted her voice, "Where's Sophie?"

Maria shook her head. "I don't know, Mama. She went off on her own."

Louisa looked at Anna in exasperation. "You see what I mean?"

Sophie was at that moment in her favourite spot at Bissetts. Beyond the lawns and kitchen gardens at the back of the house, by the overgrown, thicketed boundary that gave on to meadows and a distant church spire was a small ruin. Once it had been a two-roomed cottage, then a makeshift stables. Now the building had all but fallen down and was nothing more than a nettle-infested, ivy-grown heap of tumbled bricks. Two walls still stood, however, and enclosed what had once been a small yard-garden. It was sheltered and sunny and had within it a tiny pool, scummed now and overgrown with weeds and water plants. Sophie had discovered this place many years ago, once, whilst staying with Uncle Josef, and had shared it with no one. She had believed it then, when the world had been kinder, an enchanted place. She loved it still, and still, too, half-believed in the magic with which her childhood had invested it. She sat, gingham green-stained and crumpled, knees drawn up, watching the busy insect life of the little pool. She picked up a small handful of gravel stones and held them high above the surface, letting them drop one by one, watching the wide ripples for the magic pattern that she had once believed meant a wish fulfilled.

— I wish I could stay here — just here — for ever;

— I wish horrible Miss Bantry had never been born;

— I wish I could be like Victoria;

— No, I don't. But I wouldn't mind being less like me;

— I wish I were grown up. I wish I were Aunt Anna;

— I wish Papa hadn't lost his arm;

— I wish people wouldn't be so absolutely awful sometimes.

A cuckoo called in the distance. Something scurried through the undergrowth beside her.

— I wish, I wish, I wish that there was no such thing in the world as boarding schools.

CHAPTER SEVENTEEN

In the course of her first year at St Hilary's Sophie ran away twice. On neither occasion did she get any further than the station of the small village near which the school was situated. The headmistress, Miss Salisbury — an unusually enlightened woman who showed, in the opinion of many of the more conservative members of staff, more understanding and tolerance than Sophie deserved — did everything that was reasonably within her power to help the child to settle, but to no avail. Sophie, caught between the world she knew and one that she considered neither knew nor cared about her, and in which she felt a stranger, was unhappily — and predictably — badly behaved. Whilst the world beyond the high walls that bounded the school grounds stirred and trembled with a groundswell of revolutionary change as the unrest of the working classes built towards bitter industrial strife and women besieged Parliament and engaged in pitched battles with a police force whose avowed intention was to break the women's movement once and for all, Sophie suffered helpless homesickness and a largely self-inflicted loneliness. She was popular neither with her fellow pupils, who found her arrogant and difficult to get to know, nor with most of the staff, to whom she showed an even worse face. St Hilary's was a school for the solidly middle-class — Sophie's first shock came when her father told her firmly that in his application to the school he had described the Red Lion as an hotel, and that, like it or not, that fabrication would have to stand. It was unfortunate, too, that she arrived as a new pupil in a class of a dozen or so girls whose friendships and loyalties were particularly well formed and cemented. Not that there were not, at first, those to make overtures to the tall, interesting-looking girl whose ability on the games field put her into the first team for netball and for hockey within a month of her joining the school. But Sophie would have none of what she quite mistakenly construed as their patronage, and unsurprisingly they soon left her to her own devices. So, during that first year she was more miserable than she had ever imagined it possible to be, which simply aggravated an already difficult situation.

The summer of 1911, however, brought some relief — the long school vacation, most of which was spent, at Josef's suggestion, at Bissetts with him. Louisa and Boris were only too thankful to accept, happy to keep the girls away from the events that were stirring in London. It was a stifling summer, and the city sweltered in heat and tension. In Parliament a constitutional crisis involving the curtailing of the power of the House of Lords caused chaos for the government. In the country at large industrial unrest was seething — seamen, dockers, miners, transport workers, all were bitterly dissatisfied, and resentment and discontent were building to explosion point. During that uncomfortably warm June, the month that the new King, George the Fifth, was at last crowned, there were strikes, riots and fire-raising all over the country. A month later, however, these domestic troubles were for a time at least overshadowed for two tense weeks by an outside threat as a Germany that was pursuing ruthlessly a policy of expansion confronted France in Morocco. Off the coast of Norway, uncomfortably well-placed for a sudden strike across the North Sea, the German Fleet steamed, an overt threat to British security. David Lloyd-George, speaking at the Mansion House, asserted publicly that if Britain felt her interests anywhere in the world to be threatened, she would fight. An outraged Germany growled, and Europe teetered on the edge of conflict. In the bar of the Red Lion, however, the credibility of this threat soon crumbled beneath the weight of more immediate issues. What was the Navy for if not to defend our shores? Leave it to them. More pressing was the need — some were now saying the right — of every working man to a living wage and security for his family, for improved conditions in the docks and in the mines. One by one they went on strike: the miners, the dockers, the transport workers. There was rioting in Liverpoool, in Manchester and in London and the troops were called out. By the middle of August, with the threat of war thankfully receding, the whole of industrial England's railway system was paralysed. London itself had been brought almost to a complete standstill and was like an armed camp, with soldiers patrolling the streets and camped in the parks.

Safe at Bissetts, however, Josef and the girls were little affected by the disturbances. They learned what little they knew from newspapers and from Louisa's letters, and buried there in the tranquil peace of the rural Essex countryside it all seemed far, far away. Sophie lived that long summer day by day, grateful for the peace and pleasure of the place in which she found herself, refusing to look back or ahead, spending the warm days in exploring the countryside, reading beneath the tall old trees, dreaming by the side of 'her' little pool. With youth's almost unique ability to live purely for the present, she dismissed the thought of the coming year and lived for the moment. The big house itself was empty, apart from a small staff — Alex was working in the city and living in the London house, Alice and the boys were summering in Italy. Mrs Brown, the Roses' cook, took great pleasure in exercising all of her considerable culinary talent upon feeding the occupants of the cottage. At least — as she confided to Mrs Lawson, the housekeeper — her good offices were much and openly appreciated by old Mr Anatov and his two young guests, which was more than could be said with regard to some others she could mention —

In the valleys the miners were starved back to work: but the dockers won their battle and put new heart into Trades Unionists all over the country.

Sophie Anatov lay dreaming upon the summer grass and ignored the rest of the world.

The rest of the world, however, flatly refused to be ignored forever. Time, that intractable enemy that cannot be defeated, moved inexorably on and inevitably the day came for her to return to school.

Louisa arrived from Plaistow a couple of days before she was due to leave, with her school trunk, it being felt that a trip all the way to London and back would be a tiring waste of time for the child. And then, despite Sophie's best efforts to pretend that it would not happen, the moment finally came when she and her mother stood upon the platform of the tiny country station, the labelled trunk at her feet, and looked for words to say goodbye.

"I've hardly seen anything of you," Louisa said.

"No."

"But — you did understand? About staying at Bissetts? It's been awful in London. It was so much better that you should be here."

"Of course. And we didn't mind. We enjoyed it — apart from not seeing you and Papa of course —"

In the distance a small plume of smoke reached a vapour-like finger above the massed green of the treetops.

Louisa took her daughter's hand. "Sophie — please? Try to be happy. It'll be better this year, you'll see. You know the place, and the people —"

"Yes."

"Papa had a very nice letter from Miss Salisbury. She's very concerned about you. And she hopes that you'll settle this year."

Sophie said nothing. They could hear the train now, distantly and cheerily puffing up the incline towards the station. The rails hummed. People on the platform began to collect together coats and baggage.

Louisa struggled on. "And next year — with any luck — Maria will be joining you. She's so looking forward to it."

"I'm sure she'll enjoy it," Sophie said, with truth. There seemed to be, somewhere lodged in the pit of her stomach, a cold stone, chill and heavy.

Her mother clasped her suddenly to her. The child was already a good two inches taller than she. "You'll be fourteen soon. Quite grown up."

"Yes." Sophie stepped back from her, smiling woodenly.

"I'll send you a cake. To share with your friends."

"Thanks." The brief word was all but lost in the busy clatter of the train's arrival. It sighed steam and was still. Sophie climbed into a carriage, banged the door and let the window down, leaning out to watch as her mother saw to the safe stowing of her trunk in the guard's van. Louisa came to the carriage window, reached an anxious hand and lifted her face for a last kiss. The engine let out an imperious shriek and the train began to pull away. Louisa moved with it, still holding her daughter's hand. "You'll be all right?"

"Of course." Sophie managed a too-bright smile. She let go of her mother's hand as the train gathered speed and, clamping her shapeless uniform hat on to her mane of blonde hair, hung from the window watching as the small figure who stood upon the platform, hand upheld, diminished to doll-size and finally disappeared as the train swayed around a bend.

Sophie sat back into a seat, bolt upright, and stared ahead, bleakly, into space.

A woman sitting opposite her smiled companionably. "Going back to school?"

"Yes."

"Do you have far to travel?"

"No."

The woman appeared not to notice the unmannerly brusqueness of the replies, nor the suspicious brightness in the girl's eyes. She fluttered a gloved hand. "How much I envy you modern girls! My own daughter simply *adores* her school — she'll be Head Girl next year, I do believe. How very different from my own childhood — only the boys were lucky enough to go away to school in those days, my dear. So see how lucky you are —"

Sophie, very deliberately, turned her head away and stared stonily out of the window.

The third time that Sophie ran away from school her plans were better laid and she made it all the way to that person and place that to her personified refuge, Uncle Josef and Bissetts. It was a wild and wet winter's night in the December that followed that sultry, violent summer that Sophie, victim of yet another clash with authority in which she had inevitably come off worst, climbed from her dormitory window, scaled the school wall and set off to walk not to that station that was closest to the school and where she had been so easily apprehended twice before, but across country to the next stop down the line. It was a cold and frightening journey, and a child of less obstinate courage would have given up long before her destination was reached. Sophie, however, chilled, tired and more than a little frightened, had set it grimly in her mind that this time she would reach Bissetts. Surely — surely — Uncle Josef would stand up for her? He wouldn't let them send her back? Uncle Josef was getting old. He needed someone to look after him. Why shouldn't they live there, at the cottage, just the two of them? She wouldn't give up. She wouldn't.

The woebegone figure that turned up at last in the sheltered porch of the cottage that night, was however, far from an heroic one. The long dark walk from the station had leeched the last defiant self-confidence from her; she had never felt so much an outcast as when she had plodded, drenched as a drowning cat, past the secured windows and doors of the cottages along the road, never been so grateful for the sight of that familiar, studded door. Even the unexpected sight of her Aunt Anna's face, sleepy and questioning, at the open door did not surprise her enough to overcome the enormous relief at having at last come to warmth and safety.

"What the — Sophie! For Heaven's sake! What are you doing here? Lord — you're soaked! Absolutely soaked! And shivering — come in. Here, let me help you —" Anna, pulling her dressing robe about her against the cold air that streamed into the house from the open door, stopped suddenly as the implications of her niece's unexpected appearance filtered through to her sleep-clogged brain. "Oh, Sophie," she said.

Sophie was crying. She had lost her hat in the scramble over the wall, and her hair was sodden rats' tails, water-dark and bedraggled. Her heavy woollen coat had simply soaked up the rain, and hung heavily, chill and unpleasant-smelling. Her feet were wet. She was, as Anna saw, shaking like a leaf, from cold and misery. Her skin was pallid, blue-tinged.

"Come along." Anna was suddenly brisk. "Get those wet things off before you catch your death. I'll get the eiderdown from my bed. It'll be warm and dry at least. And Sophie — be quiet, dear, please. Papa – Uncle Josef – hasn't been at all well. Oh, don't worry," she added as the young, woebegone face turned to her in fresh alarm, "it isn't serious, and he's much better. But he has been rather unwell and it's best his sleep isn't disturbed." She bent to poke the dying fire briskly. Small flames licked around an unburnt log and the flare of it lit the familiar, homely room briefly. "Hurry — you're drenched. We can't have you catching pneumonia —"

Sophie silently climbed out of her sodden clothes and accepted the eiderdown her aunt offered. She curled into an armchair in front of the fire, her long legs folded beneath her. Anna took the wet clothes into the kitchen, where the range at this time of year was always kept burning, and came back a short while later with a steaming cup and a handkerchief. Sophie accepted both with muttered thanks, and blew her nose resoundingly.

"Well," Anna said, pensively, "here's a to-do."

Sophie ducked her head. She had stopped crying. Her mouth was stubborn.

The silence lengthened.

"Are we going to sit here like this all night?" Anna asked at last, mildly tart. "Or are you — eventually — going to say something?"

Sophie lifted her head. The young, strong bones shone in the fire-light. "I'm sorry."

Anna considered. Then, gently, she shook her head. "Not good enough. We're going to have to do better than that. But first —" she stood up "— we must get a message through to the school. They must be worried sick about you. Papa doesn't have a telephone here, so I'll have to walk up to the house. Don't move —" she lifted a firm finger "— you hear me? Don't *move* until I get back."

"But — Aunt Anna — it's awful out there — you'll get drenched."

Her aunt surveyed her, not unkindly. "My dear child — it's a little late — isn't it — to be considering the welfare and convenience of others?"

Sophie had no answer to so obvious a truth.

"Just stay where you are. We won't be long. And then — we'll see what's to be done about all this."

Several hours later Anna surveyed her niece's blotched, unhappy face with exasperated affection and sighed. The built-up fire flared and flickered between them; the buffeting of wind and rain against the window reinforced the air of cosy privacy that had encouraged intimacy and confidences. For hours — and for the first time in her life — Sophie had poured out her troubles with honesty, into a more or less sympathetic ear. Now she sat, still huddled into her eiderdown, nose and eyes reddened by emotional weeping, but much calmer. Anna remembered — oh, how well she remembered — the age, and the sense of confusion that went with it. She remembered too a child younger than this one who had run away and had been comforted.

Joss.

The thought of him, as always, intruded suddenly and disturbingly into her mind, like a rock that breaks the water of a smooth, fast-running stream.

Sophie sniffed disconsolately.

Anna smiled. "Could you drink another cup of cocoa?"

"Yes, please. If it isn't too much trouble."

"Of course not. I won't be long." Anna picked up the cups and went back into the kitchen. Although all their meals came from the big house, Mrs Lawson always made sure that the larder was well stocked with snacks and beverages. She put a small saucepan of milk upon the range, reached for the cake tin. Then she stood for a moment, a hand to her tired eyes, her mind distracted from her niece's predicament to her own — to the enigma of her relationship with the man who was her husband.

For what seemed now to have been a long time — after Nicolai, and the near-ruin of her father — she had believed herself to hate him. That cold-blooded insistence that she bear him a son had exacerbated that emotion and had driven the wedge deeper between them. And yet — always it seemed she found herself using those words about Joss — and yet the fact remained that he had not discarded her as he might have when he had discovered her to be carrying another man's child. Neither had he, as he might have done, made her life a purgatory of penance and penitence. On the contrary, after Ben had been born she had been left to live her own life in a way that she knew to be the envy of a lot of women.

She straightened. Ran her hand through her hair. Opened the cake tin and reached for a small plate.

Then why was she not satisfied? Why — despite the freedom that he afforded her to live her own successful life, despite her insistence to herself that his attentions, physical or otherwise, would be entirely unwelcome, did she perversely find herself lately more than ever resenting that cool emotionally barren relationship that at first she had welcomed? Resenting his absences. His secrecy. His women.

She arranged some of Mrs Brown's small, appetizing-looking cakes carefully upon the plate.

There. She had admitted it. For the first time. She smiled wryly to herself. It must be a night for honesty. Poor, miserable little Sophie had bared her soul. It must be catching.

She nibbled at a cake, hardly tasting it.

And now, again, as she had known it would, her mind was teasing at the puzzle of that odd occurrence last week. Why could she not forget it? It wasn't, after all, as if anything had actually happened. Was that it? Was it that the odd, disturbingly dissatisfied feeling that recollection of the incident invariably brought was something close to disappointment? She stood, still and cold, and tried to force herself to honesty.

It had been the night before she had heard of Josef's illness and had come to the cottage to nurse him. Joss, as he usually did, had come home late, long after the rest of the household had retired for the night. The sound of the cab in the street had awakened her. She had heard the shutting of the front door, and then his light step on the stairs, had registered the slightest hesitancy in his tread that had suggested to her that at least one of his companions this evening had been a vodka bottle. She had lain in the darkness, listening, seeing in her mind's eye the slight, austerely handsome figure, a little dishevelled, as he climbed the stairs and made his way to his own rooms at the other end of the house. Then it had for a moment seemed that her heart had ceased beating; his footsteps had turned not away from her door but towards it, and then had stopped. A moment later a chink of light had appeared, a needle of lamplight that had pierced the darkness and then widened to a shadowed shaft as he had pushed the door silently open and entered the room. With no conscious thought she had closed her eyes, with an effort kept her breathing even. Yet surely — surely — he must have heard the pounding of her heart? The light of the shaded lamp he held had glowed rosily through her closed lids. He had stood in silence over her for a full minute, that to Anna might have been an hour. And then, neither touching her nor speaking, he had turned and left the room, closing the door very quietly and leaving behind him the faint aromas of his night; the smell of spirits, of cigar smoke and a slight, cloyingly sweet perfume that lingered like poison in the air above her bed.

She had not slept well that night, and had been ashamed of her dreams.

"Damn!" The word was vicious and aimed not exclusively at the milk that was boiling and sizzling on the hot plate. She retrieved the saucepan hastily, held it, dripping, over the sink until its seething had stopped, then with what was left made a full cup of cocoa for Sophie and half a cup for herself.

Settled back in the cosy little sitting room, she pushed her own troubles to the back of her mind and regarded the girl with pensive, questioning eyes.

Sophie fidgeted for a moment under her regard, and then asked abruptly, "Aunt Anna — what am I going to do?"

"I think," Anna said quietly, "that that's rather up to you. Don't you?"

"I s'pose so." The words were glum. "But, Aunt Anna, I don't know where to start. I'm never going to fit in — I can't."

"Nonsense." Anna leaned forward, "Sophie — darling — listen to me. First; no one ever solved a problem by running away from it. I think you know that in your heart of hearts already. Second; if you've spent all this time thinking about yourself and you've come to no constructive conclusions, then why not try looking at things from a different angle? Why not try thinking about someone apart from yourself for a change?" Though the words were a little harsh, the tone was gentle. Sophie was watching her intently. Anna searched tiredly for the words that might help the child. "You seem to think that your parents have sent you away and abandoned you — that they don't understand, that you're alone in all this. You know as well as I do that that simply isn't true. Your parents want to do what they see as best for you; not necessarily for now, this minute — but for the rest of your life. They see things that you don't. They know things that you don't. And if they have made mistakes — and personally I don't believe they have — it's only in their eagerness to help you. You're a lovely girl, lively and intelligent," she stopped the girl's self-conscious words of protest with a wave of her hand, "of course you are. And times are changing, thank heaven. There will be a place for girls like you in tomorrow's world, please God; that's what people like Arabella are fighting for. But if you're going to take advantage of that you have to acquire a decent education. You surely don't want to work at the bar of the Red Lion all your life?"

The girl lifted a quick, mutinously defensive head. "If it's good enough for Papa —"

"But it isn't. Is it?" Anna asked quietly. "We both know it. We all know it. Your father knows it himself. It's his stiff-necked pride, his total inability to back down once he's embarked on a course of action —" She broke off for a moment, a sudden thoughtfulness in her eyes. Then continued, "You of all people should understand. You're like it yourself. I'm coming to believe it's an Anatov trait. Your father doesn't belong in Plaistow running the Red Lion. He should be working in the business with Joss —"

"He won't do that."

"I know he won't. And I think it perfectly ridiculous. But I understand to a certain degree and I know there's no use in arguing with him. But I also know that he'll break himself to ensure that you and Maria don't suffer because of his obstinacy. He knows the difficult position he's putting you in — but he's trusting to your courage, your good sense, that you'll make the best of it — of what he's trying to do for you. And then how do you repay him?"

Sophie was silent.

"They deserve better of you." Anna's voice was still gentle.

"But — it's all so difficult! So — so stupid! Why must I lie about what Papa does? I'm not ashamed of it —"

"And neither should you be."

"And why should I bother with people I don't like —" the girl hesitated, then added, honestly and desolately "— or rather with people that don't like me?"

"Oh, for heaven's sake, child!" her aunt scolded. "Don't like you? How on earth would you know? How much chance have you given them to like you? If you snub people — show no interest in their friendship — how hard can you expect them to try? You don't get anything for nothing; you have to work at this the same as anything else. No one's going to go on bended knee and beg, 'Sophie Anatov, please be my friend'! You have to show people that you want them. You have to fit in with the society in which you're living. You have to compromise —"

Sophie shook her head. "You don't do that."

Anna stared at her. "My dear Sophie! Of course I do! More than most if you really think about it. I just do it in my own way. And that's what you have to learn to do. To use not only your own talents, but those of the people around you, the support of the group you're living with. Sophie — you have to stop fighting the world. You can't win. You'll never win, not the way you're going about it. And it isn't fair — to yourself, to your parents, or to Maria. She's joining you at school next year, isn't she?"

"Yes."

"Then there's an aim for you. When Maria joins you, let her be proud of her big sister. Don't make yourself a liability to her. You have to change your attitude. To *try* — to be happy, to fit in, not to judge people so harshly. You have to soften a little. Don't be so stiff-necked. So ready to be hurt. Learn to bend a little with the wind. Dead wood breaks, the willow does not —" Once again she had that strange feeling that had assailed her earlier on — that she was talking not only to Sophie, but to another, more obdurate ear.

There was a long, thoughtful silence. Then Sophie, completely calm now, turned her head to look at Anna. "Is that truly what you do? Bend with the wind? Compromise?"

"Of course." Anna brought her attention back to the child. "But then I believe that we all do, whether we recognize it or not."

"But you're so different! So individual! You're the last person I'd think of as —" Sophie shrugged "— as following the herd."

Anna shook her head sharply. "I said nothing about following the herd. That isn't what I'm talking about at all. I said you don't have to take on the herd single-handed." She leaned back. The wind had died a little and the room was quiet. "When I discovered that the world expects its women — quite unreasonably — to be physically attractive, regardless of how bright, or talented or intelligent they might be — I didn't make myself uglier in an attempt to show the world that I didn't care for its ways. I did care. I cared a lot. So — I did something about it? Do you think any the less of me for it?"

"Of course not."

"Then — can't you see that the same applies to you? Except that you haven't thought it through. You are — at present — making yourself 'uglier' — not physically, but in your attitude and character. And yet there are so many people who are ready to help you, if you'll let them. The headmistress of your school, when I spoke to her this evening, sounded charming, and was obviously very concerned about you. Fortunately, by the way, she hadn't had a chance to contact your mother and father, so at least they've been spared a night of worry."

Sophie ducked her head.

There was a short silence. "My dear," Anna said at last, "I think you know — you're beginning to see — how very silly you've been."

"Yes."

"And — are you going to do something about it? It won't be easy."

"I'll try." The young passionate face was touchingly determined. "I promise I'll try. I'll remember everything you've said tonight. No one's ever really talked to me about it all before."

Anna half-smiled. "And whose fault might that be do you think?"

"Mine. I never asked anyone. Never knew how to ask." Sophie paused, then added, "I don't think I knew that I wanted to ask."

"Well," Anna was brisk, "it's all agreed, then. A new start. Now, you'd better get off to bed. There isn't much of the night left and I promised I'd get you back to the school first thing in the morning."

For the first time the enormity of her crime seemed to strike Sophie. "Was — was Miss Salisbury very angry?"

"Of course she was. And worried too, You won't get off scot free —"

Sophie pulled a face.

"— but I promise I'll do my best for you. I'll have a word

with her. Tell her that we've talked. That things are going to be better now."

Tiredly Sophie got to her feet. "Thank you." She bent to kiss her aunt's cheek. "Thank you for everything. Good night."

"Good night, my dear. And Sophie —"

Sophie, at the door, turned.

"Don't let me down."

"I won't."

"And if you ever need help — someone to talk to — I'll always be there, if it helps."

"It does," the girl said, softly. "Thank you. Good night."

Anna sat for a moment, listening to the girl's footsteps as she slowly climbed the creaking stairs. The fire was dying. She leaned forward, chin on hands, to the last of the warmth. "I never asked anyone," Sophie had said, "I never knew how to ask —" and strangely the words had twisted in her like physical pain.

The fire tumbled at last to ash. Anna gathered her gown about her against the chill, and went to bed.

Sophie surprised herself with the determination that grew and blossomed from that night. Never one to do anything by halves, grimly at first but then with gathering confidence, success and enjoyment she set about directing that headstrong energy that had been turned until now largely to rebellion and mischief into more positive channels. She learned — not without difficulty — to curb her temper and her tongue, at least for most of the time, learned too to be more tolerant in her reaction to her own and others' failings. By the time Maria joined the school in 1912 it was to find herself the sister of something of a school heroine on the sports field — hadn't she scored that famous last-minute goal against the High School and saved the day? — and a girl who, if still not everyone's favourite, at least and at last was the centre of a small circle of loyal friends. If, still, she sometimes led those friends into mischief it was of a different order than before. There was, Miss Salisbury observed with truth, a world of difference between slightly anarchic high spirits and miserable and bitter rebellion.

That year, that Sophie and her friends spent playing cricket and tennis, and studying Shakespeare and Wordsworth, saw the further deepening of the country's industrial troubles and the launching by the Suffragettes of a militant campaign of violence. In March, Sophie learned from a letter from Anna that Arabella had been arrested on a window-breaking expedition to London's West End and, refusing — as all Suffragettes on principle refused — to pay her fine, had been sent to prison for a month, where she had promptly gone on hunger strike. "I do fear for her," Anna had written, "truly I do. Constitutionally she is not strong, and if half the awful stories one hears of forcible feeding are true, then I shudder to think what she might be going through. But — while Mr Asquith and Mr Lloyd George refuse to honour their promises then Arabella and her friends will keep fighting. To the death, if need be, I fear — though sometimes I wonder, disloyally perhaps, if their actions are not actually working against their aims —"

Arabella was released from prison two weeks later, weak from her ordeal, but still very much alive, and with a spirit far from broken. She did not share her friend's misgivings. A month later she was on her feet and breaking windows again.

That summer was again a summer of strikes, with the London docks totally paralysed from May to August and the mood of the working classes alarmingly militant, so once again the Anatov girls spent the summer at Bissetts. Josef no longer lived alone, but on Anna's insistence was looked after by a middle-aged widow named Emmeline Saunders who spoiled him like a child whilst pretending to rule him with a rod of iron. Both Sophie and the placid Maria got on well with her, and for her part Mrs Saunders was always sorry to see the youngsters go.

The following year a new threat was added to those already besetting the British Government; the real possibility of civil war in Ireland. Perhaps it was this, added to the roar of its people demanding industrial and electoral reform that deafened the ears of the country to the growing, deadly murmurs across the English Channel in Europe. The year of 1914 dawned still in domestic chaos.

Sophie Anatov was in her seventeenth year. Still headstrong, often thoughtless, she had, happily, at last developed her father's capacity for laughter, and the way ahead looked clear and good.

CHAPTER EIGHTEEN

Sophie renewed her slight and almost forgotten childhood acquaintanceship with Rupert Rose on a warm and breezy early June day when the air was fragrant with the scent of late spring flowers and busy with the hum of winged insects and the song of birds. A great chestnut tree, pink-flowered and full-leafed, rustled above the ruined cottage and swallows dipped and shrieked in the high air. Sophie was by her little pool in the overgrown yard-garden that had been her favourite place for as long as she could remember, watching with some concern a plump, clumsy baby blackbird as it hopped and staggered about the paving stones calling for its mother, when she heard, from behind her, the sound of scrambling footsteps in the tumbled bricks and rubble of the cottage. The baby bird, already frightened half to death, froze completely.

"Ssh! Maria! Do come quietly. There's a poor little bird —"

The footsteps stilled, then resumed, more quietly. Sophie held out a green-stained finger to the bird. "Tsk, tsk, tsk. Here, then. I won't hurt you."

The bird shivered and gaped. From the high sheltering wall its mother scolded with sharp, clucking sounds that rang with the awareness of danger. Sophie sat back on her heels. "What's best to do, do you think? It can't fly yet. And if we leave it here that beastly cat's bound to get it —"

"Why don't you put it up on the wall near its mother? If you don't know where the nest is, that is."

Startled, she looked up. A tall, slim youth, dark-haired, sun-tanned and pleasant-faced smiled down at her. He was wearing grey flannels and an open-necked shirt, a cricketing pullover slung about his shoulders. His smile widened as he looked at her green-stained fingers and skirt. "I say — what on earth are you doing?"

She glanced down at her dirty hands, in one of which she held a broken knife. "Gardening," she said shortly, all the old defensiveness rising.

"With a kitchen knife?"

"It's the only thing I've found that will get the weeds out from between the stones."

"Oh, I see." He glanced around. "Why, yes, of course!" His voice was warm, "You're clearing the paving around the pool! What a good idea. It's a shame to see it so overgrown." He hunkered down beside her, bouncing on his heels. "Do you know that I've known Bissetts all of my life, but I didn't know this was here? What a topping little spot."

"Yes." She could not keep the shortness of faint resentment from her voice.

Very faintly, beneath his tan, he flushed. Stood up. "I'm sorry," he said stiffly, "I interrupted you. You were expecting your sister."

"I wasn't actually expecting anyone."

The little bird squawked.

"I'll put him on the wall," the boy said, "where his mother can feed him."

Sophie watched as, very gently, he captured the bird and set it upon the wall. She knew him to be a year or so younger than herself, but he did not look it. For all his pleasant diffidence, he had about him an air of adult confidence that went with the casual, well-cut clothes and the clipped, assured public school voice. She knew, of course — or almost knew — who he must be.

"Which one are you?" she asked, forthrightly.

He grinned, unoffended. "Rupert. And you're Sophie of course, aren't you? Gosh — it must be years and years since we've met. Mind you — I always remember, once, when we were little — I think it was in the Bayswater garden — you threw a frog at me —"

Sophie looked surprised. "I did?"

"You don't remember?"

She shook her head.

"Lord — you'd think you'd remember something like that! How many people did you throw frogs at? Did you make a habit of it?"

She giggled. The atmosphere between them had suddenly eased. He looked around him, curiosity in his hazel eyes. "What exactly *are* you doing here?"

She shrugged, elaborately dismissive of an exciting idea and three days of surprisingly hard work. "Just fiddling about."

"Looks like more than fiddling about to me." He reached and pulled an enormous, coarse-leafed weed from between two stones. A strong earthy scent filled the air. "You're clearing it, aren't you? Making it a garden again?"

"I thought I might. I like it here."

"I'm not surprised. It's wonderful. So quiet and sheltered. I can't understand how we haven't found it before." He paused, a little awkward again. "I say — it's a bit of a cheek, my walking in on you like this. I mean — if you want the place to yourself I'd hate to intrude."

She had to laugh. "Don't be silly. It is your house."

"Not this bit."

"Of course it is."

"Not if we didn't even know it was here. I think you've probably got — what's it called? — squatter's rights, or something."

She laughed, and he grinned, relieved. She began again to scrape at the cracks between the stones with the broken knife.

"I don't suppose you could do with another pair of hands?"

"Help yourself. There's enough weeds for both of us, I should say."

He sat beside her, companionably, and began to haul enthusiastically on the weeds.

"We don't usually see you around here in the summer," Sophie said, after a moment, curiosity in her voice.

"No, worse luck. Mama's a born traveller, I'm afraid, and Papa isn't. Almost ever since I can remember, every summer she's dragged us off all over the place — Pa just won't go, so Ritchie and I have to sort of take his place as escorts."

"And this year?"

"Ah — well, what happened you see is that Richard and I were supposed to go on a school cricket tour for the first part of the hols. And Mama was dead set on a cruise up the Nile that started right in the middle of it. Poor Pa didn't stand a chance."

He grinned. "He's half-way up the Nile right now, and hating every minute of it. We had the very glummest postcard yesterday —"

Sophie laughed. "And the cricket tour? What happened to that?"

"Richard's on it now. He's Captain, actually." There was sheer pride in his voice, "The youngest in the history of the school. It's a great honour."

"But — what about you? Why aren't you there too?"

"Bit of rotten luck, actually. I sprained my left wrist just a couple of days before the end of term. I'm right-handed — but you need two hands for a cricket bat."

"Yes," Sophie agreed soberly, "I did know that."

"So — here I am —"

"What a shame."

He grinned suddenly. "Yes. I'm sure they're all missing their slices of lemon."

She looked at him enquiringly.

He shrugged philosophically. "Twelfth man," he said. "And I probably wouldn't have got that if it hadn't been for Ritchie." There was neither embarrassment nor self-pity in the words.

Sophie smiled sympathetically. It came to her that she could very much like this pleasant young man. "So — here you are — stuck all alone with a bad wrist."

"Something like that, yes. Though it isn't as dreary as it sounds. The wrist is much better, and I won't be on my own for long. Ritchie's due back at the end of next week." A couple of martins had joined the swallows in their swooping pursuit of insects in the summer air. Rupert sat back on his heels and shaded his eyes with his hand, watching them. "I knew something nice was going to happen today," he said unexpectedly. "Because the martins are back in the nest by my bedroom window. They're my favourite birds. They bring me luck."

Sophie put her head on one side. "Something nice?"

He waved a hand. "I found this. And I met you."

"Me and a pile of weeds."

Their clear young laughter was the very sound of friendship.

Had Sophie ever bothered to think of it — which she had not —

she would certainly not have expected to like Rupert Rose, let alone to cement within days bonds of friendship and camaraderie as strong as any she had known with anyone. She had always disliked his parents, finding Alex exasperatingly pompous, and Alice purely detestable, and knowing of the bad blood that had existed between them and her own parents for some years. Yet from that moment of meeting it was as if she and Rupert had been fast friends since childhood. They spent the days together, talking to Josef, walking the countryside, clearing the little garden. When Rupert discovered Sophie's passion for tennis he was absolutely delighted, and every day they played at least once, sometimes twice and often far into the long June evening. There was no one to oppose the blooming of their friendship — Rupert was alone at Bissetts apart from the staff; and Josef, sitting in his wheeled chair in his small garden smiled to himself at the sound of their young voices and their laughter. More often than not Maria would tag along, happy simply to be in their company. She adored Rupert from the moment she met him; Sophie, in private, teased her unmercifully about it. "I do believe you're in love with him!"

Poor little Maria coloured to the roots of her light brown hair. She was a slight, rather plain child with her father's blue eyes and pale skin. Sophie often declared that her delicate little sister made her feel like an over-active elephant — a comment that never failed to reduce the adoring Maria into uncontrollable giggles. "I'm not!" she said now. "Don't be silly!"

Sophie surveyed her with apparently serious eyes. "Well, I'm not so sure about that. If I were you, my dear, I'd be very careful indeed —"

"What do you mean?"

"You might finish up with the most awful mother-in-law —"

"Oh, Sophie! You are just — just *terrible*!"

"What's so terrible about being honest? Come on — Rupert and I are going to play tennis. Are you coming?"

In those few days, as if they had been friends all of their lives, Sophie found with Rupert a real and honest companionship which she had discovered with few other people. His character was in general more serious than her own, yet his good humour allowed her to tease him as she might a brother, amused that often he could not tell if she were joking or not. He was sensitive and very intelligent, and in these qualities she delighted and would sit with him for hours listening in fascination as he spoke animatedly and with imagination of things that until now had interested her not at all. To hear John Milton's stirring and beautiful words quoted in Rupert's pleasant well-modulated voice and to discover that for the first time she actually understood and appreciated them was an entirely new experience for her, a large part of her literature lessons at St Hilary's having been spent in watching other, as she considered it more fortunate, beings on the playing fields outside the window. The discovery that poetry could be a means to express ideas and emotions as opposed to being simply words that marched in rhythm and rhymed she found truly exciting. Their time, however, was far from entirely taken up in erudite discussion; at times they acted like children as they almost still were, simply revelling in youth's energy and laughter and the warmth of a summer's day. Sophie, to her delight, found that she could run faster than the long-legged Rupert, and no matter how determinedly he tried he could rarely beat her at tennis. Yet this too he took in good part. "Wait till Richard comes. I'd like to watch you two play —"

"I do like Rupert," Sophie confided to Josef in her open way one still, sunny evening as she pushed his wheeled basket chair at strolling pace along the well-kept gravel drive. This was a favourite daily occupation of these two, and neither would miss the evening promenade for anything. "He's just so nice. I suppose I shouldn't say so — but he doesn't seem to me to be a bit like his parents. I think," she grinned down at him, mischief in her eyes, "I think he must take after his grandfather."

"Which one?" Josef asked, solemnly innocent.

Sophie laughed. "Why, you of course! Weren't you just like him when you were young. I bet you were —"

The laughter slipped suddenly from Josef's face. "I don't remember. I don't think so."

Sophie, intent upon her game, did not notice his change in mood. "Someone else, then. Your mother? Your father?"

There was a moment's silence. "That I don't know, my dear," Josef said quietly, "I did not know my true parents."

Sophie stopped walking, looked at him in astonished concern. "I didn't know that."

Josef shook his head a little tiredly. "It doesn't matter. It's all so very long ago." He looked down at the old, bony hands that rested in his lap, the branded thumb uppermost. "All so very long ago," he repeated, then lifted his head, his smile genuine enough so that the watching child did not see the pain beneath it. "I knew your father's parents, though. Very well indeed. And his grandparents —"

"Tell me some of the stories again, Uncle Josef. Tell me about my grandfather, who you always say was so much like me." Sophie was easily distracted, as Josef had known she would be. "Tell me about the picnic when he pushed you in the river and he'd forgotten you couldn't swim —"

"Then jumped in fully clothed and rescued me, though the water was only three feet deep."

She pulled a funny, rueful face. "Oh golly — yes, he does sound a bit like me, doesn't he?" The wheels crunched again on the gravel. The birds sang. "Uncle Josef?' Sophie said, softly, "tell me about Russia."

"Ah, Russia," Josef said, and the words were a small, thoughtful sigh. He shook his head. "It's all so very far away, child. And so very long ago."

"Aunt Anna went there, didn't she?"

"Yes."

"She never speaks of it."

A small furrow appeared between Josef's grizzled eyebrows. "No."

"I shall go there one day. I shall see all the places you've told me about. I shall visit the famous Shuvenski family, as Aunt Anna did, and be made much of. I shall see the fabulous diamond that you created all those years ago." She paused, tilted her head back to the last rays of the dying sun. "It must have been marvellous to have done such a thing," she said.

Josef shivered. "I'm getting cold, child. It's time to go back in."

Later, when they had almost reached Josef's small garden gate, Sophie, suddenly and with no preamble asked, "What's Richard like? I mean — is he as nice as Rupert?"

Josef, with an effort, brought himself back to the present. "Richard? To tell the truth I don't really know. I don't know either of them as well as I know you and Maria, for all that they are my grandchildren. I've seen so little of them. They are, I believe, very alike, although they are not actually identical. And — no, I don't believe they are all that alike in character. Richard was always the leader, ever since they were very young. Rupert, I think, is the dreamer, Richard the more positive of the two. As a small child I remember him being very lively, very determined. Anything he did he had to do better than anyone else."

"Yes. That was the impression I got from Rupert."

Josef turned his hand to look at her at the tone of the words. "Why so gloomy?"

"He's coming home tomorrow," she said, obliquely.

"So? That will make another companion —"

Sophie shook her head. "No. I don't think so. Rupert talks about Richard a lot. All the time almost. Richard this, Richard that — I'm almost tired of him before I've met him, though I know that isn't fair. I've got a feeling that I'm not going to like him. Or perhaps I'm afraid that he won't like me. I don't know . But — whatever — it isn't going to be the same, is it? With him here? Rupert's going to want to spend his time with him —"

"Of course. That's only natural. But that doesn't mean he won't want to spend time with you as well." His voice was gentle. Josef knew more than he admitted about this favourite child's problems in the past.

"I s'pose not." Sophie was silent for a moment. "They're lucky, aren't they? It must be nice to have someone so close, so much a part of you —" They had reached the narrow path that led to the back door of the cottage. Sophie stopped, clicked the brake firmly on and held out a hand to help Josef from the chair. Holding his hand she smiled suddenly, and her strong face was transformed. "That's not all I envy them."

A little breathless, but steady on his feet Josef looked at her with raised eybrows. "Oh?"

She leaned to kiss his cheek. "I envy them their grandfather. I don't care how dashing mine was. I don't care if he was a Count or whatever. I'll bet he wasn't as nice as you." She stood, young and strong and fair in the last rays of the evening light —

Alexei's granddaughter — and for a moment forty years were like a mist that shifts and clears as if it had never been. The strong, white smile, the reckless eyes, the hand of friendship. Then the mist closed again.

"We ought to go in," he said, very gently. "Mrs Saunders will be fretting and my chocolate will be cold."

Rupert and Sophie were playing tennis when Richard arrived the next day. Sophie saw him first — a tall, blazered figure swinging across the lawns towards them — and fluffed a sitting duck of a shot like a novice, her eye distracted from the ball. Rupert finished the point off in short order. "My advantage," he called, cheerily, and turned to walk back to the serving line. "Richard!" Balls and racquet went flying from him. "Richard old chap! You're back! How perfectly spiffing to see you! How did it go? Did you win the Varsity? Gosh — you seem to have been gone an age!"

Sophie stood, alone and awkward, a total outsider as these two, brothers and more than brothers, greeted each other enthusiastically, shaking hands, slapping each other on the shoulder, talking excitedly. Her eyes were upon Richard's face. Josef had been right; the twins were like and yet unlike each other. In Richard the bones were sharper, the laughing hazel eyes clearer, the movements more positive. The two boys were still thumping each other on the back, laughing in sheer pleasure at the reunion. Sophie, watching, caught a swift impression of a dark, lifted head, an open smile, a tall, slight, sportsman's body. To her utter astonishment something extremely strange had happened to her breathing and to the beating of her heart. She bent to pick up a ball at her feet. The trembling of her legs had absolutely nothing to do with her recent exertions. She felt a mortifying blush of colour mounting in her already exercise-flushed cheeks. She straightened, smoothed her calf-length grass-stained white linen skirt, rescued the navy blue tie that had slipped almost round to her ear. Her white shirt was grubby and had slipped from its constraining belt. Her hair was a bird's nest.

"Come and meet Sophie. You remember? Sophie Anatov. Aunt Anna's niece. She's here for the summer —"

She transferred her racquet to her left hand, rubbed the right one furiously and furtively on her skirt. He stood before her, cool, unruffled, smiling easily, a young god on his own ground. She felt the awkward falseness of her own smile. "Hello."

He took the proffered hand. "Hello."

"Rupert says you've been on a cricket tour." The words were stiff. "I hope it was successful."

Richard grinned at his brother. "Won every match, that's all."

Rupert whooped. Sophie watched him. She had never seen him so excited, so lively. It was as if the coming of his brother had injected new life into him. "I'd better go," she said, abruptly.

"Oh — no — please —" Rupert was all concern. "We haven't finished our game."

"We can finish it later. You and — and Richard —" to her confusion she discovered that she had some difficulty in speaking the name "— must have a lot to talk about." Woodenly, and aware of two pairs of faintly surprised eyes she turned from them and walked away. Behind her she heard Richard's voice, lighter than Rupert's, a little worried.

"I say — I hope I didn't break in at an awkward moment. I could have waited up at the house I suppose —"

"No, no. Of course not. Come on — let's see if we can cadge tea and cakes off Mrs Brown —"

Sophie's steps, without conscious thought, were directed not back to the cottage, but to the tiny, cleared garden and shimmering pool. She stood for a moment, looking into the water, then dropped her tennis racquet and sat, straight and still, beside the pool. Above her the pair of martins swooped and called. The ridiculous thumping of her heart had eased a little. She sat for a long time, contemplating the still water. What on earth had happened to her? The sight of Richard Rose had hit her like a physical blow. She had acted stupidly. Made a complete fool of herself. And — oh, Lord! — she must have looked a positive sight!

She frowned ferociously at her dim reflection. At St Hilary's there had been a girl named Lucy Burton, whose passion for forbidden, fatuous penny romances and simpering attitude to any member of the opposite sex regardless of age or attraction had made of her a despised laughing stock amongst Sophie's particular group of friends. The undoubtedly exaggerated — not to say completely untrue — tales of her romantic adventures during the holidays were doted upon by some girls and dismissed as ludicrous by others, including Sophie. Since Lucy had turned thirteen, it seemed that every young man she had met, from visiting cousins to butchers' boys, she had fallen irrevocably in love with. "Oh, but I could simply have *swooned*!" she was in the habit of saying, "Simply *swooned* when he looked at me. And when he touched my hand —" The cataclysmic event would be illustrated by dramatic gestures and upturned eyes. Sophie had always considered her and her stories to be puerile, childish and utterly silly.

But it had happened.

She shook her head, confused and strangely angry. It couldn't have happened. It wasn't reasonable — wasn't logical — that one person should have that kind of impact on another. She had always believed firmly that such things existed only in the overactive imaginations of silly little girls like Lucy Burton.

But — it had happened. The sight of Richard swinging lightly across the lawn towards her had all but stopped her heart. His simple presence had choked her voice in her throat. She must be going mad.

She stood up abruptly, and brushed herself down.

He'd certainly take Rupert from her, of course. She'd be alone again.

She didn't care. Why should she care?

He was quite the most beautiful person she had ever seen. The thought came from nowhere and lodged within her, strangely, an indefinable ache.

She snatched up her racquet. She'd stay away from him. Right away. That was the answer. How dare he make her feel as foolish as silly Lucy Burton?

Her resolution, however, lasted for less than five minutes. Richard, with Rupert, was at the cottage with Josef and Maria when she got back.

"Ah — Sophie my dear — see who's come to visit." Josef

lifted his face for her kiss.

"Yes. We met earlier." She felt huge. Huge and clumsy and untidy to the point of ugliness. "Excuse me. I really must change." She turned, to find Richard's eyes upon her. He smiled, charmingly.

She fled.

Changed, and at least somewhat more composed, she rejoined them in the garden some fifteen minutes later. To her own utter disgust she had taken a great deal of trouble with her appearance. Her white muslin, trimmed with green, became her well she knew, and her heavy hair was caught softly back from her face with a matching ribbon. Maria's eyes opened wide when she saw her. Sophie studiously ignored the look. She did not notice Josef's quiet smile.

"I say —"

She turned at the already-familiar, light voice. He stood behind her, and to her surprise there was a certain diffidence in his manner. Over his shoulder she could see Maria and Rupert, bending to where Josef sat, laughing with him. She waited, unsmiling, hoping that he did not suspect the uncertain hammering of her heart.

"I say — I do hope I didn't upset you this afternoon?"

"Upset me?"

"Interrupting your game the way I did. It was terribly rude of me. I really shouldn't have just barged in like that —"

"Nonsense. It really didn't matter."

He looked unfeignedly relieved. "Oh, good. I'd hate for us to get off on the wrong foot. Rupert's been telling me all about you."

"Oh?" Something warm and happy was moving in Sophie. "What's he been saying?" She smiled brilliantly. He liked her. She did not know how she knew it, but she did. He liked her.

He cleared his throat self-consciously. "Oh — just what good friends you've become. What fun you've been having. Quite made me feel as if I'd missed out on something —" He laughed, a little too loudly, and cleared his throat again.

Sophie, for no apparent reason, felt suddenly as if she stood upon a rainbow. She could have sung. Shouted. Danced. She lowered her eyes. "I'm sure your cricket tour was much more exciting."

He did not answer. She lifted her eyes to his. He was looking at her intently, an expression in his hazel-flecked eyes that brought a slow rise of colour to her cheeks. They stood for a long, still moment, unspeaking.

"Grandfather's coming up to the house for dinner tonight," he said, and his voice was faintly husky with a strange kind of excitement that she knew to be mirrored in her own face. "Would you join us? You and your sister?"

Sophie hesitated, the sudden picture of an outraged Alice in her mind's eye. "Well — I —"

"Please. Oh, please come. We'd both love to have you."

"All right."

His boyish smile was bright with delight.

"Richard!" Rupert called, "Come on and tell Grandfather about your fifty in the Varsity match —"

That evening Sophie dressed with great care. Her simple, Grecian-style gown, the most grown-up dress that she owned, was in a soft pale green that complemented her fair hair and dark eyes. A wide chiffon scarf, long gloves and kid slippers completed the ensemble. In her hair she wore a spray of sweet-smelling hawthorn.

"Golly," Maria said, graphically, when this vision descended the narrow stairs.

"My dear, you look charming." Josef too had dressed for the occasion, formally, in dinner suit and white shirt with tiny gold and pearl buttons that had been designed by Anna. "Utterly charming!" His eyes twinkled as he surveyed her, "And so very, very grown up!"

They paraded up the drive, a strangely assorted trio, Sophie pushing Josef's basket chair, Maria in her best pink silk that had dimmed just a little in her own eyes since she had seen her sister's splendour, slowing her pace to theirs. At the door of the big house the brothers met them, both handsome in their dinner suits, both solicitous for Josef as they helped him from the chair and up to the wide shallow steps.

Sophie had never been inside the house before. As Rupert guided Josef through the tall door that led into the drawing room, followed by an unusually voluble Maria, she stopped for a moment and looked around her. The house was big but pleasantly proportioned and in no way overawing. Opposite the drawing room was an identical tall door through which she could see a high-ceilinged room, well-lit and lined with bookshelves.

"The library."

She turned. Richard stood, smiling, at her elbow. "And the door over there is the dining room. The passage beyond the staircase there leads to the kitchen and servants' quarters. That door there —" he pointed up the wide, curved staircase "— see it? On the half-landing? That's the old school room. Pa's had it turned into a billiard room. I wonder —" he stopped.

"Yes?"

"— if you might like to see over the house later? I'd love to show it to you."

"I'd like that very much."

That evening was an occasion that Sophie Anatov was never to forget. Mrs Brown outdid herself, the company was convivial, and from across the table, candle-lit as the evening light faded, Richard's eyes were warm and bright with interest. She sparkled. She teased Rupert, flirted a little inexpertly with Richard, held sway over the table with her vivacity and laughter.

Richard, a shade daringly, had raided his father's cellar. Josef shook his head, delightedly reproving. "Champagne, young man?"

Richard laughed. "Pa wouldn't mind. It's a special occasion."

After dinner they returned to the drawing room, where Josef, comfortably ensconced in an enormous armchair, promptly nodded off.

"I thought," Richard said, elaborately casual, "that I might show Sophie the house."

"Lovely idea!" Maria bounced out of her chair, beaming. "I've always wanted to see it!"

Rupert, ever observant, did not miss the faint look of disconcerted disappointment on the other two faces. "Later, poppet," he said evenly, his own small heartache ignored. "Didn't you say you wanted to see the guinea pigs? There'll be no light left at all. Come on — I'll take you out to see them first, then I'll show you the house."

Richard led Sophie out into the hall. "This is the hall," he said solemnly.

"I rather thought it was." The champagne had lightened both their heads. They laughed like children. "The portraits," Richard said "are absolutely nothing to do with us. Mama got them as a job lot because she thought they looked grand."

"They certainly do that."

"And this —" he pushed open the tall door "— is still the library."

"What a lovely room! And what a huge fireplace! It must be marvellous in here in the winter."

He looked at her, pleased. "It is. It's my very favourite room."

"And all these books." She walked alongside a bookshelf, running her finger along the ranked spines. "Don't tell me you've read them all."

"Good Lord, no! Not half, actually. They came with the portraits —" He was looking not at the books but at her.

Self-consciously she spun gracefully upon her toes and looked out of the tall window. "And such a pretty view. You can see right down to the stables and the cottage —"

"Yes."

There was a sudden silence. From the hall came the sound of Maria's and Rupert's voices, and a door banged. Panic suddenly and unexpectedly took Sophie. "I want to see the room half-way up the stairs," she said, gaily, "that you said was the old school room." She was past him and, lightly, had started up the stairs before he could move. Laughing, he followed.

The old school room was a long, well-proportioned room with a high ceiling and tall windows. A large billiard table above which hung two long, fringe-shaded lights, took up the centre of the room, whilst several comfortable armchairs lined the walls and there was a heavy mahogany bar at the end of the room. Faintly in the air hung the smell of stale cigar smoke. "Did you and Rupert ever use it as a school room?" Sophie asked.

"Oh, no. We had a tutor at the London house and then we went away to school." He was looking at her again in that intent and intimate way that both excited and frightened her. "Sophie —"

"And do you like it? School, I mean? I hated it. Absolutely hated it. I ran away, did you know? Three times. Once I got all the way back here —" She was gabbling. She pressed her lips firmly together to stop herself, her too-loud voice echoing in her own ears.

"No. I didn't know."

"Aunt Anna was here. She was very kind. I do like Aunt Anna."

"Yes."

It was almost dark now, the small lamp that Richard had lit threw long shadows on wall and ceiling. The moment stretched between them, waiting for words that neither of them could find.

Downstairs a door banged. "Hello? Richard? Sophie? Are you there?"

Sophie raised her voice "Up —"

"Ssh!" Richard, his face suddenly alight with mischief had sped to the lamp and turned it out.

"What on earth —"

He came swiftly back to her, caught her hand and pulled her into a crouching position behind an enormous wing armchair. In the faint light he put a warning finger to his lips. She stifled a giggle. He grinned. "Ssh!"

"Richard? Sophie?" Rupert's puzzled voice was just outside the room. The door opened for a moment, then closed again. "No," he called to Maria, "they don't seem to be up here."

Richard waited for a moment, then caught Sophie's hand again and crept with her through the darkness to the door. He opened it very quietly, peered out and, the coast clear, towed her at a quiet run up the stairs. On the wide landing he paused and leaned over the heavy banisters, looking down to where Maria and Rupert stood in the hall below. "Grandfather's nose!" he hissed.

"What was that?" Maria's voice was startled, and clashed with Rupert's quick call.

"Done! Come on Maria — they're upstairs somewhere. The attics most likely —"

Richard, laughing almost too much to run, was however

towing Sophie not towards the small flight of stairs that led to the warrened attics but along a narrow landing towards the back of the house.

"Grandfather's *nose*?" Sophie gasped, giggling as she ran.

"That's the target. We have to touch it before they can catch us. Come *on*!" He opened a door that led on to an uncarpeted corridor with plain, painted walls adorned by pictures, quite obviously the upper floor of the servants' quarters.

"Are we supposed to be here?" Sophie asked, a little nervously.

"Not strictly," he conceded with a grin. "Look out — here they come —"

Behind them Rupert called, above Maria's excited laughter.

Richard opened another door. A narrow flight of steps led up and down. "Take a chance," he said, and they clattered downwards and burst through a narrow doorway into a vast kitchen, at one end of which, in comfortable armchairs set around the kitchen range, sat Mrs Lawson and Mrs Brown nursing large, steaming mugs whilst at the other Mary, the little housemaid, tackled a veritable mountain of washing up in the deep old sink.

"Mr Richard!" Mrs Brown raised scandalized hands, "I do declare! Whatever do you think you're doing?"

"Downstairs!" Rupert called from above. "They're downstairs! Quick — run and guard the drawing room door —"

"Dinner was topping, Mrs Brown," Richard called gaily, "thanks a lot. One of your very best! Come on, Sophie —"

Sophie made a small, half-embarrassed and apologetic gesture to the two women as she allowed herself to be dragged to a small door at the far end of the room. Once through it she found herself to be back in the dining room, cleared now, the polished table gleaming in lamplight. Richard stopped, put his finger to his lips, and tiptoed to the big door that led out into the hall. He peered through it, then slipped back to her side, shaking his head. "The window," he said.

The tall windows stood open still to the evening air. Richard flung a leg over the sill and stepped easily into the garden. Ready for anything now, Sophie with no hesitation kilted her skirt about her knees and followed him. "That's the girl!!" The whisper from the darkness was jubilant. "Here — give me your hand. And watch your step — it's very dark."

They crept through the shrubbery and round to the front of the house. The drawing room windows stood open. Lamplight flowed softly. Josef still slept in his chair. For an odd, quiet moment the two young people stood watching him, very close to each other. It seemed to Sophie as they stood there that the warmth of Richard's body was reaching through her flesh to kindle a small fire, a core of lovely warmth, deep within her.

Then, "Can you manage?" Richard asked. In his voice Sophie thought she heard the same trembling excitement that coursed in her own blood.

"Of course." She sat on the windowsill and swung her legs through the window. Richard scrambled in after her.

"What's that?" Maria squealed from outside the door. "Rupert — I'm sure I heard something —"

Richard streaked across the room just as the door opened. "Home!"

"What the —" Josef opened his eyes at the light touch on his nose, eyed the four hilarious young people in puzzlement. "What have you young scoundrels been up to, eh?"

"They hid from us —" Maria said, almost beside herself with happy excitement at having been part of such a game "— and we chased them. And they had to touch your nose —" She went off into peals of laughter. Sophie's attention, however, was not on her sister. As if it were the most natural thing in the world Richard had taken her hand again. She did not try to disengage it, but lifted her head and looked at him with huge, dark, suddenly serious eyes. The hand that held hers tightened and he smiled.

"Well," Josef said gently, his old eyes soft, "it seems that you've all had a very successful evening."

It was perhaps predictable that Sophie should fall in love in the same headlong, open-hearted and passionate way that she did everything else. From that first day she would have died for Richard, to ensure his welfare and happiness. That he should feel the same way about her was almost incredible to her; she had not believed such happiness existed. In the enclosed, idyllic surroundings of Bissetts over the next weeks their innocent, exciting love blossomed free and unafraid. They spent every moment together, mostly in the company of others, occasionally — and how precious these occasions were to both of them — alone. Shyly, then, they would hold hands and talk of their past lives that, incredibly, had not included each other and, vaguely, of the future which surely always must. Their first sweet, hesitant kiss was exchanged beneath a tree in the little walled orchard; Richard's lips were warm and firm, the feel of his body infinitely exciting.

"I love you, Sophie," he said, quietly, as he drew back from her. "Truly I do."

"And I you."

"I'll always love you."

"Yes."

"You'll wait? You don't mind that we're so young?"

"Of course not."

"We'll never be parted. I promise you."

Smiling, she lifted her lips to his again.

Why it never occurred to them that parental opposition might be incited by more than the simple matter of their youth, Sophie never afterwards knew, but at that time it did not. They were young and in love, and the carefree, happy plans that they made for the future during those June weeks seemed totally logical and achievable. Sophie, quite simply, lived to see Richard; every moment spent out of his company, out of range of his voice, was a wasted one. She loved him more than life itself. Nothing, she was certain, could ever change that. Nothing and no one could keep them apart. It would be too cruel.

Of outside events she took little notice, until the late June day that she awaited Richard by the little pool in the secret garden that had lately become their habitual meeting place. Not even she, that morning, could have missed Uncle Josef's agitation at the news that had filtered into their closed small world. She pondered it now as she watched the water insects busy about the glimmering surface of the water. They reminded her of the lovely jewellery her Aunt Anna designed, their bodies gleaming in the sun against the metallic background of the water.

"Sophie! Sophie!" The unmistakable footsteps on the path

beyond the cottage were swift, the voice breathless, "Sophie — are you there?"

"Here — yes, I'm here."

Richard scrambled through the tumbled bricks. "Have you heard?" he asked with no preamble.

"What — that some old duke's been assassinated in Sara-something by some beastly anarchist? Yes — Uncle Josef seemed very upset about it all. But what —"

"No, no! Ma and Pa — they're home! Came home unexpectedly early this morning!" Richard's face was flushed and excited. He reached for her hand.

It was as if someone had rudely shaken her awake in the heart of a dream. Her pulse had taken up an irregular hammer-beat of apprehension.

"But — surely — they weren't due home till the end of next week?" All the light-hearted certainty that had attended the last delightful weeks had deserted her entirely.

"That's right. But Pa detested Egypt, and with all the stupid war talk that's been going on — well, they just decided to call it a day and come home."

Sophie spoke with some difficulty. "It wasn't — wasn't because someone told them about us?"

He threw back his dark head and laughed. "Of course not, silly! Oh, I can't wait to tell them! Don't worry, my darling, darling Sophie! They'll love you. Just as I do! What else could they do?"

She stood in shaking silence, and at last her apprehension touched him. He stepped to her and caught her in his arms, resting his face on her tumbled air. "Don't worry!" he said again, more seriously. "It will be all right. I promise it will. For heaven's sake, Sophie, Ma and Pa aren't ogres, you know —"

As they drew apart a cloud slid over the sun and the garden around them darkened.

"No, of course not." Sophie summoned a not very convincing smile. "It's just that —"

"What?"

"I don't know — something's changed, hasn't it? And nothing is ever going to be exactly the same again. I'm just not ready for it, that's all. Richard," she caught his hand suddenly, urgently, "let's not tell them? Not yet —"

He smiled his brilliant, confident smile. "Not tell them? Don't be daft — why shouldn't we tell them? They'll be delighted, you'll see. And as for things changing —" he took her hand and they strolled towards the cottage, "— things change all the time, don't they? Nothing ever really stays the same. It can't."

"I suppose not."

For both of them the events in far-off Sarajevo were already forgotten.

CHAPTER NINETEEN

"The girl, quite obviously," Alice said, her voice perilously calm, "has learned well the lessons of the gutter in which she was bred."

"I say, old girl, steady on." Alex was uncomfortable.

Richard, white to the lips, stood as one struck entirely dumb.

Alice continued as if her husband had not spoken. She totally ignored the speechless Richard. "She has seduced our child whilst our backs were turned — one can only assume in the hope of some financial gain —"

"Mother!" Richard stepped forward, "Please — stop talking like this. You don't know what you're saying!"

Coldly she turned on him. "On the contrary, Richard. I know very well what I'm saying. It is you — you, Richard — who have been gulled by this girl. Nor is that the only bone of contention between us." She paused, her gaze forbidding. "Quite apart from this — unsavoury — matter, the reports of your behaviour have been scandalous. Truly scandalous. Besides your outrageous and feckless behaviour with this girl you have stolen from your father's cellar — *stolen*, I say," she repeated as her son opened his mouth to protest, "you have invaded the servants' quarters, acted like a young hooligan —"

"Come, now, Alice. Mrs Brown was not complaining when she told us of the incident —"

"Then she most certainly should have been. Is this any way for a gentleman to behave? Is it?" Alice brushed her husband's half-hearted remonstrance aside and still faced her white-faced son.

"Mother — please — won't you listen to me? Sophie and I —"

"Silence, Richard! And understand, once and for all, that I will not have that — that hoyden's name mentioned again in this house. Do you hear me?"

"But — you don't even know her —"

"No, Richard —" her voice was very quiet "— it is you who don't know her and her kind. Be thankful that we came home in time. The Lord only knows what mischief she might have achieved had we stayed away longer."

Richard stepped back from her. "I won't listen to this."

"You will listen to anything that I choose that you should. Alex," she turned her head, but her eyes remained upon Richard, "that girl must be made to leave. Immediately. I won't have her here."

"It's a little difficult, my dear — she is father's guest, after all."

"A guest who has abused your hospitality — seduced your son — played fast and loose with the morals of the household —" Alice's tone was vitriolic.

"Stop it! Will you stop it! I won't listen!" Richard's face had suddenly flamed with anger. "You shan't say such things about Sophie —"

Alice turned back to her son, an expression of almost theatrical astonishment on her face. "I — beg — your — pardon?" she asked, icily.

"Mother — please — you have to listen to me. To let me explain —"

"I don't have to do anything of the sort."

They faced each other in fury. Richard backed towards the door; mortifying tears stood in his eyes. "If you make Sophie go, I'll — I'll go too. I swear I will. I'll leave. You'll never see me again —" He heard, himself, the emptiness of the childish-sounding threat, and his frustration and anger grew. "I won't have you saying these awful things about Sophie! I won't! He had reached the door. Blindly he reached for the handle.

"Richard! Come back here at once!"

But he was gone, his running footsteps echoing behind him. They heard the front door open, saw the tall, flying figure as he ran down the drive towards the cottage.

"Don't you think you were — perhaps — a little hard?" Alex, awkwardly, asked the furious silence. "He's right in a way, my dear — you really don't know the girl."

Alice stood like a statue, staring out of the window. "I don't need to. Her schemes are perfectly clear to me — as they would be to you if you weren't so absurdly short-sighted. The girl is out to get Richard — his position, his — our — money. Well —" her fine mouth drew to a straight, harsh line "— she shan't succeed. I'll make absolutely certain of that. We must get rid of her. Immediately. Josef's guest or no. Once out of sight this — this ridiculous infatuation of Richard's will die. She must leave at once." She turned and fixed portly Alex with a steely eye. "You'll see to it?" It was a statement rather than a question.

Alex subsided, reflecting as he had done more than once in the past weeks of close contact with his wife that Alice and that damned Kaiser fellow that was causing so much trouble had a lot in common. "Yes, my dear. Of course."

They stood together in miserable silence. Sophie's face was tear-streaked, Richard's fierce and bone-white. Sophie bowed her head, looking at the hands that were twisted and clenched before her, and a heavy lock of hair fell across her eyes. He reached for her and drew her almost roughly into his arms again. She stood rigid, fighting fresh tears.

"I won't let them do it," he said into her hair. "Don't think it. I won't let them part us."

She shook her head miserably. "There's nothing you can do about it."

He stepped back from her, looked into her face. "That doesn't sound like my Sophie. You aren't going to let them beat us?"

She sniffed.

"The worst that can happen — the very worst —" Richard's voice was calmer and in face of her distress his own desperation was giving way to determination "— is that they win temporarily. We'll have to wait, that's all. Once I'm twenty-one —"

"Twenty-one! Richard — that's more than *four years*!"

"I know." Doggedly he kept the misery from his own voice. "But — it isn't the end of the world. We knew we'd have to wait —"

She flung from him. "To wait, yes — wait to get married, perhaps. But not that long. And — not like this! They'll keep you from me. We'll never see each other — oh, Richard, I can't bear it! Why are they so beastly? What have I ever done to them? Oh — I hate them! Hate them!" Her voice shook with the sudden rise of rage. "They've no right to do this to us!"

He was silent.

"They'll send you away. You know they will. And they're trying to make Uncle Josef send me home — poor little Maria, too, though I don't see what she's done to deserve it."

"What did grandfather say to Pa?"

She calmed a little. "He said that we were his guests, and that he could see no reason why we should leave. He stood up for us. Tried to explain to your father the way it's really been —"

"And what did Pa say?"

"He didn't really say anything. To be truthful, if I hadn't been so angry — so miserable — I might have felt a bit sorry for him. It isn't him, is it? It's your mother. She's always hated my mother and father, and now she hates me." There was desolation in her young voice as she turned from him and dropped on to the grass, her skirts spread about her, and picked at the slender stems with long, brown fingers. Her mouth was set into an unhappy line, and her breath still caught a little, tearfully, in her throat. She plucked a dandelion clock and held it in front of her. The delicate bowl of the seedhead was soft and fragile in the sunlight. She blew, sharply. Some of the seeds lifted and sailed into the still air. "One year," she said, and blew again, and again. "Two years. Three. Four." She lifted her head. She was suddenly very calm, and her voice was intense. "We can't wait that long, Richard. We can't. Something awful will happen. We'll lose each other. They know it."

He seemed to have run out of words. He sat beside her, half-turned from her, knees on elbows, shoulders hunched, head bowed.

With restless fingers she tore the blown dandelion head to pieces. Above them a robin sang, piercingly sweet and in the distance a cuckoo called.

She lifted her head, an odd, defiant expression upon her face. "Richard?"

He turned his head. She was looking not at him but at what remained of the stem of the dandelion, twirling in her fingers.

"Do you know — what you do — to —" She stopped,

nibbling her lip, then said, very fast, "That is — what people do — to have a baby?"

Silence lengthened. She turned to look at him. He had flushed a deep embarrassed brick red.

"Well," she asked a little sharply, "do you?"

"I — well — yes."

She looked away again. "It's no good pretending that I do, because I don't. I looked in a book once — in the San at school — a medical book. But — I didn't understand it."

The quiet this time was fraught with question and implication.

"I thought —" she said at last "— that if you knew, we could — could —" she lifted a brave head and looked at last directly at him "— could do it. Then — they'd *have* to let us marry. Wouldn't they?"

He was staring at her. She flushed, but her eyes were steady. He it was who turned away, abruptly, shaking his head. "No. We can't do that."

"But — why not?" Perversely his opposition overcame her own qualms, and her voice was suddenly positive and determined. "Why not? If it is the only way to make them let us be together?"

"It — isn't that."

"What then?"

He reached for her and hugged her to him, fiercely and awkwardly. "Oh, Sophie, darling Sophie! Don't you know? Don't you know what people would think — what they'd say of you?"

She was very still against him. "Of course I do. I'm not stupid," she said, very quietly. "But what does it matter? What people say — what they think — I don't care about them. I only care about you. And if it's the only way —"

He thrust his face hard into her hair. "We can't," he said. "We can't."

Sophie was right; they were prevented from meeting for anything but the most fleeting, stolen moments in the next few days. At last, and inevitably, Richard allowed himself to be persuaded that their only chance to see each other was to meet at a time when there could be no one to stop them. The loft of the stables that adjoined the cottage was the designated place. Sophie, slipping from her bed, down the creaking stairs and across the brick-paved yard, got there first and sat, alone and terribly afraid, in the rustling darkness, her eyes and ears strained for a sign of Richard's coming. The misery of the past few days, the quarrelling, the awful things that Alice had said of her when she had stormed down to the cottage on being told of Josef's attitude to her demands, were still with her. She ached with unhappiness. Her eyes were hot and tired with tears. The moonless night was a threat and a loneliness about her. She knew, with sudden awful clarity as she sat, chill and huddled and afraid, that she had made a mistake. He would not come. She knew it. Her rash suggestion had, after all, confirmed the truth of his mother's accusations. He was at home at this moment safe in bed. They were going to lose each other; they stood no chance against so hostile a world. Sooner or later he would begin to listen to what they said about her. He would believe it. He would despise her —

He wasn't coming.

She drew her dressing gown about her, shivered a little, though the night was not cold. Beneath her the great hunter and the two carriage horses moved softly in their stalls, chains clinking. It seemed to Sophie that they were the luckiest of creatures. Mindless and obedient, they were never called upon to take a decision, to take responsibility for their actions —

There was movement then, and through the trap of the loft she saw softly moving shadows. Someone had come into the stables carrying a carefully shaded lantern. For a moment her heart stopped. Then in the uncertain light she saw the familiar, lifted, dark head.

"Richard? I'm up here."

He climbed the ladder, the lantern swinging and sending shadows dancing wildly about the rafters. Once in the loft he set the glimmering light safely upon a cleared space on the floor, and then turned to her. Wordless, she flung herself upon him and they clung to each other, more like fearful children than like lovers.

"Your mother came," she said. "Oh, Richard — it was awful!

she said the most terrible things —" The last thing she had intended to say to him, yet the words tumbled out and she could not prevent them.

"You mustn't listen. Mustn't take any notice."

"I thought you weren't coming. Thought you must have listened to her. She hates me so —"

"Nonsense." His voice was gentle. "She just doesn't understand, that's all. Give her time. I'm sure she'll come round in the end."

"No! She won't! Richard — you didn't hear her —" Sophie drew away from him and dropped back into the heap of straw. Their whispers were counterpoint to the rustle of the breeze around the tiled, unlined roof. Sophie huddled disconsolately, her arms about her drawn-up knees. "She'll part us. For ever. She will."

"No!" He was beside her, his arms about her, his mouth close to her ear. "No! She won't. Because we shan't let her. Or anyone. I love you, Sophie — don't you believe that?"

She turned her face to him and with a desperate, unpractised urgency he kissed her, bearing her back into the warmth of the straw, his weight crushing the breath from her body. She was crying again, silently and wretchedly, as they embraced. He rained small, frantic kisses on her wet face, her hair, her neck. "Sophie — darling — don't cry. Please don't cry —" Brought up in a household of three men and a woman who rarely — if ever — shed a tear, he could not bear the sight of the girl's distress.

But she could not stop; as if they had been his own her tears wetted his lips and his cheeks. He lay beside her, his face buried in the fall of her hair, holding her, silently and tightly, until she quieted. Then they lay so for a long time, scarcely breathing, their young warm bodies pressed closely against each other. The lantern lit the mossy, cobwebbed roof above them. The horses moved again, hooves scraping upon the brick floor. Very, very gently Richard slid his hand under her dressing gown and caressed her body, warm and smooth beneath the voluminous fine cotton nightdress that she wore. She trembled a little and her breathing was uneven, but she did not pull away from him. His hand moved quietly, stroking, touching, gentling. The excitement that rose between them was fired by his hard-held restraint. Sophie it was who, with a sudden movement of her body, brought his hand into contact with her hardened breast. He could feel the beating of her heart, the lift of her breath. For a moment neither of them moved, and then his self-control broke and he kissed her again, hard and a little clumsily, his teeth sharp against her soft mouth, his body sprawled across hers. She held him to her with fingers that bit strongly through his shirt to his skin.

"You said you knew," she whispered at last into his ear. "You said you knew what we should do —"

He pulled away from her. "No!"

"Yes! Please!" She clung to him. "Richard — it's the only way! I don't care what they say! I don't care what anyone says! I want you. I love you. I won't let them part us! Please, Richard —" With a quick, unexpected movement she caught his hand and thrust it into the loose neck of her gown, to her bared breast. His fingers brushed the rigid nipple and she shuddered. "Please, Richard!" she said again, and in the lamplight he saw that the tears had started again, streaking her cheeks, damping her hair.

"Sophie don't — please — don't —" The whisper was pleading; but his body was already reacting to her demands, and he knew himself lost.

Sobbing still, with a swift movement she sat up, slipped her dressing gown from her shoulders and almost in the same movement stripped the nightgown over her head. Then she sat, straight and still and white as bone, watching him, a turmoil of embarrassment and longing in her eyes.

"Christ," he whispered.

A gust of wind scurried through the overlapping tiles. She shivered. Very slowly he put out his hand, traced with his finger the line of her shoulder, the sweetly drooping breast. Her skin was cold. He stood. Took off his clothes. She watched him, silent, unblinking, unsmiling, fear in her face, but determination too, and the softness of love.

"This is our wedding night," she said, as he leaned above her, "isn't it?"

He kissed her. "It is. And I swear it: no one shall keep us

apart. I'll marry you, Sophie Anatov. And we'll live together for ever and ever, with no one to come between us."

He was far from a practised lover, but Sophie, innocent too, did not know that and their young ardour needed no art to perfect it. She gave herself to him with no reservations, instinct her sure guide: and the tears that she shed were no longer bitter ones. He leaned above her, afterwards, and kissed them away, a little worriedly. "Why are you crying? Did I hurt you?"

She smiled. Shook her head. "No," she said, untruthfully.

He reached for her dressing gown and drew it about them, then, on one elbow, looking down at her, he reached a finger to her hair and wound a strand of it about his finger. "There. A golden ring. Our wedding ring."

She took a long, trembling breath. "Richard?"

"Yes?"

"Do you think — I mean —" she paused "— have we made a baby?"

He shook his head. "I don't know."

"I hope so. Oh, I do hope so!"

They were silent for a while.

"We ought to go," Richard said at last.

Her arms tightened about him, but she said nothing.

"Sophie? We really have to go."

Reluctantly she released him. He stood and, a little awkwardly, began hunting for his clothes. She slipped her nightgown over her head and drew her dressing gown about her, then sat watching him. "Richard?"

"Mmm?"

She hesitated, pulled a piece of straw from the pile and smoothed it with her fingers. "How did you —" she looked at him quickly, and away "— how did you know what to do?"

Tucking his shirt into his trousers, he paused.

"All right," she said, hastily, "it doesn't matter."

He crouched before her, took her hands. "It's no mystery." His hesitation was barely noticeable. "A boy at school told me." It was almost the truth.

She looked relieved. "You mean — you've never actually done it before, either?"

He shook his head.

She smiled, softly and happily. "I'm glad."

He stood again, pulled her to her feet after him. "Tomorrow night? Here?"

She nodded and smiled as if tears had never been.

They met every night for almost a week before the storm broke. Richard it was who was caught — and by of all people his mother, who, woken from light sleep by a noise, left her husband snoring in bed and walked out on to the landing just in time to confront Richard as he climbed the stairs, shoes in hand and an expression on his face that screamed guilt almost before she had had time to connect his actions with their most probable cause. She lifted the night-lantern high and studied her son, her face forbidding. Then she raised her voice. "Alex? Here — at once, please. Send to the cottage. Quickly. Catch that creature before she reaches her bed. And as for you," she addressed Richard in a quieter, flinty voice that made his skin crawl, "get to your room at once. Your father will deal with you later."

The flogging he received was bad enough; the castigation of Sophie and of what had been between them was all but unbearable. And this time there was nothing to be done; they had no champions — none that is but Rupert and Maria, and their young good will was hardly effective against the hostile condemnation of everyone else, including a hurt and disappointed Josef. Sophie, in undertaking her rash action, had not considered this, and was desolate. But worse was to come; this time Boris and Louisa could not be kept out of it. They arrived the next day, Louisa distraught, Boris raging. Sophie had never seen him so angry. She was appalled, however, to discover that his anger was directed if anything more at Richard than at herself.

"I'll take a horsewhip to the young scoundrel! I'll kill him —"

"Papa! No! It wasn't Richard's fault! It wasn't!"

He turned on her, his face blazing. His tender pride was touched by this, and that it should be Alex Rose's son doubled the humiliation. "Keep a still tongue in your head for once girl! Not his fault? Of course it was his fault. His — and mine," he added grimly.

"Yours? What do you mean?"

"I mean," he said, his voice corrosive with contempt and fury, "that in all these years I have been blinded by my own stubborn stupidity. I have loved and indulged you. Now I get my just deserts. I would not — could not — listen to what others said of you. What my own common sense should have told me. And if you repay me in this way for my foolishness then I have no one to blame but myself."

"Papa!" Sophie was horrified.

"You're spoiled. And arrogant. And selfish. You care for no one and nothing —" His harsh voice was cold as a steel blade.

Shaking now, Sophie covered her face with her hands. Louisa turned away.

"Your actions have brought dishonour not just upon yourself but upon your mother, your sister and upon me," he continued, remorselessly savage. "I swear, Sophie, that I will never forgive you for this. You are no longer my daughter."

"Papa!"

He turned from her. Louisa's slender shoulders were shaking. At the door Boris turned again, looked coldly at Sophie. "Go now to your room. And stay there." He turned to Louisa. "Lock her in. We'll have no more of her harlot's tricks."

Sophie flinched. The shock of her father's anger had leeched the blood from her face.

"Where are you going?" Louisa asked her husband quietly.

"First I have an apology to make," Boris said, stone-faced, "to Uncle Josef, whose kindness and hospitality have been so flagrantly and heartlessly abused —"

"Papa doesn't need an apology, Boris. Truly he doesn't."

Boris turned. Anna stood behind him, unsmiling. "He's upset, of course. He feels responsible. But he certainly doesn't blame you for what's happened." Her gaze had moved to Sophie. The girl said nothing, but her eyes were eloquent. Very, very slightly Anna shook her head. "Oh, Sophie," she said, as she had said once before, and at her expression Sophie's heart sank.

Louisa hurried to Anna, hands outstretched. "How pleased I am to see you! You've heard?" Her eyes were still bright with tears.

Anna leaned to kiss her warmly. "Yes. At least one member of the family had the good sense to see that you needed an outsider — a comparative outsider at least — down here to calm tempers and ease the situation. Rupert," she added at Louisa's enquiring look. "He rang me first thing this morning. I came at once."

"It's kind of you," Boris said, stiffly. "But unnecessary. We can manage our own affairs."

Anna raised caustic eyebrows, in no way deterred by the tone. "What are you going to do?" she asked midly. "Horsewhip the boy? Pound Alex to a pulp? Put Sophie on bread and water?"

Colour rose in Boris's handsome face.

"You'll only make matters worse, Boris," she said, gently. "The thing is done. Richard has been punished — very severely punished — by his father," she ignored the small, choked sound that Sophie made at that. "Alice and Alex — of course — blame Sophie. You — of course — blame Richard." She glanced at Sophie. "It seems to me that such mischief takes two." Sophie could not sustain the look. Miserably she hung her head. "So — surely," Anna continued, "it is the future that we must now think of. What are we going to do about the situation?"

"The boy must marry Sophie." Surprisingly, it was Louisa who had spoken. Her husband's volatile anger had kept her quiet until now, but Anna's presence lent her strength and her voice was firm.

There was a small silence. Sophie looked from one to the other, hope dawning in her eyes.

"Exactly my thought," Anna said quietly. She looked at Sophie again, her pale eyes unusually chill. "And if we're playing the game the way that you planned it, Sophie, then I hope you're proud of yourself. I wish you joy of your manipulations."

Sophie coloured a deep and painful scarlet.

Boris, for the moment, appeared to be at a loss for words.

"Now," Anna was brisk, "I would suggest that for the moment — until tempers have cooled — I should speak to Alice and Alex. Accusations and recriminations will do no good at all. Is that acceptable to you?"

"Of course," Louisa said, promptly and gratefully.

"Boris?"

Boris hesitated. "It's the only way," Anna said gently. "The boy must marry her. There can be no doubt about that. And words spoken in anger now will never be forgotten. We'll have to live with them for ever. All of us."

The fierce light of anger was dying in the fair, handsome face. He nodded.

Anna looked at Sophie, exasperation in her eyes. "Isn't there enough trouble in the world at the moment — don't we all have enough to worry about — without you making it worse?"

"I'm sorry," Sophie said, and her voice was sincere. But glimmering in the dark eyes was the beginning of an undisguised gleam of happiness.

"No," Alice said. "You may talk, Anna, until you are blue. No."

Anna stared at her. "You can't mean that?"

Alice returned the look, cold as stone. "On the contrary, Anna, it is I who find it hard to believe that you mean what you say. That we should allow this — guttersnipe — to trap Richard as her mother trapped her father —"

"Alice! That's an outrageous thing to say! And as for Sophie — she may be silly and headstrong —"

Alice laughed, and the sound was unpleasant. "Oh, come now, Anna! Silly? I should say not! She's far from silly. In my belief she knew exactly what she was doing — knew exactly what the reaction would be. Well, she has miscalculated. Under no circumstances whatsoever will we give our permission for Richard to marry. Isn't that so, Alex?"

Alex looked helplessly at Anna.

"Well?" his wife prompted sharply.

He nodded. "I'm afraid so."

Anna held her temper, with difficulty. "And what," she asked, "If the child should be pregnant?"

Alice's expression did not change in the slightest. "That has nothing to do with the case. Nor with us."

"Nothing to do — for God's sake, Alice!" Anna could restrain herself no longer, "It would be Richard's child! Your grandchild!"

Her sister-in-law lifted a cool, contemptuous face. "Can you be so sure of that? We only have her word for it. How do we know who else she may have been," her lip curled, contemptuously, "romping with in the hay?"

"Now that's unfair, and you must know it."

"I know no such thing. I simply know this. Under no circumstances whatsoever will we give our permission for Richard to marry that girl. He is to be sent away — to the military establishment at Woolwich. I have no doubt that the discipline there will restore his sanity and his sense of proportion. He will forget her."

"I shouldn't count on that," Anna snapped, all her dislike of the woman openly in her voice. "Has it occurred to you that the youngsters may really love one another? Is it so hard to believe? What they've done is wrong — of course it is — but it's hardly the worst crime in the world, is it? God Almighty, with the terrible things that are happening, that may happen, around us you can hardly blame them for —"

"Now you're being ridiculous," Alice interrupted sharply. "Are you suggesting that every absurd rumour of war should be used as an excuse for wicked immorality? Have you taken leave of your senses? If war breaks out tomorrow — and I have to say that I for one do not for an instant believe that it will — it excuses not one jot of that chit's behaviour."

"I didn't for one moment suggest —"

"Then what are you suggesting? That we allow them to marry? That we should let the scheming little minx get her own way? What a good idea that is! As mismatched a pair as you could possibly wish to find —"

"You don't know that. In point of fact I should have said that they were quite well matched."

Alice smiled, viciously sweet, and let off her final salvo. "I hardly think, Anna my dear, that you are an expert on what makes a successful match."

Anna stared at her, speechless.

Alex cleared his throat.

"I think," Anna said, "that I'd better go. Before I throw something."

The dashing of scarce-raised hopes was cruel, and Sophie —

defiantly brave until now — broke under this final blow. Locked in her room at the cottage she cried, first hysterically, then more quietly, and finally soundlessly and wretchedly, as if she would never be able to stop. Boris's bitter anger and disappointment, however, were too great to be softened by this behaviour. "If the girl won't pull herself together," he said harshly, "then she'll have to travel as she is. I'll not remain in this place one moment longer."

"Boris — please, my dear." Louisa's still-pretty face was pale and worried, "of course we must go. But give Sophie a chance to —"

She trailed off as her husband turned a closed, hard face to her. She knew Boris: softhearted and indulgent as he was, his pride, temper and trust affronted in this manner might take months, if not years, to appease. She looked in silent appeal at Anna.

Anna thought she had never seen lighthearted Boris look so much like his brother. The thought changed a vague thought into determination. "I've an idea," she said.

No one spoke.

"Perhaps — for now — it might be better if Sophie came home with me. I promise I'll care for her —"

"She has been cared for," Boris said, coldly, "and see what's come of it. She needs discipline. Punishment."

Louisa winced.

Anna, gently, shook her head. "No, Boris. That simply isn't so. And in a few weeks — perhaps months — I'm sure you'll see that too. That's why I think it would be better if you allowed Sophie to come to us. To give everyone a chance to calm down. I, for one, don't intend to let Alice get away with this so easily. I'll get Alex on his own — try to persuade him to —"

"No!" The word was violent. Boris stepped forward, his one hand raised, index finger stabbing aggressively at her, "No one — *no one* — begs on behalf of an Anatov! You hear me? If Richard Rose were the last man on earth I would not give my permission for him to marry my daughter after this."

"Oh, for God's sake!" Anna, too, was really angry now. "Can't you *see* what you're doing? You're as bad as they are! Can't you see how destructive it all is?" She stopped, fighting her temper down. She of all people should know that she would get nowhere shouting at an Anatov with his pride up. She spoke more calmly. "Boris. Please. Let Sophie come to me. Everything else we can talk about later. But — for now — we have to get her away from here. She'll have Victoria and the boys for company. It will be better for everyone."

"She's right, Boris," Louisa said.

Boris turned away, anger still veiling the terrible hurt in his bright eyes. "I don't care where she goes," he said.

Sophie left Bissetts the following morning, subdued in the company of an equally quiet Anna. Half an hour before she was due to leave, still locked in disgrace in her room, she stood at the window and looked up the curving drive towards the big house.

Richard. What have they done to you? What have they said? Do you hate me now? The hot, easy tears rose again. It seemed to her that there could never be a time again when she would smile.

A movement caught her eye, on the fringe of the shrubbery. A tall, dark figure — she dashed her hand across her eyes and leaned, suddenly eager, to the window. Not Richard — even from here she could tell it — but Rupert. He stood for a moment looking towards the cottage, glanced at his watch, as if waiting. There was a scurry of movement in the garden below and Maria slipped from the door and along the path to where Rupert stood. They came together for only an instant, and that furtive and hurried, with Maria glancing constantly and nervously over her shoulder. Rupert gave her something, then swiftly bent and kissed her upon her cheek and was gone. Maria scampered back to the path to the cottage. Sophie's tears had died. Her heart was thumping in fierce excitement. She heard the door slam, heard her sister's quick footsteps on the stairs. A moment later a slip of paper was pushed under her door. She flew to it, snatched it up.

DARLING SOPHIE. THEY WON'T WIN. BE BRAVE. R.

She read it again and again. Touched the scrawled words, gently and reverently, with her finger.

"Sophie?" Anna's voice, outside the door, "It's time to go."

She folded the precious note carefully, tucked it into the pocket where she could touch it. "I'm ready."

Two weeks later Austria-Hungary declared war on Serbia, and the confused and grim train of events that was to lead like a lit fuse to general conflict burned on. Russia mobilized in support of her Serbian allies. Germany — her acquisitive eyes as always on French soil — followed suit. Within days these two nations were at war, and Germany's attack on France was launched. Ignoring the guaranteed neutrality of a tiny and totally defenceless country, the German army marched into Belgium, raping a country and brutalizing a people whose simple misfortune was their geographical situation. Roused at last, the British bulldog raised a belatedly outraged head and growled a warning. Supremely confident that his grandmother's country would never actually take arms against him, the Kaiser ignored the threat. Twenty-four hours later, on an unprecedented wave of jingoistic fervour, Britain declared war upon Germany and her young men began to queue at the enlisting posts for fear of being left out of the fun.

It was upon that very day that Sophie began to suspect that she was pregnant.

CHAPTER TWENTY

London, in those first few weeks of war, was a city of strange contrasts; a city of confidence, her streets full of young men in uniform, fresh and unblooded, off for a not unwelcome bit of excitement after these past years of peace and politics, her girls too caught by the high-hearted urgency of the time, their enthusiasm kindled by the opportunities offered by war to break from the confines that peace had imposed. Yet, of course, there was fear too, and heartbreak, and those to shake their heads at the dauntless naïvety that foresaw no possibility of defeat, to wonder in the darkness of the night what their sons, lovers, husbands, brothers might have to face before the so-blithely-forecast day of victory arrived. There were fears of another sort, too — fears that no civilian population in Britain had ever had to face before: in the first month of the war Zeppelins, menacing giants of the sky, brought fire and death to beleaguered Antwerp and the reports of the raids that appeared in the British newspapers caused more than one thoughtful eye to lift to the skies of London, more than one ear to strain for the thrum of a distant engine on a clouded autumn afternoon. The possibility — some would have said the probability — of an air attack on the civilian population could not be ignored. By the darkling evenings of early October city streets were dim, their lights shaded or extinguished altogether, trams and omnibuses travelled all but unlit and private houses were blinded and curtained against the lamplight. And with the darkening of the streets came the darkening of the horizon of war. The debacle of the French defeats in August had been no more than a chauvinistic public — already sadly biased against these, their comparatively newly acquired allies — had expected. The British retreat from Mons, though a shock, could be accepted as a temporary setback. But for those with eyes to see and knowledge of the terrain over which the armies marched and fought the first signs that this was to be no swift and gallant encounter to be decided by a few brief and bloody battles were already there. At Verdun in September the French forced the Germans back to a ridge on the north bank of the River Aisne, and in the indecisive and tragically costly battle that followed for fourteen days thereafter lay the first inklings of the terrible stalemate of trench warfare. Along the rest of the Front the struggle for dominance swayed fiercely in those first few months, and unheard-of names that were to become all too familiar to British ears found their way into conversations over the dining table, the shop counter and the public bar. The Marne. Le Cateau. Guise. Flanders. And — in October — Ypres. The casualty lists grew with each day and each fierce attack. Ypres was held — just — and the small, pretty city unwittingly and unwillingly became both a symbol of freedom and a focal point of horror. The fight to save it decimated the old regular British Army. Only the remnants remained — remnants whose urgent job it would now be to train the young men who had so cheerfully obeyed their country's call to arms, and whose experience of fighting was on the whole confined to school yard scuffles or the occasional bloody nose on a Saturday night. By November the flaming, clamorous line of the Western Front had been drawn in shed blood and barbed wire through France and Flanders and the armies were dug in as best they could be. Yet the situation could not be said to be equal, for the enemy had gained a good deal of his objective in those first fierce months and was now ready grimly to defend it, and so the German dispositions were made in concrete and steel and with an eye to permanence. Not so the Allies. To win this war they must attack, advance — so there were few well-serviced or solid bunkers for Jacques or Tommy or his Commonwealth mates. On the whole he crouched in and swore at a hastily-scraped hole in the ground shored up with corrugated iron and sandbags and — more and more frequently as the weeks moved on and the constant bombardment smashed the ground — knee-deep in filthy water. For now the gods had taken a hand in man's ill-managed affairs, and the rain had started.

For Anna — as indeed for most women — the greatest and

most immediate effect of the war was in seeing some of the menfolk of her family don uniform and leave for France. The first — and perhaps the most surprising — departure was Ralph's, his chaplain's collar incongruous beneath his khaki uniform jacket, his gentle smile unchanged.

"But — Ralph! Why?" She was at a loss for words.

They strolled in the garden at Bayswater. The grass and paths were heaped and scattered with fallen leaves that skittered in small swirling whirlpools in the light breeze. The sky was bright and peaceful with sunshine.

For the space of perhaps half a dozen quiet paces he did not reply. Then, "I'm not sure I can answer that myself," he said. "It has nothing to do with — with bravery — or patriotism —"

"What then?"

"It's," he hesitated, "I think it has something to do with James," he said very quietly.

She looked a question.

He shook his head. "Dead — buried friendless in a strange land. Someone must have prayed for him. I hope so, anyway."

She glanced at him again, sharply. She had always believed Ralph to be closer to James than to any of them, yet in those years since her brother's death she had never suspected this haunting.

"And perhaps too," Ralph continued, "it's that if my flock goes to war then it ill becomes me to hide beneath Mother Church's skirts."

"Oh, don't be silly. No one would have accused you of that. And anyway you're surely over age? They're calling for volunteers between eighteen and thirty years old. I'm thirty-seven. If my arithmetic serves me well that makes you thirty-five."

His smile this time had in it the faintest hint of self-mockery. "They aren't so particular about parsons."

She shook her head stubbornly. "I still don't understand."

"Anna — in war, always, men are close to death. To pain. To fear. God can help them. Heal them. Strengthen them. Keep them whole." He gestured, a small, self-deprecating lift of the hand. "Perhaps through me. I have to try."

She could find no counter to that. They paced for a moment in silence, then stopped by the small overgrown pool that had been such a childhood favourite. "Michael's going, you know," Anna said.

"Yes, he told me."

"It's ridiculous. He doesn't have to go, either. He's a year above thirty." She broke off a small dead twig from the tree by which they were standing and snapped it, quickly and nervously, in her fingers. "I can't think what's happened to everyone."

"War's happened to everyone."

"I suppose so." She threw the pieces of twig into the clouded water, watched them spin in slow, lazy circles. "Ralph — what do you think? I mean — will it all be over by Christmas as some people are saying? I read in the paper the other day that it could go on for as long as three years." Nicholas, tall, fair, handsome Nicholas with his bright, bright eyes was nearly fourteen years old and already mad for a Subaltern's uniform. She turned troubled eyes to her brother. "It couldn't last that long could it?"

He laughed, gently exasperated. "My dear Anna — I'm a chaplain, not a general. How would I know? We must just pray that it does not."

"Yes, of course." Her tone did not indicate that she took much encouragement from that course of action.

"What will you do?" he asked. "Have you thought? Will you stay in London?"

"Why yes, of course. The boys are safely away at school, so we don't have to worry about them. And we're hoping that Victoria will join some friends in the country. Joss is doing something mysterious with all that money he's making — armaments or something, I believe. It's all very hush hush and he spends a lot of time away, in the north —" Her voice was even; any wife talking about her busy, absent husband. Ralph — no man's fool despite his gentle nature — felt a twinge of sympathy for his sister. Anna needed warmth, love; he doubted that his brother-in-law had ever provided her with either. "And as for me," Anna continued, and grinned suddenly, reminding him, briefly, of the mischievous, teasing older sister of childhood, "I'm not altogether useless, you know. I've already been co-opted on to God knows how many committees — Red Cross, Belgian Refugees, Ambulances for the Front — there must be half a dozen at least. Mind you, that's nothing compared to Arabella. She's careering around London on a motorcycle, you know. Must be rather fun, I should think."

Ralph looked as near to shock as his calm, pleasant face allowed. "Good Lord! You aren't thinking of doing something like that, are you?"

She laughed aloud at that. "Of course not! What do you take me for? I'm no Arabella to believe that we women should don uniform and fight shoulder to shoulder with the men —"

"Heaven forbid."

"Quite. Someone's got to look after things at home. While there's still something to look after, that is. Still — I do suppose that if this business goes on for very long women are going to find themselves as involved as men. If General Kitchener keeps taking our men and the armaments factories entice our domestic help away we're going to find ourselves doing a little more than twiddling our thumbs and watching for Zeppelins."

"You've never twiddled your thumbs in your life."

She grinned again. "That's true."

"And what of your own work?"

She shrugged a little. "That I'm afraid will have to take a back seat for the duration. Designing expensive jewellery could hardly be said to be the most patriotic or useful thing to do at the moment. My talents lately, such as they are, have been turned to designing posters and raising money."

"And what of Sophie? How is she?"

The small, sudden silence was enough to make him turn and look at her. Then, "She's pregnant," Anna said, flatly. "With Richard's child."

He stared at her, his kindly face stricken. "Oh, no."

She nodded. "There's no doubt, I'm afraid."

"But that's — terrible. A tragedy for the child —"

"Yes. So everyone thinks. Except Sophie. Her father had to be physically restrained from grabbing the nearest pistol. Louisa is devastated. Alex nearly had a heart attack. And Alice — well, I'd better not go into what the charming Alice said, or I might have a heart attack myself." Anna sighed, and the false, bright edge to her voice died. "But Sophie — Sophie is perfectly happy. Richard will marry her, she says, as soon as he is able. Perhaps she's right. I don't know. Alice can't keep him from her forever, can she?"

"Do they see each other? Sophie and Richard?"

"No. Alice has seen to that. At the Military Academy — you know both the boys are at Woolwich now? — he's been put on his honour not to approach the girl. You know Richard. That's as effective as locking him in a cell. Sophie writes to him, I know. But he isn't allowed to answer. Yet she has perfect and utter faith that he'll come to her when he can."

"Perhaps he will."

"He'd better," Anna said, unexpectedly grimly. "Or I'll shoot him myself."

He smiled at her vehemence. "You're very fond of her, aren't you?"

"Yes I am. More than I knew." More than of my own daughter — not for the first time the guilty thought flicked through Anna's mind. She could never understand why Victoria's pleasant docility could aggravate her to screaming point whilst Sophie's headstrong and volatile nature, which others found so difficult, sometimes exasperated her, but at the same time always endeared the girl to her and touched her heart. "Our Sophie, I'm afraid," she added wryly, "is that kind of person. She brings out extremes in other people."

"Do you think —" Ralph hesitated. He looked faintly uncomfortable, "Do you think I should, well, talk to her?"

Anna could not stop her sudden laughter. "Oh, Ralph, dear! And say what? That she's a naughty girl and should not have done such a thing? Or that God forgives her wickedness? She'd laugh at you."

"I didn't mean —"

"Of course you didn't." She was instantly contrite. "But — that's what Sophie would think you meant. Whatever you said. No, Ralph, leave Sophie to go her own way. I'm coming to think that's the best thing to do." She turned to him and took his hands in hers, her face suddenly serious. "When do you leave?"

"In two days."

"You'll be careful? Truly careful?"

He kissed her cheek. "Of course."

He left her there by the pool that had so many associations with their childhood, and she watched his retreating back with a gleam of anxiety in her pale eyes. The uniform he wore — so strange — so very alien to all she knew of her peace-loving brother — was like a symbol of all that had changed in the world, all that was threatened. She felt the faint and surprising sickness of fear creep through her bowels. Nothing she had read, nothing she had heard or seen so far, not even the tragic lists of the dead had so brought home to her the reality of the war. "God keep you." She was startled to discover that she had spoken the words aloud.

The celebration of Christmas 1914 was at home inevitably overshadowed by nostalgia for the past and fear for the future, and in the trenches by the mud, the enemy bombardment and the bloody weather. For a few brief hours along a few brief miles of battlefront enemies met, exchanged cigarettes, addresses, photographs and then went back to their guns and their avowed intention of wiping each other out; a strange interlude that illustrated the best and the worst in human nature. Ralph Rose, his well-attended evening Communion over, sat, still and alone, looking out across the barbed wire, allowing himself the luxury of his first cigarette of the day and wondering at the lunatic inconsistency of man.

It was in January that the much feared airships made their first foray across the Channel and attacked the English east coast. Four people were killed and much damage was done to property; and Londoners slept even more uneasily in their beds when they heard the news. Across the water the guns rumbled, the shells sang their song of death and blood seeped into the ditch-pitted slime and filth that had, just a few months before, been peaceful cultivated countryside. At Neuve Chapelle the British Army lost thirteen thousand men in a battle in which all the ground that was gained was taken in the first three hours yet that lasted for a costly and exhausting three days. For one small, wrecked village it was a desperate price to pay; a price it was becoming increasingly obvious would be demanded again and again for every square foot of advance.

In Bayswater, Anna found herself fighting an unexpected battle of her own.

"I'm sorry, Mother. I don't want to upset you. Or — defy you." Victoria, flushed with the stress of a confrontation she would have given blood to avoid, clenched her hands hard upon an already ruined lace handkerchief and, contriving to look contrite and defiant at one and the same time, stumbled obstinately on through an obviously prepared speech, her eyes avoiding her mother's astonished face. "I will not run to the country and hide my head whilst the rest of the world fights a war. I'm not a child." She stopped, the sensible and reasoned words running dry on her.

Anna, as much amazed as actually angry at this defiance, waited.

Victoria lifted her head. The softly pretty face was as intense as her mother had ever seen it, the wide, violet eyes dark with unwonted agitation. "I want to be a nurse, Mother. I want it more than anything in the world. I don't want to go to France, or drive an ambulance, or be a heroine. I just want to be a nurse. Here, in London. I want to help. To do something."

In the silence, rain drummed against the window.

"You're very young —" Anna started to say.

"I'm seventeen years old. I'll wait till I'm eighteen if I must, though I'd rather not. Boys of my age died at Neuve Chapelle, Mother. No one told them they were too young."

Anna, nonplussed, shook her head. "Shouldn't you wait? Perhaps go away for a while — think about it."

"No. I *am* sure. I've never been so sure of anything in my life."

And she was. To everyone's astonishment Victoria stuck to her guns with a stubborn determination that no one — not least herself — had suspected she possessed. Faced with such obduracy Anna gave in; indeed, for the first time in her daughter's short life she found herself regarding her as an individual, and one to be admired. Victoria's training, at St Bartholomew's Hospital, Smithfield, was gruelling, and nothing in her sheltered life had in any way prepared her for it: no one who knew her well believed that she would stick it out for more than a week. Yet she scrubbed floors, emptied bedpans, ran messages, washed soiled dressings for fourteen hours a day and cheerfully thrived upon it. Her meals were snatched and her sleep interrupted. She lost weight, gained blisters and confidence. By choice, to be close to her work, she roomed with another girl near the hospital; and from her very first visit home it was obvious that Victoria had found a vocation and the strength to pursue it. Anna's respect for her daughter grew, and Victoria — tired, thinner than perhaps suited her, her hands red and rough — nevertheless glowed in the warmth of her mother's approval at last.

For the men in the trenches spring brought little relief. Whilst at home the cuckoo called and the buds of April swelled and burst in the growth of a new season, the shattered woodlands of France and Belgium were stripped of life, trees and earth blasted to the very image of death by the relentless bombardment and the traffic of war. Yet even there could be found strange, odd little pockets of green, pockets where nature struggled to keep her promise despite man's madness; and it was in one of these that Ralph Rose found himself pausing one late April day — a small copse, still miraculously green, in which could still be heard, incredibly, above the rumble of the guns, the sound of bird song. In the distance, set in that saucer of fertile land that had become a death trap beneath the German guns on its rim, the little, shattered town of Ypres reached skeletal masonry fingers to the wide evening sky. Ralph had been to visit a friend — an unlikely friend some would say — a Roman Catholic Padre attached to an Algerian division of the French army. The two men had met on the football field, friendly rivals, had shared a glass of wine later and had found a companionship together despite the difference of dogma that divided them that each had found difficult to achieve with the men to whose spiritual well-being they tended in such utterly impossible circumstances. On the way back now to his own dugout Ralph stopped to view this small, miraculous oasis of green and to enjoy the luxury of a solitary cigarette. He settled back comfortably at the foot of a small tree, his back against its trunk. A shell whistled above him. He did not even duck. Seconds later he heard it explode. He tilted his head back against the tree and watched the smoke from his cigarette drift fragrantly in the light wind.

Another shell. And another.

He drew a long, weary lungful of smoke. They're stepping it up. What's that in aid of, I wonder? Another attack? Another barbarous exercise where men are forced to advance over the bodies of their dying comrades or their dead enemies — or to fall beside them, to mingle blood and guts and brains upon the putrid ground of this useless, indefensible Salient.

He drew up his legs and for a brief instant dropped his head to his knees, curled in a foetal position, his shoulders slumped. God, it's awful. So truly awful.

He lifted his head, drew deeply again on the cigarette. How did I ever believe that I could serve God in this hell? Where is He here? What good am I? To Him? To anyone?

The bombardment was noticeably heavier. Automatically he reached for his helmet and clapped it on his head; although behind the front line the copse was well within the range of the German guns. The birds had stopped singing. He stood up, took one last pull at his cigarette then dropped it to the ground and crushed it with his foot, smiling wryly to himself at his own foolish carefulness. He should be getting back. If this kept up there would be need of him in the dressing station, if nowhere else.

He left the shelter of the trees in a fast, ducking run that had become second nature when this close to the forward, sniper-ridden trenches. In a shower of stones and dirt he slid into a trench. A dark-skinned man in unfamiliar uniform grinned cheerily at him and started to speak. Then the smiling mouth gaped, the eyes bulged and the man's body lifted and buckled as the ground disintegrated beneath them and the concussed air roared. The body hit Ralph, knocking him flat. He clenched his eyes and his mouth against the warmth and wetness that invaded them. Revulsion churned in him and savagely he wrenched from beneath the corpse, burying his face in his hands, wiping the blood and slime from his skin.

The world was suddenly, heavily, quiet.

Somewhere close, a man moaned.

Ralph gathered his knees beneath him, with enormous effort straightened his arms, levered himself to a kneeling position. The Algerian soldier who moments before had been ready to greet him so cheerfully grimaced emptily at the menacingly still sky. Two others lay sprawled in death, the one headless, the other untouched and apparently sleeping. An arm, encased still in a dark blue sleeve, lay a foot from where Ralph crouched, dazed and terribly afraid. All the fear, all the terror that he had known and fought against in the last months, rose now to his throat in sickness and he vomited violently. He was trembling uncontrollably. He staggered to his feet, his mind wiped clean of thought by panic. He stumbled along the wrecked and bloody trench, his teeth clenched against the sobs of horror that were forming in his throat.

"*Maman. Maman!*"

He almost trod upon the boy who lay sprawled upon his back, the terrible injuries glinting red and black upon his body, his soft child's face untouched except by terror and by tears. "*Je veux Maman.*"

Ralph lifted a foot to step over him. The blinding eyes detected the shadow and a small hand lifted. "*Maman — aide-moi.*"

The man stood for a still moment looking down at the dying boy.

Run. You can do nothing for him. Run. Save yourself.

The child was crying still for his mother, tears on his smooth cheeks, one hand lifted beseechingly to the tall form that towered above him.

Ralph dropped to his knees, took the hand in his own. The young fingers clung like death.

Ralph lifted his head. That strange tense silence still held, infinitely threatening, infinitely terrifying. "The Lord is my Shepherd, I shall not want." To his own surprise his quiet voice was firm. The small hand clenched and unclenched upon his. The boy muttered, but he was calmer, the human contact and the gentle voice comforting him.

"He leadeth me beside the still waters —"

Somewhere in the distance a man shouted, the voice brutal with urgency and warning.

The boy was quiet now, his eyes focused upon Ralph's face.

Men ran past, shouting — ran towards the beleaguered town, their weapons discarded in panic, their streaming eyes fear-filled.

"He restoreth my soul —"

Still steadily reciting the comforting words, both of his hands trapped in the boy's, Ralph lifted his head. The air was acrid. Eerily in the dusky half-darkness a heavy, greenish vapour wreathed upon the evening breeze across the blasted landscape, drifted balefully towards him. Men were shouting, mortal dread in their voices.

"Yea, though I walk through the valley of the shadow of death —" There was a tremor now in his voice that it was utterly beyond him to control, but if the boy heard it he showed no sign. The strange, rhythmic foreign words, spoken in that even, gentle voice were comfort enough. The hands held strong. The young mouth relaxed, beyond pain.

"Yet will I fear no evil."

The gas enveloped the great coils of barbed wire, rolled through the outer defences, advanced silent, inexorable and utterly merciless. Ralph lifted his head and his voice now was strong.

"Thy rod and Thy staff they comfort me. Thou preparest a table before me, in the presence of mine enemies —" He paused for a brief moment at that. "Thou anointest my head with oil, my cup runneth over."

Noiseless, deadly, all his fears crept towards him.

"Surely goodness and mercy shall follow me all the days of my life. And I will dwell in the House of the Lord for ever."

The boy was dead before the chlorine reached them.

The news of Ralph's death reached the house in which he had spent his childhood within a day of a new life entering it. Sophie held her daughter close and looked at Anna.

"I'm sorry, Aunt Anna. Truly sorry. I didn't know Uncle Ralph very well — but I think he must have been very brave." The young eyes could not hold grief for very long when the soft head of her baby with its fine, downy hair, nestled softly and warmly in the crook of her arm.

"Yes," Anna said. All her tears had been cried. Oddly, the news of Ralph's death had come as no surprise. It was almost as if she had expected it from that moment he had walked from her by the pool in the garden. She reached a finger to the baby's tiny hand. "How is she?"

"Wonderful."

"Have you decided on a name yet?"

"Yes —" Sophie hesitated. "That is — I know what I'd like to call her —" The emphasis was on the personal pronoun. "I thought — Felicity."

Anna smiled. "What a lovely idea. Happiness."

"That's what I thought."

Early May sunshine streamed through the window. The room was decked with flowers. Anna sat on the bed and regarded her new great-niece with favour.

"Aunt Anna?"

"Mmm?" Anna's eyes were still on the baby.

"I can't ever thank you enough. For everything."

Anna shook her head.

"Truly I can't. I don't know what might have happened to me — to us — without you. It isn't everyone who'd take a —" her wide mouth ever humorous, twitched to a swift smile and with a pang Anna thought that she looked the very image of her estranged father "— a fallen woman into their home."

Anna stood up briskly. "Nonsense. I do it all the time. Now — what would you like for tea? I've some eggs. Queued for them myself. Could you manage one?"

"That would be a lovely idea." Sophie watched her to the door. "Aunt Anna?"

Anna turned.

Sophie's strong young face was suddenly uncertain, her eyes, avoiding her aunt's, turned upon the child. "Do you think they might let him see us? Just once?" The frailty of need rang in her voice no matter how hard she tried to disguise it.

Anna swallowed. "I don't know, my dear," she said at last. "I really don't know."

She faced Alice in wrath, the impatience and dislike she had for the past hour been at pains to hide clear upon her face. "You can't mean it. Alice — you *can't!*"

Alex moved uncomfortably in his chair. Both women ignored

him. Alice turned to the window, stood with her back to the room looking down on to the wide lawns of Bissetts. Beneath the trees a uniformed man upon crutches stood in conversation with another in a wheelchair. A nurse bustled across the grass towards them, a tray in her hands.

Alice turned back to face her sister-in-law. Her gaze was absolutely steady. "I have already told you, Anna, that I do not accept that — that girl's child as Richard's. The whole unsavoury affair has nothing to do with us, or with him. As to the idea of his visiting the girl — it is preposterous. He is well settled at the Academy. He has forgotten her. There can be absolutely no question of our giving our permission for him to go to Bayswater. The answer is no. Absolutely no. And I'll thank you not to mention the girl's name in this house again. For your own sake I should advise you to send the little hoyden and her fatherless brat back to her parents and leave it at that."

Anna controlled her surging temper with an effort, and a few deep breaths. "Alice — has it occurred to you that in a few short months Richard could be caught up in this beastly war? Doesn't that change your attitude one little bit?"

"Don't be absurd. Why should it? In the first place I have no doubt that the war will be long over before the boys are commissioned, and in the second — circumstances do not change facts." Alice's voice was severe and reasoned, utter conviction underlay every word. Anna met Alex's eyes. He looked away. Whatever happened to brave General Gordon, Anna found herself wondering tartly. "The child is not Richard's." Alice said, firmly and in Anna's ears the words had the ring of a determinedly repeated phrase. "And there's an end to it. Now, Anna, will you take tea before you leave?"

Anna stood up. "No. Thank you." She found it hard to be civil. She reached for bag and gloves. In her mind's eyes the image of Sophie's face hovered, as she had seen it last, obstinately cheerful, apparently uncaring, the eyes desperate with oft-denied hope. "Damn you, Alice," she said. "You'll ruin these youngsters."

Alice said nothing, and no trace of expression disfigured the taut, attractive features of her face.

In the silence, Anna left. With the downstairs rooms and most of the servants' quarters given over to a convalescent home, the family were living in those first floor rooms through which Rupert and Richard, Sophie and Maria had hunted so happily the year before. On the landing she heard movement behind her and paused, turning.

"Anna." Her brother stopped, his heavy face flushed.

She waited.

"Tell Richard —" his voice was low and he could not hide his anxiety that his wife might overhear "— tell him he has my permission to visit Sophie. Just the once, mind you. And only, of course, if he wants to."

She stared at him. Then, impulsively, she stepped forward to fling her arms about his neck. "Bless you," she whispered.

Embarrassed, he extricated himself. "Explain to Richard," he said hastily, "that it's — best kept between ourselves."

"I will." She kissed him quickly on his cheek then ran swiftly down the stairs.

"Alex?" Alice's voice was sharp. "Are you there?"

"Coming my love," Alex said.

They had not seen each other for more than nine months; an age, a lifetime — and yet, yesterday. He stood a little uncertainly just inside the closed door, unfamiliar in his uniform, his cap in his hand, yet so dearly, so achingly familiar that it was as if every dream of him had crystallized into reality here before her, flesh and bone and smiling hazel eyes. They were both, for a long moment, speechless.

"Goodness," she said at last, lightly. "You do look smart!"

The cap spun on to a chair and he crossed the room in three strides. "Sophie! Sophie!" He hugged her to him, hurting her, taking her breath. When he released her at last, her eyes were shining with laughter and happiness. "May I breathe now?"

He held her at arm's length. "You look wonderful! Absolutely wonderful! More beautiful than ever."

She flushed, grinning. "But not as beautiful as you, Mister Officer Cadet Rose! Just look at you! How long did it take you to clean those buttons?"

He grimaced, then laughed. "Hours!" They looked at each other then for a long, quiet moment, each searching the other's face with love and with a certain anxiety that neither had the guile to hide. Richard saw before him a girl who in the months past had grown to womanhood; she for her part saw a young man immaculate in his khaki, brass and leather gleaming; a young man whose negligent slouch had been replaced by the carriage of a soldier, and whose face had leaned and sharpened.

"Oh, Richard," she said, and her voice despite all her efforts trembled.

He caught her to him again, crushing her, pressing his cheek into the soft crown of her hair, his eyes shut, his face clenched against unmanly tears.

At last she pulled away, dashing a hand across her eyes, half-laughing. "There's someone here just dying to meet you." She caught his hand and led him across the room to where a small, pink-draped crib stood beside the window. Richard stood for a long time, staring down at the sleeping scrap whose fine, fair lashes curled against apple cheeks and whose milky mouth pursed, firm as a rosebud.

"Good God," he said at last.

Sophie laughed, the tension broken. "You can touch her, you know. She won't break."

Very gingerly he reached a long finger to his daughter's curled hand. His skin looked dark and calloused beside the pale softness of the child's. Felicity twitched and stirred, her mouth making small sucking motions, and he pulled his hand back quickly. Sophie laughed again, sheer happiness in the sound. She leaned to Richard, he put an arm about her shoulders, and they stood looking down at their daughter. "We have two more hours," Sophie said softly. "Two whole hours. And I want to hear everything — absolutely everything." She caught his hands and tugged him to the sofa. "Are you happy at the Academy? What do you do there? Is it hard? Do you —"

"Whoa!" He stopped her busy mouth with a laughing kiss that quickly became more serious. When they drew away from each other at last Sophie's colour was high and his breathing was uneven. "Now," he said, his voice almost steady, "I'll answer your questions. Yes — I love it at the Shop."

"The Shop?"

"The Academy. As for what we do there — we get up at the

most beastly unearthly hour you can imagine, work till we drop and fall into bed exhausted each evening. We get hardly any time to ourselves and I've never been so tired in my life. We march, and ride, and polish and clean, we're lectured and shouted at and drilled till we drop — and —" he gestured, laughing "— and I just love every minute of it. There's something I have to ask you —" He took her hands, drew her to him. "Sophie, darling, could you be a soldier's wife? I don't mean just for the duration of the war — I mean a real soldier's wife. For that's what I should like to be. A regular soldier. Could you take it, do you think? Would you marry a poor soldier?"

"Yes," she said simply. "And yes, and yes, and yes. So that's settled. You'll have to do more than take the King's shilling to get rid of me, my lad."

Their hands were linked. They sat for a moment, locked in each other's smiles. Then, "We still have to wait," he said. "My parents — especially Mother — are still —"

"I know," she said, swiftly, stopping him. "And I don't care. I'll wait for ever if I have to. For ever. Especially now. Now that I know —" She ducked her head suddenly, avoiding his eyes.

"Know what?"

"That you still love me. Still want me." Her voice was low. "I told everyone you did. That I knew you wouldn't forget me. Wouldn't let them part us." She lifted her face and he saw, in that instant, all that his loved and lovely girl had gone through — was still willing to go through — for his sake. His hands tightened upon hers. In her crib Felicity stirred, hiccoughed a little, and let out a yell that might have been heard three streets away. "Our daughter, I'm afraid," Sophie said almost composedly, disentangling her hands, "has inherited my temper. Shall you be able to stand both of us do you think?"

Their precious time flew. They spoke of personal things — of the time next year when both Rupert and Richard would receive their commissions, of Sophie's plans to remain here at Bayswater with the baby, of Anna's kindnesses and Alice's intransigence, of Sophie's wretchedness at the unhappiness she had caused her father. Inevitably they spoke too of the war, of the sinking a couple of weeks before of the Cunard liner *Lusitania* with the loss of more than a thousand lives, of the recent and long-expected heavy raid upon the East End of London and of Sophie's fears for her parents and sister, living as they did so close to the river — the airships' road to the heart of London — and the docks. But Anna's clock prettily chimed the quarter-hours away and before they knew it the enemy, time, had defeated them and they fell silent. At last the moment came when they approached the crib together and stood, hands linked, gazing down at their daughter.

"May I hold her? Just for a moment — before I go?"

"Of course." Sophie bent and expertly scooped the warm, soft bundle from the cot, deftly arranging voluminous skirt, shawl and lacy bonnet. "There." She laid Felicity in her father's arms. He cradled her awkwardly, studying the tiny face intently. Sophie, watching them both, blinked.

"She's going to be just like you," he said.

"Heaven forbid." The words were heartfelt and only half-humorous.

His mouth twitched at that. She relieved him of his burden, laid the child back in the cot. "And what shall you do when she comes to you and tells you that some strange and daring young man has stolen her heart?" she asked softly.

He reached for her, rocked her gently against him. "I shall ask, 'Does he love you?'"

"And if the answer is yes?"

"Then he shall have her with my blessing. For I shall have her mother; and nothing in the world could mean more to me than that."

They stood, each encircled in the other's arms for a moment, utterly wordless. Then he stepped back. She picked up his peaked cap, brushed it off with gentle fingers, handed it to him. "Will we see each other again, do you think? Before —" she could not say it "— well, before you're twenty-one?" She tried to grin, and failed.

"I'll try. I promise I will. But — you do understand? I gave my word — I had to give my word — I couldn't see any other way."

She stopped his mouth with her fingers. "Of course, I understand. You know I do. And one day we'll be together. All three of us. No one will stop us."

He kissed her swiftly, settled his cap upon his head. She watched from the door as he ran swiftly and gracefully down the stairs. At the foot he looked back, raised a hand to his cap, and was gone.

She did not go to the window to watch him down the street. There would have been little point: she could not have seen him for her tears.

CHAPTER TWENTY-ONE

By January 1916 Britain alone had mustered one million men in the field, and the deadly and stubborn war of attrition had truly begun. The situation in Europe was deadlocked: campaigns the previous autumn by both the Allies and their opponents had failed. Within a month of the birth of the new year attention was focused upon the French lines at Verdun — the French, the Germans considered, were the most weakened of the Allies, and the most likely to break if subjected to a concentrated and determined attack. So it was at this hard-pressed point that, during those first months of the year, they unrelentingly battered the exhausted French forces. The French defence, however, was grim, courageous, and — to their enemies — dismayingly and surprisingly obstinate. Through bitter weather and beneath the heaviest bombardment of the war so far they held, despite crippling casualties. As bleak winter turned again to unpromising spring the snow melted, waterlogging the desolate landscape, and men lived, fought and died knee-deep in mud, while the wounded, helpless, drowned in flooded shell holes. Throughout the spring the fighting was the most furious of the war; attack, counter-attack — the same blighted piece of land taken, lost and taken again, and all at the most terrible cost. Quite clearly it would not last; something had to be done to relieve the intolerable pressure. German attention must be distracted from Verdun. British eyes turned towards the Somme.

It was Sophie who informed Anna that her daughter was in love. Anna looked at her in disbelief. "Victoria? Oh, no, Sophie. You must be mistaken. You've been reading too many penny romances."

Sophie laughed, watched with resigned exasperation as

nine-months-old Felicity, beaming, systematically destroyed a small rag doll. "You mark my words. Something's going on, or I'm a Dutchman, Aunt. It's obvious."

"Has she actually said anything?"

Sophie shook her head, deftly extracted a piece of sodden material from her daughter's still almost toothless mouth. "Not in so many words. But she will — you'll see —"

Sophie was right. And perhaps it was just as well that Anna had had at least a little forewarning before her daughter made her shy confession.

"I wanted to tell you first — before Papa comes home next week —"

With sinking heart Anna smiled brightly and patted her hand. "Don't worry dear. I'm sure Papa will be delighted —"

Victoria, despite an obvious effort, did not look overly convinced. Anna could not pretend that she did not understand why. She knew the girl to be more than a little nervous of her unpredictable father, much as she loved him. And this somewhat unconventional romance would not be the easiest thing to confess to him. Victoria twisted her fingers together. She looked very tired. Her fair, fluffy hair was scraped back beneath her cap and her violet eyes were no darker than the shadows beneath them. Her fine skin was pallid. Unexpected sympathy stirred.

"Would you like me to — explain — to Papa? Before you speak to him." Anna could hardly believe herself that she had said it. She and Joss had exchanged barely half a dozen personal words in as many months. The prospect of confronting him with this was far from inviting. But it was too late to withdraw her impulsive offer. Victoria was looking at her with shining eyes.

"Oh, Mother! Would you? I'd be so very grateful. I never really seem to know how to talk to Papa. And I do want him to understand — to be prepared when Samuel calls —" She spoke the name with shy hesitancy. "He's a truly remarkable man. I know you'll both love him."

"I'm sure we shall, dear." Anna hoped that her lack of conviction was not too clear in her voice.

For once Anna's prediction of her unpredictable husband's reactions was absolutely right. He folded his napkin, lifted his head and regarded her forbiddingly across the breakfast table with dark, disbelieving eyes. "A widower? A man old enough to be her father? Has the child taken leave of her senses?"

"He's a doctor at the hospital. A brilliant one, she says —"

"With children older than she is."

She hesitated. "Yes." Heartily she wished she had never taken this on; but having begun she stuck doggedly to her task.

He shook his head. "No. Absolutely not."

"Joss — please — at least talk to her. Listen to what she has to say —"

"What she has to say cannot change the situation. The man is too old for her."

"And is that all that counts?" Anna spoke quietly. "Is it such a great hurdle? Joss — what of love? Of Victoria's happiness? She loves him. She loves him very much. Does that count for nothing?" Her voice faded as their eyes met in a sudden disquieting communion that for no explicable reason brought a quick lift of blood to her cheeks.

Abruptly he reached for his newspaper. "All right. I'll talk to her. But I'm not promising anything."

She let out a small breath of relief. She had done her best. Victoria, now, must fight her own battles. "Are you in London for long?" Part of her mind registered, wryly, that the question might have been asked, politely, of a casual acquaintance.

Joss had picked up his newspaper again. "No. A few days only."

"I see." The lack of communication, of warmth, never failed to dismay her. She wished she had not asked.

He had looked up at her tone, his eyes thoughtful. She applied herself to her toast, with its bare scraping of butter and marmalade. "This is the end of the marmalade. We must try to make it last."

He ignored the comment. Anna played with her toast. "Joss?"

"Mmm?"

"What exactly are you doing?"

He looked up in quick surprise. She lifted her shoulders in a strangely defensive half-shrug. "I'm just interested, that's all."

After the briefest of silences he said, "I'm making sure that the men who are laying down their lives for us in France have the armaments and ammunition to fight with."

"And are you making an enormous amount of money whilst you're doing it?" The question, with all its inferences, was out almost before she knew it. She stilled the immediate, conciliatory urge that followed it. Let him make of the words what he would. She crumbled her sticky toast on her plate. Joss said nothing. Anna at last lifted her eyes to meet his. A dark glint of anger sparked in their depths. She held his gaze steadily.

"Yes," he said at last, briefly and without expression. "I'm making money."

I thought you might be. She did not actually speak the words, but knew beyond doubt that he heard them as clearly as if she had.

He picked up the paper, folded it to another page, laid it on the table before him and within a moment was apparently completely absorbed. Anna watched him, irritation growing. Nothing exasperated her impatient nature more than this man's provoking ability not to argue with her: an ability remarkable in one so volatile and which illustrated to her — perhaps perversely — the lack of commitment or passion that had been the hallmark of her marriage since the ruin of her father and the birth of Nicholas. She simply could not bear to sit here watching him in docile silence as he read his paper with apparent unconcern, as if the short exchange of words had not taken place.

"Michael is greatly improving," she said, seemingly inconsequentially.

He did not look up. "Good." Michael had been wounded the month before and thanks to a little gentle string-pulling was now recuperating at Bissetts.

"I had a letter from him this morning."

Silence.

Normally by now she would have given up, the chill of his lack of reaction stilling her tongue. Doggedly, however, she continued. "He seems worried about Papa. His health is as good as can be expected, he says, but his mind wanders sometimes —"

As always when she mentioned her father she thought she detected a faint reaction in the man, a slight and sudden suspension of movement.

"That isn't surprising," he said, evenly, after a moment. "Josef is, after all, an old man."

Faintly surprised that he had answered at all, she shook her head. "He's only seventy-six. That isn't so very old." The scars left by what Joss had done to her father had, mostly because of the determined encouragement of the injured Josef, almost healed within the family. To her own surprise Anna herself rarely thought of it now. Only occasionally, sparked as now by some reference or comment, did the memory return in the full force of its conflict and confusion.

Very precisely, Joss shook out his paper, refolded it, prepared to settle to reading it again.

Anna's impulsion to quarrel died abruptly. What on earth was the point? She pushed her plate away, and stood.

He lifted his head. "Anna —" His voice was sharp.

She waited.

He picked up his knife, measured it against his plate, replaced it precisely beside it. When he spoke his voice was cool, his words measured. "At the start of the war — and for some of the time since — our forces were hopelessly handicapped by the incompetence of those who should have been backing them. And in particular in the field of munitions. If the Government — the country — had not been so criminally complacent, so wilfully foolish, the war might well have taken a different course by now. Last year, whilst our fighting men were at war, our working men were not. There were strikes and disruption — excessive wage claims, overtime bans, refusal to accept the use of women workers. Men died on the barbed wire in France because our armaments industry was in chaos and — worse — its products faulty. Did you know that at Neuve Chapelle the shells provided to the army were all but useless? Many of them didn't even explode. Men were asked to fight with bayonets and bare hands because of the inadequacy of the artillery back-up. And they died for it in their thousands. Now — just a year later — the situation is entirely different. We are in the position of being able to supply our fighting men with literally millions of shells a day. Shells that will do the job for which they were intended. And no matter what you think of the morality of that it surely can't be as bad as allowing men to die with no defence because of incompetence and lack of investment. Because British industry did not possess the accurate machine tools necessary to the manufacture of modern armaments we have had to re-equip whole factories using American tools. With men now being conscripted from the industry we have persuaded the unions to accept women in their place. The Government needs money to invest in new factories of its own —"

She was watching him, thunderstruck, only barely listening to his controlled, yet strangely passionate words, understanding simply that her words after all had penetrated that apparently uncaring and invulnerable shell that was so often all that she saw of her husband. He was explaining himself. To her.

"And that's the whole point. It all takes money. The machine tools from the States. The new factories. The equipment. Yes — I am making money. To invest in the future. In the winning of this foul war. What would you have me do? Ignore what I am best at doing? Cut fifteen years from my age and trade my desk and pen for a private's uniform?"

"Of course not! I wasn't criticizing —"

"Not in so many words, perhaps. But by inference —"

Deliberately she let the silence lengthen. Then, "I'm surprised that you care," she said at last, evenly and softly. "I'm surprised that it matters to you, what I might think of your actions."

"No man likes to be criticized unfairly." His voice was neutral, conceded nothing.

"I'm sorry. I didn't meant to." The hint of warmth had gone, her voice was brisk. "I have to go. I have a meeting. And I promised I'd look after Felicity for Sophie this afternoon."

"Oh?"

"Sophie has lost yet another nursemaid to one of your munitions factories — the new one seems far less trustworthy. It's so hard to get good staff at the moment."

"Yet it hardly seems necessary for you to care for the child."

Anna hesitated. "I thought — for this afternoon — Sophie had quite enough on her plate. The last thing she needs is to be worrying about Felicity. She's meeting Richard. The boys have joined their regiment. And they've got their posting. They leave for France next week."

*

They were not the only young couple to be strolling by London's river that afternoon all but blind to their surroundings and to the presence of others. The sky was overcast, the clouds of a colour with the battleship that lay at anchor on the far reach of water. A sailor and his girl leaned upon the stone parapet of the embankment watching the river traffic, wordless. A young man, dressed, as was Richard, in spruce new army uniform, sat upon a bench with his head bent to his fair-headed companion, talking earnestly. Sophie let her hand rest in Richard's and tried not to count the minutes that were ticking away so terribly fast.

"— and is she well?"

"Oh, wonderfully. Positively bouncing. She crawls like lightning — it's impossible to keep her in one place for a moment. She's a terrible mischief. She's into everything."

He grinned. "I warned you she was going to be just like her mother."

She laughed a little. "God help us all when she learns to walk."

They sauntered on, stopped for a moment and leaned by the parapet, watching the naval ship. "I was at Bissetts earlier this week."

"Oh?"

"It's so strange — so very different, with the nurses, and the soldiers — and yet so very much the same. I never realized before just how peaceful it was."

"Did you —" she cleared her throat, and he glanced at her sharply "— did you go to our little garden?"

"Of course. Rupert came down. We spent a couple of hours tidying it up. We saw Uncle Josef too. He sends his love by the way."

"Aunt Anna's worried about him. Uncle Michael seems to think that he's — well — going a little strange in the head."

"Oh, I wouldn't put it that strongly. It's true that he talks a lot of the past. And that sometimes he doesn't talk at all. But he seemed perfectly rational to me — and we spent a whole afternoon with him."

"Has he forgiven us do you think?" The question was asked softly.

Richard did not hesitate. "Yes. I'm sure he has. As a matter of fact he seems almost to have forgotten it all. As I said — he seems to live more and more in the past."

"It's natural, I suppose." They paced on. Sophie tried not to ask the question that had hovered on her lips for the past minutes, and was, as she had known she would be, unsuccessful. "And your mother? Has she —" she pulled a wry face "— forgiven us too?"

Richard shook his head. "She simply refuses to discuss it."

Sophie sighed and turned her head to look across the river.

"Sophie. It doesn't matter. They won't stop us. Not in the end."

"No. Of course not."

They stood in silence for a moment. A small, cold breeze riffled from the water, stirring Sophie's hair and chilling her skin. She turned to face Richard, leaning against the parapet, tilting her head to look up into his face with clear, direct eyes. "You're looking forward to it all, aren't you?" she asked, quietly.

The question took him by surprise. He hesitated. Then, "I suppose I am, yes," he said, frankly. "In a way, anyway. You see — we've been playing at war for such a long time — with all the time the thought of the real thing at the back of our minds. I can't deny that it's something of a relief to be on our way at last. To be doing something. I only hope —" He stopped.

"What?" she lifted a soft finger to his flat cheek. "Richard? What do you hope?"

"That I don't funk it. That I don't let you all down." He blurted the words, and laughed self-consciously.

"You won't."

"I do think about it sometimes. About what it will be like. About how I'll react — to being under fire and all that. Sometimes I get into a stew just thinking about it — but then again sometimes it seems that the whole thing will just be a great lark. Like the stories of India and Africa that I used to read when I was young. I always longed to be in them. I thought it must be easy to be a hero, if there were something to be heroic about."

"I don't want you to be a hero," she said sharply. "I want you to be careful."

"Oh, I shall, never fear." But he could not quite keep the bright eagerness from eye and voice. "And of course I don't want to leave you — but you can see, can't you, that it's an awfully big adventure?"

Sophie smiled, and said nothing. The night before, the echoes of murderous bombardment across the Channel had filled the night skies of London and, listening, she had wept. "What do you say to a cup of tea before you have to go?" she asked lightly. "There's quite a nice little tea shop up towards Charing Cross —"

They sat over their steaming tea cups, talked of the war, of their families, of the past and of the future, and finally, ran out of words altogether. Richard looked at his watch, the tenth time he'd done it in as many minutes. "I ought to go. I mustn't miss my train."

"Of course not." She carefully replaced in her saucer the small silver spoon she had been tinkering with and reached for her gloves. She was wearing blue, her favourite colour; a heavy cotton dress with a white, square collar, a small beribboned blue and white hat perched upon her piled hair. He watched her with love clear in his eyes. Stretched out a hand and covered hers.

"You mustn't worry about me. I'll be all right. And just think it won't be nearly as bad as it has been. We can write to each other every day."

She looked up at that, startled. He grinned happily. "I was saving that till last. Father gave his permission. Actually stood up to mother about it — said they couldn't treat me like a disobedient schoolboy when I was going off to war. It's the first step, Sophie. I know it. They'll give in, in the end. You'll see."

They left the shop and walked towards Charing Cross. The streets were thronged with hurrying people, most of them men in uniform, converging upon the station. A bus roared by, belching fumes, upon the open platform a woman in conductor's uniform — a sight still rare enough in London to draw stares from the passers-by. Outside the station itself a line of ambulances stood, and as Sophie and Richard drew level the first of their passengers, transferring from a recently arrived hospital train, emerged from the station. In wheelchairs and on stretchers they came, the lucky ones walking or struggling with crutches. A pale-faced lad was carried by, covered to the shoulders with a blanket that was flat as a tablecloth where his legs should have been.

"Gawd bless yer, son —" A flower seller, shabby shawl tight about her shoulders, tossed a single rose upon the stretcher. The boy smiled wanly, the mark of death upon his face.

Sophie turned away.

Richard was fishing in his pocket for his ticket, making a great show of it. She waited calmly until he had found it, then lifted her face for his kiss. As his lips brushed hers she expended every atom of willpower she possessed to shut her eyes, her ears and her heart to the noise and bustle around them and to hold him, the essence of him, in the warmth and safety of her love. God would not allow him to be harmed. She knew it: he could not be so cruel. She stepped back from him. "Do you mind if I don't wait? I'm not very good at prolonged goodbyes."

"Of course not. I'd rather you didn't. I'm not too good at handkerchief waving myself."

"You promise you'll write?"

"I promise."

"Oh, Lord — I nearly forgot —" She scrabbled in her small handbag, "I had these taken for you." She handed him a small, folding leather case, pocket-sized. Framed within it were two photographs, one of herself in the outfit she was wearing now and one of Felicity, smiling her heart-stopping smile, reaching for the camera. "I thought you might like them."

He said nothing, stood looking down at the photographs for a long, long time. Then, still wordless, he gathered her to him fiercely and held her, still and trembling, against his heart. Then he put her from him, his hands upon her shoulders, turned her gently towards the open street. "Off you go." She barely heard the husky words through the uproar around them.

She walked away from him on legs that seemed not to belong to her. Just once she turned. He stood where she had left him, watching after her, his tall, slim figure still in the bustle around him. As she looked back he smiled brilliantly and lifted a hand.

Sophie almost ran into the street.

*

Two weeks later Subaltern Richard Rose, with his brother Rupert, was at the front waiting with the rest of the British army for the start of the well-telegraphed big push on the Somme that was to relieve the merciless pressure on their French allies at Verdun. On the first of July the word was given at last. The bombardment stilled. In the eery quiet, at seven in the morning of a beautiful summer's day, the mines that had over the previous weeks been so painstakingly laid by the British Sappers beneath the German emplacements were blown. Then, for an incredible thirty minutes the infantry waited for the order that would send them over the top to follow up the advantage. At last, too late, that order was given. The enemy had been given precious time: to recover, to regroup, to re-man the wrecked positions. The British battalions advanced into a hail of death that beat them down like ripe corn in a summer storm, row upon advancing row. Twenty thousand men died on that first day, the worst single day in the history of the British army — men who had joined their battalions together, had marched from the same street or the same village self-consciously straight-backed under the proud eyes of mothers and girl-friends. Richard Rose, recklessly eager in this, his first engagement, was one of those that were cut to pieces in the first hopeless wave. His twin was beside him when he fell, bloody and almost unrecognizable, and in an almost self-destructive rage the boy stormed on the German trenches with nothing but murder in his heart. Not barbed wire nor bullets could stop Rupert on that day. By evening he was a hero and a clear candidate for honours and advancement.

He spent the night in a shell hole in no-man's-land, sobbing like a bereft child.

"There have been mistakes made before. You're always hearing stories. The papers are full of them. Men who've been posted dead sometimes turn up months later." Sophie settled the child who was squirming to get on to the floor more firmly on her lap. Her voice was firm and utterly unshaken.

Anna regarded her worriedly. "Sophie, no. You mustn't deceive yourself like this. There can be no doubt. Rupert was with him. He — saw it happen."

"He made a mistake," the girl said, stubbornly reasonable. "It's perfectly understandable. You can imagine what it must be like — the confusion — the fear — it must be like a kind of madness, mustn't it? Rupert didn't stay with Richard — so how could he be sure he was dead? No. I don't believe it. I won't believe it. I would have known if he had died. I know I would."

"Sophie — Rupert saw him fall. Saw him die." Anna bit her lip, "Darling — you have to believe it —"

Sophie shook her head, fussed with the baby. "Be still, Flissy. You'll fall."

Anna draw a long, shaky breath, then with some reluctance opened the bag that she held. Her hope, she now realized, of finding the right moment to give the bereaved girl the final proof of Richard's death had always been in vain. There could be no such thing as the right moment. She reached into the bag, drew out a dark-stained, battered leather folder. "Sophie. Darling — I'm sorry. This was sent to Bissetts with Richard's things. Rupert persuaded his parents to let you have it back."

Her face stricken to stone Sophie stared at the photographs. "Oh — my — God," she whispered at last, the slow words both an exclamation of pain and an anguished prayer. Anna flinched. Sophie did not take the folder, yet while convulsively she clutched Felicity to her she could not remove her eyes from the two smiling faces it contained. "No," she said. "No. No. No! I would have known. Surely I would have known?"

The child, frightened by the vice-like grip of her mother's arms, began to wail. Sophie bowed her face to her daughter's soft down of hair. Her shoulders were shaking, yet she made no sound.

Anna bent to take the crying child. Sophie relinquished her hold, buried her face in her hands. Her body was rigid, taut as wire. In the silence of the room her breathing rasped. When she lifted her head at last her eyes burned dryly, too deeply shocked for tears, and her mouth was drawn down in bitter pain. "He is dead," she said, quietly. "Isn't he?"

"Yes, darling. I'm sorry — but yes, he is. You have to accept it."

Sophie turned from the comforting hand her aunt reached to

her. "I'll never accept it. Never." The desolate voice was harsh. "Not any of it."

Anna watched her with growing concern over the days that followed. So far as she could tell the girl had not shed a tear. The brutal misery she suffered showed only in her eyes and in the despairingly unhappy set of her mouth. Meticulously she cared for her child and for herself: but she determinedly avoided company and would not be comforted in her loss. She had, it seemed to Anna, retreated into a prison of grief the doors of which could not be opened except from the inside; and far from trying to open them Sophie seemed set upon keeping them bolted and barred against a world that had betrayed her.

When Alex approached Anna with his diffident, astonishing request Anna was truly appalled and more than half angry.

"Alex — I couldn't! It isn't fair on the child. Not yet. You don't know the state she's in. She can barely talk to me — let alone Alice, of all people."

Her brother looked terribly haggard. Although still overweight the florid glow of good living had left him, and he looked older than his years. "Anna, please listen to me. I know how you must feel. I know you don't care much for Alice —" he ignored the small sound that Anna made "— and I don't blame you. But — if you could see her — see what Richard's — death —" his voice faltered painfully on the word "— has done to her, you'd understand at least a little. She adored the boy."

"As did Sophie." Anna's voice, despite herself, was bitter.

"I know. And Alice knows. Can't you see? That's the whole point. She wants to see Sophie. To tell her how very sorry she is about what happened."

Anna was watching him, a perilous anger growing in her eyes. "And —" she said, very soft "— to see Felicity?"

He sustained her regard for a few seconds, then his eyes dropped.

"Oh, Alex, Alex." Anna's tone was almost pitying. "Can't you even be honest about this? To yourself, if to no one else."

He turned his head jerkily. "Of course we want to see her. Why shouldn't we? For God's sake, Anna — the child is Richard's daughter."

"That," Anna said, very precisely, "is not what Alice told me last time we met."

He had no answer. His shoulders were bowed. Despite her anger, Anna could not deny a certain sympathy. "Be reasonable, Alex," she said quietly. "At least leave it for a while. Sophie has been devastated by Richard's death. And Flissy is all she has of him. She does not even bear his name. Thanks to Alice. And to you. Can't you see how she'd feel if — after all that has gone before — you turned up now, taking an interest in the child? Can you blame her?"

"No." Alex slumped into a chair, defeat in the lines of his body. "No, of course not."

Anna watched him in silence.

"Christ, Anna," he said at last, "I never knew anything could hurt so much."

She moved to him, rested a hand upon his shoulder. He shook his head, a man bewildered. "It isn't just Richard, you see. There's the worry about Rupert. He's still out there. Every day, every hour, we live with the knowledge that the same thing could — is likely to — happen to him." There was raw pain in the look he turned upon his sister. "Do you know what I've found myself doing? Praying that he'll be wounded. An arm. A leg. Anything. Just as long as it brings him home. Just as long as he isn't dead. As Richard is dead. I pray for that. Can you believe it?"

"Yes." Anna's voice was not steady.

"Anna — please — won't you just ask Sophie? Felicity is Richard's child. God, Anna, Sophie is a mother herself — surely she'll understand how we feel? If we could just see the child — Richard's child — that's all we're asking. I know what you think; but it isn't true. I swear we won't interfere —"

"Can you swear so confidently for Alice?" Despite herself, Anna's voice was dry.

He made a sharp, fierce gesture with his hand. "I tell you Alice has changed. I promise you. Please say you'll ask Sophie — just ask her."

"Ask me what?" The words came from the open doorway. Brother's and sister's head turned to the young figure who stood there. Composedly Sophie walked across the room and offered a steady hand to Alex. "Good afternoon, Mr Rose."

Alex scrambled to his feet in ungainly haste, took the proffered hand. "Sophie, my dear."

The faintest expression of cool distaste flickered across the girl's face and was gone.

"How are you?"

"I'm very well, thank you." Her voice was politely expressionless. She had not smiled. "You wanted to ask me something?"

Alex glanced from Sophie to Anna, his eyes uncertain. Anna said nothing. Sophie was owed this moment at least, however arid the triumph. "We wondered," Alex began, "that is — Alice and I — wondered if we might visit you. You and Felicity. Under the circumstances the — misunderstandings that have occurred seem —" his voice trailed off. Sophie regarded him for a long, cool moment. Alex's face showed clearly that he thought he had lost. But Anna, watching the girl, was not so sure: she wondered, suddenly, how long Sophie had been standing by the open door, how much of her conversation with Alex she had overheard.

"Of course," Sophie said. Then, "If you'd like." There was no trace of warmth or even of interest in her voice. She might have been commenting on the weather.

Alex stared at her, dawning happiness in his face.

Before he could open his mouth to thank her Sophie had turned and left the room.

They came to Bayswater two weeks later, on the September morning after London's night had been turned to day by the terrible torch of the first Zeppelin to be destroyed in the skies of Britain. A jubilant population had cheered in the streets as the flaring ball of fire slid northwards over the city, a falling star that signalled at last a breakthrough in the battle against these terrifying and so-far invincible raiders. At least now as Londoners endured the tensions of a 'Zepp Night' and watched for the sky-borne monsters to nose from the clouds with their threat of fire and death, there would be some hope of retaliation, some return, threat for threat, terror for terror. Sophie had watched the window, her child in her arms, her eyes remote with pain and hatred as they followed the fireball that hung in the sky, her expression conveying no feeling for the men, enemies notwithstanding, who were being incinerated with their craft.

She faced Alice the next day with the same detached lack of warmth or emotion. To her credit, in a very difficult situation, Alice's behaviour and self-control were impeccable. Thin-faced to gauntness, her eyes haunted, she conducted polite small talk with Anna — about the great events of the night before, Josef's health, Michael's progress — as if such things were the very centre of her thoughts. As Sophie entered the room, carrying Felicity, only the slightest catching of her breath, the paling of her already white skin betrayed her. Sophie stood in the centre of the room, unsmiling, waiting. Anna could not blame her for that; not even Sophie's worst enemy could ever have described her as a hypocrite.

Very composedly, Alice stood and approached the girl. With an effort she dragged her eyes from the child and regarded the mother. "Sophie. It was most kind of you to allow us to visit you."

Sophie inclined her head, stone-faced.

"I realize how very difficult you must have found it."

Felicity reached a small, plump hand to the enticing glitter of a diamond brooch upon Alice's lapel. The woman's eyes were hungry. Flissy's eyes were Richard's, hazel and gold-shot as summer woodlands, her smile, as his had been, sunlit and beguiling. With no word, Sophie held the child towards her grandmother. Anna had never admired her difficult, wayward niece as she did in that moment. Flissy crowed with delight, grabbed at the brooch with a small, determinedly acquisitive hand. Much as she still disliked her sister-in-law Anna could not find it in her to remain unmoved by the tears that stood, proudly unshed, in the other woman's eyes. Not so Sophie. No sign of emotion moved in her still face. It was, Anna thought worriedly, as if the warmly impulsive, headstrong girl she had once been had withdrawn from the world that had dealt her such pain and left behind an image of stone. Only Flissy had brought a faint smile to her face over these past difficult weeks, and that rarely. And yet — she had agreed to let Alex and Alice see the child; that surely must show that somewhere within her warmth and generosity still lived? Anna could only hope so. Certainly there was no sign of either in the cool eyes she turned upon Alice.

Alex had joined his wife now, offering an eager, stubby finger to his grandchild, smiling delightedly as she grabbed for it imperiously.

"Sophie —" Alice it was who spoke. High colour flushed her prominent cheekbones and her arms were clasped about the child as if she could never bear to let her go. "We wondered — would you, could you — bring yourself to visit Bissetts, sometimes, with Felicity?"

Sophie blinked, as if at a stab of pain. "Not yet."

"Of course not." The words were hasty, conciliatory. Desperate. "Oh, of course not. But — in a little while, perhaps?"

Sophie said nothing.

Alex cleared his throat. "And — Sophie, my dear — we'd like to settle a small amount upon Felicity. Just a little something, to help her — and you —" His voice faded into a discomfiting quiet.

The face that Sophie turned to him was bleak. "I'd like to tell you to keep your money. Perhaps I ought to. But I won't, for we need it. We're living on Aunt Anna's and Uncle Joss's charity —" she ignored Anna's automatic quick movement of protest "— and that isn't good enough for Richard's child. So we'll take it. For his sake." She hesitated, then added as if the simple words all but choked her, "Thank you."

Felicity, fingers tangled in her grandmother's perfectly coiffed hair, crowed with pleasure.

CHAPTER TWENTY-TWO

Nicholas Anatov had discovered the pictures that his mother kept in the exquisite nephrite box on her dressing table many years before he was old enough for their possible significance to occur to him. Always indulged by his mother he had been given — or more exactly had assumed — the right of open access to her room at a very early age and, since there was little either in the boy's nature or in his upbringing to impel constraint or respect for the privacy of others, he had long taken that to mean that anything that was Anna's was naturally open to his inquisitive eyes and fingers. The pictures intrigued him — especially the portrait that had been torn and so carefully repaired. Something in the face fascinated him, and as a small child, when his mother was from home — for however confident he might be of her indulgence, prudence nevertheless dictated even to Nicholas that there might be some things best kept from her knowledge — he would creep to his mother's room, spread the sketch carefully upon the dressing table, smoothing the paper, studying it, moving his head a little so that the warm, life-like eyes seemed to follow him, smiling. Clearly the same man featured in the other sketch and, too, he recognized his mother. He guessed that she had drawn both these pictures — for how often, throughout his childhood, had she not done similar sketches for him — sketches of a moment, or of a person that she could capture precisely and deftly with a few swift strokes of her pencil. Nicholas, in so far as his indulged and self-centred nature allowed, adored his mother. No one else's mother could do what she could do. As no one else's mother could draw every eye in a room simply by appearing in the doorway. Or design jewellery so exquisite that the insects and flowers she was so fond of incorporating into her pieces seemed to the dazzled child to be all but alive, arrested movement spellbound into precious metal and stone. At first it had been simply this that had fascinated him about the portrait: the clear, bright eyes, the expression that tempted him to believe that if he looked for long enough that half-smile might break into laughter. As he grew older, however, and a gracelessly inquisitive nature began to assert itself, he found other things to intrigue him about the pictures, not least the character of the damage to the portrait that his mother obviously valued so highly. It could not, he surmised, have been accidental: the tears, precisely across the centre, were too obviously and deliberately destructive for that. Yet the picture had been painstakingly mended — the four pieces pasted carefully upon two strong strips of paper — and undoubtedly by his mother, for where the damage had been irreparable she had used her pencil and her skill to cover it up. Even more intriguing were the words that were still decipherable on the back of the picture, in another hand than his mother's: "Anna, August 1900". Over the years, in those odd moments that the child chose to indulge his curiosity and take advantage of his undoubtedly privileged position — for neither his brother nor his sister would have dared enter their mother's room without permission, let alone touch any of her things — the strong, scrawling writing became as familiar to him as did the face. The possible significance of the strange attraction for him of that face however did not remotely occur to him until one day in the winter of 1916, a few months before his sixteenth birthday and a few days before his sister Victoria was to marry her Samuel.

Dr Samuel Bottomley — tall, balding, sparingly built, painfully reserved and himself believing until a short while before that surely he must be by now immune to Cupid's painful darts — had surprised himself, to say nothing of the rest of the world, by the determination with which he had set out to win the approval of the Anatov household for his intention to marry Victoria, having already with an equal effort of will convinced first Victoria and then his own sceptical family. Slow-spoken, kindly and a dedicated man of medicine — even Joss had been immediately impressed by the man, and no one who came within a mile of Victoria could have had any doubts as to her feelings for her Samuel. As to the difference in their ages — Dr

Bottomley had impressed Joss further by admitting freely that just a few short months before he himself might have frowned upon such a suitor for his own daughter, who was nearly two years Victoria's senior. It was, however, with no apology and irreproachable dignity that he finally made his formal request to Joss for his daughter's hand, and Joss, impressed as much by this as by the man's obvious deep attachment to Victoria, found himself acceding with little reluctance. In this day and age, after all, there was something to be said for the security and comfort to be found as the wife of an older man. Already it was becoming obvious that the flower of a generation of young men would never reach maturity. So it was with few misgivings on either side that the wedding date was fixed for the week before Christmas, 1916 — and so it was that Nicholas, on holiday from school and driven from the old nursery by his sister's continuous and fluttering talk of dresses and guest lists and bridesmaids and the exigent pressures of wartime rationing upon the nuptial celebrations, strolled without knocking into his mother's room and found her sitting at her dressing table, the nephrite box open, the portrait spread before her. At her son's entrance she gave a palpable start of shock, her pale, startled eyes meeting his in the mirror with an expression that — had he not dismissed the notion immediately as ridiculous — he might have called fear. A little disconcerted at her obvious alarm, he took refuge in the charm that never failed him, and smiled his improbably brilliant smile.

"Hello Mumps. Mind if I join you for a bit? Victoria's driving me barmy!" He spread graceful, long-fingered hands and smiled again, winningly. "Anyone would think that no one in the world has ever got married before." The use of that private nickname, he knew, invariably disarmed her.

Utterly unnerved by his unexpected entrance, Anna was still staring at him as if he had been a ghost, her forearms covering the picture that, for the first time in years, some strange impulse had driven her to take from its resting place to look at once more. Unsuccessfully she forced a smile. "Actually, darling — I'm a bit busy at the moment —"

Totally assuredly he flung himself upon the bed. "That's all right. I'll be quiet as a mouse, I promise. I won't say a word.

Just protect me from timetables and veils and ribbons and flower-girls for a while. You wouldn't stand by and watch me driven completely round the bend, now would you?"

Anna relaxed a little, laughed, turned on the stool so that her back obscured the spread paper upon the dressing table. "Don't be unkind, Nico. Victoria's happy, that's all. And so she should be. It isn't every day that a girl gets married. And I have to say that it makes a change from talking about the wretched war —"

The expression on Nicholas's bright, handsome face showed clearly that he did not agree, but he did not argue. He rolled instead upon his stomach and propped his chin on his hands, his feet waving in the air. "Seems jolly strange, I must say, acquiring a brother-in-law who's older than my own father!"

"I expect it does, dear. But then — the decision is Victoria's, after all. And I must say that, having come to know Samuel, I feel that she could have done a lot worse. He will certainly care for her. He can offer security, a good home —"

Nicholas pulled a face.

"— and I think that, at the bottom of it, these are the things that Victoria probably most needs." Anna tried to keep her face severe before her son's bright, teasing eyes. "We can't all be the same you know." With Victoria leaving home, Anna felt inclined to be generous towards the daughter that she had never herself truly understood or been close to. "Victoria's different from you, that's all. She's —"

"— dull." Nicholas said, grinning caustically. "Dull. Dull. Dull. That's what Victoria is."

"Nico!"

"Oh, Mumps — you know it's true. I can't imagine how you came to have her — she isn't a bit like you." He rolled over, dropped like a cat gracefully from the bed. "I say — I rather like that — is it your outfit for the wedding?"

Disarmed as he knew she would be by his not altogether feigned interest, she smiled. "Yes, it is. I've actually had the material since before the war. Now seemed as good a time as any to use it. Arabella designed it specially. And I thought perhaps the jet and amber pendant and earrings." She could not hide her pleasure. She joined him by the dummy upon which the new clothes were displayed. Of golden velvet, its tiered skirt and matching hat trimmed with sleek black fur, it was fashionable rather than exotic — for Anna was well aware that there were times when her more flamboyant clothes embarrassed her daughter, and had thought to spare the girl that on her wedding day.

"The jet'll look spiffing with it." Grinning, Nicholas tweaked the skirt. "Mind you — bit daring isn't it? You'll show a fair bit of leg in that. Not —" that he added with another flashing smile "— that you don't have a fair bit of leg to show, of course."

Laughing, she slapped his hand away. "For goodness' sake — look at those dirty paws! And — it isn't that short — shorter skirts are very fashionable at the moment." She was fussing with the neckline of the jacket when she caught a movement from the corner of her eye. She spun around. "Nico!" Her voice had changed, rang suddenly with alarm as her son, apparently aimlessly, wandered across the room to the dressing table, "What *are* you doing?"

"Hel-lo — who's this?" Before she could reach him he had picked up the picture, looked at it, grinning. "Bit of a devil, this one, from the look of him. Who is he?" He lifted his head, caught sight in the mirror of his mother's face, frozen in guilt, over his shoulder. Saw in that instant something else too, for the first time. Saw beneath a falling lock of hair a pair of eyes that glittered, and laughed, a well-shaped, straight mouth that tilted to a smile. Saw the face each time he looked into a mirror. Then looked down again at the picture he held.

"Give it to me," Anna said grimly, her voice brooking no argument.

Wordlessly, he folded it and handed it to her. She snatched it, regardless of its frail state. Carelessly and lucently the boy smiled. "I'm sorry. I didn't realize it was private."

"It's just — someone I knew. A long time ago."

"I didn't mean to pry."

"Of course not."

He leaned to her, kissed her lightly upon the cheek. "I suppose I'd better go and rescue Ben from our almost-married sister's clutches. Poor Ben would actually allow himself to be done to death by boredom before he'd do anything about it. See you later, Mumps."

"'Bye, darling." Her breath still caught in her throat; despite all she could do to prevent it the words were jerky.

She closed the door behind him, leaned upon it for a moment, the crumpled paper in her hand. The picture couldn't have meant anything to him. It couldn't.

Nicholas ran lightly up the stairs, his quick, precocious brain flitting from one thing to another, forming theories, testing them. Outside the nursery door he paused, his eyes very thoughtful.

"— and I do hope that Samuel's son can get back from France in time to be best man," Victoria was saying, worriedly. "And, oh dear — if he does come I do hope he likes me. He's the only one I haven't met."

"Oh, of course he will. How could he not?" Ben's voice was reassuring.

"It's just — it's all so very nerve-wracking —"

In Nicholas's head at last a small, interesting piece of the puzzle had clicked satisfyingly into place. "Anna, August 1900," he said softly. "Nineteen hundred. Well, well, well." He pushed open the door, his smile brilliant. "Hey — I've an idea —"

Two faces turned to him surprised and — from long experience — wary.

"Let's go and see Sophie. Cheer her up a bit."

Undisguised relief cleared the way for assenting smiles.

He looked from one to the other, the very picture of injured innocence. "Why — what on earth did you think I was going to say?"

The wedding, to Anna's well-hidden relief, was not the trial it might have been. Any celebration in this time when there seemed so little to celebrate, though welcome, could be so easily marred by the absence of so many who would under happier circumstances have attended. Many people simply could not bring themselves to ask after a missing face for fear of the news that the answer might bring, and so quite often Anna had noticed about these affairs a fierce and artificial gaiety that she found at the same time pathetic and wearing. Adding to this the fact that this particular occasion would bring together two very different families and their friends, the odds had seemed to her to be stacked in favour of disaster. Already she knew from a few unguarded comments from her ingenuous daughter that the Bottomleys as a family, whilst approving wholeheartedly of Victoria herself, entertained some reservations about the more flamboyant Anatovs. That the reverse might also hold true Anna suspected would not have occurred to them: but it was not only Nicholas — who referred to them invariably and to his sister's distress as 'the worthy Bottomleys' — who was convinced that Victoria's future in-laws were likely to be sober, virtuous, and deadly dull.

The day itself dawned bright and clear and very cold. The proximity of Christmas lent to the festivities an added zest. Victoria was a breathtaking picture in her white satin, fur-trimmed gown, her bouquet a brilliant, seasonal splash of colour with its red-berried holly, shining laurel and trailing ivy. The church too was decked for Christmas, and a small, charmingly candle-lit crib stood to one side of the altar. Victoria, pale with nerves, stood rigid in the porch of the church as her mother smoothed and arranged the folds of her skirt.

"Honestly, Mama, I still don't see why we couldn't have had a much quieter wedding. It doesn't seem —"

"Nonsense, dear. There. Turn around." Anna straightened. "That looks lovely." She looked at Joss who, with one of his rare smiles, extended an arm to his daughter. Anna stood for a moment, surveying them both, astonished by a sudden and unexpected constriction of her throat. She swallowed, said briskly, "I'd better go and find my place. Good luck."

Impulsively Victoria stepped to her, hugged her close. "Thank you, Mama," she said, softly and simply.

Smiling, Anna turned and walked, her breath clouding the cold air, down the long, columned aisle to her place beside the two boys. Ridiculously the light of the candles blurred and danced as she walked. She blinked rapidly, acknowledged soft greetings and smiles. In her seat she sat very straight and resisted the impulse to mop at her idiotically damp eyes. There was a stir of expectation, then, in the body of the church and the organ's first dramatic note sounded. As the ceremony started

Anna found herself watching not Victoria and Samuel but Joss, who stood, handsome as ever in his morning suit beside his daughter. Did he, Anna wondered, remember their wedding in this very church more than Victoria's lifetime ago? So much had happened since — to them, and to the world — that it almost seemed two strangers had once stood here and taken these same vows that Victoria now spoke in a tremulous voice. Almost. As Joss took his place in the pew beside her, Anna glanced at him. The look he returned was utterly unreadable. She turned her attention back to the altar.

The reception was held at home in Bayswater, and the house was filled to bursting. Men in uniform, or morning dress, a predominance of women in pre-war finery carefully refurbished, children beginning the afternoon as models of good behaviour and ending it, despite a gaggle of nursemaids and nannies, under everyone's feet. There had been no question in this time of shortages of providing a full-blown meal, but the cook and the caterers between them had managed a very satisfactory buffet and Joss, from some mysterious source known only to himself, had provided more than enough champagne to oil the wheels of celebration. He and Anna had their first real conversation of the day half-way through the afternoon as the guests gathered in the long drawing room to watch the newly-weds cut a cake that might a few short years before have been considerably bigger.

"I saw the design that you did for the new Red Cross poster the other day. Congratulations, it's excellent."

Anna jumped. Joss stood beside her, his eyes upon their daughter and her new husband.

"Why — thank you."

"I thought it very striking."

She said nothing. Joss had arrived very late the evening before, long after she had retired to bed, and they had seen each other hardly at all in the whirlwind morning.

"How are you?"

He nodded. "Well, thank you."

"Will you be — staying long?" She was struck, as she had been before, by the ridiculous formality of their relationship. How very pleasant to see you again, Mr So-and-so. Will you be staying long? Her mouth turned down, wryly.

"I'm afraid not. We've a very important contract to fill. I'll have to leave first thing in the morning."

What else had she expected? Why should she care? His absence, she found herself telling herself, has always been more comfortable than his presence —

There came a sudden shout of laughter from a group of people standing nearby. Anna glanced at them and smiled. Beth, at the centre of the gaiety, winked back. A mistletoe branch was being passed from hand to hand, and the appropriate forfeit taken. Not far from them Samuel Bottomley's daughter, a tall, ungainly girl with a plain, kindly face smiled too, and said something to the serious-faced young man in uniform with whom she was standing.

"Everyone seems to be getting on remarkably well," Anna said, lightly. "I have to say that I had my doubts."

A burst of applause signalled the cutting of the cake.

"I rather like weddings," she went on, inconsequentially, in the face of his silence. "There always seems to be that feeling that people have truly gathered to wish the couple well. Don't you think?" She was aware of his eyes upon her. Oddly, she found she could not face the dark gaze, and she averted her own, letting it slip over the sea of happy, animated faces around her. "Even now. Even with this dreadful war —" Suddenly the vivacity seemed to drain from her. She looked down at her half-empty glass, then lifted her head at last to look at him. "The third Christmas," she said softly. "How many more, do you think? How many more Christmases? How many more deaths?"

He shook his head. "Who knows?"

The crowd around them was singing now. "For they are jolly good fellows, For they are jolly good fellows —"

"Joss —"

He raised questioning eyebrows. He stood very close to her in the overcrowded room. It was a moment of strange intimacy. She wanted suddenly to touch him. Shout at him. Shake him. Shatter, at last, for better or for worse, that rigid barrier of distrust and hostility that had held them apart for so long. God in heaven, she found herself thinking, isn't there enough hatred in the world at the moment without our adding to it? And for what? Isn't tomorrow more important than yesterday? "Joss — couldn't we at least —"

"Mama! Papa! We've been looking for you absolutely *everywhere!*" Nicholas swooped upon them. His young, boy-smooth cheeks were champagne-flushed, his eyes bright as gemstones. Ben, as always, trailed in his wake. "Samuel says Papa has to make a speech. He's in quite a tizzy about it." He lifted a bright, challenging head and looked at Joss. Anna's heart sank at the look in the man's eyes. Nicholas laughed. "You're holding up the proceedings, you know. Awfully bad form."

"I'm coming." Joss, with no look at Anna, shouldered his way, politely apologetic, through the crowd to where a radiant Victoria and a Samuel, looking at least ten years younger than his age, waited. Anna sighed. Nicholas glanced at her, an odd light in his eyes.

"Come on, Mumps. Cheer up. You aren't losing a daughter, you know. You're gaining a grand-dad!"

"Nicholas!" As always she could not withstand his laughter.

He leaned to her, whispering. "Come on upstairs. We've cleared the nursery and got the old gramophone going. Dancing, and singing and —" he rolled his eyes "— all kinds of mischief. There are," he added solemnly, "even a couple of the younger Bottomleys up there. So your reputation will be quite safe!"

She laughed. "Later."

He grinned and sidled away from her through the quietening crowd. Ben hesitated, hovering at her side for a moment before with a quick, nervous smile he followed his brother.

Joss's speech was short and entertaining. Anna saw, as he finished, his eyes searching the sea of faces. As they rested upon hers he began to move towards her.

"Anna, my dear! How much it must mean to you to see Victoria so safely settled and happy —"

She turned. Hermione Smithson, portly, white-haired, stood beside her, beaming, her florid face sheened delicately with sweat. Beside her was Josef, frail-looking but smiling. "I was just saying to your father —"

Anna turned her head.

Joss had gone.

She hardly saw him again, except from a distance. In the morning he had left before she had lifted her champagne-heavy head from the pillow. He had, however, left a message for her. He would not, he regretted, be home for Christmas; the contract he had mentioned was vital to the war effort and must come first.

Of course.

Anna leaned to the mirror and thoughtfully smoothed the skin about her eyes, touching her moistened finger tip to her arched, tidily plucked brows.

She would ask Beth for Christmas. The boys adored her. And Arabella. And that fascinating man that Arabella appeared to be living with. What was his name? Something Italian. He was an opera singer. She must try to book him for the Red Cross Gala in January. Josef, of course, wouldn't want to come all the way to town for Christmas; but she and the boys could spend the New Year at Bissetts. They could go beagling on New Year's Day. With all those retired Colonels and Brigadiers. That would be fun.

She straightened, sighed, and then with a burst of impatient energy that refused to take note of her thumping head, she reached for her gown and started for the bathroom.

It was the worst winter that Europe had known in nearly forty years. The same cold that had frosted the air of the church where Victoria had become Mrs Samuel Bottonley froze men to the very marrow, sometimes to death, in the desecrated countryside that was the front line in a war that as yet no one showed signs of winning. Another Christmas; no truce this year, no comradely meeting in the barbed and deserted land between the opposing lines. The men that died that Christmas day, a sacrifice not to the Christian God to whose favour, ironically, both sides laid claim but to the flawed gods of war and national greed were just as dead, the day notwithstanding. Such things as hope, and promise and the birth of a Child had almost ceased to have meaning in those muddy, rat-ridden holes in the ground where quickness of eye, a good strong arm, a sense of humour and — above all — a highly-developed sense of self-preservation were understandably of more value and assistance to a man than the traditionally Christian virtues of loving kindness and forbearance.

Lieutenant Rupert Rose, MC, was astonished to discover, in the early spring of 1917, when the raw days and bitter nights still flayed skin to blood and froze fingers and toes from agony to insensibility, that he was ordered on leave.

"To take effect immediately, Rose. Get yourself a razor packed. There's a truck leaving in half an hour."

Rupert shook his head. "If you don't mind, Sir —"

"Oh, but I do mind." His Commanding Officer fixed him with a look that had quelled rebellion in more recalcitrant souls than Rupert's. "You're off, lad. For a fortnight. And that's an order."

"But —"

A cold eye stopped the words before they could form. "But you want to collect a few more medals before the end of the month, Lieutenant?"

Rupert flushed hotly. The bunker, despite the cold outside, was fuggily warm, and already in his unsuitable clothing — he had been inspecting the forward lookout posts when he had been summoned — he was sweating uncomfortably, the skin of his wind-flayed face stinging. "No, Sir. Of course not, Sir," he said stiffly, resentment in every formally correct line of his body.

The face softened. "Go home, Rupert," the captain said, sympathy in his tired voice. "Before you get yourself — or someone else — killed. The war will still be here in a couple of weeks' time." He smiled bleakly. "Don't worry. We won't be going anywhere without you."

Rupert saluted, spun on his heel and left. Thirty minutes later he was perched uncomfortably on a pile of dirty sacking in the back of a truck that rattled towards the reserve trenches and the railhead, his eyes upon the familiar, shell-lit night, his mind a blank.

Bissetts hadn't changed. Incredible as it seemed to him in this world where he had felt that surely nothing could have remained untouched, Bissetts was the same. The great trees, wind-tossed now, still reached to a peaceful sky, the grass was green and smooth, unpitted, the brickwork of the house solid, unscarred, soft and mellow. The Essex countryside stretched its tranquil patchwork about the house, with no raw wound of war to be seen. He had all but forgotten that such a place could exist except in memory. The very silence shouted in his ears. He stood for a moment on the drive, looking at the house. He had dismissed the trap that had brought him from the station — with the shortage of petrol had come a revival of the more traditional modes of transport — at the foot of the wide drive and had chosen to walk to the house; though whether the more to savour his homecoming or to put off the moment of his arrival he himself would have been hard-put to say. He hunched into his greatcoat, pulled the collar closer about his ears, the wind whipped at his cap, tugged at the heavy skirts of his coat. Beyond the house he could see the tennis court, the grass long-grown and winter-rough, the empty netposts green with mould.

Richard's voice: "My 'vantage. Come on, Rupe — you can do better than that." Cool lemonade. Laughter. Cucumber sandwiches. Crisp apples from the autumn orchard —

A pain stabbed, so savagely that it took his breath and stilled his blood with its agony. No. Bissetts was not the same. Would never be the same. For one instant he had to make a physical effort to prevent himself from turning, running back the way he had come. Running anywhere. Anywhere but here.

"Rupert! Christ! Son — it is you? Your mother said it was — we couldn't believe —" His father stood at the open door. Behind him a young man in uniform, a crisp, snow-white bandage about his head and covering one eye, watched with an interested, sympathetic smile.

Alex ran down the steps and across the crunching shingle of the drive at a speed remarkable in one so large. A yard from Rupert he stopped. His face was working. "You didn't let us know — didn't tell us you were coming."

"I couldn't. It was — very sudden." The bone-weariness in the young face was echoed in the voice.

Alex took an odd, juddering breath, controlled with difficulty the impulse to fling himself upon this tall, gaunt figure and hug him. He stuck out his hand. "Welcome home, lad."

Rupert took his hand, felt its tremor, smiled. "Thanks." Over his father's shoulder he saw that now his mother, thin and elegant, her changed face radiant, had appeared at the door of the house. He covered the distance between them in seconds. "Mother!" He clenched her to him, felt the strong, nervous hands clutch fiercely at his shoulders. Then he lifted his head and froze. A young woman holding a child stood on the stairs in the darkness of the hall, staring at him, an absolute agony of grief in her dark eyes. A ghost of yesterday. The very last person he had expected to see. "My God!" he said, and closed his eyes, knowing what he had done to her.

Sophie very, very carefully descended the last few steps, transferred the weight of the child on to her left arm. Extended a steady, narrow hand. "Rupert. How lovely to see you."

He did not know — how could he — that the tears that had suddenly started to run unchecked, it seemed almost unnoticed, down her cheeks were the first she had cried since his brother's death.

She avoided him for days, as far as she could, and he could not find it in his heart to blame her for it. Who knew better than he the likeness between himself and the dead; as who knew better the disparity? And in any case his own frame of mind did not prompt him to any close association with Sophie, or for that matter with anyone else. He slept as much as he could, walked the winter lanes alone when the restlessness of dread forced him out, tried — unsuccessfully on the whole — to live from day to day without thought, to enjoy this brief respite. And all the time in his mind, in his gut, in his very bones the fear crouched, waiting; waiting to leer from a shadowed corner, to grin in the darkness, to gnaw with sharp teeth at his strength, his will — sometimes he wondered if not at his very sanity.

His enemy showed itself one day, a day of gusting, gale-force winds and rain that drove against the window like hard-flung stones, when he sat before the fire in the upstairs sitting room, a book open but unread on his lap, his eyes distant upon the flames. Outside, trees creaked in protest as the wind shrieked to a crescendo. The sharp crack as one of the brittle branches of the old ash tree that stood upon the lawn not far from the house finally gave under the onslaught might have been a pistol shot.

Rupert's head snapped back in shock, and he ducked, cringing. His mother, her eyes upon the window, did not notice the movement. Sophie did, and he caught in her eyes a sudden, surprised flash of unnerving compassion that he found utterly intolerable. He stood up abruptly. "I think I'll stroll down to the village."

His mother looked around at him in astonishment. "But — darling! — it's absolutely foul out there! You'll get soaked."

He shook his head. "I need a bit of air. And I'm almost out of cigarettes."

Minutes later he strode down the drive, hands in pockets, collar turned against the wind, his footsteps crunching on the wet gravel, his face lifted to the driving rain as if he welcomed its sting. He walked to the village, bought the packet of cigarettes that were his excuse for the errand, dismissed the thought of a pint at the local pub for fear that he would almost certainly find himself paying for it in a friendly and inquisitive conversation, and turned back towards Bissetts. The rain had stopped for the moment and the wind had died a little, though it still blustered across the drenched countryside and piled the fast-moving rain clouds one upon another like mountains of dark fleece. He slowed his footsteps. If only time could be arrested. If only this tranquil moment of safety and solitude could be captured forever, riven from past and from future to exist alone, like the bubbles he and Richard had used to blow as children into the still summer air that would waft, rainbow-hued to the bright sky, there to hang and drift feather-light in the sunshine until they burst. Until they burst. He stopped for a moment, tilted his head to watch the racing clouds.

Is that what death will be like? Like the sudden bursting of a bubble? I hope so. God — I hope so. That would be bearable. At least for me.

"Rupert?"

She stood by the roadside, watching him. Her fair hair was wind-blown as a child's and in the dark storm-light the lines of strain upon her face were disguised. Almost he could have believed that they had stepped back in time, and were young again.

"I popped down to see Uncle Josef. Then I waited for you. Do you mind?"

He shook his head. "Of course not. How is he?"

Sophie half-shrugged. "He's not too bad. Physically he seems fine, in fact. But he does ramble a lot — at least, I think it's rambling. The news from Russia — the riots, the Tsar's abdication — it seems to have set him thinking about the past more than ever. It's only natural, I suppose. He talks a lot of my Aunt Tanya. Yet sometimes I think he's almost forgotten who I am."

"She killed herself, didn't she?"

"Yes, she did. Before we were born. Yet — he talks as if it were yesterday. He speaks of her — to her, sometimes — as if she were a child. She came with him from Russia, you know."

"Yes. I did know."

"I think she wasn't — quite right in the head." They had turned into the gate and were strolling slowly towards the house. She looked at him, unsmiling. "I don't suppose you fancy a bit of a walk?"

He hesitated.

"All right," she said. "It doesn't matter."

"No — please — I'd like to."

"No. You wouldn't. And I don't blame you."

Suddenly and unexpectedly, after the weeks, the months of silence, he wanted to talk. He stopped. She turned, and tilted her head to look steadily at him. "Please," he said again.

She nodded.

They turned their footsteps on to the wet grass beneath the tossing trees. "When I first arrived," he said after a moment, "I thought — I rather expected — that you might leave."

"I nearly did. Then I thought — no. It would just be running away, wouldn't it?"

Their feet whispered wetly in the short grass. "I'm glad, so very glad, that you agreed to visit them," he said, softly. "I can't tell you how much it means to them."

Her mouth turned down, bitterly, at the corners, but she did not speak.

"It must have been very hard for you," he said.

"Yes. It was." She glanced sideways at him, half-defiant. "But I don't want you running off with the idea that I'm noble or anything. I'm not. I did it for Richard. Purely for him. And for Flissy."

"Richard would have been very proud of you."

Dark lashes veiled her eyes. Her face was expressionless.

"I'm sorry — you don't want to talk about him."

She looked at him then, and he saw the pain, the desolation of loss. "There's no point, is there?" she asked, collectedly. "Richard's dead. Gone. Nothing will bring him back. One of thousands. Of hundreds of thousands. Perhaps — who knows? — of millions before this — this lunacy is ended. Flissy will never know him. God! What are we doing to ourselves?"

They stopped beneath the bare, spreading branches of a magnificent oak. The great trunk afforded at least some shelter from the wind. Rupert lit a cigarette, cupping his hands to the match. Sophie picked at the bark of the tree with her fingernail.

Rupert tilted his head to look up into the tree. "We used to have a treehouse up there. See? Where the big branch forks."

"I see it. It looks very high."

"Richard would have it right up there." He half-laughed. "To be truthful I used to suffer agonies over it. I've always been a bit afraid of heights. I used to find the climb up there pretty fearful at first."

"But — you got used to it?" She was not looking at him.

"More or less."

"Did Richard ever know? That you were afraid?"

He shook his head. "No."

She leaned against the tree. "And now?"

"Now?"

"Are you still —" she paused "— afraid of heights?" Her voice was light, her eyes intense and questioning.

He took a long breath. Above them the clouds had broken a little and the faintest gleam of pale sunshine touched the waterlogged countryside, lining it in silver and in pearl. "Yes," he said, very quietly, "I am afraid. Of everything." He turned from her, leaned against the tree, drew deeply on the cigarette, his eyes on the wetly-gleaming countryside. "I'm afraid of death. Of the grief that my death will inflict on others. I'm afraid of pain. Of mutilation. Of fear. I'm afraid of going back."

She said nothing.

"Over there — I wake with fear each morning. I eat with it, drink with it, sleep with it. It's a familiar face in the mirror. Here," he shook his head, helplessly, "it's as I feared — it's worse. Much worse. I had grown used to it. Now, I have to start again."

"But — I thought," her voice was soft, and she stumbled upon the words, "I mean — you've been so brave. The Military Cross. Mentioned in dispatches, twice."

He made a small, impatient movement with his head. "I didn't say I was a coward," he said. "I said I was afraid."

She sucked her lip, watching him. And for the first time since Richard's death the ice in which misery had sheathed her heart melted a little and she found herself sharing, almost physically, another's pain. She had after all loved Rupert as a friend before she had found a lover in Richard.

"Have you told anyone else?" she asked, not knowing why she asked, not knowing why it was important.

He shook his head.

She pushed herself away from the tree, held out her hand, the hand of love and compassion.

With no hesitation he took it, and together they walked back to the house.

CHAPTER TWENTY-THREE

On the sixth of April 1917, a couple of weeks after Rupert had rejoined his regiment at the front, the long-awaited news that America had at last entered the war on the side of the Allies cheered war-weary Britain in a way that little else could have done. Surely, now, the end could not be far off? Yet still the fight continued; bitter, deadly, indecisive. Winter refused even now to relax her ruthless grip upon Europe and men still fought and dropped in sleet and snow, their fingers too numbed to reload their rifles. The French in particular had fought almost to exhaustion: sporadic and worrying outbreaks of indiscipline and near mutiny in the ranks were dealt with severely, and the news of them suppressed. Russia's internal problems, too, were bleeding those of her soldiers still at the front of confidence and the will to fight. As summer came at last, however, Londoners found themselves rather more concerned with a domestic threat than with the problems of their allies, as a spate of air attacks was launched upon their city by a Germany desperate to end the war in victory before the might of the United States could fully be brought into play against her. No airship attack these — for the tracer bullets that had brought down the first airship the year before had spelt a fiery end for those giants — but raids by flights of a dozen or more aeroplanes, often by day, sometimes by night, that caused casualties and damage enough to make certain that a civilian population already tired and on edge did not sleep easily in their beds. As the year moved on, however, the news from the front at last began to look more cheerful. Anna was one of many Londoners to be woken in the early hours of the morning of the seventh of June by the vibrations of the huge explosion that blew the Messines Ridge and its German emplacements quite literally to pieces and paved the way for a victory that raised spirits and hopes. Within weeks it was the name of Passchendaele that was on every tongue — strange, evocative name that was for many to be the one that personified the endeavour and the suffering of this war to end wars. And through that terrible battle — that lasted, incredibly, until November — inexorable rain, chilling cold and ground that had been blasted long ago into filthy bog created conditions that no man that suffered them was ever likely to forget.

"The mud is unspeakable," Rupert wrote to Sophie. "Worse than the bombardment. Worse than the weather. Worse than the food. Yet still the men find humour in it. No one — fortunately for him — has yet discovered the identity of the man who substituted a plate of it for the Sergeant Major's mulligatawny soup the other day. The laughter over that piece of insubordination did us all more good than three days' rest!"

And then it was over at last, when at the beginning of November Canadian troops captured the small, utterly wrecked group of ruins that had once been the village of Passchendaele. But while the bells of victory rang in London news just as momentous was filtering from the East: for in Russia bloody revolution was under way, and the Russian bear was out of the war.

Joss spent a good deal of time that year in the north where two of his factories were now heavily involved in the designing and production of tanks, those armoured monsters that many thought might prove to be the final weight in the balance of victory. Anna was surprised therefore to be informed one cold December morning on arriving home that the master was there before her, and awaited her in the drawing room. She divested herself of hat and coat, patted her hair, ordered tea, and went to join him.

When she entered the room Joss was standing at the window, his back to her.

"Joss? What are you doing home? I thought —"

He turned. And at the sight of the object that depended from his fingers in a shimmering blaze of light and gleamed in the room's darkness like fire, she stopped, her eyes wide with shock. "God in Heaven," she whispered, after a moment. "Where did you get that?"

He held it up. It swung gently, each facet independently brilliant as if lit from within, the entwined doves gleaming dully above the stone. Very, very slowly Anna advanced into the room, lifted a hand, then let it drop without touching the pendant. "Where did you get it?" she asked again. Her heart was thumping painfully against her ribs, as if she were engaged in some great physical effort, and she found it impossible to control her breathing. She had not dreamt that the thought of Nicolai still had the power to hurt so; not after all these years.

"It was brought into the shop. They contacted me. It's for sale." He lifted unreadable eyes. "Congratulations, Anna. It's a truly lovely piece."

"For sale? But how? Who brought it?"

"A cousin of the Shuvenskis'. The family have suffered badly, both in the war and in the revolution. Most are dead. The rest are in prison or in hiding. Their property has been destroyed or confiscated —"

Anna flinched.

"This man escaped with his family, bringing with him what he could. What more natural than that he should bring it to us? Within the family, apparently, it was often called the Rose Stone."

"And — shall you buy it?" Anna could not keep the tremor from her voice. Joss's bald words were taking painful moments to sink in to her shocked consciousness. In her mind's eye young and happy ghosts called, and sang; careless, innocent victims of their inheritance. All gone? Oh, surely not? Surely, surely not!

His eyes did not waver, yet they were not as guarded as usual. It seemed to her that she detected a gleam of sympathy in their depths; and then it was gone, and she knew she must have imagined it. "Oh, yes, I think so," he said, softly.

Despite herself, her eyes were drawn back to the stone. Brilliant, lustrous, ablaze with a fire that was as cold as ice it swung gently. "Papa," she found herself saying, her voice strange in her own ears, "Papa has always thought — that the stone was unlucky —"

Her husband's expression did not change. "I know," he said.

Two days later she was to remember that conversation when in a telephone call from Bissetts Alex informed Anna that their father had disappeared. "God only knows where he's gone," Alex said, his voice angry with worry. "He's in no fit state to be wandering around by himself — especially in this weather. We simply can't imagine what can have got into him. We've been everywhere. He's simply nowhere to be found. The nurse says he went for a walk —"

"You've contacted the police?"

"Of course. They're out looking now."

"I'll come immediately."

In the event, however, Anna did not go to Bissetts. For before she could pack, change and make the necessary arrangements, the uniformed maid was tapping upon her door, a worried look upon her face. "Excuse me, Ma'am —"

"What is it, Madge?" Anna was impatient.

"There's an old — gentleman — down in the 'all." The girl's face was doubtful. "'e says 'e's —"

Anna was out of the door and down the stairs before she could finish. Josef stood in the hall. He was hatless, drenched, and shivering with cold.

Sophie appeared at the top of the stairs. "Good Lord! Uncle Josef! What the —"

"Sophie, dear, get a bedroom ready, will you?" Anxiously Anna put a supportive arm about her father, shocked at his appearance and at the frailness of his frame beneath the wet jacket he wore. "Light a fire. And get some extra blankets."

"Of course." Sophie flew from the landing.

Anna turned to Josef. "Papa! What on earth are you doing here? We've all been so worried!"

"I have to see Joss." The old face was earnest, and his voice surprisingly strong. Yet Anna got the impression that he had not heard the words. "Anna — I have to see him —"

"But — to come all this way — and in this weather — what on earth were you thinking of? You could have telephoned Joss —" So anxious was she that for a moment the oddity of her father's need to see a man who had barely spoken to him for fifteen years passed Anna by.

He shook his head. "No, no! I have to see him. Speak to him. Now. He's here?"

She shook her head. "No, Papa, he's —"

He turned to the door. "I must find him."

She caught his arm, held it fast. "Papa — no! You can't possibly go out again. You're shivering with cold! Come upstairs to the drawing room. The fire's lit."

Hectic spots of colour burned in his face. The hand that gripped hers, she suddenly realized with a shock, beneath the surface chill was beginning to burn like fire. "I have to see Joss. Have to see him."

"I'll send for him. I promise. But — please, Papa! — come with me now."

Suddenly it was as if his resolution deserted him. He shivered, looked around him, strangely vague, as if only just registering his surroundings. "Yes," he said. "I am — a little tired."

"Then come." She began to lead him up the stairs when suddenly he stopped, clutched at her arm.

"I must see Joss!"

"What about, Papa?" she asked, gently. "What must you see Joss about?"

"The stone. Alexis said the stone had come. From Russia —"

She bit her lip. Of course. The stone again. Damn the thing. "Yes," she said quietly. "It has."

"— and that Joss is going to buy it."

She hesitated. "That's right." What use in lying?

He swayed a little, dangerously, upon the stairs. "Don't let him do it, Anna. To himself. To you. Stop him. Don't let him." He swayed again. In desperation she caught and held his slumped body.

"Sophie! Madge! Here — help me — quickly!"

The pneumonia that came in the wake of the fever which struck the frail constitution that night took the old man quickly. He died before Joss could be summoned from the north, his son-in-law's name the last on his lips. Dry-eyed, Anna had kept a watch by him through the day and the night as he drifted in the half-world of delirium, a half-world peopled by ghosts whose names meant little to her as she listened to the all-but unintelligible babblings of fever. But Joss's name she heard, and Tanya's. Again and again. But in this final hour the adopted language of his adopted country failed the old man, and his explanations and his terrors found voice in his native tongue; with the one who might have understood not there. He was lucid just before the end. Alex and Alice were there, with Sophie and Anna. The old eyes wavered from one face to another. Then sadly, sadly, the old head shook upon the pillow. "Joss," he said softly, and died.

On a bitterly cold day three days before a Christmas that everyone prayed, with a little more hope than before, would be the last of the war, Josef Rosenberg was laid to rest. And as the coffin was lowered into the dark, frozen ground, a single flower, tossed there by Sophie, resting upon its lid, Anna lifted her eyes to her sombre, silent husband's and saw, with a shock of utter astonishment the tears of loss upon his face. She stared at him across her father's open grave. He met her eyes steadily, made no attempt to hide the tears.

"You cried for him," she said later, in bitter disbelief, when the other mourners had left the house and Sophie had gone to tend to Felicity. "After all that's happened. After all the — the hate. You — cried — for him. Why? Joss — why?" Her own tears, very close to the surface, sounded in her voice. Her father had been an old man. She had thought herself prepared for his death. Had discovered that she was not.

Joss did not reply. He was sitting in a large winged armchair, feet stretched to the meagre wartime fire, in one hand a large glass of brandy, which rested upon the arm of the chair. His face was in shadow.

"Joss!" Anna had to restrain herself from screaming. From shaking him. "For God's sake! Talk to me! I have to know!"

"Why?" Joss's voice was tired. "Why do you have to know?"

"Because my father is dead. And I didn't know him. Because you are here. And I don't know you. Because something — something — is being kept from me. Has always been kept from me. Hasn't it? Joss — *hasn't it?*"

He said nothing. Drank deeply of the brandy. Leaned to the bottle at his elbow and poured more.

She came to the chair, crouched beside it, looking up into his dark face. "You cried," she said again, painfully patient. "Why?"

"Because once I loved him." The words came out with difficulty, their tone harsh.

"And then — you hated him. Why?" She watched him tilt the glass, swallow. "Why?" She knew with absolute certainty that if she were ever to find the answers to the questions that had haunted these last fifteen years of her life it must be now, or never. His tears had unlocked a door between them that had been closed these many years. She could not — must not — let it shut again without trying to discover what lay behind it. "Joss — why?"

For a long moment he did not move, then with a movement so abrupt as to startle her he got up, went to the bureau desk that stood in the corner and unlocked a drawer. When he returned to the chair the glittering ice-fire that was the Rose Stone dangled from his fingers. She watched him, and it. He held it, swinging, his eyes fixed upon it as if hypnotized by the movement. Once again his face was in shadow.

"You," he said very quietly, "and the rest of the family — believe that Josef brought this stone with him from Kiev."

"Yes."

The dark eyes moved from the shimmering diamond to her face. She kept her own eyes steady, though her heart, strangely, had taken up a sickening hammer-blow of dread.

"The night before my sister died," her husband continued softly, "I discovered differently. Once a long time ago, Josef implied to me that there was some connection between Tanya, her —" he paused "— her strangeness, and the diamond. He thought that she did not remember. He thought that the innocent child did not know what he did. But it was there. Locked in her memory. Until Matthew turned the key, and the memory destroyed her."

Only once did she make a sound. "Oh, God!" she said, when he told of Josef's frenzy and van Heuten's death. The deeply accented, unemotional voice did not falter. The tale was told, apparently dispassionately, to the grieveous bitter end. But the hand that held the stone was knotted like wire, bone and knuckle showing whitely through the dark skin.

When he had done there was a long, heavy, silence. Anna dashed the tears from her face. Cleared her throat. "And all these years," she said shakily, "this is what has lain between us — between *us* —" she emphasized the last word "— and you haven't told me."

"It was not my story to tell," he said, stone-faced.

"Oh, but it was!" Suddenly, fiercely passionate, she was on her knees beside him, her bunched fists hitting at his arm, "It was! Josef was my father, Tanya your sister. That —" she indicated the stone with a sharp gesture which held a kind of loathing "— has been the basis of my life and comfort ever since I was born. And, worst of all, our marriage — my marriage — has been wrecked — *wrecked*, I say — by these things you have refused to speak of. How dare you say to me that it was not your story to tell? You certainly thought it was yours to brood upon — yours to allow to warp and to twist your own life and mine." Tears were again pouring down her face, and she made no attempt to wipe them away. "God, Joss, don't you see it is for that that I could hate you? For the wasted years, the emptiness, the hopeless trying —" The shock of what he had told her had set her shaking. She could not stop. She trembled so that her teeth chattered and she stuttered, as if with cold. "I c-could k-kill you."

As he lunged forward, caught her shoulders, urgently and painfully in hard hands, the diamond fell unheeded to the floor. "Anna — stop it."

Blinded by tears she struggled to be free of him. "I l-loved you so much. So very much — and I thought it was I — *I* — who had failed. I who was to blame that you didn't love me. And all the time," the shreds of her control were slipping from her, "all the time it was this that lay between us — this — s-story that was 'not yours to tell'." She clamped her mouth shut, biting her lip painfully enough to draw blood, fought the hysteria that she knew to be rising, and won. He was watching her with night-dark eyes, his hands still strong and supportive upon her shoulders. The stone glittered on the floor between them, a bright, baleful eye. She wrenched herself from his grip, sat back upon her heels, sniffing, her eyes upon the diamond. "You've never loved me, have you?" she said, the words no question. "You married me to punish my father. To take me from him. To make sure that no matter what you did your connection with him and with the stone could not be broken. So that you could torment him forever. And all the while you let me struggle — fight for a love that never existed —"

"No," he said.

"I've loved you. All of my life I've loved you. The child I was — the girl who married you —" Her head came up sharply. "Joss did you never feel any pity at all?"

She saw him flinch, physically, as if at a blow. Strangely, the sight gave her pause. She took a breath. "I'm sorry," she breathed, as if truly she had hit him. He bowed his head. A still silence fell between them, heightened by the far-off rumbling echoes of the infernal, the terrible guns. He lifted his head at last. "And Nicolai Shuvenski?" he asked, gently.

She did not hesitate. "Yes, I loved him. But not as I did you. And it never would have happened if you had cared for me. Never."

Unexpectedly he reached a hand to her face. "I believe you."

At the gentle touch of his hand, the first such gesture he had made in what seemed to her to be a lifetime, she closed her eyes. Tears still squeezed from beneath her lashes. Tiredly she bent her head and rested it against his hand. Suddenly she found herself thinking of Tanya, as she remembered her; beautiful, gentle, afraid. "Oh, God, Joss," she whispered, "it's all so horrible. And I'm so very sorry." She was in his arms then, without volition, the most natural thing in the world. And when his mouth covered hers the need that rose shook them both, relieving them of sense, of bitterness, of grief, and leaving only a physical need that it was beyond either of them to resist. In silence he took her hand and led her to her bedroom, locking the door behind them. In the light of the small lamp she looked at him, at the ravages of bitterness and of pride and knew that she loved him now above all things. As she always had. She gave herself freely, the joining of their bodies an explosion of pleasure and of pain. Their whispers, after, were those of lovers. "I've loved you always," he said, in the dark hours when pride had long been surrendered. "You must believe me. Beneath it all, I've loved you always." And she, wanting to believe, believed and cried out with the pleasure that he gave her, that she had craved so long.

*

Benjamin it was who found the stone, the next morning on the floor of the drawing room. "I say — look at this." He held up the lovely thing to the light. "What on earth's it doing here? Hey — be careful, you idiot!"

Nicholas had snatched it from him, was looking at the pendant with strangely intent eyes. "The Shuvenski diamond," he said.

"What?" Ben was thunderstruck. "Here? On the drawing room floor? You're nuts, Nicho."

"I tell you it is! I know it. I'd know it anywhere." Nicholas's voice, like his eyes, held an intense excitement.

"How would you? Why would you? You've never seen it. It's got nothing to do with you."

Nicholas lifted a bright, picturesque head. "Oh, no? Well that's where you're wrong. I know it because I asked Mama to draw the design that she did for it. I still have it upstairs —"

"What on earth for?"

"Because, brother mine," Nicholas's voice was soft, his eyes riveted to the swinging jewel, "this lovely lady is more mine that anyone's. That's why. One day she'll be mine, as she should be —"

"I don't know what you're talking about."

"No." Nicholas grinned suddenly, "I know you don't. But one day —" He stopped, stood for a moment as if frozen. Ben, slow to follow the direction of his brother's eyes, looked puzzled.

"What's the matter?"

"Benjamin." Joss's voice was very quiet, utterly authoritative. "Leave us please. I wish a word with Nicholas." He stood by the open door, his eyes fixed upon Nicholas. Ben stood for a moment as if rooted to the spot, something in his father's face setting the shaved hairs at the back of his neck prickling uncomfortably. Nicholas stood very straight and still, the pendant swinging from his fingers. Joss stepped forward, his hand outstretched. "Give that to me."

With no word Nicholas handed it to him. Slow, mutinous colour was mounting in his cheeks. He tilted his head defiantly, staring into Joss's cold face with no trace of fear.

"Benjamin."

Soft-footed, Benjamin walked to the door, paused for a moment, his eyes upon his father, then very quietly left the room, pulling the door to behind him. Before it was completely closed, however, he heard Joss's voice, chill as ice and edged sharp with a strange anger. "So. The Shuvenski diamond is more Nicholas Anatov's than anyone's? That, I think, calls for an explanation."

The temptation was irresistible. Ben stood like a statue as the voices from the other side of the door wrought their bitter damage.

Anna woke that morning to find her husband up and about before her. Recollection was instant and complete, the bad and the good. At some time during the night it had occurred to her to wonder at the terrible burden her father had carried through his life, and to grieve for it. She thought of it again now, and her happiness was for a moment tempered by pity for him. She looked at the clock, ticking upon the table as if it had been any ordinary, common-or-garden day. She had a meeting of the Refugee Committee early this morning, with barely an hour to get up, dressed and across half of London. Singing she slid from between the sheets and reached for her velvet robe.

Later, she arrived home more eager than she cared to admit even to herself for the sight of Joss's face, the sound of his voice. Like a lovelorn girl she had found herself thinking of him, on and off, throughout the day, the memory of the night bringing warm blood to her cheeks whilst the world about her talked interminably of quotas and fund-raising and shortages and clothes-collections.

She handed her small, smart hat to Madge. "Is the master at home, Madge?"

"No, Ma'am."

"Oh." She paused in her busy movements, disappointment taking the edge from her smile. "Well, I don't suppose he'll be long. I'll leave tea for a while."

The girl looked uncomfortable. "'e left, Ma'am. Packed 'is case an' left. 'E's left you a note."

Anna stared at her, then followed the direction of the girl's pointing finger to where a white, undirected envelope lay upon the hall table. "What do you mean — left?" she asked, carefully.

"Just that, Ma'am. Packed 'is bags, made a few telephone calls an' — left."

Anna walked with as much control as she could muster to the table, picked up the envelope, tapped it, unopened, upon the palm of her open hand. "Did he say when he'd be back?"

"No, Ma'am."

"All right. Thank you, Madge. I'll take tea in the drawing room."

Cold as stone she opened the letter. The girl was right. Joss had left. With no explanation and no apology, let alone a word of love. The note, brief and to the point, contained his forwarding address in Manchester for urgent matters and very little else. Very, very deliberately Anna tore it to shreds and dropped it into the fire.

CHAPTER TWENTY-FOUR

This time he did not return. Indeed within a very few weeks it became perfectly apparent that Joss Anatov no longer considered the Bayswater house to be his home; and Anna, confused, resentful and more hurt than she would admit even to herself, found herself having to face the fact that, despite that one strange night they had spent together and which had seemed to promise so much, with his hatred for Josef gone there was now apparently nothing left to hold her husband to her. In frigid anger she resisted any temptation to contact him. She was determined that this time she would neither cry recriminations nor demand explanations. She was, after all, a grown woman and no heartsick girl to pursue and to beg the man who had chosen to treat her so. In the weeks that followed it seemed to her that her feelings for Joss had been switched off as surely and completely as the light in a room that is left closed, dark and empty when its occupants leave. It was, in fact, a positive relief, she told herself sensibly, to be rid of him. Living without him had always been a lot less harrowing than trying to live with him. Life went on. And only a fool would let it pass her by because of the graceless inconsistency, the capricious bitterness of one man. The fiction was established that Joss's commitments in the north were too pressing to allow him to come to London; how many of the family knew, as she did, that upon his many trips to the capital Joss stayed at his club in St James's, Anna neither knew nor particularly cared. Let the world think what it might. She had her work, her home, her friends, her children. What had he ever been able to offer worth more than that?

In Europe, as the first American troops began to arrive in France, the Germans, in March 1918, launched a final, desperate offensive designed to crush the war-weary allies before these fresh and well-armed reinforcements could make a decisive difference. It almost succeeded. From Cambrai to the Somme the British lines were all but overwhelmed — whole battalions, taken by surprise, cut off from their fellows, enveloped in a terrible miasma of fog, smoke and choking gas stood their ground and fought with futile and ferocious courage because the orders to retreat did not reach them: in some cases they were wiped out to a man. By the end of March the long-held line of the Somme was gone and the British Fifth Army all but smashed. For a while the fate of Europe hung once more in the balance. But it was not just the British, the French and their Allies that were weary to death of this blood-letting: the German army had been in the field for too long, and their losses had been as great as anyone's. As it became clear that the hoped-for collapse was not going to materialize, and as American men and arms began to pour to the Front, the symptoms of a collapse in morale began to appear in the German ranks, isolated and apparently insignificant at first, but straws in the wind nevertheless. For two months the struggle continued unabated, and for some it seemed that it might never, after all, end — that the world was caught in a madness from which it could not escape until the last drop of blood had been spilled. Then, towards the end of June, the initiative swung the way of the Allies; inexorably they began to push forward, pressing the German armies back towards Berlin and the Rhine. Spirits lifted. This, surely, must herald an end? But for hundreds of thousands of men and their families the good news came too late. That last, despairing offensive and the stubborn resistance it had met had been terribly costly to both sides. Five hundred men of a single battalion of the Rifle Brigade simply disappeared in one disastrous day on the Somme, wiped out, with not even their bodies ever recovered.

From the French coast the hospital ships sailed, and the trains steamed into London with their loads of wrecked humanity. It was on a sweltering day in August 1918 that the train carrying Captain Rupert Rose pulled slowly into Victoria Station. He watched with strange dispassion as the boy in the stretcher beside him, who had died a few minutes before, was lifted with little ceremony and carted like a lump of dead meat upon a pallet out on to the platform. "It's all right, Sir," the orderly grinned, seeing Rupert's eyes upon them, "we'll be more careful with you."

He was long months recovering. Whilst he lay upon his hospital bed the war flames flared, flickered and died at last. On the eleventh of November the nurse who tended him wept tears of happiness as she told him that the war was over, the slaughter done. The tears that Rupert shed, later, in the concealing darkness, were not however for the joy of the living, but for the comfortlessly mourned dead, who lived still within him. Yet those bitter tears — almost the first he had shed for his dead brother — were not wasted. Sophie, visiting him the next day, saw in his face a new peace, in his eyes a new light as he looked at her. And through her own tears she smiled as she held the cool, still hand.

There could have been no gladder heart than Anna Anatov's on that long-awaited Armistice Day; and no more frustrated hero than her son Nicholas, whose heroic aspirations had got no further than an application for the Military Academy at Woolwich. To say that he was disappointed that the war had ended before he could join it would have been an exaggeration, for not the most insensitive soul in the world could have been unhappy to see the bloody business over, and Nicholas, with all his faults, was far from that. Yet still he could not help but rue the lost opportunity for excitement. Now, suddenly — and to his mother's unutterable relief — the most adventure that the future held was a university entrance examination. Characteristically and carelessly he shrugged, laughed, and set about finding some substitute entertainment. Inevitably that involved a devilry that took no note of consequences. Equally inevitably it involved Ben, though the younger boy — who had conceived an unexpected and desperate determination to win his way to Oxford University — did his best to stay out of his rash brother's wilder scrapes. Twice Anna found herself the recipient of polite but caustic letters from the boys' headmaster. The first, involving breaking bounds, a forbidden late-night party and a couple of over-willing girls she did not take too seriously. Visiting the school, her questions as to the none-too-veiled references that this was not the only incident to cause concern about the Anatov boys, were cheerfully dismissed by a Nicholas too sure of himself in his mother's affections to worry about such things. "Take no notice, Mumps love. Old Baxter's living in the last century. No one's told him Victoria's been dead these eighteen years."

Ben was quieter and very obviously more concerned about the possible repercussions of their escapade. That he had not wanted to go to the party in the first place he did not mention: but his eagerness to reassure his mother that such a thing would not happen again predictably brought upon his head his brother's blithely undisguised scorn.

The second confrontation, a month later, was more serious, and even Anna could not indulgently excuse it.

"I do not, Mrs Anatov, propose to go into unpleasant detail," Mr Baxter lifted a dignified head and fixed her with a pained, slate-grey eye. "It is not, I'm afraid, something I find easy to discuss. Suffice it to say that the offence concerns the smuggling of strong drink — alcohol, Mrs Anatov! — into the school. And — worse — we have strong reasons to believe that certain younger boys are involved."

Anna stared at him. "Are you trying to tell me that Nicholas — that my sons — are encouraging younger boys to — to misbehave?"

He raised pencil-thin, repressive brows. "Just so, Mrs Anatov, I'm afraid. And I feel that I must warn you that any repetition of this kind of behaviour will lead to your sons being required to leave the school immediately. I hope I make myself clear?"

Anna flushed. "You do, Mr Baxter. Perfectly."

"I will not have such mischief perpetrated within these walls."

"Of course not." In her mind Anna was roasting both her sons over the slow fire of her anger. How dare they put her in this position?

Unsmiling, he showed her to the door, stood for a moment shaking a grave head. "I'm surprised at Benjamin, Mrs Anatov. Surprised and grieved. The boy has a brain. Pray tell him to use it."

"I will." Anna's voice was grim. "Oh, I promise you I will."

But neither her anger nor the severe punishment meted out by the school could repress Nicholas for long. He was bored, and avid for experience. He saw no reason for self-restraint. His restless and indulged nature refused to be curbed. The chance for glory had been taken from him, so, with no regard for consequences, he would brighten up his life some other way. And no one would stop him.

It was on a cold March afternoon that Anna came home to find her sons' school trunks stacked in the hall. At first the possible significance did not strike her.

"What on earth's going on, Madge? The boys aren't due home for weeks yet, surely?"

The girl avoided her eyes. "Don't know, Ma'am."

Anna, her swift movements arrested, stood quite still for a moment. "Where are they?" she asked, very quietly.

Madge took her coat, her head still ducked. "In the drawing room, Ma'am. Waiting for you."

Slowly Anna started up the stairs. She heard their voices through the open door long before she reached it.

"Why didn't you *tell* them?" Ben sounded as if he were almost in tears. "Nicholas, why didn't you? Why did you let them believe that I — that I —" His voice broke.

"Oh, for Christ's sake, Ben, stop snivelling!" Nicholas's voice was sharp with nerves and with anger. "It's over and done with. What does it matter anyway?"

"Matter?" The tears of frustration and anger were clear now in Ben's voice. "I'll tell you why it matters! You've ruined my life, that's all! Not only have I been tarred with the same — the same unspeakably rotten brush as you —" he plunged on, ignoring his brother's acid bark of laughter "— you've ruined any chance I might have had of making it to university. I'll never get the exams now. Don't you see what you've done? Don't you care? Are you really so damned self-centred that you don't *know*?" He choked, could say no more.

Anna pushed open the door.

"Oh, don't be so puerile. What do you want with university anyway? Bunch of boring idiots playing God in the hallowed halls of Oxford."

"*I wanted it!*"

"That — is — enough." Anna's voice cut them to utter silence. Ben swung away from her, dashing his hand across his eyes. Nicholas lifted a wary, tousled head. As she stood in the doorway watching them, it came to Anna, suddenly and for the first time, that these sons of hers — both a head taller than she — were no longer children. They were almost men.

"Hello, Mumps."

She said nothing. Stared at him. Ben sniffed. "What," Anna said at last, "have you done now?"

The silence stretched, a tenuous thread strained to breaking point.

"Well?"

Nicholas blinked at the sharp word. Ben did not move. Anna looked from the wide, brilliant eyes to the hunched back, and back again. "I'm waiting."

"We —" Nicholas lifted a graceful shoulder, kept his gaze, watchful, upon his mother's face "— we've got ourselves into a bit of a pickle, I'm afraid."

Ben swung around at that, outraged, no longer caring that his mother should see his tear-marked face.

Anna held up a swift hand, her eyes not leaving the defiant blue gaze of her elder son. "Wait, Benjamin. Explain yourself, Nicholas, please. What have you done now that is so disgraceful that you should be packed off home with no warning, no communication?"

"There's a letter in the post," Ben said, his voice tight.

"Nicholas?"'

For the first time his eyes slid from hers. "We've been expelled."

"I rather gathered that." Anna's voice was dry. "I'm asking why. I think you'll agree I have a right to know."

Nicholas was very still.

"Because," Ben said into the silence, "Nicholas —" he paused "— debauched was the word that was most often used — not one but two members of the lower school. And was stupid enough to get caught at it. 'In flagrante' don't they say?" There was real and bitter revulsion in the words.

The look Nicholas threw his brother contained murder. Anna had gone very white. "Nicholas? Is that true?"

He shrugged, took refuge in defiance. "Not quite the way I'd have put it myself, but — substantially — yes."

"Little boys?" Anna asked, faintly.

"They weren't so little."

"You bastard!" Ben's control, suddenly and shockingly, broke. Years of a resentment so subtle that he had hardly himself been aware of it lifted his voice and embittered his tongue. The words tumbled over themselves, almost incoherent. "You worthless, spoiled, self-centred bastard! Don't you care what you do? What you say? Don't you *care* how much you hurt anyone? Even her?" He jerked his head at Anna. "Can't you see anything but your own needs? Hear anything but your own damned voice? You spoil everything you touch! Everything! You always have —"

Nicholas, very pale, lifted a fair, handsome head but said nothing.

"You lie and you cheat and you smile your pretty smile. Anything to get what you want. And damn anyone who gets in your way. You don't care what happens to anyone else, do you? You don't care how anyone else feels? Look at Mama's face. Look at it! Forget what you've done to me — what about her? How *can* you? Everything else I can understand — even what you did to Papa —" Ben stopped, his teeth clamping on to his trembling lip, appalled at the sudden blaze of fury that had flamed in his brother's face.

In the silence that followed the violence of Ben's voice those last, clear words hung like the echoes of a great bell. The quiet lasted for what seemed a very long time. Anna looked at Nicholas. "Is this —" she asked at last, carefully "— something else I don't know about?"

Nicholas turned his head away, ran his hand through his hair.

Anna turned from him. "Benjamin?" She asked, her voice still carefully steady.

Ben's face was scarlet. The tears had started again. Like a baffled child he looked from his brother's stiffened, turned back to his mother's face. "I swore I'd never tell," he said, his voice choked.

"It's a little late, I think, to remember that." The words were quiet. "Your father? What could Nicholas possibly have done to your father?"

"I was listening outside the door," poor Ben said, his voice a whisper. "I heard." He was watching Nicholas's stubbornly turned back. "Then — when I told Nicho — he made me swear —"

"Benjamin. What did you hear? When?" The words were clipped, suddenly.

"I heard — Nicholas tell Papa that —" Ben's voice stumbled on the words "— that he wasn't his father. That you'd told him that Nicolai Shuvenski was his father. That you'd said that was why you loved him better than any of us. Because you still loved his father better than you had ever loved Papa."

In her shock only the first few words had truly registered in Anna's brain. "That I'd told him?" she asked. "That — *I'd* — told him?"

"Yes."

In two steps Anna was by her elder son's side. With strength that was beyond herself she reached for his arm and spun him to face her. "What's this?"

His eyes were shut.

"Nicholas! What — is — this?"

The bright eyes flew open.

"How did you know?" The first, the irresistible question. "How in God's name did you know?"

He swallowed. "The sketches. The date. The likeness."

She bit her lip. "God in heaven."

Silence hung like a curtain between them.

Anna tipped her head back to look at her son. "You added two and two together. Made four. And then —" She struggled for a moment. "And then you told Joss — that *I* had told you?"

"Yes."

"But — for God's sake — why?"

Nicholas spoke very precisely, his bright, beautiful eyes not leaving her face. "Because I wanted him to leave. I wanted him to go away for ever. I don't want him here. He doesn't like me. He hates me. I know it. And that night — the night after Grandfather's funeral — you had spent the night together. Of course you did!" Flushing she had moved her head in a small, instinctively negative movement. "The whole household knew it! He was going to stay, wasn't he? He was going to walk back in here as if nothing had happened. After the way he's treated you — treated Grandfather —"

"Nicholas! Stop!"

The boy ignored her. Tears stood now in his eyes. "And then, the next morning, he took the diamond from me. My diamond. So I told him —" He stopped.

"You might as well go on. What did you tell him?" Anna's voice was shaking a little. She cleared her throat.

Nicholas shook his head.

"Tell me. I think I have a right to know."

"I'll tell you." It was Ben, his eyes on his brother's face. "He told Papa that you'd said that you loved Shuvenski still. That you could never love anyone else. That Nicholas was all you had of him, and that because of that he and you were a conspiracy. Against the world. Against Papa —"

"Oh no."

"He told Papa that you'd promised the diamond to him. Told him that it was his by right, that Papa had no right to it."

"That stone again." Anna said, tonelessly bitter.

Nicholas's bright head did not move.

"He said —" Ben ploughed on.

Anna made a swift movement with her hand. "All right, Ben. I don't think I need hear any more." She took a long breath. "Would you leave us, please?"

"But —"

"I need to speak to Nicholas alone. And Ben —" The boy looked at her. "These examinations that are so important to you. Isn't there something we can do about them? Tutors, perhaps. Could you get through if we could find someone to coach you privately?"

The tear-stained face lit. "I might. I could try."

Anna nodded. "We'll talk about it later."

As Ben left the room, closing the door behind him, she turned to look at Nicholas.

"You haven't denied it," he said at last, into the stillness. His clear-boned face was ashen.

Anna sighed. "That Nicolai Shuvenski fathered you? No, I can't deny it. But —" she divined with sure instinct what would cut most deeply, and used it "— you didn't have to tell Joss. He already knew. He always knew."

That shook the boy, as she had known it would. He glanced at her, and away. He said nothing.

"He knew, yet still he treated you as a son. Still protected you, clothed you, fed you, educated you. Gave you his name."

Silence.

"Whilst I," she continued quietly, "have ruined you. Ironic, isn't it? Ben's right — you go through life taking what you want, giving nothing. And it's my fault."

Nicholas was visibly trembling now, blinking rapidly. Anna looked at him, tiredly, her anger and all the words she had intended to say draining from her. "Go to your room," she said. "I'll speak to you later."

He turned, stopped at the door. "Mama?"

She looked at him, her face closed against him.

"What was he like? My real father."

She did not speak for a long moment. Then, "Perhaps one day I'll be able to tell you," she said. "But not now. Just one thing I will say." Her voice was even. He watched her, waiting. "He would have been ashamed of you. As I am."

For a week she tried to write. For hours at a time she sat at her small, elegant desk with the crumpled paper of failure mounting in the waste-basket. She could not put into written words the things she felt she had to say. To be truthful she did not, indeed, herself know from one day to the next exactly what it was that she wanted to say at all. Then, a week after the confrontation with Nicholas, she woke one dark, wet and windy morning, and knew that there was only one thing to be done. She was out of the house within an hour, a small portmanteau on the seat beside her as the cab drove throught the rain-lashed streets to Euston Station. Her ticket bought, she had an hour to wait. She bought a magazine, sat in the dull-lit waiting room flicking absently through it, trying not to think about what might await her at the end of this absurd and impulsive journey. In her bag was the card upon which Joss had scrawled his address on the morning that he had left: '22, Albert Road, Manchester.' She did not even know if it were his home address or his office; she might, she thought, have been on her way to visit a total stranger. And a hostile one at that. As she sat in the stationary train, the excited bustle of approaching departure about her, her nerve almost failed her. She did not have to go. She owed him nothing. Had he come to her? Had he asked about — or even questioned — what Nicholas had told him?

A whistle shrieked. Someone ran past the window. Panic took her. She stood, reached for her bag from the rack above her head, staggered as the train jerked forward. The sudden movement forced her backwards, and she stepped on the toes of an elderly gentleman who had taken the seat opposite her. "Oh, I — I do beg your pardon."

"Not at all, my dear. May I help you?"

"Oh no. No, thank you." She sat down, feeling stupid. London, dreary in the murky rain, slid past the window. She would get off the train at the first stop, and go back. Yes, of course. That's what she would do.

She did not. Through unremitting rain the train raced north-westward, through the shrouded Chilterns, across the flat, rainwashed county of Northamptonshire, on to the sprawling industrial towns of the Midlands. She watched the drenched countryside stream past the window beneath a sky so leaden that it might have been resting upon the shining slate roofs of the houses. She ate lunch in the dining car, politely refusing the offer of the company of the elderly gentleman. She did not care how rude she appeared. She had to think. Yet, it seemed, the more she thought the more confused she became. All too soon she found herself standing amidst the bustle of Manchester Exchange Station, her portmanteau at her feet.

"Porter, Ma'am?"

"Yes. Please."

"Where to? Taxi rank?"

"Yes."

She followed the porter. This was it; her last chance to give up this idiotic wild goose chase upon which she had launched herself. She stepped into the taxi. "Number twenty-two, Albert Road, please."

It was his office. Number 22 was a large, old-fashioned building, its brick smoke-blackened but its interior, which housed several suites of offices, splendid with marble and mahogany and shining brass. She was shown up a handsome, sweeping staircase to a landing along which were several doors.

"There you are, Madam. That's Mr Anatov's."

"Thank you." She was infuriatingly nervous. She hesitated for a moment and then knocked, a little too firmly.

"Come." A woman's voice, young and pleasant.

Anna entered a large office, book-lined, wood-panelled and well lit. To one side was a door with a glass panel through which she could see several young men in shirtsleeves working at drawing boards. At the far end of the room was another door, solid polished mahogany, standing a little ajar. Through it she could see another comfortable room not unlike the one in which she stood but with the addition of deep leather furniture and an enormous desk.

"May I help you?" A young woman, brisk and extremely pretty came from behind a small table upon which stood a typewriting machine, a large black telephone and several neat piles of paper.

Anna set down her bag. "I'm — looking for Mr Anatov. Mr Josef Anatov."

"I'm afraid he isn't here. May I be of assistance? I'm his secretary, Miss Adams." The girl's eyes held curiosity, politely veiled.

Anna took a sharp, steadying breath. "No, thank you. It's a personal matter. I'm —" she paused, absurdly embarrassed "— I'm Anna Anatov. Josef's wife."

The girl stared, recovered herself. "I'm so sorry, Mrs Anatov. Mr Anatov didn't mention —" Her eyes had flickered to Anna's bag and back.

"No. I don't suppose he did. This is something of a flying visit. He isn't expecting me. Will he be long?"

"I don't think so." The girl seemed at a loss.

"I'll wait." Anna was feeling better. A reprieve. A chance to compose herself.

"Of course. Won't you take a seat?" Miss Adams waved to a small armchair next to the table at which she had been working.

Anna lifted her head, nodded to the half-open door. "That's my husband's office?"

"Well yes — but —"

"Then I'll wait in there if you don't mind." Anna took a step forward. Nothing in this world would force her to stay here where her first confrontation with Joss would take place beneath Miss Adams's wide, forget-me-not eyes.

"I'm sorry." The girl stepped quickly in front of her. "Mr Anatov never allows anyone in his room alone. It's a strict rule."

Anna side-stepped her neatly. "But not one, Miss Adams, I think that he would apply to his own wife?"

"With respect —" the girl said, determinedly "— I only have your word for that —"

"I didn't bring my marriage lines, certainly," Anna's voice was tart, "but then I hardly expected that I would have to prove my identity."

It was a victory of poise and confidence. Miss Adams stepped back. "No. Of course not, Mrs Anatov."

Anna swept past her and into Joss's office, pushing the door almost closed behind her. She found herself in a large, comfortable room with two sets of long, small-paned windows, velvet-curtained, that looked out on to a vista of grimy, rain-wet roofs and spires. A fire burned in the grate. Upon the enormous, tidy desk stood a fine model of an army tank, perfect in every detail. Anna touched it, thoughtfully, with a long finger, then wandered to a bookcase and stared unseeing at the regimented leather-clad spines. From beyond the door came the sound of the typewriter, clattering fiercely. Anna almost smiled — perhaps just a little too fiercely? She had the distinct impression that the attractive Miss Adams was not used to having her territory invaded. She could not settle: ignoring the comfortable-looking armchairs she walked to the window. God — was it never going to stop raining?

She heard the outer door open and close decisively. Quick foot-steps clicked upon the wooden floor of the other office. "Ah, Miss Adams, did the Minister ring? It seems I missed him yesterday."

Anna turned to face the door at the sound of Joss's voice.

The typewriter had stopped. "Mr Anatov," Miss Adams

said, quickly, "you have a visitor. Your —"

Too late. Joss stood in the open door, and just for a second his face was such a picture of utter astonishment that Anna, nerves strung like wires, found it hard not to laugh.

"— wife," the girl finished, lamely.

"Yes, Miss Adams. Thank you." Joss shut the door behind him with a sharp movement. They looked at each other in the shadowed light for what seemed to Anna to be a very long time indeed. She could not think of a word to say.

"Well, well." Joss walked to his desk. He had recovered himself; his voice was light. "How did you get past my young watchdog?"

She did not reply. All her misgivings had returned in full force. Fool. Fool! What was she doing here? "I had to talk to you," she said.

He nodded, his face guarded. "Will you sit down?"

"Thank you, no. I'd rather stand." Her voice was jerky.

He gestured — that characteristic half-shrug that was so much a part of his mannerisms. "Of course. Whatever you like." He waited, politely.

"It — isn't good news," she said at last.

He was watching her steadily. "I didn't somehow suppose that it was."

"The boys. They've got themselves expelled from school. Some awful scrape Nicholas got himself into. Involving —" she added with some difficulty "— a couple of younger boys."

"How very unsavoury." The words were non-committal.

"Yes."

A faint puzzlement had drawn his brows together.

She found herself talking without taking breath, very fast, the words all but running into each other. Her hands were tight-gripped before her. "I feel so sorry for poor Ben. I don't believe that he was involved at all. But Nicholas just let him take half the blame anyway. He doesn't seem to see — doesn't seem to care — what he's done. Oh, God, it's my fault isn't it? My fault —I've ruined the child." Her voice died to silence. Rain drove against the window panes.

He said nothing. Shook his head, very slightly.

She looked down at her clasped hands, and took a long,

sighing breath. "That wasn't really what I came to say," she said softly, not looking at him. "Oh — it's all true, and perfectly horrible. And I do feel dreadful about it. But I can cope, I expect. I didn't have to come running to you." There was a kind of defiance in the words.

"Of course." He waited.

She lifted her head at last, and held his gaze steadily. "Nicholas told me what he told you on the morning after Father's funeral. When you found him with the diamond."

There was a long moment's silence. Anna heard her husband's slow release of breath. "I see."

"I wanted you to know — I had to tell you myself — that there was absolutely no truth in what he said. I have never at any time spoken to Nicholas about his father. Nor told him that I still loved him. Nor formed any —" she hesitated, then spoke the word firmly "— any conspiracy with him against you or anyone else. The boy guessed about Nicolai. He found the pictures, and he guessed. The rest he made up. I don't know why. Mischief, perhaps. Or — I don't know — some obscure need." She stopped. "Anyway, I just wanted you to know that whatever has been wrong between us in the past, whatever has stood between us, that is something that I never would have done." At the look on his face her voice faded and she caught her breath. He turned from her and looked out of the window.

"I think — that I have known that for some time. After I had left. After I had had time to think —"

The words sparked swift anger. She stared at his back. "I beg your pardon?"

He said nothing.

"Are — you — trying to tell me —" the words were slow, almost choking with anger "— that after you had had time to calm down you realized that Nicholas had been lying?"

"I suppose so. Yes."

"And yet — you said nothing? You didn't come to me — to tell me?"

"No." The low word was scarcely audible.

"Why? Joss — why?"

Silence.

"I don't understand you." The words were flatly quiet. "I

never have understood you. I never will, if I live to be a hundred. First you let your hatred of my father come between us. And then, with that gone, you manufacture something else —"

"No!" He turned at that.

"And I say yes! What other explanation is there?" Her voice was rising. She fought to control it.

He shook his head, turned from her again.

"Joss!"

He did not answer. But this time she would not make it easy for him. She gritted her teeth, held her silence, let the quiet stretch between them, dark and empty and full of the sound of the driving rain.

"It isn't easy for a man like me to love." He said at last, very quietly, as if in that single sentence all was explained. As perhaps it was.

"For God's sake!" Anna, without thought, spoke savagely. "Do you think it's easy for anyone?"

He shook his head. "No."

Quite suddenly the rain eased a little. Large, dirty drops slid down the glass of the window, glinting in the light.

"Pride," she said. "That's the key, isn't it? Sheer, stubborn, bloody-minded pride! You make up your mind to do something, and that's it. You won't back down, won't admit you might be wrong, won't ask for explanations. Your stupid man's pride has stood between us like a wall since the day we were married." Unexpectedly her breath choked in her throat. She swallowed. "Hasn't it?"

"Yes."

"You're always ready to believe the worst. Don't you know that that in itself can sometimes make the worst happen? You're like that hateful diamond. Hard as rock, and cold as stone."

"You really believe that?"

"You've never given me reason to believe anything else." To her horror she felt hot tears rising. She had promised herself — vowed to herself — that she would not, above all things, cry. Fiercely she fought them down.

He turned at last, back to the room and to her. "Anna." His voice was gentle.

"Don't," she said, sharply. "I didn't come here for your pity."

She could not, absolutely could not, stop the tears.

Surprisingly he almost laughed. "Pity you? I don't pity you, Anna. I never have. As a matter of fact I can think of few people I'm less likely to pity than you."

She looked at him. "What, then?"

"I told you once before. But you didn't listen. Not that I blame you for that —"

"Told me?"

"That I loved you. That I have always loved you. No matter —" he added softly "— how I tried not to."

She made a small, sharp sound of disbelief. "And that's why you left me? And stayed away for all this time? Because you *loved* me?"

"Yes," he said.

She shook her head, violently.

He sighed. "I left in anger — and then — I suppose it became a — a kind of habit. To stay away. It seemed to me that we could not get near each other without hurting each other."

She sniffed. "You never seemed to be hurt." For her life she could not keep the bitterness from her voice.

"That, perhaps, is my misfortune," he said. "Not to seem to be hurt."

She straightened, took a handkerchief from her small handbag, blew her nose. "Well," she said, a little more composedly, into the silence. "There it is, I suppose. As usual I've done all the things that I swore I wouldn't — cried, lost my temper, caused a scene. All the things, I expect, that you find so difficult to understand. But at least I've told you what I came to tell you." Her voice was commendably steady; but she could not look at him. "So now I suppose I'd better go." She turned to the door.

"Anna."

She stopped, head high.

"Have neither of us learned anything in twenty years?" The words were very soft. "Please. Don't go."

That almost broke her. She stood unmoving, her hand on the door-knob.

"You surely didn't come all this way just to turn around and go back home again?"

She ducked her head.

He moved to her, standing behind her, not touching her. "Anna —"

She shook her head. "Don't! You don't mean it. And I didn't come here to — to —" The tears came again, sliding down her cheeks as the rain slid down the windows.

In the quiet, beyond the door, Miss Adams's typewriter rattled loudly.

"Please," Joss said. "Come and sit down for a moment."

She sat down beside him, rigid, upon the edge of the leather sofa.

He surveyed her with dark, quiet eyes. "Why did you come here today?" he asked unexpectedly.

She looked up in surprise. "I told you. To tell you —"

"Yes. But why?"

She flushed, deeply.

"Tell me," he said, insistent.

She turned her head from him.

"Then let me tell you."

That snapped her head back. "No!" Then, chin lifted. "All right, tell me. If you can."

"Because you love me still," he said softly.

She sucked her lip. "No."

"Look at me and tell me so."

She raised her eyes to his. Remained silent. The mouth that could be so harsh turned down in a strange, deprecating little smile. "Who spoke of pride a moment ago?"

"Well, you aren't the only one —"

The pressure of his hand upon hers stopped the words. "I know," he said, "I know." In the most gentle gesture she ever remembered him offering he extracted the damp handkerchief she was twisting between her fingers and wiped the tears from her cheeks. Then he handed her the handkerchief, caught her wrists lightly in his hands. "There is an excellent tea shop," he said solemnly, "not far from here. It's warm and cosy and a very good place for talking. I think you'll like it. Would you care to take tea with me?"

"I — yes," she said, bemusedly.

"Good." He stood, helped her to her feet. "I think perhaps

you should get to know a little of Manchester. Come."

She took the proffered arm. Miss Adams looked up as they entered her office. "Ah, Mr Anatov, the Minister's been on the telephone. He's free later today."

"I shan't be able to make it, Miss Adams."

"But — what shall I tell him?" The big blue eyes were wide with astonishment.

"Tell him," Joss tucked Anna's hand firmly into the crook of his arm, "tell him that Josef Anatov is taking tea with his wife." Half-way to the door he stopped, as if suddenly recollecting something. He looked at Anna thoughtfully. She lifted enquiring brows. "A moment, Anna. I have an idea. A small gift. Something that I think I must have been keeping for you." He walked to a large safe set in the wall, opened it, took out a long, familiar box.

"For you," he said, simply, and ushered her from the office, closing the door firmly in Miss Adams's amazed face.

"And what," Anna asked, snapping the case open and gazing with some distaste upon the brilliance within, "am I suppose to do with this?"

He shrugged. "Wear it. Sell it. Give it away. Whatever you like."

She stared. The Rose Stone's rainbow refractions flashed upon wall and ceiling. "You mean that?"

He took her arm. "I mean it."

She snapped the case shut. Half-way down the wide stairs he stopped. "If you sold it," he said.

She looked at him warily, "Yes?"

"You would raise enough money to invest in a quite nice little house, would you not?"

She frowned. "Joss — it can't have slipped your mind — I already have a house."

"Ah, yes. But that one's in London. I was thinking of something a little different. A little — further north?"

She took his arm, started down the stairs again.

"You mean somewhere like — Manchester, perhaps?"

His smile was slow and wide. "Somewhere like that, yes."

They stepped through the doors into the busy city street. The rain had stopped at last.